Dragon and Mr. Sneeze

Witches of the Horseshoe Book One

A Blue Skeleton Novel

Dragon and Mr. Sneeze: The Witches of the Horseshoe, Book One by Blue Skeleton, published by Blue Skeleton Inc.

www.blueskeleton.com

© 2020 Blue Skeleton
Print Edition

All rights reserved. No part of this publication may be reproduced, distributed, or transmitted in any form or by any means, including photocopying, recording, or other electronic or mechanical methods, without the prior written permission of the publisher, except in the case of brief quotations embodied in critical reviews and certain other noncommercial uses permitted by copyright law. For permission requests, email the publisher, with the subject line: "Attention: Permissions Coordinator," at blue@blueskeleton.com

All the characters in this book are fictitious, and any resemblance to actual persons living or dead is purely coincidental.

Foreword

Thank you, dear reader, for doing whatever you did to find yourself here on the first page of book one of my Witches of the Horseshoe series. If you want to steam ahead once you've finished the read, **Books two and three are now available exclusively on Amazon**. I have woven together a rather intricate tale under the umbrella of Dragon and Mr. Sneeze (you'll have to stick with me to learn all about that), and I hope you will enjoy its twists and turns.

Some of you may have already ventured into the first book in the companion series, ***Charli's Story***. Charli is the daughter of the main character in this book. If you'd prefer to start with the second generation of the family, you can pick it up here. Either way, I'm confident that you'll enjoy the entire family, however you get introduced.

One other heads-up, the dialogue of a few of the characters carries a Creole accent. I've tried to present it as it sounds, and I hope you can hear its authenticity and that it enhances your appreciation of the characters.

Before I let you dive in, I want to thank the team that helped bring this series together. The best two editors ever: Sara Bodinar and Shelley Holloway. (Under no circumstances can you use them!) My dearest friend Matt Wong who created the fantastic illustrations. Wonderful and patient beta readers: Leila Harper, Vesta V-RO May, and Mary Balogh. (Your input is invaluable.) And mostly to my wife, Zinnia, who should probably murder me at this point. Lastly, to my Advance Reader team. (You are the best group of Skeletons this half-crazy person could hope for.)

Now, go forth and enjoy!

The Beginning

THERE CAME A knock at the door. Not that I heard it. I was passed out cold. I had only just fallen asleep, too, so when my wife Zinnia nudged me awake, I was less than thrilled. It was the crack of dawn, and I'd been up for hours re-working the songs for the latest Skeleton Dance record.

Squinting, I open my eyes, and an ugly little creature comes into view. Humphrey, my family's Drolling Dragon, is floating inches from my nose. His bulbous orange eyes poke out of his ugly stone face like big tennis balls. He's barely over a foot tall, old as sin, and nearly completely deaf. I'm reasonably certain that he can hear just fine despite his feigning otherwise. I think he's just lazy.

"What is it, Humphrey?" I ask, pushing his face out of mine. He floats a little ways off.

"Someone is knocking at the front door," says the little stone beasty.

"Well, what do you want me to do about it?" I ask, annoyed.

"Humphrey does not care. Humphrey thought you would like to know."

"Well, I don't," I snap at him. "Goodnight!"

SWISH!

The little Drolling Dragon disappears, followed by a funny sound.

"Who do you think it can be?" Zinnia asks in a worried whisper. Her long black hair falls across her face, and she reaches for her glasses on the nightstand and then picks up a wooden compass. I know what she's thinking; more enquires from the Ghostal Holly, our oppressive government. Recently, I wrote the first Dragon and Mr. Sneeze book called *Charli's Story*. Unfortunately for me, it drew their attention. The book chronicles a young girl named Charli Wonkers, whose extreme powers define her as a Dragon, which is the most powerful being on this side of the Graveyard. The Fire Thief, too, was a Dragon.

He nearly destroyed the world.

"Can't be good," I say to Zinnia. "It's 5:12 in the morning. Too early for a social call."

I lie there for a second before I put my slippers on and turn back to her. "I could just ignore it. Maybe they'll go away."

"Oh, Blue, what if someone needs our help?"

"What if they don't?" I say, as she opens the lid to the compass.

"If we're not going to help folks, then can we turn the recording studio into a nursery?" she warns. "It takes up most of our home. Maybe a spare bedroom? Then my parents might like to visit."

"Your parents hate leaving their island, especially your dad. When was the last time they visited this side of the Graveyard, anyway?"

"Would you go check the door already?"

"I'm just tired," I say, standing up. "I had a late session."

"I know, honey, but it's safe," she says looking down at the compass again. "The Blumpass says that the person outside is mildly non-threatening. Look!" She turns the little wooden scope toward me. I lean forward and look at the two tiny blue hands. One is pointing to a teddy bear and the other a lion cub.

"That's reassuring," I say. "Sorta."

"Just don't open the door all the way."

"I won't. But in case I'm wrong, go wake Uncle Keeno. Between him and Humphrey, there is almost one whole extra person."

I make my way out of our tiny bedroom and catch my reflection in the glass door leading into the recording studio. My long black hair is a mess, and the bags under my eyes are visible even through my blue skin. Oh, well. Whoever's knocking is going to see me at my best! Once through the dance hall, to which our home is attached, I step outside into the courtyard. The smell of BBQ smoked meat lingers from last night. The stranger knocks again in three quick raps.

"I'm coming. I'm coming," I say under my breath, and for some reason, I speed up. Of course I whack my shin right into a picnic bench, which doesn't improve my already fantastic mood.

"Who is it?" I snap through the closed door now that I'm across the courtyard.

"Someone who needs to talk with Blue Skeleton," says an

oddly low, rumbling tone. Whoever is on the other side of the door is somehow distorting their voice. The stranger could be one of the neighborhood kids using a child's toy; something purchased from Pawn 'n' Cauldron perhaps. Or the stranger could be someone much more dangerous, looking for a Dragon. I think back to my childhood best friend, Marshall. He was like Charli. He was a Dragon. That is before he disappeared.

"He's not here," I lie. I don't feel good about it, but I'm just not in the mood right now.

"I think you'll be interested in what I have to say," the voice rumbles.

"Come back at a decent hour," I say. "Who should I say is looking for Blue?"

"A friend," says the stranger. "Please, this is very important."

"So is my sleep, which you're currently interrupting."

"You're Blue Skeleton, aren't you?" says the voice through the door. "I know about you. Your parents were murdered when you were a child. You and your brother, Jimmy Bum, were the only survivors. For two years, the Ghostal Holly kept you under watch at Saint Jude's Blessing, because you claimed that the Fire Thief killed your mother and father. It wasn't until you signed an affidavit stating that you made up the entire story that you were allowed to go free."

I bang the door with my closed fist and say, "That monster killed my parents. I saw it!"

"I am right then?" asks the stranger.

"How do you know these things?" I bark.

"Open the door and I'll tell you."

I remain silent, contemplating if I should let this stranger inside.

"You found the first Dragon in centuries. Or should I say, she found you?"

"All right, so you read the first *Dragon and Mr. Sneeze* book. A lot of people did. So what."

"Yes, but how many of them believed you?"

"Not many," I say.

"I believe you."

"Your voice is distorted," I say. "How do I know you're not from the Ghostal Holly?"

"I am from the Ghostal Holly, but I'm not your enemy."

Honesty, I think to myself. This person is being honest, sort of. The voice distortion doesn't inspire confidence though.

"Humphrey," I whisper, but the Drolling Dragon doesn't appear. I guess those big floppy ears on his ugly stone head are about as useful as wings on a penguin. I place my hand on the door and debate again whether or not to let this stranger inside. If he's a powerful Sky Builder sent by the Ghostal Holly, they've at least honored the protective charms that would keep lesser witches out. Any Builder worth their salt can break in here once they've managed to find this place, which this stranger obviously has.

"I can tear the door down if you prefer," says the stranger, as if reading my mind. "Your protective charms are rudimentary. But I'd rather walk in as a friend."

"Fine," I say, slightly irritated that I'm being forced to open my door. "But if you don't behave, you'll have one very angry Drolling Dragon to deal with." *What a joke.* I can't imagine Humphrey doing much beyond watching reruns of the *Brothers Grim* on his Busyboo.

As I slowly open the door, a tall, hooded figure stands in the winding alleyway.

"You're covering your face too," I say, braver than I feel.

"May I come in?" asks the stranger.

"Do I have a choice?" I reply, gesturing the person inside.

"One always has a choice," says the stranger, walking in as I close the door.

When I turn around, the stranger is holding a Wyndomier Wick: the Sky Builders' weapon of choice. It's capable of besting the greatest witches, destroying ghosts, and even killing immortals. I have never seen one up close, as they are very rare now. Similar to a policeman's baton, a Wyndomier Wick is a foot and half in length, mostly black, but with glowing red carvings along the side. I'm only a Skeleton, so I think I'm done for.

I'm surprised when the stranger says, "Take my Wick as proof of my intent. I wish to set your mind at ease."

"Really?" I pause, looking down at the deadly weapon. "Keep it. If you really wanted to kill me, you'd have done it by now. Are you going to show me who you are?"

The stranger pulls back the hood, revealing a beautiful witch in her early forties. Long, wavy dark brown hair falls, framing her brown face and green eyes; the same striking green eyes I've seen in publications like the *Thirteenth Saint* and history books on Tuning since I was a child. This witch was responsible for overthrowing the last Wiggler risings and successfully bent an invisible shield called a Trankler's Hold It around herself, which renders her nearly impossible to harm. Achievement awards in her name are given to young students of the Sky Builders' Guild for excellence in Tuning. If there is a better example of a witch on this side of the Graveyard, I have never heard of one, at least not one that is alive.

"Famka Meadows," I say, amazed. "No one has seen you in twenty years… or more."

"For good reason," she says looking around at the empty courtyard.

"You're a legend."

"I don't deserve such high regard. I have things to tell you. Might we continue inside?"

"Um, sure," I say, still not quite believing that she is actually here. "Follow me."

We make our way across the courtyard, through the dance hall, and into my recording studio, before we sit at an old round table. She is across from me with her hands on the table drumming her fingers almost nervously. Two microphones hang from the ceiling, facing each of us.

"I record everything. It's the way I work. Non-negotiable."

"I'd have it no other way," she says.

"So, Famka Meadows," I say, leaning toward the microphone. "Where have you been all these years?"

"I've been under a Speaker spell."

What a terribly dangerous spell, part of the Fallen Arts, I think to myself. If she isn't careful, the words that she speaks aloud will kill her.

Chapter 1

Two Little Witches Plus One

IN A SMALL town in Texas, live three little witches: one is a diamond waiting to be discovered; the second an innocent babe full of life; and the last one, despite her charms, is a ruthless killer.

Famka Meadows and Ophelia Laveau are childhood friends living in a run-down trailer park called the Horseshoe. It's on the outskirts of a small Texas town called Wink, on an island nestled in the Gulf of Mexico. You may not have heard of it and that's all right. Not very many people have. The Horseshoe is the sort of place you'd never see when vacationing in Wink, because it's too big of a dump for the locals to point out. But like many small and out of the way places that are tucked in forgotten corners, the Horseshoe is the sort of place filled with charm and virtues. You know the quaint little places you miss when you're paying too much attention to things that probably don't matter? Yep, it's one of those.

Famka and Ophelia were reared in the witchy arts of Tuning even before they could walk. They were taught by

Ophelia's grandmother, the country witch, Momma Nay. Their first lesson was the most important one—to see the dead is to do as the dead do. They understood that one day they, too, might learn to walk through walls, fly in the sky, or disappear from sight, like ghosts. This is what is known as Tuning. But in some ways, there was much more to Tuning.

Of the two young witches, Famka was the first to hear it, the Song of the World. When she asked Momma Nay about it, she was told that the Song of the World is what makes all things possible; the birds, the trees, and even the air in the sky. And Tuning was simply the best way to hear it.

"Gawd, I hate it here!" says Famka shortly. She slams a spell book down on the warped porch floor and abruptly stands, sending her flimsy metal lawn chair bouncing out behind her. "*Gravedigger's Handbook* my eye. Handbook to what? Certainly not getting out of here. More like how to waste your life away in this dump. I've read it from front to back, and nothing. Nothing! Every new spell I author doesn't work. How are we going to join the Sky Builders' Guild if we can't get out of here, Ophi?"

"You know Try Outs are just over a week away, and we haven't gotten invitations from the Sky Builders yet."

"I know. I know," gripes Famka.

"And a *Gravedigger's Handbook* isn't supposed to tell you what you *want* to know, but what you're *capable* of knowing," says her best friend Ophelia, who's seated on another metal chair. She wiggles her back as a way to unstick her moist shirt from the metal. "You know that."

"I dunno," says Famka, frustrated.

"You learned to be Animouth," says Ophelia.

"Sure, but I talked possum to a turtle for hours before I

figured it out," says Famka.

Ophelia laughs then says, "Yeah, that was kinda funny. That poor turtle thought you were as a crazy as a badger."

"Thanks for reminding me," says Famka.

Burning inside, Famka paces the porch. Bare feet pad along the squeaking wood, and her long brown hair flows out behind her, falling nearly to the middle of her back. As is typical, she wears a faded black T-shirt and a loose ankle-length skirt. Across her shirt is a band name, Led Zeppelin. Famka has never heard of them, and she's often wondered how she might buy a Stairway to Heaven. To make it weird, however, the band won't exist for perhaps another ten years. Now that she's older and has grown into the shirt, she wears it almost every day.

Wind chimes ring from the roof as a welcome breeze flows in off the ocean. She stops at the edge of the porch and looks out at the surrounding trailer park, which to her is nothing more than a shackle. Disappointment blazes in her piercing green eyes as she counts twelve trailers for the millionth time. The run-down homes sit in the shape of a horseshoe facing the beautiful Gulf of Mexico, but the view is mostly blocked by sparsely covered sand dunes. A new playground was erected several summers ago, but already, the sun has bleached the merry-go-round in spots. It's now a little less red than when it was new.

The burning inside her never really goes away. It has always been this way with Famka. She isn't really sure where it came from or why she has such a fire in her belly, but it has been there ever since she can remember. Always there, always present, and never allowing her to pause long enough to relax, she sometimes thought of the fire as tortured-soul syndrome.

Some people are simply born with desire, a longing, an emptiness that needs filling. But it isn't really emptiness that she feels, for she knows that she is loved. So, what is it, she wonders, as she looks upon her home with disappointment.

"Famka," says Ophelia. She folds her runner's legs, one over the other. "Momma Nay said to give it time. When you're ready to know more Tuning, then the book will show you more. That's the way it goes."

"I know," says Famka frustrated. "I just want us to get out of the Horseshoe. It feels like we're going to be here forever. I don't want to be like Momma Nay, fixing everyone's problems because they keep trying to do Tunings they don't understand. I want to leave here and join the Sky Builders' Guild, so I can do something important with my life."

Ophelia starts laughing. "Do you hear yourself? Momma Nay does important things. She helps folks when they're sick or hurt. She helps out the little guys. I want to join the Sky Builders, too, but I don't think they're going to help Mr. Billbray with his sore feet."

"Yes, I hear myself," says Famka grumpily. "It's not the same, Ophi."

"I'm sorry, but seriously, Famka, you can't rush Tuning. You know that," says Ophelia as she wipes sweat from her dark face. Her large afro circles her head like a tilted halo. "You remember that kid Bamford Ghoulsbee? I think that was his name, or John or something? Anyway, he lived over on Mustang Island. That knucklehead tried Devil Digging through a solid wall. He could've used the front door of his house like a normal person, but he was hasty, and Devil Dug right into the wall itself. Ended up stuck between two wooden studs. That must have hurt until it killed him good. By the time Momma Nay got to him, there was nothing she could do. She said a two-by-four was sticking right through his chest."

"Well, maybe he was an idiot," offers Famka as she starts pacing the porch again.

"Speaking of idiots. What about when you tried Devil Digging right out there in the Gulf? You can't just appear in the middle of the ocean without knowing what you're doing," says Ophelia, pointing toward the nearby ocean. "Nearly killed ya just like that Ghoulsbee kid. You try a stunt like that again, and you'll end up with water or wood, or whatever, running right through you where it shouldn't. And then what? You'll be dead as a doornail, and I'll be stuck here without you."

"That was an accident," says Famka. "And I wasn't Devil Digging. I was trying to wrap a Trankler's Hold It around me like a shield. And I know what you're going to say, but just 'cause no one ever tried it, doesn't mean it can't be done."

"Isn't a Trankler's Hold It a Fallen Art?" asks Ophelia with concern in her gray-green eyes.

"Well, kinda, but it doesn't have to be," says Famka. "Trankler may have invented the spell so he could imprison witches…"

"And torture them," adds Ophelia.

"Yes… yes," says Famka, waving her brown hand, annoyed. "But it can be used for something more productive than hurting folks."

"Listen, Famka." Ophelia's tone softens. "I know you want to try new kinds of Tuning and invent spells no one has ever thought of, but try to be careful, please!"

"Well, it almost worked," says Famka firmly. "If I only had a Wyndomier Wick."

"Have you ever even seen one?" asks Ophelia.

"In pictures mostly," says Famka. "And that one time we were in the Plaza of Giants for about a second. It looked like a cop's baton on fire."

"Well, until you have one, if you ever have one, try not to kill yourself. I'd hate to think what would've happened if Momma Nay hadn't saved your skinny butt. You'd be as blue as that ocean."

"You are just as *skinny* as I am, and what does my butt have to do with it, anyway? I'm gonna try again," states Famka flatly.

"Again? I will kick your butt from here to Travis County if you die and leave me here without you. Honestly, I couldn't think of a worse thing."

Famka smiles at her best friend. "I love you, too, Ophi."

"And you remember that, Famka. You get careless with your Tuning because you want out of the Horseshoe so badly. And I'd like to point out that messing up like that isn't going to get the attention of the Sky Builders' Guild. Not the good kind, anyway. I want out of here, too, but I'm not willing to try unsanctioned Tuning just so I don't have to wake up here in this trailer park. God forbid one of us ends up imprisoned in the Sea of Chall by the Ghostal Holly. You know the Fire Thief is locked up there too? Fine place that prison is. I'm sure."

"Yeah, I know," says Famka sullenly. She pulls her long dark hair back and fixes it in place with a rubber band.

"And it's not that easy to get into the Sky Builders' Guild. I know they are the greatest instructors of Tuning and all that, but honestly, Momma Nay isn't such a bad teacher," says Ophelia closing her *Gravedigger's Handbook* and placing it on the worn crab trap beside her. She stands and walks to another wooden trap at the foot of a pile of traps, which are stacked against the trailer. Ophelia looks around before she says, "Watch this." She then lightly taps the top of the trap, and it explodes into splinters around her feet.

Famka jumps back and then says, "How did you do that?"

"I used a Mending spell," says Ophelia.

"A Mending spell, but you broke the trap to pieces. How is that Mending?"

"I strengthened my muscles, so that when I tapped the wood, it broke apart. I figured it out on one of my runs when I had to ditch the Smelth brothers. They thought it might be funny to run me off the road with their pickup, so when I turned down Wink Tree Lane and I was sure that I was out of sight, I took off as fast as I could, which turns out is faster than their truck."

"They didn't hurt you, did they?" Famka scrunches up her brown face.

"Oh no," says Ophelia. "I think they were surprised when I disappeared."

"If they had hurt you, I'd have to kill you for dying and leaving me here."

"Don't use my lines on me," says Ophelia with a smile. "You know Momma Nay said that a witch has to complete two of the five Mending spells and one of the Making spells before the Sky Builders will even consider letting a witch join."

"I can only do one of the Mending spells, but Momma Nay won't teach me the rest. Why? I never thought to use one to get stronger. That's a good idea." Famka nods her head. "If I can just figure out a couple more, then maybe I can go to the Sky Builders and see if they'll consider me. Or if I can show the Builders some of my experiments, I just know they'll accept me." She points to the book on the table. "That thing is useless."

"Come on, grumpy." Ophelia stood and stretched. "Let's go find Momma Nay. It's lunch time and I'm hungry. If we're late again, she won't teach us any Tuning today. She's pretty strict."

"You mean purist," says Famka.

"Yeah, my grams can be that way. I bet she's stewed up some of Uncle Guncle's crabs by now."

"Speaking of Uncle Guncle…" Famka looked at the entrance to the Horseshoe. A faded green pickup pokes along the dusty road, dust trailing out behind it. Coming to a stop beside the girls, the truck door creaks open, and an older man steps out. His dark face and bald head are weathered from long hours in the sun. His hands are cracked, and large veins snake down his strong forearms. At barely forty years old, Uncle Guncle appears much older.

"Hi, Uncle Guncle," says Famka.

"Morning, girls," says Moses Guncle. "You still worked up, Famka?"

Ophelia laughs and says, "Boy, he sure knows you!"

Famka looks at her best friend with a frown and then says, "Yes."

"Here. I have somethin' for ya," says Uncle Guncle, reaching into the bed of his truck. After some clanking, he withdraws a length of thin leather with something dangling from it and hands it to Famka. It's a gold pendant with the image of the Fire Thief engraved in the surface. Burning matchstick eyes glow greenish yellow within a circle. "I don't know much about all that Tuning stuff Nay talks about, but a fellow in town said this is a good luck charm."

"Uncle Guncle, is this real gold?" Famka asked, feeling all

kinds of uncomfortable. "I can't take this."

"Girly, how many times have you looked after me when I was too tired to take care of myself," says Uncle Guncle.

"No more times than you looked after me when I was little," says Famka. "And Ophelia."

"True," says Ophelia.

He shakes his head. "You are too strong-willed and smart for your own good, Famka. Know a gift when you see one. Do this old man a favor and take it."

"You're not that old," argues Famka.

"She's right, Uncle Guncle," says Ophelia.

He stares at Famka, standing a little crooked as he often does. The whites of his eyes shine like tiny spotlights in his dark face. Famka knows from his posture that he's in pain again. She knows that he's spent his entire morning, probably starting around 3:30 or 4:00 a.m., dragging nets, checking traps, and packing coolers full of fish, so he can sell them in town. She also suspects that he's spent a pretty penny on this necklace for her.

"Your back is hurting again isn't it?" asks Famka.

"A bit," he says. "Could use some of that potion of yours again."

"I'll make some today," says Famka.

"Moses. Moses Guncle," yells a neighbor from next door.

"Good morning, Mrs. Billbray," he says as he turns to the trailer next door. An old woman is hanging half out of her kitchen window and waving. "I got a couple trout for you. I'll bring them over later, once I've cleaned them."

"Thank you, Moses," she says.

"And you tell that one-armed fool of a husband of yours to keep his trap shut. Else he's going to find himself in a heap of trouble."

The old woman smiles nervously then disappears inside.

"Well, girlies," says Uncle Guncle. "I'd better be off. I gots work to do."

"Thank you, Uncle Guncle," Famka says, then gives him a kiss on the cheek.

"Bye, Uncle," says Ophelia.

He doesn't smile, but Famka can see the smile in his eyes as he climbs back into his truck.

The two girls begin to leave when Mrs. Billbray pokes her head out of her kitchen window again and yells at them, "Where are you girls going?"

"Oh boy," mutters Famka.

"Hi, Mrs. Billbray," says Ophelia, shooting a frown at Famka and then looking at the old woman. "We're headed to the swamp. Momma Nay's waiting."

"You mind taking this to her?" asks Mrs. Billbray. She's holding something in her hand that the girls can't quite make out.

The young witches walk toward the trailer for a closer look.

"Are those socks?" asks Ophelia as she examines two soggy pieces of cloth.

"Sure are," says Mrs. Billbray with her arm flexed outside the kitchen window. "Mr. Billbray's feet swoled up again."

"Dirty socks?" asks Famka looking disgusted.

"Dirty old-man socks," says Ophelia under her breath.

"Sure. We'll take them," grumbles Famka as she grabs them.

"Thank you, girls," says Mrs. Billbray. "N' you watch out for snakes while you're out there."

"Don't remind me," yells Famka as they walk away.

"And come back before it gets too late. I'll have some fresh pot pie waiting for you both."

The young girls walk between the two mobile homes, which butt right up against a thicket of trees, and walk down a trail leading toward a swamp. Small tangled trees reach across the path just above head height and interweave through one another like pulled pork. The hot muggy air hangs heavily, making every step a sloppy wet mess. Sweat quickly builds up at the base of Famka's neck and runs down into her black T-shirt. She's used to the heat, having grown up in the great country of Texas, but she's never liked it. She pulls her long hair higher still, into a bun, careful not to get it caught in the low-hanging branches. Unseen critters scurry away from them as they approach. Famka very much dislikes snakes after her dog Hank was bitten and died when she was just a little girl.

"Slow down," says Ophelia. "Why are you in such a hurry?"

"Because Momma Nay promised to teach us the next Mending spell," says Famka.

"Oh yeah," says Ophelia. "I forgot."

"Anyway, you know how Momma Nay gets when we're late."

"Ophelia Laveau. Famka Meadows. You two are the most ungrateful witches this side of the Graveyard," mocks Ophelia in the thickest southern accent she can manage.

Famka laughs. "That's pretty good. You almost sound like her. Don't let her hear you, or you'll be in a heap of trouble."

"You aren't kidding?"

"I can't believe I'm holding a pair of stinky socks." Famka scrunches up her nose. "Maybe we should try talking with the turtles again. They might teach us more than Momma Nay does. These socks really smell bad."

Ophelia sniggers behind her. "Hey, you wanted to know more about Tuning. You got your wish. You know Momma Nay puts a spell on them, so Mr. Billbray's feet feel better when he puts his socks back on? Maybe that's the second Mending spell you could try?"

"Yeah, I get it, but at least Mrs. Billbray could wash them. And this wasn't what I was thinking when I asked Momma Nay about Mending spells," she replies. "Don't tell me she's only using the first Mending spell on these horrific-smelling socks."

"Don't worry. All the big stuff like flying through the air, talking with the wind, or visiting with the giants will come."

"Bombadoes? I'd love to talk with them. Did you know that Bombadoes were the last people to see the Dragons before the Fire Thief killed them all? I wish I could have met a Dragon or seen one of them Tune. I bet it was amazing." Famka sounds excited for the first time all morning.

"Why do you think they were called Dragons?" asks Ophelia.

"What do you mean?"

"Just that. They were people, you know. Or that's what they looked like, anyway. It wasn't like they were winged lizards flying around the sky and breathing fire. So why Dragons?"

"What would you suggest?" questions Famka with a giggle. "Super crazy powerful Tuning humans?"

"Yeah, sounds dumb doesn't it?"

"We could ask Momma Nay. Maybe she knows," offers Famka.

"If she'll tell us," says Ophelia.

"Good point."

"I bet Dragons knew all the Mending spells," says Ophelia casually.

"I'd at least like to know one more of them." Famka ducks beneath some low branches crossing the path.

"Me too," says Ophelia. "Maybe then I could get rid of these blisters on my feet."

"If you quit running so much, you wouldn't have blisters."

"I like being healthy. You need to start training too."

"For what?"

"Bombadoes mostly live in the mountains at high elevations. If you want to go talk to them about your Dragons, then you need to get in shape."

"We have to get out of here first and then get to the Other Side of the Graveyard." Famka stopped and turned to look at Ophelia. "You really think we can visit Bombadoes one day? All the way in the Fogalsong?"

"Sure, why not?" says Ophelia. "Momma Nay took us to Louisiana last year."

"Yeah, but Louisiana is on this side of the Graveyard and practically next door. Fogalsong isn't," argues Famka. "And you can almost walk to Baton Rouge from here."

"Still, I think we'll go some day," says Ophelia. "What's the big deal?"

"Well, for one, we aren't even allowed into the Hallowed Halls without Momma Nay. How are we supposed to get to the Other Side of the Graveyard, drive a truck? Yeah, that'll work. And using the Halls is the best chance out of here. Even if we were allowed to use them, we'll still need a Wyndom Window to get into the Halls, and we can't afford to buy one.

And another thing..." She points a finger into the air. "We don't even know how to use the Window to get into the Hallowed Halls in the first place. Gawd, we're never getting out of here," complains Famka.

"Baby, you're just having a bad day." Ophelia places a hand on Famka's arm. "I promise that Tuning will take us out of here one day soon. Once we get better at it, we'll use the Hallowed Halls to get us anywhere in the world. The first thing we'll do is visit the Bombadoes... not in a million years from now, but soon. Okay? Now let's go. Those socks really smell bad."

"At least you're not holding them," says Famka as she turns toward the trailhead.

"Give me one of them," Ophelia offers.

"No, it's fine," says Famka over her shoulder. "I'm sorry. You're right. I'm just having a bad day."

They continue down the path, which bends around a large crooked tree with limbs sticking out at every possible odd angle like a giant mess of spaghetti.

"Hello, Grandfather," says Famka to the tree.

"Hello, Grandfather," echoes Ophelia. "Why do we say that every time we pass that old tree, anyway?"

"It's the oldest wormwood tree around," Famka says as she stops to look up at the spiraling limbs climbing overhead. Sunlight can barely poke through the Frisbee-sized leaves, and tiny purple blossoms sparsely cover the gray bark, which resembles the skin of a very old man.

"It's maturing," says Famka.

"I'd say it's mature enough. If this poor old tree gets any older, it's going to fall right over."

"Ophi, Wormwood trees age in reverse as they grow taller,

so it's getting younger... at least physically," Famka says, sounding disappointed. "Seriously, you need to study more if we're going to get into the Sky Builders' Guild together."

"And where are our invitations to join the Guild?" asks Ophelia. "Ain't it kind of weird that we haven't gotten 'em yet?"

"You think Momma Nay might have something to do with that?" asks Famka skeptically.

"Oh, come on. She loves us. She would never do something like that," argues Ophelia.

"Well, I for one, think she would. You know she's not a fan of the Guild. She's convinced that the Sky Builders are just the muscle branch of the Ghostal Holly, which I'd like to point out she also hates. Especially Chairman Boo."

"He does seem like a crotchety old fart," says Ophelia. "Does make you wonder how he's been the chairman of the Ghostal Holly for centuries."

"Even the president of the United States has an eight-year limit."

"Good point," says Ophelia. "Maybe the Ghostal Holly is just a lame ghost government."

"I've read a lot of their history," says Famka.

"Of course you have," says Ophelia teasing.

"First off, the Ghostal Holly does more than simply govern the dead. They also keep the peace between all the other magical races. I have to agree with you a little though. Chairman Boo should have retired a long time ago." Famka wipes her sweaty brow. "Boy, it's hot today."

"I agree. Doesn't seem like the Ghostal Holly has much sense," adds Ophelia.

"Maybe not," says Famka as she begins walking up the

path again.

As they continue onward, the ankle-high grass grows taller, reaching nearly waist height on either side of the path. Famka begins clapping her hands and stomping her feet with every step as she tries to scare snakes away.

"You don't have to do that," says Ophelia behind her. "Snakes done heard us already."

"I don't care if I need to or not," says Famka. "It makes me feel safe."

Finally, they come to a fork at the edge of a large spring-fed pond.

"Left," yells out Ophelia.

"I know," says Famka annoyed.

"Well, your sense of direction is awful."

"I got us lost one time, and suddenly, I don't know where I'm going."

They turn and continue alongside the greenish water, which flows like Mountain Dew over large white rocks, some breaking the surface. Frogs croak nearby, welcoming them to the shallow swamp. Buzzing fireflies zip playfully between blue flowering plants, which smell oddly like cotton candy when the wind catches the pollen at the right moment. Famka watches a turtle dive into the water from a fallen tree branch. The girls bend around the pond and leave the water as the trail winds toward an old, dark wooden cabin. Two large trees that resemble gigantic open hands seem to almost cradle the cabin. The ground slopes slightly upward until they reach the first of two steps at the foot of a slightly crooked porch.

The door flies open, and a large dark-skinned woman bursts onto the porch. In her plump hands is an ugly stone statue the size of a teddy bear, and it's wailing at the top of its sorry little lungs.

Chapter 2

The Fire Thief and the Last Dragon
(Long before you were born)

THE FIRE THIEF, like all shadows, was filled with malice and cruelty. He stood in the entranceway of the Macabre's family home, for only the briefest of moments, before setting out on his task. Despite their dark name, the family was the happiest anyone had known.

The house was old and smelled of baked desserts, candles, black tea, and a hint of mold. The dark wood floors were covered in rugs and handcrafted furniture with fine inlays. A large ornate chandelier hung from the high ceiling above, the walls appearing to shimmer with flickering light from the full moon that peeked through the stormy clouds outside. Winds blew and howled angrily, as if to warn those who slept inside the happy home, that all was not well.

In one corner, there stood an old antique grandfather clock.

It chimed twelve times.

It was midnight.

It was time.

First, the Fire Thief went to the eldest child's room, a daughter. With brutal resolve, he removed what future she might ever have. She quietly slipped from this life as she dreamed of Zinnias and summer balls. Satisfied, he then moved slowly up a massive curved stairway toward the parents' room. He was careful not to make a sound, and not being entirely human, he had no need to actually touch the stairs, removing any concern that a squeak might wake the sleeping family.

This was an old house after all.

At the top of the landing, the Fire Thief disappeared like a swarm of black moths being sucked into a tiny black keyhole. He reappeared in the parents' room as a tall man in a worn riding coat with long greasy hair, his face obscured in shadow.

He stood above the parents as they slept peacefully. Slowly, he brushed his greasy hair away from his eyes and tucked it under the brim of his hat. Something about the father seemed familiar. A curious expression on his now-human face reflected an even more curious emotion, and for a moment, he tilted his head in quiet contemplation.

"No matter. This will all be done soon."

Carefully, he removed a long, sharp knife from a sheath that was tucked neatly inside a pocket of his riding coat. This was no ordinary pocket, because the inside, or rather the other side of the pocket was in a different place altogether; a place much further away, many thousands of miles away in fact. He had stored the knife and many other such tools for just such an errand as this cold and stormy night had called for. So, when he reached into this unusual pocket, which was not really a pocket, he could have at his disposal whatever he needed, regardless of shape or size.

"It makes travel an easier practicality in the end."

Of all his unusual talents, he preferred the cold simplicity of the blade to anything else. He found it oh so very satisfying. Yes, very satisfying, indeed. *One stab, two stabs, three stabs, four.* It was like a song to him, a sonata in its full bloom. And just as the crescendo reached its apex, the parents passed on, never to see their children grow up to be adults with their living eyes. They would not see them fall in love for the first time. They would never be able to spoil their grandchildren. Sadly, they had reached the end in the clearing.

All too soon, their song was over.

He wiped the edge of the blade on their goose-down comforter before returning the knife to its sheath.

"Never let blood dry. It stinks when it does."

His form dissolved back into the shadow it had been, and he moved silently out of the room and down the hall toward the remaining child, a boy. Only one left now, but the most important one, yes.

A Dragon!

Must complete this task, this very important task. One stab, two stabs, three stabs, four... It echoed in his head, his very wicked head. He enjoyed the rhythm, so he continued to repeat it over and over as he slowly moved toward the boy's room.

Chapter 3

A New Drolling Dragon

"Pass the cornbread!" shouts Momma Nay as she hands the little fleshy statue to Famka. It's heavier than she expects and she nearly drops it. "Take him!"

"What on earth is this thing?" shouts Famka over the little creature's wailing.

"Drolling Dragon. New born," shouts Momma Nay. "Now set him down over there." She points to a wooden table nailed in a corner between the outer kitchen wall and the porch railing. "Ophelia, go get the Sarsaparilla Sometimes from the fridge."

"Yes, ma'am," says the young girl as she sprints inside the cabin.

Famka places the crying Drolling Dragon on a checkerboard cloth spread across the table. The creature reminds her of an ugly little elf. Big ears flop around its bald head, and its large orange eyes resemble pool table balls. Sticky slime from the baby's gray body covers Famka's hands. Its tiny protruding stomach is bruised purple and looks like it might burst open at any moment.

"Here, Momma Nay." Ophelia hands her a tall metal canister.

Momma Nay quickly uncaps the container and tips it toward the Drolling Dragon's mouth. Green liquid spills onto its face as it spits out what little of the concoction got past its lips. She tries again, but the baby coughs out green liquid, which splashes Famka right in the face. *Yuck*, she thinks as she wipes it away.

"Ophelia, hold the child in place," barks Momma Nay. Humming a melody, Momma Nay closes her brown eyes tightly, then hovers her thick open hand, palm down, over the tiny Drolling Dragon. Famka immediately feels the air tingle against her skin. Flickers of blue light spark around Momma Nay's dark hand, and the baby goes silent.

Momma Nay's eyes pop open. "This poor child." She lets out a long breath and looks sadly down at the baby.

"What's the matter?" ask Famka.

"Torn up inside," she says. "Things ain't where they're supposed to be."

SWISH!

Another Drolling Dragon suddenly appears. It's floating in midair just above the baby on the table, looking worried and clearly female. Her ears flop down around her stone face like hair, and her dress is smeared in the same sticky goo covering the baby.

"Heiki! Get back inside!" snaps Momma Nay.

"Please save her, Momma Nay," cries Heiki.

"I'm trying. Now get back in the house. You're in no condition to be out of bed," says Momma Nay.

"What can we do?" asks Famka as the little creature grabs

her finger.

Momma Nay's eyes flash to Heiki, and she says, "I don't know. This is the first Drolling Dragon born in three centuries. There ain't no manual on birthing these little munchkins."

"Her name is Heaven," says Heiki as she wipes her ugly bulging eyes. She floats down to the table and rubs the little baby's sticky head. "Hellman and I have named her Heaven."

"Momma Nay, what about Leadbelly butter?" Famka asks.

"That's for wounds," says Momma Nay. "It won't work."

"You said the baby is torn up inside," says Famka.

"Yes, but Drolling Dragons aren't organic the way we are. They are nearly pure Tuning. It ain't nothing to fix broken legs or ripped up skin with Leadbelly butter, but it won't help a Drolling Dragon."

"But you said it yourself. You don't know what's wrong with the baby. Maybe it'll work."

"It can't hurt—can it?" asks Ophelia.

"No, I suppose not." Momma Nay lets out a long breath. "But I highly doubt it'll have any effect. Famka, that baby seems to like you. Keep holding that little hand. I'll be right back."

A moment later, Momma Nay steps out of the cabin holding a small wooden barrel. She places it on the table above the baby's head and twists open the spigot. What looks like twelve long golden guitar strings flow out like they have a mind of their own. They wrap around the baby, vibrate, and then lay still like spilled spaghetti before dissolving through her gray skin. The baby coughs, goes quiet for a moment, but then begins whimpering again.

"Momma Nay, I have an idea," says Famka. "Hang on. I'll

be right back." The moment Famka releases the baby's hand, however, she begins wailing loudly.

"Hurry up!" yells Momma Nay.

Famka rushes inside the cabin and stands before a tall, open cabinet beside the kitchenette. Each shelf is lined with gizmos, books, and clear jars filled with an assortment of odd things. Labels scribbled on white pieces of paper are tacked beneath each one.

Whiperwill: For talking with the chronically dead even when they are still alive.
Blumpass: For locating that which cannot be found.
Chronic Canker Sore Concoction: For folks you hate.
GumDrum: For beating sense into sick children.
Mugwart: For the new girlfriends of ex-boyfriends.
Mancork: For wives in long, boring marriages.

Her eyes scan Momma Nay's favorite self-help book, *I'm Stinky, but with Purdy Toes*, until her she finds what she's looking for.

Salamander Matter: Extremely dangerous. Use with caution.

Famka steps back to the cabinet and finds the jar labeled "Salamander Matter" and, with two very steady hands, places it on the kitchen counter. Slowly she removes the lid, and a black salamander with bright yellow circles on its back leaps out onto the counter.

"What do you want, Famka?" asks the salamander.

"Don't bite me, Edwin," she says.

"What's going on in there?" yells Momma Nay.

"Gimme a sec," Famka yells back.

"Come on. I need your help, Edwin."

"Do you have any cookies?" asks the salamander.

"I'll bring you some later." Famka grabs a glass from off a shelf. "Now spit in this."

"Not without a cookie."

"Don't get smart, Edwin," warns Famka. "If you don't help me, I'll never bring you another cookie. If Momma Nay knew how many I've brought you already, I'd be in all kinds of trouble. She's convinced you're no good as it is."

"Maybe I'll bite you anyway." He jerks toward her like he's about to jump onto her arm.

"You're willing to give up fresh-baked chocolate-chip cookies for a little spit? I'll even bring you some of those chocolates you like from Miss Turtlebalm's soda shop the next time I'm in town."

"Ohhhh," says the salamander. "Fine, but I also want a dozen cookies."

"You're going to get fat."

"I sit in a jar all day. Unless you can break the charm holding me there, I don't care. Momma Nay can get me a bigger jar after I've gobbled down your dozen and a half."

"Good point," she says as she holds the empty jar up to his lips. "And you said a dozen. Now spit."

The salamander fills the glass jar half full with something akin to jelly. It looks like it was made with a blend of strawberries and orange slices, then stirred with a dirty boot. If it hadn't just come out of the mouth of a magical lizard, one might be tempted to spread it on morning sourdough, but then again, maybe not.

"Thank you," says Famka. "Now back in your jar."

"Two dozen, Famka," says Edwin.

"Two? Good grief, you're going to be as big as a house. Now get in the jar." He leaps inside, and she quickly closes the mesh lid.

"Hurry up in there," yells Momma Nay again.

As Famka rummages through a drawer, she nearly spills the Salamander Matter. Not finding what she's looking for, she's about to pull open another drawer when she notices two invitations sticking halfway out of a thick envelope. They request that Famka and Ophelia attend Try Outs for the Sky Builders' Guild, this year. Behind them are two more for the previous year and two more before that. *You've got to be kidding me.* Frustrated, she shoves the two invites for this year into her front pocket, tosses the rest on the floor, and then flings open more drawers.

Tap tap tap.

"What?" yells Famka turning to Edwin. He points to the shelf above him.

"Of course," says Famka as she grabs the jar labeled Gum-Drum.

Edwin climbs up on his hind legs and talks into the mesh lid. "Two drops then stir it counterclockwise four times."

"How do you know that?"

"That's an old combination," says Edwin. "You're not the first person to think of it. But I'll give you credit for reaching that conclusion on your own. Momma Nay doesn't teach you squat. You should go talk to the turtles, dummy. They're old and know all sorts of things. Three dozen cookies."

"For real," Famka agrees, following the salamander's instructions to the letter. She finishes and is about to rush outside when another thought occurs to her.

"I know…" she says as she adds a pinch of Grumple Moss to the concoction.

"Clever girl," says Edwin.

"Thanks," Famka yells as she rushes outside and hands the concoction to Momma Nay.

"Smells awful. What is it?" asks Momma Nay skeptically.

"Salamander Matter, GumDrum, and Grumple Moss," says Famka.

"Famka Meadows," says Momma Nay shaking her head. "That is a bowl of mish mash."

"Will that work?" asks Ophelia.

"I don't know," says Momma Nay, who looks at Heiki. "I can't tell you what to do with your child, Heiki. It's up to you."

"What happens if we don't use the potion?" The Drolling Dragon looks up from the table, the baby's head in her lap. The child named Heaven sniffles between shallow breaths.

"She dies," says Momma Nay. "Plain as that. I'm sorry to be so blunt with you, but this ain't the stage for half-truths."

"It'll work," says Famka. "I know it will."

After just a moment's pause, Heiki says, "All right. Do it."

Famka scoops out a spoonful of the mixture and places it gently to the baby's lips. Then she bends forward and blows across her face. Blue sparks flow from Famka's pursed lips. The baby's bulbous eyes follow the sparks until they pop like a tiny 4th of July celebration. Ophelia places a hand on the child's chest and begins humming a lonely melody as Famka takes another breath and blows out more of the sparks. As ugly as Heiki is, the fear is clear in her orange eyes. For just a second, the baby stops breathing and goes completely still. Heiki looks up at Famka desperately, but Famka backs away and smiles. Heaven instantly takes in a big breath and starts laughing as the remaining sparks pop in front of her little ugly elfish face.

"Oh dear Lord," says Momma Nay relaxing.

Ophelia laughs and throws her arms around Famka and gives her a big kiss on the cheek.

"That was amazing," says Ophelia.

"Look at that," says Momma Nay. She leans over the table, and her round face nearly touches the baby, who reaches up and pinches her fat nose. "The first Drolling Dragon born in three centuries. Why, I'll be darned."

"Thank you," says Heiki as she dabs her eyes.

"You know what this means?" asks Momma Nay.

Heiki shakes her stone head. "There'll be a Dragon soon."

"Never in my life did I think I'd meet another one. Not after what the Fire Thief did to those poor Dragons."

"Not actual flying, fire-breathing dragons?" asks Ophelia.

"No, you silly child," says Momma Nay. "That's make believe. The Dragons that I'm talking about were folks with powers like you can only imagine. There are stories that some of them were world builders. They've been extinct for centuries."

"What happened to them?" asks Famka.

"They were butchered during the last Great War: the Battle of Bloodberry Bloom during the 1600s. Some even left the Motherland seeking asylum from the Fire Thief. Those might only be stories though."

"Why isn't there anything in our books about Dragons?" asks Ophelia. "That doesn't make any sense."

"Because the Ghostal Holly doesn't want you to know about them," says Momma Nay.

Famka looks down at the baby Drolling Dragon and nudges her under the chin. Heaven grabs hold of Famka's forefinger tightly and swings her little feet. Famka's taken by the sweetness of the child, but it's doing little for the betrayal she's feeling from Momma Nay.

"That's cute," says Heiki. "Clever of you to combine Salamander Matter with GumDrum. You would make a great addition to the Sky Builders' Guild."

"Back to bed with you, Heiki," Momma Nay barks. "Bring that little precious baby of yours inside. We'll get you tucked in nice and cozy." Momma Nay disappears inside with Heiki and Heaven floating in behind her.

"Ophi, come here," says Famka. She clutches her best friend by the wrist and drags her off the porch. They walk toward the pond before Famka says, "Look!"

She hands Ophelia the two invitations to Try Outs.

"After much deliberation the Bevy of Decomposing Composers, along with the esteemed members of the Ghostal Holly and in accordance with Jorge the Alien as head of the Sky Builders' Guild, do officially invite Famka Meadows and Ophelia Laveau to this year's Try Outs, which will begin at midnight October 25th and end on November 1st, the Day of the Dead, in the Plaza of Giants."

"That's only a few days away," says Famka.

"I can't believe it," says Ophelia. "I never thought my grams would do that to us."

Chapter 4

A Fight

Several days go by before the girls return to the cabin in the swamp. Famka has been silently brooding and, in an odd departure from character, hasn't bothered to pick up her *Gravedigger's Handbook* even once. Instead, she plays with a strange zipper-like device called a Winzi that Heiki gave her for saving Heaven.

It's early in the morning, and the girls are sitting in the tiny playground at the center of the Horseshoe. Most of the residents have left for the day to work in town, so besides a few of the old folks, they're alone. Famka looks at the trailers surrounding her and counts them again. This does nothing for her bad mood and reinforces that she's absolutely and positively miserable. Fortunately, the Texas summer sun has yet to turn the bright yellow seats of the plastic swing set into the consummate blister makers they'll become sometime around noon.

"Are you going to sulk for the whole day… *again*?" asks Ophelia, her annoyance seeping through her tone. "Just like you did yesterday and the day before and the day before that." She's sitting at one of the three picnic tables, running her bare feet through the sand. Famka watches as grains fall between Ophelia's brown toes as she lifts her feet only to do it again.

"Yes," says Famka. She turns toward the trail into the swamp. The dusty path splits a small parcel of ankle-high crabgrass in between two trailers; the one that Famka shares with Ophelia and her folks, and the other one, which belongs to Mrs. Billbray.

"Yes, we're going to talk about it, or yes you're going to sulk?" asks Ophelia lifting more sand with her toes. "Because if you're going to sulk, then I'm going for a run before it gets too hot."

"I'm not sulking, Ophi. I'm angry. Let's go find Momma Nay. Come on, she should be back by now." Famka leaps from a swing and storms across the Horseshoe.

As they approach Mrs. Billbray's trailer, the snoopy old woman sees them approaching. "Thank you, girls," she yells from her kitchen window. "Mr. Billbray's feet are feeling much better now."

Famka is so angry as she and Ophelia pass the trailer that she doesn't even acknowledge the old woman.

"You're welcome, Mrs. Billbray," Ophelia yells out running to catch up with Famka. "You're being rude."

"It doesn't matter right now," says Famka over her shoulder.

"Fine. Slow down," complains Ophelia.

"You're the runner. Catch up," snaps Famka.

The two girls make it out to the cabin in record-setting time. At least that's how Famka feels, because all she can think about is finding out why Momma Nay has been hiding their invitations to attend Try Outs with the Sky Builders. The Sky Builders! Famka's dream. Her brown face is a bright shade of red as she bursts through the front door of the cabin, the crumpled invitations in hand.

"What's this, Momma Nay?" yells Famka holding her hand out.

"That's nothing that you need to be concerned about," she answers flatly, barely glancing up from the kitchen table.

"You shouldn't have kept these from us. We get to decide," says Famka. "Not you!"

Momma Nay casually turns a page of the paper she is reading without looking up.

"I told you, Ophelia." Famka looks to see her best friend still standing in the doorway. "She doesn't want us leaving here."

"Momma Nay," says Ophelia surprised. "You've been lying to us?"

Famka sidles up beside Ophelia, points to the invitations, and says, "Look right there, Ophi,"—she puts Ophelia's invitation on top—"in the top left corner, that's your name in bold ink. It's addressed to you."

Ophelia Laveau
Cabin in the swamp.
Horseshoe near Wink, Texas.

"I can't believe this!" shouts Famka, waving her own invitation in the air. "We come out here to this dump every day to learn the tiny bits of Tuning you dish out."

"Dump!" says Momma Nay suddenly, slamming her thick hand down on the table. "What on earth do either of you fool-headed girls know about anything?"

"I know you're afraid," says Famka. "You're afraid we might leave you all alone in this godforsaken swamp. Or that we might be better than you at Tuning."

"You watch your tone with me, missy." Momma Nay points a thick, stern finger at Famka.

"This place *is* a dump, and you're an old woman who is too afraid to let us go." Famka crosses her arms over the chest and stares defiantly at the old woman.

"Come with me," demands Momma Nay. "Right now!" She jerks up from her seat, quickly rounds the table, grabs Famka by the wrist, and drags her out onto the front porch.

"Look at me, child," says Momma Nay standing in a beam of sunlight. "Look close and tell me. How old do you think I am?"

"What's that got to do with anything?" snaps Famka as she rubs her sore wrist.

"Come on now. Tell me," says Momma Nay.

"I don't know, early fifties, maybe?"

"Very generous of you," says Momma Nay. "But I'm four hundred and seventeen years old." She pauses and looks up like she's working out a problem in her head. "Make that four hundred and eighteen. Ya lose count when ya get past a certain age."

Famka and Ophelia both look at her skeptically.

"I am old enough to be Ophelia's grandmother ten times over. Don't ask me how I got to be so old without dying naturally, because I don't rightly know, but I suspect that an immortal I once knew had something to do with it. Now turn around and tell me what you see."

The girls face the swamp and Famka says, "A stinky

swamp, more trees, bushes, and bugs than I care for, and snakes hiding just waiting to bite me when I'm not looking. Oh, and this dumpy shack you call a home."

"You're blind, child," says Momma Nay. She points her thick finger toward the water and asks, "How do you think a spring-fed pond ended up on an island in the gulf? Ever consider that? I don't think so," Momma Nay says with a frosty glare. "I made it. That's how. How do you think the water gets here and then doesn't flood our home? Tuning, that's how. All around you, there are things to learn, things that the Sky Builders won't teach you. Go talk to the turtles, the fish, *and* the snakes. They'll each teach you something of Tuning if you'd just wake up and listen. Sky Builders are soldiers despite what you may think. I was here for the last war with the Fire Thief when the Sky Builders' Guild was brought to life by Wyndomier to fight the Fire Thief for the Ghostal Holly. Don't for a moment underestimate a government's need for control. The political control of the Ghostal Hollyis no different from any other.

"What I teach you out here in this *so-called dump*, as you consider it, is far deeper knowledge than you could gain at the Guild. I built this place for Ophelia, then you came along, Famka, and as far as I'm concerned, you're part of our family. Look around for once in your selfish lives and ask yourself why are there so many Wormwood trees?"

"I don't know," Famka says. "Maybe because the leaves are used in making Sarsaparilla Sometimes and that's about all you're good at?"

"Not bad little Miss Know-it-all, but that's only part of the tree. Do you even know what Wyndomier Wicks are made from?"

"Let me guess. Wormwood trees," says Famka.

"You got it," says Momma Nay. "This place is a gold mine, and one day, those trees will mature. I planted them over three hundred years ago and kept them a secret all this time. There are almost no Wyndomier Wicks remaining in the public's hands. The Ghostal Holly destroyed them after the war at the order of Chairman Boo.

"The few that still exist belong to the wealthy families that are close to the chairman and are handed down from generation to generation. When those trees mature, they will be in your hands. Ophelia's folks don't have a knack for Tuning, so you two better get your acts together and quit complaining about your poor little lives."

"What about you, Momma Nay?" asks Ophelia concerned. "Isn't the swamp for you too?"

"Child, I'll be gone soon. I'm old. My days are coming to an end, and I'll be closing up shop soon," she says. "I'm trying to leave you with what I can, but I fear that the days of Tuning are coming to an end, as well, and all the Sky Builders create are soldiers." She lets out a long breath and leans heavily on the porch railing. "Now I need you thickheaded, unappreciative girls to study, and study hard. Walk out there and talk with them turtles, the snakes, the trees. I've taught you both how to be an Animouth, so go ask the critters what they know and, God willing, learn something useful."

"I don't want to talk with turtles. I want to join the Sky Builders," says Famka stubbornly. "I don't want to be stuck here anymore, and I don't for a second care what snakes have to say."

Momma Nay's plump face, which is usually cheery, turns dower. "Then you do so without my consent. And don't come back if you leave here." She walks back into the cabin and slams the door shut.

"Fine!" yells Famka. "I'm going to Miss Turtlebalm if you won't help me. She's the best Sky Builder around, and she'll get me and Ophi into the Guild."

A sprinkle of dust falls on Famka's nose, and she sneezes loudly.

"That's not good," says Ophelia.

"Oh, don't be superstitious," says Famka. "Nothing bad is going to happen."

Chapter 5

The Fire Thief: Absent Drolling Dragon
(Long before you were born)

"YES, THIS IS a good night," said the Fire Thief. "Centuries of killing Dragons. Finally, the last one."

It is a fact that spirits do not move on from this earthly plane until their lives are completed, and on this night, the dead, particularly the recently dead, were restless and steadfast in their resolve. Yes, very restless, indeed they were.

"You can't go in there," said a young girl. "I will not allow it."

The Fire Thief stopped. He became a filthy man once again. He turned and looked toward the voice. The ghostly image of his first victim stood defiantly at the bottom of the stairs. The stain of her death wound spilled across her chest, painting her white nightgown blood red. Her long brown hair was disheveled, making her head look just a bit lopsided. He turned around and continued on his way. Random thoughts ran through his wicked mind in a nonlinear fashion. This was the problem with immortality. Sequential time became irrelevant.

One stab, two stabs, three stabs, four. Unperturbed, the Fire Thief ignored the girl and continued on his way.

"I said you cannot go in there!"

She was no longer at the bottom of the massive stairway and now stood at the top of the landing between the Fire Thief and the boy's room. The shadow raised his wicked hand and smashed it against the ghost of the young girl, hard. She flew across the room and disappeared through the wall of the old Victorian house.

"No!" yelled a man. "How dare you touch my daughter! How dare you!"

The Fire Thief turned lazily. A man with a bloody chest stood in the doorway next to a woman, also covered in blood. The man's watery image shimmered with anger. The doorway in which he stood appeared to strain. Every fiber of his body seemed bent on destroying the cruel intruder.

Could this be a challenge? thought the Fire Thief.

The man turned to his wife and said, "No matter what, keep our son safe. I love you." Then he kissed her goodbye.

The Shadow looked at the couple in the doorway for a moment and tilted his head again in quiet contemplation. They were doing something that he did not understand. Sacrifice. Love. Shouldn't he know about these things? Perhaps he once did.

No matter. This will all be done soon.

The father rushed the Fire Thief. His force took them both over the balcony railing, smashing through the ornate chandelier and onto the living room floor with a crash. The splinters of the railing lay scattered around their fierce struggle while the chandelier swung back and forth wildly. The father tried with all his might to keep the Fire Thief from destroying what little he had left, but the Fire Thief had lived a long time now and was much stronger than the man. So, with one cruel hand wrapped tightly around the man's throat, the Fire Thief pinned him to the floor and reached carefully into the pocket, which was not really a pocket, and removed what looked like a black stick, which was not really a stick.

"Dear God," gasped his wife from the balcony above.

The man looked at the ghostly image of his loving wife. As tears streamed down his face, he choked out his final words to her, "Go, woman."

For the second time that night, the Fire Thief stabbed the man in the chest, this time with the strange black weapon. Pain coursed through the father's ghostly body as he began to dissolve into nonexistence.

"What are you?" he asked before he was entirely gone.

I'm what's killing you, replied the Fire Thief inside the man's head.

Chapter 6

Lady'Witch Turtlebalm

It's early. The main boulevard in Wink is mostly empty, but already, it's blisteringly hot. Across the street, anxious tourists wanting a good spot near the water are already spreading their towels on the beach as sacred placeholders. That is when Mocha Turtlebalm, who is sweeping the sidewalk in front of her shop, overhears a conversation of interest. Two ghosts fly close by. Normally, ghosts aren't ones for the daylight hours here on the Middling Side of the Graveyard, but these two seem to be in a hurry.

"Families murdered. It's started again."

"I don't know about you, but I'm not staying on this side of the Graveyard any longer."

"And all for the Kitab…"

"Don't say its true name, Wilber. It's the Bastard Book."

"Ssssorry—"

Mocha continues sweeping the boardwalk, not bothering to look up until they are a safe distance away. She would rather not bring attention to herself as a Resident Witch. Often, she finds it best not to let on that she can see and hear the dead, a secret which has become more difficult to keep as her reputation has grown over the years. All sorts of juicy details slip out when the speaker is unaware of an eavesdropper. Mocha finally looks up as the two ghosts disappear into a five and dime several doors down. She considers their words for a moment before returning to her shop.

Mocha Turtlebalm is a traditional witch if ever there was one. A fly-through-the-air, disappear-from-plain-sight, and make-things-move-on-their-own sort of witch. She is not the sort of witch that wears a tall black hat, dresses in a cloak, or streaks through the night on a broomstick silhouetted against the moon. Those in the know are aware that brooms are an awful mode of transportation because they always go up your butt before you're even two feet off the ground. Ouch! Eventually, they were outlawed by the Ghostal Holly for chaffing.

She is a tall, thin woman with a long, stern face, but not unattractive. A perfectly proportionate nose, if not a little pointy, and not a single wart in sight. There are light wisps of gray through her long dark hair, which is always in a bun at the back of her head. Silver-framed glasses cover her light blue eyes, and despite what you might think of witches, she has a very pleasant smile and appealing teeth. Not a single yellow one and certainly not one out of place.

Mocha Turtlebalm isn't the sort of witch that huddles over a boiling cauldron, throwing in all sorts of things with funny names, like Root of Hemlock or a lizard's tail, into a potion. Unless of course she was making a disgusting bowl of soup for some uninvited guests. If you think that is what witches do, then you will get exactly what you deserve: an eye roll and a disappointed head shake, followed by a hefty bout of bouncing-belly laughter.

Lady'Witch Turtlebalm, as she was often called on the Other Side of the Graveyard, is a term of respect. One forged after years of training at the Sky Builders' Guild, the preeminent institution for learning all things witchy, or Tuning as it is more commonly known. Having been the first woman to win the infamous Hoodoo Man award for excellence in Tuning, she was offered a position of her choosing within the Ghostal Holly by none other than Chairman Boo! This is why no one understood why, after so many distinguished years at the Sky Builders' Guild, Lady'Witch Turtlebalm chose to become a lowly Resident Witch and patrol a remote speck of dirt. Then, as now, Wink was nothing more than a small tourist town on a tiny island in the Gulf of Mexico, just a few miles from the shores of Texas. There was certainly nothing special about it, unless you enjoy overeating while baking in the hot summer sun. Certainly, no place for a witch, thank you very much.

So, Lady'Witch Turtlebalm set up a shop selling sucking candies, ice cream shakes, and burgers to tourists along the bustling avenue of Wink Tree Lane. She called it Turtleburgers, which is ironic as the service is anything but slow. A peculiarity to be sure.

Despite her dedication to creating delicious chocolate malts, sprinkled with a touch of Tuning, it was a young girl she had rescued just days before relocating to Wink that kept her attention. The girl was a tiny thing filled with giggles, warmth, and smiles. How she had survived was nothing short of a miracle. Someone had mastered one of Wyndomier's Nine incredibly difficult spells. It was a Breaking spell, the likes of which was most challenging. It left nothing more than a crater-sized hole where the little girl had once lived with her parents. By the time Mocha had arrived, all that was left was a crying child at the bottom of the hole.

Mocha Turtlebalm knew that the girl's family had been hunted and murdered by those seeking an ancient book. This book was stolen right out of heaven by an immortal, who became a monster known as the Fire Thief. Mocha knew the girl's family had been entrusted with the knowledge of the book's whereabouts after the Great War with the Fire Thief had ended, because she, too, had been told this dangerous, but privileged information by her own parents. Neither of the families knew one another of course. It was the surest way to keep the book secret and the safest way to keep the families alive. It was only by chance that Mocha knew the girl's parents. *Bad luck*, she thought, as she reflected on that morning's events. She had sifted through the rubble of their once beautiful home until she found little Famka crying beneath a blanket holding a small stuffed animal.

That was over fifteen years ago.

These memories run through Mocha's mind as she puts away her broom in a closet that isn't really attached to the building and re-enters her shop. She is opening up for the day. Taking a deep breath, she steps into her store through an opening that disappears behind her, then she snaps her fingers and the lights overhead come to life. She flips over a sign so that it reads OPEN, unlocks the front door, and places several plastic chairs outside along the boardwalk.

Once inside, and with the ghosts' words echoing around her head, Mocha instantly feels that something is off. The air in the room has changed, feeling more electrified. Tiny hairs raise on her arms, and there is now the distinct scent of cinnamon. She smiles to herself, turns toward one of the booths, and says, "Momma Nay. I'm glad to see you."

The large, round woman materializes seated on a bench squished against the table.

"Every time, Mocha," says Momma Nay. "How do you do it?"

"Just a feeling I guess," says Mocha. "Might I get you something to eat?"

"Well, you did win that award for Tuning or some such nonsense," teases Momma Nay with a smile.

"You know I do not care for those sorts of things," she says, stepping behind the counter. "It allowed me to retire."

"Oh, we both know that ain't true," says Momma Nay. She pushes herself from the bench and walks over to a bar stool, where she plops back down and rests her dark arms on the counter. "I wouldn't mind a cup of coffee and a piece of your cobbler."

"Cobbler for breakfast?" says Mocha with a raised eyebrow.

"Mocha Turtlebalm, don't sass me. I was a big girl as a little chitlin, I was big when I raised my babies, and I'm big as an old woman. N' too old, in fact, to care what pie might do to my backside. Now warm me up a piece, would ya?"

Mocha wiggles the fingers of her left hand, and two small plates rise from a stack behind her. A knife shoots across the room toward a glass cake dome, which rises into the air, exposing a recently baked pie. Two warm pieces float into the air and land on plates, which are now between the two witches. A coffee pot bounces across the counter, followed by two cups trailing like puppies.

"Careful," says Mocha. "You're spilling it all over the counter."

"Slorry," gurgles the coffee pot and slows its approach.

After the coffee pot fills the two mugs, Momma Nay says, "Too early for pie, huh?"

"I didn't say I was a saint."

The two witches eat in silence until Mocha says, "So what can I help you with, Momma Nay."

"Famka is coming to see you," says Momma Nay. "About joining the Sky Builders. And you know Ophelia will be right on her heels."

"That's not a good idea," says Mocha.

"I couldn't agree more. You know I don't care for the Guild, but why exactly do you feel that way?" questions Momma Nay suspiciously. "You are a Sky Builder after all. I'd think you people would be happy to have Famka."

"Normally, I would agree with you," says Mocha.

"You had to know this day would come. All these young witches dream of joining the Sky Builders, and despite my arguments, I can't stop either of them girls from wanting to go. So once and for all, Mocha, why exactly did you leave that little girl at my doorstep fifteen years ago? You need to be coming clean with me."

"She was a three-year-old orphan, and I thought you best suited to raise her."

"Mule matter!" says Momma Nay. "One week after you left that child at my door, Mocha Turtlebalm, YOU, one of the most famous witches the Sky Builders has ever produced, settles just a few short miles away. And on my island of all places. Don't you find that peculiar?"

Frowning, Mocha pauses before saying, "I know we haven't always seen eye to eye over the years, but I believe you an honest witch, if a bit unorthodox in your approach to Tuning."

"You Sky Builders are always up on your high horse," says Momma Nay shaking her head. "You ain't the final authority on Tuning, you know. Most of us country folks figured out all sorts of things ya haven't even thought of."

"I don't want to argue with you," says Mocha after another pause. "There are dangers coming whether we like it or not."

"Yes. Yes," says Momma Nay. "I feel it too. Been hearing all sorts of rumors from fuzzy floaties for months now. Them ghosties can't help but be scared too. So, what's this all have to do with the girl?"

"Her father was a Letters of the Living. As a Letter he was guarding the *Kitab'i'Mordanee*."

Momma Nay slams her thick hand down on the counter. "Do you have to say its name out loud?"

"I do not wish to give it power over me by adhering to superstition."

"Then respectfully call it something else in my presence," says Momma Nay.

"As you wish," says Mocha.

After a long pause, Momma Nay says, "I've wondered if those stories were true."

"They are quite true. There were six families. One from each magical race. The Poppets in the north, Bombadoes in the middle, Wigglers in the west, Drolling Dragons in the East, Witches in the south, and of course, Dragons. Each was entrusted with the knowledge of the book's location after the Great War. They were each given a sealed case. None of them knew if their case held the book or not, nor did they know about the others, but I've been following particular patterns of murders over the last eighteen months or so. The first one that got my attention was the murder of the two Bombadoes."

"Horrible," says Momma Nay.

"And it's very rare that anyone succeeds in killing a Bombadoe. As you know, they are ancient, and for good reason. There was a string of witches murdered shortly thereafter, with houses torn apart in a way that reminded me of how I found Famka's parents' house all those years ago. I am not certain why this is happening again. I had believed that Famka's father was the last living Letter."

"Are you suggesting that Famka is a Dragon then?"

"No," says Mocha. "Though she is exceptional, I do not believe her to be a Dragon."

"You said each of the six races was given a case, but only one supposedly held the book. There are no Dragons left, so I assume that two of the cases were given to one race."

"Yes, you deduce correctly. As it happens, however, I knew the Drolling Dragon that was given one of the six cases. He came to me, fearing for his life. I'm the one that took him to Famka's father for help. He was one of the best Sky Builders the Guild had, but more important, he was an honest man. I thought he might hide it in the past."

"So, what happened to her parents… was your fault," says Momma Nay.

"To my everlasting regret," says Mocha. "You have no idea the weight I carry."

"Oh, I have some familiarity with it," says Momma Nay looking downward. "So, what happened to the Drolling Dragon?"

"He was right. Someone was after him. Two days after giving up the case, he was murdered. A day later, the Meadows' home was attacked."

"Did you bring the book to my island?" asks Momma Nay.

"No. I do not have it. I only arranged the meeting with Lockland," says Mocha flatly. "Regardless, I suspect that these dangers will come to your home eventually."

"Perhaps after I'm long dead," snaps Momma Nay.

"I know that you have reason to care despite being angry."

"You leave Ophelia out of this. My grandbaby ain't got nothing to do with this fuss of yours." Momma Nay points a thick finger at Mocha.

The two witches sit quietly for a long moment. Both are lost in thought. The coffee pot leaps into the air and refills both mugs, spilling only a little on the white counter top. Mocha looks out the front window. Tourists are already filling Wink Tree Lane, and soon it will be crowded. A shirtless young man dashes by the window laughing, followed by two boys. Mocha is certain they are up to no good. What she would give to be out there with them, carefree and unaware of the darkness slowly descending on them all.

"So, it's starting again?" says Momma Nay interrupting the silence.

Mocha turns back to the large woman and says, "It would seem so."

"And Famka?" asks Momma Nay.

"I believe that she is somehow hiding the book. Her father may have authored a spell that is attached to her."

"You think she's a Caramel Key?"

"No, nothing so dark," says Mocha.

Momma Nay pauses, then says, "Dang it! I lived through the last war. I can't take another one."

"The only thing you can do is prepare the girls for what is

coming. You cannot keep them from joining the Sky Builders forever. You will only alienate them."

"I know," says Momma Nay in a rare resignation. "But I love them two girls. And even if Famka ain't mine, she's still mine."

Chapter 7

Turtleburgers

Famka and Ophelia dash into Turtleburgers, Miss Turtlebalm's soda shop. Sweat runs down Famka's back, drawing a moist line in her black T-shirt. Music plays from a jukebox against the far wall in between two doors that lead to the restrooms. Waitresses run burgers, fries, and shakes out as fast as the cook can throw them together.

"I'm so sorry that I missed you girls last week. I had an errand in the Plaza of Giants that needed my attention," says Lady'Witch Turtlebalm from behind the counter. She's seated on a bar stool, wearing a long white apron. "Might I get either of you something to eat or perhaps a soda?"

"I'd love a Dr. Pepper, thank you," says Famka.

"Ophelia?" Miss Turtlebalm raises her eyebrows, silently asking the same question.

"Sweet tea, please," Ophelia replies.

"I assume you are here because Momma Nay doesn't want either of you to join the Sky Builders," says Miss Turtlebalm as she pops the cap from a bottle then slides it to Famka.

Famka takes a big gulp of her drink and says, "Yeah. It's not fair."

"We're witches," says Ophelia under her breath. Her eyes dart to the other customers seated nearby. An old-timer beside her sips from a cup of coffee but doesn't appear to hear her. She wipes a bead of sweat slipping from her big poof of curly hair and down her temple.

"No need to worry about the other customers," says Miss Turtlebalm noticing Ophelia's apprehension. "What is said in my shop stays between us witches. The man sitting next to you hears us talking about football."

"That's so cool," says Ophelia, her eyebrows raising.

"Shouldn't we be in the Sky Builders' Guild by now?" asks Famka.

"Yes, you should have at least been to Try Outs by now," says Miss Turtlebalm. "Have you received invitations yet?"

"Months ago," says Famka.

"And last year and the year before that," adds Ophelia.

"Hm, that is a concern." Miss Turtlebalm furrows her eyebrows, and a crease appears between them.

"Momma Nay hid them from us," says Ophelia.

"She's only trying to do what she thinks is best, girls," says Miss Turtlebalm. She smiles reassuringly, her blue eyes twinkling behind her silver-framed glasses.

"She's just jealous because she never went," says Famka angrily.

"Well, I may not agree with Momma Nay's methods, but she is a fine witch. Her approach to Tuning is unique, and I believe that her feelings about the Guild are not down to jealousy."

"Unique... That's a nice way to put it," grumbles Famka.

"I thought we weren't ready to go, because neither of our *Gravedigger's Handbooks* show us any spells, but maybe Famka is right," say Ophelia looking concerned. "We need to go, or we'll never become good witches."

"Miss Turtlebalm, can you help us?" asks Famka.

"Lucky for you both, I've already spoken to Momma Nay. She was in here just last week," says Miss Turtlebalm. "I think some things will change for you two girls soon."

Famka lights up with delight and grabs Ophelia's dark hand.

"That's wonderful," says Famka.

The two girls exchange a smile.

"What's it like?" asks Ophelia. "The Sky Builders' Guild, I mean."

Miss Turtlebalm looks away, as if staring into her memories on a TV only she can see.

"I suppose that it is both exhilarating and terrifying," says Miss Turtlebalm. "When I first joined the Guild, I was only fifteen. I wasn't ready to leave home and my parents. Even though they were both Sky Builders, they didn't want me leaving so early. They felt that I should stay home for another year."

"Really?" says Famka feeling uncertain. "We're both seventeen. Are we going to be the oldest students there?"

"No no," says Miss Turtlebalm. "The Guild doesn't work like that. A prospective student is sent an invitation when Jorge, he's the head of the Guild, feels that you are ready. That can be anywhere between thirteen, although rarely that young, and up to nineteen years old."

"How does he know when you're ready… this Jorge person?" asks Ophelia.

"That is a mystery," says Miss Turtlebalm. "There are many things about Jorge that are unknown. Some people refer to him as Jorge the Alien because some think that he is from another planet. That is plain silliness to me; part of the Sky Builder folklore, I think. Anyway, my parents were apprehensive about me leaving home at fifteen. My father specifically forbade me to work Wyndomier's Nine spells until I was at least seventeen. It was different then. Momma Nay tells me that you girls already know at least one Mending spell. Even then, the Breaking spell didn't come to me until much later."

"But you're one of the most famous witches. How could that spell be difficult for you?" asks Famka.

"Don't let the opinions of others shape your reality of things. Fame is fleeting at best, and at its worst, it clouds the mind."

"Is that why you came to Wink?" asks Ophelia.

Miss Turtlebalm suddenly looks sad as her blue eyes droop subtly at the edges. Famka wonders what could suddenly turn Miss Turtlebalm's light demeanor into a heavy one. She notices that Miss Turtlebalm's eyes rest on her for a couple of seconds.

A little voice squeaks in the back of her mind, *Does her coming to Wink have something to do with me?*

"Oh, I'm sorry," says Ophelia. "That's probably none of my business."

"It's quite all right," says Miss Turtlebalm. After a brief silence, she adds with a little smile, "I came here to take care of you two. My favorite young witches."

Famka smiles at the older woman. In some ways, Miss Turtlebalm has been like a mother figure. She has always been kind, generous with her time, and willing to address any questions about Tuning, which is not something Momma Nay cares to do. Answering a million questions only annoys the old Cajun witch. Famka can't think of a time when she hadn't known Miss Turtlebalm. To her, the retired Sky Builder has always been a part of her life.

"Do you miss the Guild?" asks Famka.

"Not at all," says Miss Turtlebalm. "I'm still involved, just not on a day-to-day basis, and I'm a Resident Witch, so I have my duties to attend to with witches and ghosts in the neighboring communities."

"Can you fly, Miss Turtlebalm?" asks Famka, her eyebrows rising high above her green eyes.

"Of course, although I don't care for it," she says. "I much prefer the Hallowed Halls for getting about. Much faster than flying."

"Don't you fly through the Halls?" asks Famka.

"Yes, I suppose that's true, but somehow, it feels different to me," says Miss Turtlebalm. "Perhaps because I'm surrounded by my fellow witches. The problem with flying in public is that you also have to be visible. That has its own difficulties. If anyone should see you then, the Ghostal Holly is likely to arrest you."

"Are they strict?" asks Ophelia.

"Well, they are our government, so they must enforce the law," says Miss Turtlebalm.

"I gotta pee," says Ophelia suddenly. "I'll be right back."

Once she's gone, Miss Turtlebalm says, "There is something that I should have told you a long time ago and I am sorry that I didn't. But I knew your mother and father."

"You did?" says Famka surprised.

Miss Turtlebalm pauses. She clasps her hands together,

places her elbows on the counter, and leans against her closed hands. Famka knows that something is troubling the old witch. After a moment, Miss Turtlebalm sits up straight again and says, "They were wonderful people. Your father in particular was one of the best Sky Builders I ever knew."

"Really! He was a Sky Builder?" asks Famka excitedly.

Ophelia returns and sits beside Famka.

"Did you hear that, Ophelia?" says Famka. "My dad was a Sky Builder."

"What?" says Ophelia. "How do you know?"

"Miss Turtlebalm knew my folks."

"Listen, girls, I've put in a request with Jorge to allow you both to Try Out privately since you missed the deadline."

The two young witches jump up and down excitedly, hugging each other.

"Thank you, Miss Turtlebalm," says Famka.

"Yes, thank you," adds Ophelia.

"Don't get too excited. I don't know if he will accept my request," says Miss Turtlebalm. "If he doesn't, then I will begin your training here."

Chapter 8

The Fire Thief: Horrid Malamander
(Long before you were born)

WITHIN SECONDS, THE father dissolved into a series of blurry images, each resembling a moment in his life. The last was of him as a child accepting a small book from a proud parent. The book was brown with words written in bright orange light on the cover that read *Gravedigger's Handbook*. He must have been about his son's age. Then the image faded, and he was gone. Once a strong, educated, and caring man, he was now nothing more than a series of memories destined to fade. The Fire Thief had taken more than just his body, for the body is temporary at best. He had done something much worse.

He had taken the man's soul and erased him from existence.

"Dear God," the woman on the landing gasped. Tears leapt from her eyes and flooded her cheeks.

"No God. Only Nyre King," said the Fire Thief. His hat covered his head, and his long, greasy hair clung nastily to his face. He did not look at her as he spoke but watched the man's life disappear before him.

"Nyre King will not help you here. Fool! So, let's leave Nyre King out of this, shall we? There are only circles. It always comes back, yes. Circles."

The woman ran to her son's room. She made a funny swooshing sound as she burst through the solid wood door. The boy sat up in his bed, rubbing his inquisitive green eyes. "Mum, what was that noise—Oh, what happened?" he asked as he pointed to her bloody chest.

"We have to go, honey, something horrible has happened."

She tried to push the window open, but her hands disappeared through the glass. "Where is Poppa and sis?"

"Hurry, help me with the window," she said, ignoring him.

"Mum, we can't leave them behind." He opened his bedroom door just as the Fire Thief was slowly ascending the long, curved staircase. The shadow stopped and looked up. The boy stared at eyes that seemed to glow in the darkened face. He could feel the Fire Thief's brutal intent like worms in his veins, he knew the monster had come to carry his soul away.

"Don't look at it!" She tried to shut the door, but her hand passed through it. The boy slammed the door and ran to the window and forced it open. Air came rushing in like an uninvited guest. It was cold, and the rain was coming down at a peculiar angle. It spilled into the room and onto the dark wood floor near his feet.

He climbed onto the windowsill.

"I don't understand. What is that thing?"

"I don't know, Mum, but we have to make it to the barn. Poppa said that if anything every happened, a Wyndom Window would be there to help us escape."

The boy sat and hung his legs over the roof. He wanted to get as low as he could before he jumped off. He landed with a thud, but everything remained intact.

"Mum, don't be afraid. You can't get hurt now."

Like a feather, she landed soundlessly on the grassy court below.

"Are you all right, Mum?"

"Yes, I think so." Bravely she hid the rush of sadness nearing the surface of her heart. It was threatening to come out all at once, but she knew she had to be strong for her son or he would meet the same unfortunate demise.

They heard a noise and looked up. The Fire Thief stood in the boy's bedroom window staring down at them. Empty sockets remained where eyes had been. In each socket was only a single matchstick burning brightly.

"Where is this God of yours now?" came his dark, ominous voice.

The Fire Thief pointed lazily toward the sky, as if heaven were a nuisance to him. His fingers were long, longer than those of the average person.

Chapter 9

A Sky Builder

"I DO THIS against my better judgment, but you girls have much to learn outside of this here swamp," says Momma Nay. She stares at Famka and Ophelia, who are standing in front of her in the cabin.

Despite having fought over the Guild, Momma Nay was never one to hold a grudge. Famka appreciated that Momma Nay often let things go. She often said that life was too short for such things, and love is far more important than being right.

"Do what exactly?" asks Famka squinting.

"We're going to meet a powerful witch," says Momma Nay, "in Crow's Landing above the Plaza of Giants. I've been sent a desperate message, so we need to hurry."

"Really?" blurts out Famka excitedly. "Did you hear that, Ophi?"

"Come on, girls," says Momma Nay walking toward the back door of the cabin.

"Crow's Landing," says Ophelia to Momma Nay. "But you

always tell us not to go there."

"That's true," says Momma Nay with a sigh. "Perhaps that has more to do with my own prejudices than any dangers. Many of the witches residing in Crow's Landing…" She pauses then continues. "Well, let's just say many of them have made choices that I disagree with. Regardless, you girls are adults now, and you can make up your own minds. Circumstances are changing, and there are things I need to show the two of you."

Momma Nay sounds dire again. A couple of weeks ago, she'd revealed that she was over four centuries old and had fought in the Hundred-Year War known as the Battle of Bloodberry Bloom against the Fire Thief. That was startling enough, but then she followed it up with her impending death. Famka couldn't help but notice that Momma Nay kept speaking as if her time was truly coming to an end, and she didn't like it one bit.

They step up to her back door, and Momma Nay takes out a worn pewter key, which hangs on a piece of twine around her neck. She slides it into the keyhole of the old doorknob, and the door swings open, revealing not the swamp behind the cabin as one might expect, but a large dark room lined with shelves. Momma Nay snaps her fingers, and light bursts to life in the room, illuminating a shop, which is filled floor to ceiling with shelves stacked with glass mason jars, baskets, and a whole lot of books. The two girls follow Momma Nay through the entryway and the door closes behind them on its own. Famka looks back, and the cabin is gone. The shelves are crammed with healing curatives and potions, with labels beneath each item.

"Now I know where all the stuff we make goes," says

Famka looking up at the high ceiling, which is crossed in thick wood beams where even more baskets hang filled, some nearly overflowing.

"Famka," says Ophelia under her breath. "Don't be rude."

"I'm not, Ophi," she shoots back. "This is amazing."

"She's right, Ophelia," says Momma Nay. "Everything I've taught you girls how to make, since you were little chitlins, has ended up here. This shop is my shop, and soon, it will belong to you both."

"What's it called?" asks Famka trying to ignore the tone in Momma Nay's voice.

"Lotty Laveau's," says Momma Nay squeezing behind a counter and ducking down. She pops back up holding a mason jar labeled *dangerous* and places it on the counter. Behind her on the wall is a long chalkboard detailing the day's specials.

"Apparently, my concoction is popular," says Famka reading the words written neatly in white chalk…

Meadow Wells: Just the right amount of Salamander Matter, GumDrum, and Grumple Moss.

"You named it after me?" says Famka, suddenly feeling a little sting of guilt for fighting with Momma Nay.

"Yes of course, child," says Momma Nay. "You thought to combine those elements, which was very clever of you. I've sold out of it twice already. I suspect that if we don't make more soon, I'll have a line of angry witches to deal with. Now come on. We need to head up the hill to Crow's Landing before it gets much later."

"Don't let it go to your head," teases Ophelia as she nudges Famka.

A sudden noise followed by a tall man stepping out of the shadows draws their attention. The stranger is dressed in black from head to toe, including a mask over his face. Only dark eyes are visible and a single scar across his left eye, giving it a milky white appearance.

"Hold It!" yells Momma Nay. Her hands shoot up reflexively as a near invisible shield comes to life in front of the figure. It places a protective barrier between the stranger and the three witches. It's supposed to be invisible, but to Famka, the air is cloudy like looking through water in a glass jar. She wants to reach up and touch it, but from her last experience with the shield, she is reluctant.

"Better to meet you here," says the stranger. "My time is running short."

"That wasn't the agreement," says Momma Nay angrily. "I've made my opinion very clear. I don't care for you Sky Builders. No deal. Get out."

"I never said that I'm a Sky Builder," says the man.

"When you're as old as I am, some things are plain as the day is long. Now leave!"

The man falls to his knees with a grunt. Even through the Trankler's Hold It, Famka can see that he is bleeding. A stream of red runs from beneath his long black sleeve and onto his hand. The drops quickly pool on the wood floor beneath him.

"It's eating away at me," slurs the man. "Without your assistance, I'll…"

Momma Nay lets out a long breath and looks on with a heavy, furrowed brow. Her dark round face is stiff with anger, and Famka knows from the look in her eye that she's made up her mind. Famka has seen that look more than once, and Momma Nay rarely turns back. She will not help this man. Whatever history there is between her and the Sky Builders is bad enough to let him die. Famka, however, has no previous history, so she walks up to the invisible shield and places a hand on it.

"Step back, Famka," snaps Momma Nay, but Famka ignores the old woman and closes her eyes. In her mind, she imagines the shield like a large sheet pinned to a clothesline. She breathes out and calls on the Song of the World. She'd heard it once before when she tried pulling the shield around her as she swam in the ocean. She hopes to hear it again. It takes a few moments, but the Song of the World becomes faintly audible, humming in the distance like a car passing with its radio blasting. She reaches up with her other hand and pulls on the shield as if yanking a blanket from a bed. Much to her surprise, it snaps loose.

"Famka Meadows!" says Momma Nay with amazement in her voice. "How on earth?"

Famka tries to fold the Trankler's Hold It, but it bursts in her hands like a bubble popping.

Dang it!

"How did you do that?" the bleeding man slurs from the floor. "Not possible."

"We can't let him die, Momma Nay," says Famka, turning back to the old woman. "I know you're mad at the Sky Builders, but he's still a person, and he needs our help. You always taught me and Ophi to show kindness, love, and empathy."

"Famka's right, Momma Nay," says Ophelia stepping forward.

"You girls are my dearest blessing, but this will come back on us. Mark my words." Momma Nay takes out another jar from beneath the display case. She places it on the counter and removes the lid. Edwin the salamander jumps out and sits up on his hind legs as if he's a person. He crosses his arms and looks up unimpressed. At least that's what Famka thinks his little expression is saying.

"Edwin," says Momma Nay. "I have a favor to ask."

"Oh, do you now?" he says sarcastically. "Edwin, I need this. Edwin, I need that. Edwin, just a little more of your spit, so I can make *yet* another batch of Salamander Matter. I think not, Momma Nay. Go find another Malamander. I am done with your requests. You've shackled me to this jar long enough."

The stranger groans from the floor. When Famka looks at him, his eyes are closed and he's on his side favoring his good arm.

"I could make the jar smaller, Edwin," threatens Momma Nay. "Or I could bury it in the ground and leave you in the dark for a few decades. How would you like that?"

"Fine," he says. "And while you're at it, you can suck a fart right out of my butt."

"Edwin!" snaps Famka. "Don't be rude."

"That's really gross," says Ophelia scrunching up her dark face.

"Edwin," says Famka leaning against the counter just out of biting range. "What is it that you want?"

His little face perks up. "Oh, don't act like you care, Famka," says the little black and yellow Malamander.

"Despite your sarcasm, Edwin, I think you like living at the cabin. I think you like me and Ophelia and you might even love Momma Nay. You're just hurt," says Famka.

The little Malamander's black eyes flash to Momma Nay then back to Famka.

"Tell me what you want," says Famka, "and I'll get it for

you."

"I want hot dogs and pizza swimming in barbecue sauce," he says, then looks up at Momma Nay. "And I want you to say thank you from time to time. You don't appreciate me at all. Do you know what it's like to be all alone? No, you don't, because you have a family. You have friends and witches that reach out to you because they need you like that poor slob on the floor. I'm the only Malamander left. Have you seen another one since the war? No! That's because we're all gone, thanks to the Fire Thief. It's just me now, and your invisible shackles don't allow me to get five feet from this jar."

"You're too dangerous to let loose," says Momma Nay.

"Since when did I ever bite anyone?" argues Edwin. "You think that I like watching you puny witches balloon up like a bloated blueberry, float into the sky and die? You're content to let snakes slither freely in the swamp, but not me. Snake venom is practically useless. At least mine can be combined into a healing balm."

"The last time I let you free, you ran off," says Momma Nay.

"Ran off?" says Edwin. "I had to poop."

"Well, you were gone an awfully long time, and I had to come find you."

"Do you see what I eat?" he says. "Of course it would take me a long time. It would take you a long time to pass five cheeseburgers too."

Famka reaches out to Edwin and places an open hand on the counter before him. "Don't bite me, Edwin."

"Famka, don't." Momma Nay slaps her hands away.

"Ugh," he snaps. "You witches and your biting. Do you have any idea how bad you taste?"

"It's okay, Momma Nay," Famka places both of her hands down. "Come on, Edwin, let's go help that man over there."

Edwin looks at her uncertainly and says, "What are you doing, Famka?"

"I don't think that you're going to bite me. I think that you're lonely. You miss having family, and the simple touch of another living being might be comforting. So, climb onto my hands."

He sits forward and takes a step toward Famka's hands. He places a tiny, clawed foot onto her finger. At first, he feels cold and his claws are like tiny nails. Then he leaps up and lands squarely in her palms. Momma Nay jerks up but doesn't move.

"It's all right, Momma Nay," says Famka. She turns away, walks to the dying man, and bends down before him. Edwin scurries off her hands and sniffs the blood on the floor.

"What do you think happened to him?" asks Momma Nay stepping up behind Famka.

"Attacked by a Pilgrim," says the man in a barely audible whisper.

"He's lying," says Edwin. "His wound smells like it came from a Wyndomier Wick. No, that's not it. A spell backfired on him."

"All right, girls, help me roll him off his side." Momma Nay bends down beside the man. They carefully turn him onto his back, revealing a large bloodstain on the floor pooled underneath his left arm. His hand is frozen in a claw-like shape, as if he is gripping something invisible.

"Can you move your hand?" asks Momma Nay frowning at his bent fingers.

"No," says the man.

"Ophelia, there's a pair of scissors behind the counter.

Fetch them, would you?"

"Momma Nay, is he dangerous?" asks Famka.

"Not in his current state," says Momma Nay. "But I wouldn't want to meet him in a dark graveyard."

Ophelia dashes away and quickly returns. "Here you go."

As Momma nay begins cutting the front of his shirt, she says, "Don't uncover his face. I don't want to know who he is. It's safer that none of us know."

Opening his black shirt, she reveals a pale white chest covered partially in blood. A stab wound in his abdomen is growing as if it's eating him.

"No Mending spell will heal this," says Momma Nay to the man. "You should be dead already. What did this?"

The man hesitates, so Momma Nay adds, "If you don't tell me, I can't help you."

"Cauldron of Names," whispers the man.

"Fallen Arts," says Momma Nay. "Lord love a duck! You Sky Builders will resort to anything won't you?"

The man moans but says nothing more.

"What happened to him, Momma Nay?" asks Ophelia looking like she might throw up. She leans against Famka as the three of them stare down at the stranger.

"By the look of his wounds, he tried to find out who the author of a particular spell was. And whoever the author was didn't want to be found out, so the Cauldron backfired on this Builder." Famka notices that Momma Nay says *Builder* with disgust.

"Is he going to die?" asks Famka.

"He might," says Momma Nay.

The man lets out another moan, and Famka can see that Momma Nay is torn. Famka knows that Momma Nay is a healer. It's in her nature to help folks, but there is something about this man that's making her hesitate.

"All right, Edwin," says Momma Nay after a moment. She turns to the black and yellow Malamander perched on the floor near the puddle of blood. "He's all yours."

He quickly scurries over. His little claws tapping along the wood floor. Momma Nay leans away as Edwin crawls onto the dying man. The Malamander sniffs the wound and says, "His own Wyndomier Wick did this."

"You stabbed yourself with a Wyndomier Wick?" says Momma Nay to the man. "What on earth is so important that you would risk doing that?"

The man mutters, "Trying to heal myself."

"Foolish," is all that Momma Nay adds.

Edwin says, "Two parts GumDrum, One part Leadbelly butter, four parts Wormwood."

"Wormwood!" says Momma Nay surprised, then looks down at the stranger. "Mister this is going to cost you double."

"I'll pay it," he mutters.

"Momma Nay, you can't charge a dying man more money!" says Famka outraged.

"I'm not charging him money, child," says Momma Nay. "I'm charging him protection for you and Ophelia. Money, I couldn't care less about."

"Oh," says Famka feeling a little stupid.

"Girls, fetch the GumDrum and Leadbelly butter. You'll see them labeled on a shelf over there," says Momma Nay, pointing to a splintered green cabinet behind the main counter, tucked in a corner. Famka and Ophelia rush away as the old woman pushes herself up, then hobbles across the room to an empty space on the worn brick wall. She waves her hand, and rows of shelves appear clear to the ceiling. Staring up, she raises herself off the floor and hovers in the air until she has reached the top shelf. She takes a strange bundle of weeds, then slowly descends. Shaking them vigorously as she walks back to the man, they turn purple, glowing brightly, but strangely, they don't cast any light onto the floor.

"Is that Wormwood?" asks Famka coming up beside Momma Nay.

"Yes, it's very rare," answers Momma Nay. "So little of it is left."

"But in the swamp..."

Momma Nay nudges Famka to remain quiet, and Ophelia shakes her head nervously.

"Now then," says Momma Nay bending down. "Remove the lids. Place the Leadbelly on his left side and the GumDrum on his right."

Once the girls are done, Momma Nay places the Wormwood across the man's stomach, balancing each end on the two jars. Edwin jumps down and sits beside Famka and Ophelia. The three of them watch as Momma Nay begins humming a melody. She closes her eyes and waves her hands in circles, each hand moving in opposite motion of the other. A faint light emanates from her thick palms and begins to glow brighter. As it does, the man groans more loudly. Her dark face grows serious as she squeezes her brow together, deepening a wrinkle between her eyes. The Wormwood dissolves into his stomach, and the wound slowly begins closing until it is completely gone. His left hand, however, remains frozen in a grip. He opens his eyes again, which are dark brown, almost black, and he exhales loudly like he'd been holding his breath the entire time.

Extinguishing the light from her hands, Momma Nay bends down and glares angrily at the man. "We're going to leave now. I don't want to ever see you again. Make sure that you steer clear of my shop. Should you be tempted to return here, be aware that there is now a specific spell I've authored just for you, as I healed you. Forget my warning, and your wounds will reappear at an accelerated rate, and I promise that you will die within seconds." She pushes herself to her feet as the man manages a seated position and looks down at his now-healed stomach. "Wormwood is very expensive and nearly extinct now, so make sure you pay me in full. Understood?"

The man nods and begins to stand.

"Come on, girls. You too, Edwin," says Momma Nay walking toward the back door they came through moments ago. Trailing behind Ophelia, Famka looks back at the man as he stares down at his clawed hand. He is very tall and thin, with a lock of black hair poking out from his head covering. Famka turns away and is about to step through the doorway when Edwin begins making high-pitched sound behind her. She spins around to see the man holding a glowing Wyndomier Wick and Edwin standing on his hind legs.

"You will die from my bite," warns Edwin.

The man holds steady, and Famka can see his dark eyes peeking through his facial covering, but he doesn't move. Famka isn't sure the Sky Builder is threatening them, but she doesn't hesitate to quickly scoop Edwin off the ground and slip out the door. As the door closes, the shop vanishes along with the Sky Builder.

Once back in Momma Nay's cabin Ophelia asks, "What is that man hiding? What happened to him?"

Momma Nay sits down on a chair at the kitchen table, sighs heavily, and says, "bad stuff."

"Come on, Momma Nay," says Famka as she sets Edwin on the floor. "We're not little girls any more. You need to tell us the truth of things."

The old woman remains quiet for a moment, looking more tired and far older than usual. Her dark skin seems to sag a little. Famka worries that maybe she's telling the truth and her time really is coming to an end.

"Sky Builders' Guild," says Momma Nay, her voice weary. "It was started by Wyndomier during the Hundred-Year War, but you both know that already. What you don't know is that within the Builders' Guild, there are those that long for the Fire Thief to return to power. Some of them have continued to search out ways to free that beast from the Sea of Chall. I don't know what that particular Sky Builder was up to, but he was obviously poking at a spell that wasn't supposed to be poked at. You see, when witches hide things, they typically use spells, which have counter curses attached to them. That way, if anyone comes looking for what they're hiding, that person gets a real hurting put on them. The keeping of secrets is one of the most dangerous aspects of Tuning. In some cases, it's a Fallen Art, and by using a Cauldron of Names as that man did, he was fiddling with something shady." She stands up, then hobbles to one of the beds and sits down. "I'm tired, girls. You run on home now. Oh, and Edwin…?"

The Malamander looks up from the floor beside Famka.

"You are hereby released from your bondage," she says. "You are free to go where ever you wish."

The little creature looks up at Famka and then at Momma Nay. "That's a fine thing to say to me. Where would I go,

Momma Nay?" says Edwin. "Despite you being a big grump and keeping me trapped for exactly two hundred and thirteen years, you are the only family I have now."

"Two hundred and fifteen," Momma Nay corrected, then lies down and closes her eyes. Ophelia walks across the room, places a blanket on her, and tucks the sides in around her as Famka closes the curtains above the kitchen window and the two on either side of the front door.

"Famka," says the little Malamander once they're outside on the front porch.

"Yes, Edwin," says Famka turning to him.

"Could you make me some more of those chocolate chip cookies?"

Famka smiles and says, "Sure."

"And please don't forget the walnuts this time."

"I won't," she says with a giggle.

"It's very important to achieve the perfect bite, you know. You need the right ratio of sweet to salty. It's no joking matter," he says very seriously.

"You're going to get fat, Edwin," says Ophelia.

As Famka and Ophelia walk through the swamp toward the Horseshoe, Famka can't help but feel a sense of dread. She's been excited to meet a Sky Builder, but now that she has, she wonders if perhaps Momma Nay was right about them.

Chapter 10

The Third Witch

THE THIRD WITCH was a cute, plump, blonde-haired, blue-eyed girl named Milly Rien. She lived in the finest part of Wink with many luxurious things. With white columns towering over two-stories high, her home spoke of a time in history some folks might want to forget and others are proud to boast about.

As a ten-year-old, she saw her first ghost one sunny afternoon from the upstairs window of her parents' palatial home. And as the saying goes... To see the dead is to do as the dead do. At first, she thought it was only her imagination. She'd spent so much time alone that she sometimes talked to herself. The ghost was a gaunt man with bloodstains smeared across the back of his dress shirt. The front was clean, however. Peculiar if one thought about it.

The barely visible man floated across the duck pond, reflecting bluish light off the water. He paused over a gazebo before disappearing entirely. Terrified, Milly immediately hid in the dark recesses of the broom closet, munching on a bag of chips until the butler found her huddled in the corner, well after bedtime. These sightings of the dead man went on for years, and often, he paced near the gazebo. She tried telling her mother once, but she instantly reminded Milly about crazy Aunt Clair, who had been locked in an insane asylum for decades.

One day, Milly hid behind one of the tall white columns and watched him from the back porch, too frightened to be seen, but too curious not to peek. Most days, he would appear instantly in what she imagined was a puff of frustration, his face red as a turnip. Other days, he'd simply float away beyond the edge of the sprawling grounds, getting smaller and smaller, then becoming a speck as he went out over the Gulf, like a helium balloon let go too soon by a stunned child. Finally, however, she worked up the courage to talk with him.

And talk they did, until they actually became friends. Can you imagine such a thing?

Sitting for hours inside the sheltering gazebo, the dead man taught her all manner of magic spells that no child had any business working. She spent so much time with him that her typically absent parents sent the butler to question her one summer afternoon.

"What are you doing out here all the time, Milly?" the servant asked.

"Just playing with my friend. His name is Berny," she responded.

"You're getting a little old for imaginary friends, don't you think?"

"At least Berny talks to me. That's more than I can say for my parents," said Milly. "I'm always alone. I hate being alone."

Several years passed, and as her lessons continued, Milly

grew fascinated with the Fallen Arts; that is to say the darker side of Tuning. On this particular evening, Milly is filled with delight after once again being ignored by her high-society parents. Earlier, she had called out to all sorts of slithering creatures on their property. They rose from their burrowed cocoons in the dirt and watery homes in the nearby swamp and slithered their way to the house, where her parents were hosting a dinner party that night.

Milly is seated on a couch beside a young man by the name of Bradshaw McKlintock. It is strictly ornamental, with thin cushions, and is not in the least bit comfortable. Even the back is too uncomfortable to lean against, so Milly sits upright; her posture like a board. She is careful not to give too much attention to Bradshaw, who is nervously fidgeting beside her. She steals the occasional glance at him, but every time she does, she is just as disinterested as the first time she'd seen him.

Bradshaw had fancied her ever since they were young children. She'd first met him when she was sent off to San Marco's Baptist Academy, a boarding school in central Texas. Milly would see him in the hallways between classes. Unfortunately, she never thought much of him despite his obvious attraction to her. He was a tall boy that other girls often pined over, so why hadn't she felt the same? She certainly tried to. Even at twelve, he towered over most other boys his age. At seventeen and well over six feet tall now, he is reasonably attractive. Although Milly isn't sure she is all that interested in boys at the moment.

In the room full of guests, Milly stares absently at the large windows bordered by tall white columns that rise to a domed ceiling painted with a war scene—cowboys overtaking a tribe of Indians. Milly had never given the mural much thought and just sorta found it ugly; something she would have painted over when she eventually inherited the house.

The wood floor had been polished that day, the day before, and the day before that, so that when the guests arrived, it gleamed like it was brand new. Now that the room was full, however, it could well have been any old floor. "What a waste," she mumbles as she glares down her small nose at all the folks dancing or milling about. Men in suits, women in dresses—all of them in wealthy finery—laugh, talk, and dance into the evening. She watches her mother's mouth drops open in her biggest, fakest laugh of the night, which along with her makeup-caked face makes her look like a clown. Even above the music from the jazz band in the corner, Milly can pinpoint her mother's annoying laugh. It is more of a cackle; almost as if her mother were an evil witch, ready to cook all the guests into one giant pie. The over-sprayed blonde hair doesn't help Milly's opinion of her mother, either. Even from across the expansive room, Milly knows what it smells like, and just thinking about it turns her stomach.

Her father moves about the room constantly shuffling from one guest to the next like a bee might dip into one flower before moving onto a second and third. His dark brown hair is always combed back perfectly against his square head, his suit meticulously wrinkle-free and his shoes... Well... they gleam nearly as brightly as the wood floor had that morning before the guests had arrived. Sometimes, he would introduce Milly to a city official from the mainland, or the head of a large business. Once, he introduced her to the governor of Texas, but that was before Milly had flunked out of the Baptist Academy. Her parents had barely spoken a word to her since coming home from school this past summer. With that thought, Milly is delighted when she hears the first scream. A woman at the far end of the ballroom leaps up from a table unnaturally fast, screaming that something wet and slimy had just run across her feet. The incident is like music to Milly's ears, sending her bitter little heart jumping for joy. Inside, she's practically dancing with delight.

"I wonder what's going on over there?" asks Bradshaw, snapping Milly back into the present. She'd forgotten that he was seated beside her. Inwardly, she rolls her eyes, but she doesn't show it. He leans forward for a better look as the woman dashes from the room, trailed by two servants.

"I don't know," Milly lies with excitement, because she knows exactly what just happened. And there's more to come.

Another scream rings out, and this time, all the guests turn in the direction of the sound, as if everyone in attendance is of one mind. "For goodness sakes," snaps a young senator-looking fella. He steps away from his table just as a woman beside him yells out. She pushes away from the table and nearly falls back in her chair. Had it not been for the man beside her, she would be lying on her back with her dress sprouted around her like a flower. Now on her feet, she runs from the room. The band stops playing when the drummer leaps up. With all the sudden commotion, Milly nearly laughs out loud but purses her lips together to keep the laughter trapped inside. She watches her mother and father calmly walk from opposite sides of the room, weaving between the guests to reach another frantic woman.

Neither of them makes it as the entire ballroom erupts into chaos. All the guests rush toward the exit, which leads into the main part of the house. The crowd files through as plates clank to the floor behind them. Glasses shatter and forks get kicked across the room by hurried feet. Milly sits calmly as snakes, turtles, and insects slither into the room through one of the many doors, which opens to the expansive backyard. The slimy intruders march inside in a single wide line, leaving a watery trail behind them. The smell of swamp and stagnant water wafts through the room creating a thick, musty, and very disgusting aroma.

Milly remains glued to her couch even after the last guest has vacated the room. She is reluctant to leave, having won this tiny victory over her parents. She would rather sit and relish this perfect moment. To her, it's one of those times when the universe is working in her favor. The stars are aligned, the planets are smiling, and even God has tipped his hat in her direction. She looks out across the disaster in the ballroom. The once-polished floors resemble a war-torn battlefield covered in half-eaten steak, lobster, and potatoes.

Bradshaw grabs Milly's hand and yanks her up off the couch.

"What are you doing?" she snaps and yanks her hand away.

"Look, Milly, the guests are all gone," says Bradshaw. He points toward the doorway through which all the frightened guests had disappeared. "It's nice that you stayed until they all left, but those creatures are getting closer. Let's go."

When she looks up at him again he seems different. His forcefulness is suddenly attractive. Something about him taking charge makes Milly see him differently, or perhaps she is seeing him clearly for the first time. His black hair is cut short, his broad shoulders have grown thick from playing football, and the stubble along his chin seems to call to her. He takes her hand again, and this time, she lets him lead her away.

For days, Milly giggled to herself whenever she thought of the well-dressed guests falling over one another as they dashed out, screaming in horror. Her ghostly mentor, however, was furious.

"It is dangerous enough that I teach you, a petulant child, the ability to Tune. Should the Ghostal Holly get wind of it, I would be locked away. Your stunt was not only foolish, but dangerous as well," snaps Berny. He is floating above a decorative armchair in her bedroom, which in itself is the size of a small apartment. His oily black hair sits tightly on his small head. Milly cannot imagine him walking, having only ever seen him float, but if he did, he would stand no more than just a few inches over five feet. A little man, Berny has the temperament of a small yipping dog. Even his hands are almost laughably small. His nose is the only thing that is large. Milly, having only recently discovered that boys are strangely interesting, could never imagine a woman having any interest in her teacher or *mentor*, as he likes to be called.

"What's the problem with teaching me Tuning? I don't understand. The Ghostal Holly is dumb. They're not even here." Milly kicks her feet as she lies against a stack of feather pillows stacked up in her canopy bed. White drapes are pinned in each corner to tall mahogany posts. "What is the point of knowing how to Tune if I can't use it?"

"Pranks on your parents, because you feel neglected, are *not* the proper use of Tuning! Do not think for a moment that what I teach you is child's play. The Ghostal Holly requires that all Tuning must be lawfully sanctioned, and I am not a lawfully sanctioned mentor. The Holly tries to limit and control everything by placing a Resident Witch in every county. It is their job to inform the Ghostal Holly of any unsanctioned Tuning. Should one of them find me, I will surely go to prison. Calling insects from the swamp is the simplest of tasks and, might I add, pointless. Properly instructed, a witch can use Tuning to crush their adversaries rather than simply call forth insects to disrupt a soiree."

"I don't care. I would do it again. You don't know what it's like to be ignored all the time by Mom and Dad," says Milly angrily.

"Your mother and father suspect that you might be mentally deranged. They've made several inquiries with doctors. I suspect they care more about you than you think."

"Really?" Milly wonders if there is any chance that he's right. She leaps through her memories of her parents and quickly concludes that Berny is, in fact, wrong. Her parents are awful parents, and there should be some kind of government institution looking into them and not her Tuning. "Anyway, how's the Ghostal Holly going to know what I did? It's not like they're here."

"As usual, you only hear what you want to hear. Every county, little town, and city is watched. The Ghostal Holly, by way of a Resident Witch, monitors even an out-of-the-way jurisdiction like Wink. It is their job to make sure that things like calling critters to disrupt parties doesn't happen."

"Really? Someone is actually watching us?" asks Milly naively.

"The little candy shop in Wink. I'm sure you know it."

"Oh yes. Turtleburgers," says Milly. "Miss Turtlebalm always gives me candy."

Berny shakes his head. "I should never have taught you."

"Are you saying that Miss Turtlebalm is a witch?" asks

Milly.

"Not only a witch, but the biggest snitch there is. She is blindly loyal to the Ghostal Holly and would gladly drag me before the Tribunal of Burning Banshees if she knew that I was here. My only saving grace is that you don't seem to be very good at real Tuning. If you were anything like those two young witches living in the swamp, I'd be caught by now."

Milly squeezes her eyebrows together and says, "You mean the Horseshoe?"

He waves his hand annoyed.

"Oh, come on, Berny," says Milly. "Don't be a sourpuss. I'm getting better."

"This is no joke, Milly," says the ghost angrily. "You are a spoiled child, who is accustomed to getting what she wants. You put little effort into anything you attempt. And I am not another one of your playthings. So, today is different. Goodbye, Milly."

He bows, then snaps his ghostly fingers and disappears.

"Berny. Berny," she calls outs shocked that anyone would stand up to her, but he does not return. Certainly, he is only proving a point. He will be back! "Please, Berny. I'm sorry. I won't do it again. I promise," she says, not believing a single word that comes out of her own mouth. Milly slides her feet to the edge of the bed and slips off, then pads in her socks across the large bedroom. "I know you're just joking, Berny," she says opening a closet door. "Are you in here? No... Hm." She pushes between dresses, coats, riding jackets, pants, more coats, and even more dresses, but still no Berny. She looks underneath her bed, the drawers of her dresser, in her second and even third closet, but still no Berny. Getting frustrated, she runs downstairs into the greeting room, through the kitchen into the sitting room, and out the back door to the gazebo at the far edge of the property, but still no Berny. She looks out over the Gulf, wondering if by chance her ghostly friend might actually be serious. And for the first time in her life, she realizes that someone, other than her parents of course, has told her no.

Somehow, it doesn't really make sense to her. She can't quite figure out what has actually happened. Her mind sort of comprehends it, but her emotions are very slow to catch up. So slow in fact that she stands confused and stares out over the ocean for at least an hour until she is called inside.

"Milly. Milly."

For a split second, she feels a moment of excitement, because she thinks it's her father calling her home. When she turns, it's only the butler. She slowly drags herself back toward the house. Once inside, she sits at the table and eats her dinner alone. Again. She isn't hungry and pushes her food around the plate with her silver fork. For the first time that Milly can remember, she breaks down and cries. She isn't entirely sure why, because she doesn't really like Berny, but there is a chance that she doesn't really like herself, either.

"I'll show you, Berny!" she yells into the silence. "I'll do more Tuning, and you'll have to come back."

Chapter 11

An Unconventional Coven

After Bernard's scolding and weeks of moping alone, Milly decides to go in search of the two witches Berny had mentioned. Having spent the whole of onemorning studying, she is certain that she doesn't care even for a second about Stephen Austin and his inherited land grants, so she ventures out. Milly crams the only spell book she has and nearly everything else she can manage to carry into her bright pink leather purse, which includes makeup, a compact, lipstick, eyeliner, a brush, a comb, a bottle of perfume, and of course, a toothbrush. Milly is always careful to brush her teeth multiple times a day. She loves her white teeth and strangely admires anyone who can gleam a shiny smile.

Unnoticed, she also crams her mother's favorite cat into a wire crate; an overpriced all-white Scottish Fold named Princess. Milly hates Princess because the cat receives more love and attention from her mother than she does. It doesn't help that Princess is very overweight, something Milly is hyper aware of becoming as she tends to pack on the pounds by simply looking at the wrong kinds of food. The pudgy cat also has the dumbest-looking half ears of any cat she's ever seen.

She pedals casually; careful not to go too fast as the thick tires of her Schwinn might shoot dust onto her freshly shaved legs. She was a sight for anyone that drove by her. Big, puffy blonde hair, a bright pink purse slung over her shoulder, and an all-white cat bouncing inside of a crate perched awkwardly in a basket at the front of her bike.

Every so often, she jerks her steering wheel just to annoy the cat. Making her way down a lonely dirt road, which borders the beautiful blue Gulf, she comes to the entrance of a dumpy trailer park, whose name she recognizes from a conversation with Berny. It's called the Horseshoe. Thankful that she did not live in such a run-down place, Milly removes the crate from the basket, stashes her bike in the bushes, and finds a trail leading through the brush. The air is thick and sweat pours down her round face. However, she is determined to find the two witches Berny had mentioned when he was so angry. She would prove him wrong and rise above his low opinion of her. It is one thing for her parents to ignore her, too busy to be bothered with the child they had brought into the world, but it's another for Berny to simply disappear without any further word. What did her parents know of Tuning, anyway?

After a total of five minutes and forty-seven seconds, she gives up. Finding herself in a small grassy clearing, circled by thick, strangely spiraling, trees, she decides to practice a spell known as a Bility Burglar. It is capable of paralyzing muscles, rendering the victim stiff as a board. Originally authored by one grisly S.O.B. named William Tution, all one has to do is invoke his name while concentrating on the intended victim's muscles. But try as she might, Milly has been incapable of evoking even the simplest twitch. She hangs the cat crate from a low branch, which does nothing to calm Princess after the bumpy bike ride. This of course makes Milly happy. Rubbing her sweaty hands together she speaks aloud the name "Bill Tution" and thrusts her open hands out toward the cat, but alas Princess only meows. To Milly, the meow clearly says, "You're an idiot."

For exactly nine minutes and twenty-eight seconds, which to Milly might as well have been the whole day, she repeatedly attempts the spell. Time and time again, the cat only meows or ignores her entirely. As Milly is about to give it one last try, she overhears two teenage girls talking nearby. She snatches the crate and crouches down into the crabgrass, but Princess keeps meowing.

"Shut up," she whispers to the cat.

"Why won't any ghosts talk to us? They float around here every night doing nothing, so they might as well teach us some Tuning," says a dark-skinned girl with athletic muscles. Her arms poke through a worn red tank top, and her big bushy hair reminds Milly of a black clown. She almost laughs at the image in her mind, but Princess meows again and she smacks the crate.

"Ghosts? Come on, Ophi. They're completely useless and beyond lazy," says a very pretty girl, who immediately makes Milly envious. The girl's striking green eyes shine almost magically in her light brown face. And her long dark hair looks like she stepped right out of the salon, perfect. "Ghosts think Tuning doesn't belong to the living. And you should know that by now. They're snobs, so they hate it when we use it. They aren't going to be helpful."

"Yeah, I know that, but not all of them hate the living. I mean, without finding a ghost to teach us, how will we learn more Tuning?"

"From Momma Nay, I guess," says the pretty girl suddenly looking very annoyed.

"She's not going to be back for six months."

"Gawd. We're never going to learn anything."

"Well, Momma Nay is the only teacher we have, and she's careful."

"You mean slow."

"I was trying to put it nicely."

"Where do you think Momma Nay goes every year?"

"No idea. Hey, do you think she has a whole 'nother family like those traveling salesmen you hear about sometimes in the news, maybe in some other state, like Nebraska."

"Nebraska. That's a funny word for Northern Texas," jokes the pretty girl.

"I'm serious. Don't you think it's weird that she's gone half the year, every year?"

"We talk to ghosts and learn spells in a swamp from a supposedly four-hundred-year-old voodoo queen, who's apparently also your grandmother a bunch of times over. So no. I don't think that's weird at all."

"Yeah, good point."

"Come on, we've got to catch some Whirly Birds before they all fly off. If we haven't harvested the new crop before Momma Nay gets back, we'll never hear the end of it," says the pretty girl as they disappear behind several trees.

Milly is nearly giddy with joy. These two girls are just like her. Even though Berny, her mentor, had always admonished her to keep her powers a secret, she was lonely. Realizing that she was tired of spending so much time alone, Milly steps out from behind a tall tree, right then and there, forgetting Princess altogether.

"Hello," she calls out, but quickly retreats and grabs her prized pink purse. Running to catch up, she calls out again, "Hello."

The two girls turn around and look at Milly with a mixture of, you're-not-welcome-here and genuine curiosity, because a rich white girl in the middle of the swamp isn't something they had ever seen before. To say the three girls were curious about each other would be correct.

"I'm sorry," says Milly in the sweetest voice she can muster. So sweet in fact that she actually surprises herself, even if she is left feeling a little disgusted by it too.

"Are you lost?" asks the dark-skinned girl, Ophi, whose red shirt barely hides her stomach, which Milly notices is flat and firm. "The road is that way." She points back toward the way Milly had just come.

"Um no. I'm not lost, I don't think," says Milly looking around at the thick trees hanging overhead. "But I guess I don't really know where I am, either."

"Well, you look lost to me," says the pretty one in a not so nice way.

Ophi jabs her in the side, then says, "I'm Ophelia, and this is my grumpy best friend Famka."

"Hi," says Milly walking forward and holding out her hand. "I'm Milly."

They exchange an awkward, but quick greeting.

"What are you doing out here?" asks Famka eyeing her pink purse.

"Um, well," says Milly fidgeting. "I sorta messed up at

home. So, I came out here to practice some… spells."

Both Famka and Ophelia exchange a quick disbelieving glance.

"Really?" says Ophelia excitedly.

"Do you really know any spells?" asks Famka crossing her arms over her chest.

"Just one," says Milly. "I can create a golem. Sort of."

"Really! Can we see it?" asks Ophelia wide eyed.

"All right, but I'm not very good at it," says Milly.

Famka looks down her pretty nose while Ophelia smiles encouragingly.

Milly picks a long thin branch from the ground and draws a circle at her feet. Then she draws a line from the bottom of the circle about two feet long, two more half as long at the mid-way point, and two more at the bottom.

"Is that a stick figure?" asks Famka tilting her head.

"Shhhhh," shushes Ophelia.

Milly mumbles quietly as her face scrunches up tightly. After a moment, she taps the grass, and a stick figure, right out of a game of Hang Man, sits up, leaving an imprint of its body on the dirt. It's made of grass and twigs and manages to stand up before being blowing apart by a light breeze. Blades of grass fly through the air, and several land in Famka's mouth.

"Told you I wasn't very good," says Milly disappointed.

"I thought it was great," cheers Ophelia as she steps toward Milly and places a hand on her shoulder.

"It was all right," says Famka.

"We don't know much Tuning, either," says Ophelia. "Maybe we can teach each other what we know."

"I'd like that," says Milly.

"We have to collect Whirly Birds," says Ophelia. "You can

come with us if you want."

"Sure," says Milly. "What are Whirly Birds?"

"They're flowers with wings that fly, basically," says Ophelia.

"They're a lot more than that," says Famka shortly. "Come on. Let's go before we lose any more time," says Famka grabbing Ophelia by the wrist.

The three girls make their way deep into the swamp. They take so many twists and turns through bushes, around trees, and over fallen stumps that Milly begins to wonder if she'll ever find her way back. For about three quarters of a second, she considers going back for Princess.

"I hate snakes," complains Milly following behind.

"They won't bite you," says Famka over her shoulder.

"How do you know?" asks Milly.

"Because I ask them not to."

"You can talk to snakes?" asks Milly surprised.

"Sure," says Famka. "I'm an Animouth. So is Ophelia."

"It's true," says Ophelia.

"It's not that difficult to learn, but snakes are kind of stuck up," adds Famka.

They reach a clearing filled with six raised flower beds, which are barely held together by warped planks of wood. Four rows of winged red flowers chirping like birds from bright yellow beaks line the beds. Several rows are already empty, exposing tiny holes and loose dirt where the Whirly Birds had been.

"Hurry up," says Famka rushing forward to an old wooden shed. She props opens the crooked door and pulls out a net bag. A rake falls out behind her as she lunges toward a flower, which has just leapt into the air. She grabs it and quickly tosses it into her bag despite the angry chirping protest.

"Ophelia... Milly," says Famka as she squats beside one of the flowerbeds. "Get two more bags and be fast. If we don't catch at least a third of these, we can't sell enough to pay rent through the summer. Momma Nay will kill us."

"Who's Momma Nay?" asks Milly as she follows Ophelia to the shed.

"Our mentor," says Ophelia, handing Milly a bag. She snatches a Whirly Bird just as it leaps into the air. "And my grams," she adds.

"You have a teacher?" says Milly surprised. She crouches beside a flower bed and exclaims, "You're so lucky."

"You might not feel that way if you knew her," says Famka snatching another Whirly Bird out of the air.

Milly reaches out toward one of the still rooted Whirly Birds and says, "Why don't we just grab them before they fly off?"

"DON'T!" Yell both Famka and Ophelia at the same time.

Milly's hand jerks back. "Why not?"

"You really don't know anything, do you?" says Famka disappointed.

"I know some things," says Milly.

"Whirly Birds are deadly poisonous while they're in the ground," says Ophelia. "They only become restorative when they take flight."

"Kind of like people," jokes Famka snatching another one. "Gotcha."

"Oh," says Milly. "I guess you just saved my life then. Thank you."

"No point in killing you yet," says Famka. "We just met."

"Oh, Famka," says Ophelia as she snatches another Whirly

Bird. "I'm glad you're here, Milly. Don't listen to Famka. She's miffed because well… because we're here, I guess."

"We're not just *here*. We're *stuck* here. And we don't know enough Tuning to get out of this place. Gawd, I hate it here!"

"It's like my home," grumbles Milly. "I hate it there too."

"If we had a spell book or anyone besides Momma Nay to teach us, we might get out of here," says Famka.

Milly considers sharing her book with the two witches but decides against it. She'd feel more comfortable if they were all at her home instead.

The girls spend the next few hours trying to collect the few Whirly Birds they are able to catch. Many of the flowers leap out of their hands and fly up between the trees before disappearing. Regardless of the poor yield, the girls laugh together, joke about how dumb boys can be, and complain about their lack of Tuning. Milly so enjoys herself that she doesn't realize the sun is setting and that she should get home.

"Oh no, it's getting late," says Milly and stands to go. "Um, can I come back again?"

"Of course," says Ophelia smiling brightly.

"That'll be great. Thanks," says Milly feeling happier than she can remember. "I have one."

"One what?" asks Famka closing up her bag of Whirly Birds before any escape.

"A spell book," says Milly.

"What?" Famka instantly drops her bag. "You're joking."

"Really," she says. "It's at home."

"Bring it with you tomorrow," demands Famka.

"Um, yeah. Well, it's not that simple," says Milly. "There's a spell on the book."

"Do you know what it is?" asks Ophelia.

"Not really. Only that it jumps every time I try to pick it up. Last time I tried, it whacked me right in the chin. Hurt like the dickens. Samuel, my butler, thought someone had hit me. I told him that I fell down so he wouldn't tell my parents. Not that they would care."

"That's a Jumping Jack spell. I can break it," says Famka confidently. "It's easy."

"This is very exciting. We'll come over tomorrow," says Ophelia.

Milly hesitates and nervously grabs a lock of her blonde hair and twists it between her fingers.

Ophelia looks up from her bag, having just tied of the top, and says, "You don't want us coming to your house? That's all right. Most white folks don't want us coming around, either." For a moment, Ophelia's usual positive demeanor is replaced by something sad.

"No, no, no," says Milly waving her pudgy hands. "That's not it at all. My parents hate everyone unless they're rich. They don't care about color. Just money. I don't even think they like me."

"I don't remember my parents that well," says Famka.

"Really?" says Milly.

"Yeah, Momma Nay found me one morning at her doorstep, wearing this Led Zeppelin T-shirt. I was three years old. No note. Nothing."

"That's so sad," says Milly.

"It's all right," says Famka shrugging her shoulders. "I have Ophi."

"And Momma Nay, my folks, and everyone in the Horseshoe. They're a big noisy and very annoying family."

"Sounds wonderful," says Milly.

Ophelia stands up and hugs Milly. "You're welcome here anytime you want."

Embarrassed, Milly wipes her eyes, and Ophelia pulls away. Milly has never felt so welcome by anyone before, because at home, she has always felt like a visitor temporarily living in her own house.

"Thank you," says Milly. "Come by tomorrow morning after ten. My dad is leaving town for Austin, and my mom should be at the country club. Bye." Milly turns to go, but then realizes that she's probably lost and asks, "Oh, which way do I go?"

"Through there," says Famka. She holds out her hand palm down and wiggles her fingers. The grass goes flat, creating a narrow path that leads out of the clearing. Several trees leap out of the way, and at least one bush steps aside.

"Wow!" says Milly as her blue eyes go wide. "See you tomorrow."

Milly follows the narrow path through the grass, bouncing with nearly every step. She is beyond excited as she heads back toward her bike. She'd met two other witches, and they might actually become friends, although she isn't so sure about Famka. Something about her makes Milly feel bad about herself. Milly is suddenly hyper aware of her body: that little extra fat around her waist, the looseness of her arms, and the tiny bag beneath her chin. That is a feeling she's had enough of already, courtesy of her mother. Regardless, she is so excited that she practically skips out of the swamp. When she reaches her cruiser, she almost pedals off, forgetting about Princess. She runs back to retrieve the stupid cat. The moment Princess sees Milly, the cat looks up at her in that special way only a cat can manage. A mixture of *I can't be bothered with you* and

Where on earth have you been? Today is not the day for Princess to behave in such a condescending way. It reminds Milly too much of her home life.

Bending down to pick up the crate, Milly decides right then and there that Princess is never going home again. She opens the crate door, kicks the side, and walks away without looking back at her mother's overpriced all-white Scottish Fold cat.

Chapter 12

Grumpler's Growgan

"That can't be Milly's house," says Famka. Her mouth hangs open as she looks across the sprawling acreage that leads right up to the biggest, grandest, whitest house she has ever seen. "I've known about this place for years. I can't believe she lives here."

A large round fountain gurgling water is proudly perched at the end of a long, paved driveway, and tall columns reach over three stories tall. A wide balcony offers a perfect lookout to watch for anyone who might intrude uninvited. Behind the house, the ocean blends seamlessly with the blue sky like a giant's blanket.

"Do you really think she has a spell book?" asks Famka.

"Who knows," says Ophelia with a shrug of her muscular shoulders. "But what do we have to lose?"

"About ten pounds. It's going to take us a month just to walk down her drive way. And what are her parents going to think of us?"

"Who cares about that!" asks Ophelia walking forward.

"Come on."

"Stop!" Famka snatches Ophelia's wrist and yanks her back. "Do you feel that?"

"Yeah," says Ophelia breathing heavily. "This place is booby trapped."

"Big time." Famka closes her eyes and concentrates on the grounds before them. In her mind, she sees purple flames spring to life all across the palatial yard. Keeping her eyes closed, she pulls Ophelia forward. "You think Milly did this?"

"You really think her Tuning is that good? Milly could be in danger!" Ophelia says.

"She could have been deliberately misleading us… making us think she's… I mean, what do we really know about her?"

"I dunno. She seems so nice," says Ophelia. "but someone doesn't want witches here. Maybe we could go back to the Horseshoe."

Famka opens her eyes and turns to her best friend. "And do what exactly? Pick more Whirly Birds? Try rereading the *Gravedigger's Handbook* for the billionth time? It's not going to tell us anything we don't already know. Let's go and discover something we don't know!"

"I know, but maybe we should respect these protective charms and leave."

"Ophi, we need that book. It might be the only way we get off this island. Come on, we have strong abilities too. And the Sky Builders think so. Otherwise, we wouldn't have gotten invitations for Try Outs."

"All right, but if even for a second you think we can't get past those spells, we turn around. Don't be careless."

"I won't be," says Famka clutching Ophelia's hand.

"Seriously. Sometimes, you get things in your head, and

the next thing I know, we're in some kind of trouble. Don't forget your Devil Digging experiment out in the ocean. You nearly got yourself killed."

"Would you quit reminding me of that? And don't be such a worry-wart. You're braver than me, most of the time."

"Not when it comes to walking into a mine field filled with spells," says Ophi nervously.

"It'll be fine," says Famka. "Come on."

Famka closes her eyes again and carefully takes a step forward. The green grass softly cushions her bare feet. All around the two girls, columns of purple fire burn like torches. Famka can feel the personality of the witch who cast the spells. Whoever it may have been was vindictive, callus, and just downright mean. As Famka and Ophelia near a plume of purple fire, the feelings grow intensely stronger, leaving Famka feeling dirty inside. She jerks away, careful to keep her eyes closed and Ophelia close. The girls wind their way across the big empty yard in an odd zig-zagging pattern until they finally reach the front porch, which reminds Famka of a large hungry mouth.

Once there, Famka instantly releases Ophelia's hand, keels over, and throws up right in front of the door. Ophelia grabs Famka's long hair and pulls it away from her face as she spills the contents of her morning grits all over the nicely stained wood. As if the two girls are simply there to entertain fate, the front door opens, revealing a very stern-looking butler, who scowls down at them.

"I assume that you two will be cleaning that up," says the butler pointing his dark finger at the vomit.

"Sorry," says Ophelia, "Sure, is Milly home?"

"She is no concern of yours," says the butler.

Famka looks up feeling dizzy and leans against Ophelia. "There's something wrong with this house," whispers Famka.

"I beg your pardon?" The butler furrows his brow, a thick line forms across his forehead, creating a tiny overlapping fold. "This is the estate of the esteemed Franklin and Gilda Rien. I'll have you know that Master Rien is the finest attorney on the island. You two need to leave here now before I have you both thrown off this property."

When a creeping feeling crawls up her spine, Famka looks over his shoulder, but doesn't see anything out of the ordinary. She's certain that they are being watched, however. She turns and scans the front lawn, but no one is there.

"Leave now," demands the butler. "As a lawyer, my employer has many options at his disposal."

Famka is instantly annoyed. She straightens herself up despite feeling queasy and looks right into that butler's eyes. "So your boss is a liar?"

"No, young lady," says the butler angrily. "He is a lawyer."

"Liar is just *lawyer* spoken with an accent. It's the same thing!"

The butler is clearly about to explode when luckily Milly runs down a wide set of steps from the upstairs landing, saving the two girls from one very angry butler. Her light blue sundress flows up slightly, revealing her recently tanned thighs. Her hair is perfectly made up with so much hairspray that it resembles a feathered helmet. The tapping of her flat shoes on the cherry-colored wood steps echoes throughout the large room, and above her, a golden chandelier hangs from a long golden chain. Small white prisms sparkle on the wallpapered walls as the crystals above catch moments of sunshine.

"Samuel, you may leave now," says Milly indignantly and

raises her eyebrows as if to say, *Or you'll be in big trouble, mister.*

The butler's face hardens as he scowls down at her, but he doesn't move.

"Now, Samuel!" snaps Milly.

Despite having just thrown up, Famka feels bad for the old butler. He's only doing his job, after all, and being yelled at is absolutely not fun for anybody.

"As you wish," says the butler, who turns with a final scowl at Famka and Ophelia.

"Ew, gross," says Milly noticing the vomit. She covers her mouth and nose and asks, "What happened?"

"Your front yard is filled with spells," says Ophelia.

"Why didn't you warn us?" asks Famka. She wipes her forehead and begins to feel a little better.

"Really?" Milly says naively. She looks past Famka and Ophelia at the empty grass behind them. "I don't see anything."

"Can't you feel them?" asks Famka.

"The only thing I feel is the heat. Come inside. I'll get one of the servants to clean this mess," says Milly.

The three girls walk up the stairs. Famka holds on to the ornate railing and looks up at the towering ceiling rising three stories above them, as Milly and Ophelia walk ahead. A scene from the Civil War is painted on the ceiling encircled in a golden ring. Confederate soldiers on horseback are firing guns at fallen soldiers in blue, depicting the South's fictional victory over the North. Indians and dark-skinned African men lay scattered around the field in a bloody mess. Famka feels like throwing up again. Something about this house is wrong, and she isn't exactly sure what, because it's dark. Even worse than that, it's hungry too.

They walk down a long hallway, which is covered in paintings of people dressed in ornate eighteenth-century clothing. Famka figures that they're dead relatives of Milly, but doesn't really care, because she just wants to get the book and out of this house as soon as possible. Golden trim runs along the tops of the walls where they meet the ceiling, reminding Famka of a pretty cage. Finally, they come to a humongous bedroom.

"Is this your bedroom?" ask Ophelia in awe. She steps onto the thick pink carpet, and her gray-green eyes widen in her brown face.

"Yes," says Milly proudly.

"This is bigger than my entire trailer, Famka." Ophelia looks back at her best friend. "You all right?"

"I will be as soon as we get out of here," says Famka looking pale. "Where's that book?"

"What's wrong with my house?" asks Milly insulted.

"Famka is very sensitive to the Fallen Arts. It makes her sick if there's too much of it around," says Ophelia taking Famka by the hand and leading her to Milly's canopy bed. Famka falls back into the thick comforter and closes her eyes.

"So, there's bad Tuning here?" asks Milly. She begins shifting her weight from foot to foot as she pulls on a lock of her blonde hair and twists it between her fingers. "Are you sure? I've never seen anything bad here."

"Positive," says Famka.

"Think of the Fallen Arts like spoiled food," says Ophelia. "It's poison. I'm not as sensitive as Famka, but your house is filled with it. You can't feel it?"

"Gawd, would you two quit yapping and get that dang book," snaps Famka unexpectedly. "We need to get out of here." Her arm is resting on her forehead, placing just enough pressure, so that she doesn't vomit again. With her other hand, she points to a closet and says, "It's in there."

"How'd you know that?" Milly asks amazed.

"Because I do," says Famka. "Take this." She fishes out a piece of chocolate from her pocket and hands it to Ophelia.

"What's that for?" asks Milly.

"Your book," says Famka.

With Ophelia's help, Famka slowly sits up like a drunken pirate and leans forward against her knees. "Your book has a rudimentary spell placed on it," says Famka. "It's actually a spell meant for a toy."

"Sometimes, the Jumping Jack spell is used as a practical joke too," adds Ophelia.

Milly looks angry and says, "Berny must have done that before he left. That's not very nice."

"Who's Berny?" asks Famka.

"He's a ghost. He taught me for a while."

"A ghost taught you Tuning?" asks Ophelia walking toward a window. "They never talk to us except to tell us about their boring lives."

"Or they're half crazy," says Famka swallowing hard.

"I wonder if he placed all the protective spells outside," says Ophelia looking out the large window.

"It's likely," says Famka. "Get that book already."

Ophelia walks across the room to the closet, opens the double doors, turns on the light, and looks down at an old book sitting in the middle of the floor. Across the worn leather cover the word *Grumpler* is etched into the faded brown face. Rotting twine barely holds the manuscript together. As Ophelia bends down, the smell of mold rises from the book.

Milly comes up behind her and leans over her shoulder as Ophelia reaches out toward the book holding the chocolate. Like a shy puppy, the book sniffs cautiously then backs up a few feet.

"Come on," says Ophelia. "It's very tasty. See." She takes a small bite, then holds the chocolate toward the book again. Carefully, the book wiggles forward, sniffs it, then bites off a chunk, nipping Ophelia's finger at the same time. A corner forms a mouth, and it chews the chocolate for a moment and then spits out a dark wad onto the pink carpet. Next, it springs into the air like a cat and flies over them and out of the closet. Ophelia spins around as Milly tries grabbing it. Milly chases it around the room barely missing it with each lunge. Each time her hands are about to clasp the book, it jumps right out of her reach, taunting her. It crashes into a mirror above one of three dressers and smashes the glass to pieces. Shards fall all over the wood top.

"Watch out for the glass, Milly," cheers Ophelia clapping her hands together.

"I thought you said a Jumping Jack spell was easy to break," says Milly giving up and looking at Famka. "And it's wrecking my room."

"The chocolate usually works. Give it a minute," says Famka calmly, but Milly ignores her and gives it one more try. This time it bounces off the wall and flies across the room, landing in Famka's lap.

"Hey, that's mine," says Milly, her eyes narrowing.

Famka leaps off the bed, then drops the book to the floor and kicks it away.

"Show yourself, Growgan," demands Famka. "Do it now!"

The book suddenly begins unraveling itself.

Chapter 13

Bawd Bawd Man

THE PAGES OF the book arrange themselves into the figure of a paper man. Cursive writing runs all across its odd makeshift body in squiggly lines of black ink. It stumbles clumsily into one of Milly's three dressers, knocking over her picture before righting itself correctly.

Famka stands to attention, her body stiff. Adrenaline has forced her nausea away. She is aware of her best friend and Milly standing nearby, but Famka doesn't dare take her eyes off the Growgan.

"Finally," says the paper man, "I'm awake. What year it be?"

"State your name!" Famka demands.

"State'cho name, Momma!" The paper man looks at Famka then quickly scans Milly andOphelia. It blinks its paper eyes, creating a rustling sound, then turns back to Famka.

"Famka Meadows of the Horseshoe." Her eyes flash to Ophelia, who looks worried.

"Parran Papillon," says the paper man.

"You're French creole?" asks Ophelia.

"Bit a'dis. Bit a'dat," says Parran.

"Who's Grumpler?" asks Famka suspecting that Parran is lying.

"Ho ho. Dat is an unfortunate side effect of my captivity. Forever a joke labeled upon me by my captor."

"So, what does it mean?" asks Famka skeptically.

"Take me out of dis place, and I'll tell ya." Parran looks around the room as if he's searching for something. Famka isn't certain, but Parran looks frightened.

"This house is a dark place, isn't it?" says Famka.

"Ya feel it too?" says Parran. "The master of this stead is bawd bawd man."

"That's my father you're talking about," says Milly. "I don't appreciate that."

"He ain't the master of dis place," says Parran, shaking his paper head.

"Who is then?" asks Ophelia. She walks carefully toward Famka.

"Bernard Trankler," says Parran. "Bawd-bawd man."

"My Berny? He's been gone for months," says Milly. "I would know. He was my mentor."

"Ho ho. He's been here. Just don't show hisself to ya. He ain't no one's teacha, dat man."

"Did he trap you? Is that why you're a Growgan?" asks Famka.

"Aye, Momma," says Parran. "Did his biddin' for centuries, I have. Got tired. Went to sleep tired."

The paper man walks lightly to the window—the sound of crumpling paper heard with every step. Pushing back the curtains, he peers outside.

"He'll be coming back soon too. Bernard neva leaves here for too long," says Parran. "We got to be gettin' outta dis place."

"How can we trust you?" asks Ophelia.

"Ya can't," says Parran matter-of-factly. "Trust be built in time. N' we ain't got none between us. Ya have to risk it."

Famka is conflicted as she looks at Ophelia, who is staring back, shaking her head. On one hand, Famka is starved to know more spells and she suspects that Parran knows plenty. He seems to have more life, more Tuning, and probably knows more things that aren't anything to do with the Horseshoe. She longs to learn more Tuning, but Parran could be dangerous, and Momma Nay can't protect them since she's gone off to who knows where. Even if she was here, she hasn't been forthcoming with new spells, anyhow. Famka suddenly wonders if Momma Nay simply doesn't know any more and the only way she and Ophelia will get out of the Horseshoe is with Parran's help.

"Make haste, young witches," says Parran suddenly. "He's back."

"Where?" says Milly dashing up to the window. She stands beside Parran and peers between the curtains. "I don't see anything."

Famka and Ophelia squeeze in beside them and look out the window. A large well-manicured lawn filled with bushes cut into animal shapes stretches out to the ocean. A large rock walkway splits the center and ends at a small sandy beach at the water's edge.

"What is that?" asks Famka shocked.

"What is what?" asks Milly.

"Around the gazebo," says Ophelia. She takes a step away

from the window. "We've got to get out of here."

Famka remains transfixed on the white-domed gazebo. It sits on a mound of earth encircled by rose bushes near the edge of the beach. A normal person would see it as a nice place to sit and watch the sunset as it dips into the rolling Gulf waters. Lovers might share a first kiss here. Children would play hide and go-seek, but that's not what Famka sees. She sees columns made of reddish-brown beams covered with blood rise many thousands of feet into the air, twirling like giant licorice candy. Famka follows them with her eyes as they disappear into the clouds high above, spiraling into a dark angry sky. Below them, the blood stretches out in tentacles that spread out all across the otherwise beautiful grounds. They move like snakes as if pulling an invisible mesh netting tightly around the gazebo. Famka knows instinctively that she could never approach the sitting place. No real witch could. They'd be dead instantly.

At the base of the gazebo, covered in blood, is a doorway. Pounding on it is one very frustrated dead man. He's a miserable-looking sort too. The sort of person you'd never let inside your house if he rang your doorbell on a Tuesday morning. Even if he was holding two bottles of milk. His oily black hair is slicked close against his small head as if he's recently been drenched in water, and he's paler than his otherwise white dressing gown, which is stained with three blossoming strawberry-red stab wounds.

"Who is that?" whispers Famka.

"The bawd bawd man," says Parran.

"Where?" asks Milly, louder than necessary. She smacks her hand against the window trying to get a better look, but unfortunately, the dead man hears her. He turns around and scowls in their direction. His brown eyes speak loudly, shooting venom like beams of angry light. Famka now knows who authored the spells through the front yard; the ones that made her sick. The ones made by a man who is just plain mean. Her stomach spasms. She reaches out and clutches Ophelia's hand.

The dead man rises into the air and floats toward them. His dressing gown flows out around him, exaggerated by the distortions in the air circling him. His thin legs are covered in black pajama pants, and his pale feet dip downward.

"Oh Lord," says Famka sensing darkness seep out of the man like shadows covered in oil. She takes a step back from the window and drags Ophelia with her. "We have to get out of here."

Famka isn't certain what will happen but considering the ghost's appearance she doesn't want to find out.

"We can't out run him," says Ophelia. "Do you have any Earthquake Glue with you?"

"No," says Famka.

"What are you two talking about?" asks Milly still looking out the window. "I don't see anything."

Famka reaches out toward the window and wiggles her fingers. She mumbles a protective charm, and the curtains slam shut in Milly's face. "What was that for?" asks Milly. Famka ignores her and does the same to the remaining windows throughout the bedroom. Everything goes dark except for the light glowing above them.

"That'll hold him out for a minute," says Famka.

"Into me pages," says Parran pointing to his paper chest. "With your strength, I can fly us from here, but you must come now. Make haste."

"That's a really bad idea," says Ophelia looking at Famka. "Momma Nay would not like us jumping into some strange book. We don't even know him. For all we know, he's filled with Fallen Arts too."

"He's not, but do we have a choice?" asks Famka.

"Seriously, what is wrong with you two?" asks Milly.

Famka looks over her shoulder at the window behind her and says, "You're about to find out. Duck."

BOOM!

Something akin to a large boulder hit the window, then bounced off, the impact vibrating through the house like an earthquake. Famka and Ophelia grab each other and stumble to the floor. Milly falls onto her bed and bounces onto the pink carpet. Parran floats into the air unaffected.

"Your charm isn't going to hold him for much longer," says Ophelia holding Famka's hand tightly.

"What was that?" asks Milly. She sits up as another boom ricochets off the window.

"Your mentor," yells Famka. "What the heck were you thinking letting him into your home?"

"But I didn't see him outside," she argues.

Famka ignores her and looks toward the door. "Come on. I have an idea."

"I can take us from here if you are willing," Parran offers again.

Famka looks at the paper man book and says, "You were turned into a Growgan for a reason. No thanks."

Famka grabs Ophelia's hand, and they run for the door. Once outside, Famka pauses in the long hallway. She scans the paintings lining the walls until she decides on one filled with two old fuddy-duddies sitting side by side on a long, curly-armed couch. A man with a thin comb-over, holding a pistol, sits beside a plump woman, who resembles Milly.

"We can hide in here," says Famka pointing to the painting.

"How do you know how to do a Purdy Thing?" asks Ophelia skeptically. "That spell isn't easy."

"I don't," says Famka. "But I read about it last night in my *Gravedigger's Handbook*. So technically I should be able to do it."

"Last night?" says Ophelia, her brown eyes going wide in her dark face. "So you've never tried it?"

BOOM! The house rattles again.

"Nope, but I'm about to," she says and grabs Ophelia's hand. Concentrating on the image of the old couple, Famka imagines her body turning into air, but try as she might to call upon the Tuning running through her soul, she is too distracted by the house as it continues to shake violently. She mumbles, "Pretty as a fancy picture. Pure as breath. Healthy as death. Compress us into this canvas."

Then she opens her eyes, reaches up toward the painting, and swirls the surface like watercolor. She tries to push her hand through, but it gets stuck in thick goo.

"Yuck!" she jerks back her hand, which is now covered in black, red, and yellow paint. She flicks her wrist and splatters the carpet runner beside her bare feet.

"My dad is going to be so angry when he sees that," Milly says as she inspects the fist-sized smudge in the face of the older man sitting on the couch.

Parran shuffles up beside them, rustling with every step. "I can take us into the painting."

BOOM!

"I'm home, Milly," yells a voice from downstairs. "Did you miss me?"

"Is that Berny?" asks Ophelia.

"Yes," says Milly. "Let me go get him. Really, he is quite harmless."

"Are you out of your mind?" snaps Famka. She grabs Milly by the arm. "Don't you dare move."

The paper man opens his paper hands and asks, "Ho ho. Are ya ready?"

"Fine. Do it!" says Famka. "But if you pull any shenanigans, I promise you that Momma Nay will come looking for you."

"Aye, Momma. I have no fear of ya Nay," he says looking at Famka. "You real witch enough. I would be more concern of ya."

"I see that you have some new friends," says Berny getting closer. "Moonlighting are we?"

"Now, Parran!" says Ophelia.

The four of them disappear from the hallway and dissolve into the painting. They are now in a room that Famka imagines might have existed over two hundred years ago. Several dark wood beams split the plaster ceiling and the couple sitting on the couch are now three dimensional but remain frozen. The four of them run behind the couch and duck as Berny floats into view. Famka peeks around the curly arm of the couch as Bernard stops right where they were just standing. The right side of his face is burned, leaving his cheek melted downward onto his mouth. He turns and peers into the painting, but Famka doesn't dare move.

"He doesn't look right," whispers Milly.

"Shut up," mouths Famka silently.

"You woke my Growgan, little witches. That implies a little talent, but not enough," says Bernard nastily. "Come out of there, Parran. Now that you're awake again, we have much work to do."

"Aye, Bernard," says Parran. He rises from behind the couch and stands in full view.

"What are you doing?" snaps Famka at the paper man book.

"Go ahead and shove ya own tiny head right up ya backside," growls Parran at Bernard. "Then perhaps, we could have a civilized sit down."

"You're getting testy in your old age, Parran," says Bernard. "You were always grumpy, but never so mouthy when you were alive."

Bernard floats right up to the painting, presses his ear against the canvas, then backs away and looks at the painting from top to bottom. Famka notices that the tip of his pointy nose is red, as Bernard licks the end of his forefinger. Then he jabs it into the painting. His index finger pops through, and it's nearly the size of the couch they are hiding behind. Famka leaps out of the way as a giant blackened fingernail rams through the painted couple, cutting them in half. The three witches look at the painted couple in horror, fearing that in a few seconds, that could also be their fate.

Chapter 14

Flight

"Duck, Ophi!" yells Famka. Bernard's crusty fingernail slides across the painting, cutting through the air above them. Drops of blue, red, and yellow paint drip off his forefinger and onto the couch. A black blob lands on Milly's blonde hair, and the wall behind them melts into a puddle of green goo. Parran shoves Famka out of the way just in time. She falls into a big puddle on the floor, covering her in a rainbow. She looks across at Ophelia, who just barely yanks Milly out of the way as Bernard's finger slides above them again.

He withdraws his finger and says, "Had enough little witches? Inside the painting, my finger is as solid as you are. Get too close, and you could lose something. Pretty young witches won't be so pretty after missing a body part. Or perhaps, a nice little scar across your faces to match mine."

Famka looks out at his tiny greasy head. She gets her first clear look at him. His matted black hair is plastered around his distorted face, which is scarred from a possible burn. Above

Famka, drops of paint drip from the ceiling into her hair, which really annoys her.

"Ready to come out of there?" asks Bernard with a self-satisfied smirk. "If you stay much longer, you might end up looking like me."

"Yes! We'll come out," yells Milly, but Famka isn't ready. She is burning up inside. She doesn't like being pushed around and certainly not by some dead man, whose sense of superiority greatly outweighs the current demand for it.

"What are you going to do if we come out?" Famka asks, not believing a single word that Bernard says.

"I simply want my Growgan back. He's finally awake after so many centuries! I assume that I have one of you to thank for that, so bring him out and you may go free," says Bernard attempting to smile, which only adds to his sinister appearance. He opens his hands in a welcoming manner, but that doesn't make Famka feel any better about him. "Please."

Parran crawls beside Famka and whispers, "Aye, Momma. He be a word thief. He not let you go so easily."

"You left the Growgan in Milly's closet, so why is he so important now?" Ophelia yells out. She is crouched with Milly behind what remains of the couch, looking at Famka. She shakes her head, no. Famka knows that her best friend doesn't trust Bernard one itty-bitty teeny-tiny bit.

"I had hoped that Milly might have the strength to be able to wake my Growgan after I'd taught her a thing or too, but she did not," says Bernard.

"You're a ghost," says Famka. "What do you care if a witch can Tune or not? Most of you hate us for using your abilities."

"I wasn't always dead," says Bernard. "When I was alive, I was a great witch myself. Teaching was always dear to my heart."

Parran leaps to his bookish feet and points a stern finger at Bernard. "Ya lie like the feathers of a bird fly. No great teacher ya were. A greater criminal than even I."

Bernard squints his beady black eyes, then immediately reaches back before thrusting his entire fist into the painting. His giant hand nearly reaches Parran, but Famka yanks the book man out of the way. They roll together toward the corner of the room; an action that leads to them both being covered in a kaleidoscope of colors.

Before Famka is able to regain her balance, an explosion goes off. POW!

"Ahhh!" screams Berny.

When Famka looks up, Bernard's hand is gone from the painting and he's clutching his bloody fingers out in the hallway.

"Seems that you're right. In here, you're as real as we are! Thanks for that tidbit," yells Ophelia. She's standing stiffly and holding an old flintlock pistol. Smoke pours out of the end.

"That might be so, but unless you can get past me, you're trapped in this house," he says, glaring before floating out of sight.

"Where did you get that?" asks Famka surprised.

"He had it." She points to what's left of the painted man sitting on the couch. The upper half of his body is melted, and the woman beside him is gone completely, leaving only a blob of swirled wet colors in her place. "But how did you turn a painted gun into a real gun?"

"No idea," says Ophelia. "I just didn't want him to hurt you, so I grabbed it, and when I did, it felt solid."

"Let's just go back to my room," complains Milly. "I'm

covered in paint. I want to change my pants. Berny is not going to hurt us. I swear he won't."

"What do you call what he did to this painting? Just poking fun?" says Famka sarcastically. "Your little ghost friend is as friendly as a gaggle of Wigglers. We need to get out of this house now!"

"Aye, Momma. I offer me services again," says Parran. He stands and brushes the paint away from his paper body like it's dust: specks slowly float to the floor, which is now warped into waves.

"No, thanks. You said you were a criminal," says Famka firmly looking a Parran then turning to Ophelia. "You remember how to do a Summer spell?"

"I think so," says Ophelia. "Do you think that will work?"

"He's hurt," says Famka. "And if he can't see us, either, then we might get away."

"What about the protective charms out front?" asks Ophelia. "It took us a half hour just to walk up to the front door. Can't see us running out of here without hitting them."

"We don't go out the front," says Famka. "We go out the back."

"Through that column of blood?" says Ophelia. "Come on, Famka. We don't know what could happen if we get too close to that."

"Column of blood?" questions Milly naively. "What column of blood?"

"Outside in your backyard. It's surrounding the gazebo," says Ophelia.

"I've never seen it," says Milly picking the drying paint from her hair. "My backyard is beautiful. Are you sure?"

"Yes! We're sure," Famka snaps at Milly, then turns to

Ophelia. "Ophi, if we try a Summer spell together, then maybe we can blind that ghost long enough to make it out the front."

"Hm… All right," says Ophelia after thinking it over. "Let's go, I guess."

"How do we get out of the painting?" asks Milly.

"That's easy," says Famka. "It's getting in that's difficult. Follow me."

"Keep da pistol," says Parran to Ophelia. "You created a Tuning Tensil. It be valuable."

"You mean it will work outside of the painting?" Ophelia is amazed as she looks down at the old gun in her hand.

"Aye, it will, little witchy," says Parran. "N' if you should see ol' Berny, don't'cha hesitate on pulling that there trigger."

Cautiously the four of them step to the edge of the painting. The surface resembles a thin piece of plastic pulled tightly across the hallway with lines and lumps distorting the opposite wall. Famka pushes against it with an open palm, and with a pop, it bursts like a bubble and they drop to the floor with a thud. Famka looks up and down the walkway for Berny, but he's nowhere in sight.

"Now what?" asks Ophelia.

"Come on. Follow me," says Famka and bolts down the hallway. Feet thumping heavily on the carpet runner, they round a corner and clumsily make it down the stairs. Seconds before they reach the final step, Samuel the butler walks out of another room, glaring at them sternly. Parran slides past them in book form like a frisbee gliding across the floor.

"What may I ask is happening here?" says the butler picking up the book. "You are tracking paint all over the master's house."

"That is none of your business, Samuel," says Milly. "Just

clean it up!"

Feeling bad for the butler again, Famka steps forward and says, "Sir, we're being chased by a bad man. Sorry that we tore up the painting on the second floor and dirtied up your floors, but we needed a place to hide."

"Tore *up* a painting?" mocks the butler. "What on earth did you girls do up there?" He looks up toward the second-floor landing. "Milly, might I remind you that I am employed by your father." The butler rubs his thumbs on the book. "And I report to him and him only."

"So, what?" says Milly taking a step toward the butler. "It's not like he's ever here, anyway. It could be weeks before he returns from Austin. By then, Samuel, you'll probably just forget this ever happened."

Without another word, the butler suddenly walks away.

"I'll take that," says Famka grabbing the book from his frozen hands as he brushes by them.

They dash for the front door, but as soon as Famka opens it, Berny is floating outside on the porch. The sun catches his distorted face, clearly showing burn lines running down into his mouth. The whites of his eyes are gone, now replaced by red, glowing orbs. Behind him, the protective charms flare up like purple torches then connect to each other, creating a mesh barrier at the edge of the property, which blocks any possible hasty exit.

"Three stupid little witches," says Berny, his words slurring like a drunken sailor. "All you had to do was give me the Growgan, and you could have left by your own accord."

"You're a lawyer," says Famka. She shoves Milly back into the house and grabs Ophelia's hand.

The two girls instantly burst into bright sunlight that

blinds the ghost. The blast lasts only a few seconds before it's gone again. Berny screams, covers his eyes, and starts twisting wildly through the yard like a tornado. Then, as if on cue, he starts laughing as though he were hearing a joke.

"Did you really think a Summer spell would work on me?" He slowly floats back toward them. "I alone invented over half of all the Fallen Arts known on both sides of the Graveyard. Seeing you Tune is like watching an invalid try to walk having never taken a step in the first place. Your form is awful, your clarity of mind nonexistent. I'd hoped that I might meet a witch with some measure of talent. You did get past my protective charms, after all. And Milly..." He looks at her as she steps up beside Famka and Ophelia. "Bless your fat little heart, but you're as useless as a starved pig."

"Hey, that's not very nice," says Milly not realizing just how dangerous a position the three witches are in.

Famka flashes an angry look at Milly before looking toward Berny again.

The door slams shut behind them. With no place to run, Famka looks at Berny as he floats out into the yard. His small frame slowly grows in size and stretches out like a sheet, grossly exposing the lines of his rib cage. His sleeping gown goes flat against his legs and his feet, which are pointed downward and dragging along the yard, burning two lines in the grass.

"My dad is not going to like that," says Milly.

"Parran!" yells Famka.

The book leaps out of her arms and transforms into the paper man again. Standing beside Famka, he looks out at Berny approaching, then at Famka.

"Ho ho, Momma," says Parran. "Ya ready now?"

"Yes," she says. "Can you get us out of here?"

"With ya help, I can," he says, reaching a paper hand out to her.

The moment they touch, Parran's head, torso, arms, and legs break into a whirlwind of single pages. Hundreds of sheets swirl around the three girls like a Texas dust devil. They move faster and faster until the girls rise from the porch. Milly clumsily grabs hold of Ophelia's hand and clutches tightly. Ophelia in turn grabs Famka's hand. The two best friends look at each other with a mixture of surprise and excitement. A second later, they take flight and shoot into the air.

Chapter 15

Trankler's Hold It

BERNY ROARS BENEATH them.
It's not a sound that Famka can hear with her ears. She is certain that no one without a Knack can hear him, but it's a sound that she feels in her bones. It sends a shiver through her core, spasming in waves. Her stomach leaps into her throat when she looks down through the bottom of the whirlwind that is now Parran. The ground is dropping away quickly, and papers fly by in a blur, allowing for only small glimpses of what lies beneath her suspended feet. Berny is a giant angry mess, with burning red eyes, each the size of a pickup, and he's flying up beneath them like a rocket with his humongous mouth open wide, exposing a distorted black hole inside. He's so large that the stains on his teeth look like giant yellow blankets draped over white crooked rocks. Beneath him, Milly's massive house shrinks into a single marshmallow resting on bed of lettuce. Berny reaches out, and his giant, callused hand closes in on them, but they twist out of the way and gain momentum as the deadly ghost falls behind. As they

accelerate, Parran growls painfully around the girls, vibrating like an old car speeding down a dirt road. The sound of the rustling of paper grows nearly deafening.

"Where are we going?" Famka yells. She looks at Ophelia, who's looking downward, her eyes wide. Milly is still clinging to Ophelia like a terrified cat.

They continue upward until their island is a patchwork of odd green shapes in a sea of blue water. Famka can barely see the little town of Wink with its little tourist shops and beach bums burning in the hot sun. Following a curvy dirt road, she locates the Horseshoe sitting in its usual half circle facing the water. The white trailers gleam in the sunlight. Waves flow out across the Gulf in a rush to nowhere. Small boats bounce up and down in the tide as fishermen sit perched at the edges of their little crafts, searching for a meal. A speedboat jets across the water. Their long, frothy wakes disturbing the fishermen. Famka knows that if Uncle Guncle is down there, he'll be furious. She thinks of him as a way to distract herself from the insanity of flying through the air. She takes a breath and tries to calm her racing heart. The air is still warm and thick despite traveling so fast. It feels like an oven exhaling on Famka's face. Beads of sweat run down each side of her face, down her neck, and into her T-shirt. Her long brown hair feels like cords of rope weighing her down.

She closes her eyes and calls on the Song of the World and hopes that it will not abandon her now.

"Parran," she calls out to him in her mind.

"Ho ho!" he responds excitedly. "Momma, ya have a fine Knack."

"It worked!" she says.

"Ya not try that before?" he asks.

"Once with a possum," she answers.

"Not very helpful, possums," says Parran. "Always eating."

"Where are we going Parran?" she asks concerned.

"Just running, Momma," says the book man. "Not be caring. Want to get away from the bawd bawd man."

"Can you take us back to the Horseshoe?" she asks.

"Safe place?" he asks skeptically.

"Yes," she answers, before imagining the Horseshoe, so that Parran can see it. "Momma Nay protects our home from Fuzzy Floaties like Berny. They can't get in if they have bad intent."

"Ya sure 'bout that?" asks Parran. "Berny will come looking. Promise ya he will."

"Yes," she says not feeling so sure now.

"I can feel ya hesitating," says Parran calmly. "Ya can't lie when we speak in da mind. We share more dan words, Momma. We gets to know each other in ways da words don't allow for."

Famka realizes that it's true. She can sense that Parran is a regretful man. Having lived much longer than his deeds, however, there is guilt that follows him like a stalking butler. She can feel it sitting with him just out of eyesight, but never completely gone. He was turned into a Growgan because of something that he did, perhaps several hundred years ago, but now, he longs to be free of his dark past. The matchstick eyes of the Fire Thief flash in her mind for a brief moment then recede into darkness. She pokes around trying to figure out what could drive a person to feel so deeply regretful, when she comes to a locked door in his mind. It is sealed solid from edge to edge without even a single hinge, which would allow it to swing open. Strangely, however, there is a golden knob in the center, glistening brightly. She reaches out toward the doorknob just as Parran swings hard to one side.

"Hold on," says the book man, and they curve in a large arch through the air. The Texas mainland comes briefly into view with its green-pastured farms dotting the horizon like a granny's oversized homemade quilt. A roller coaster and Ferris wheel come into view, jutting out on a pier into the ocean. The sun catches Famka's eyes, and she blinks away the sting before looking down. They're above the Gulf again, moving quickly downward toward the Horseshoe. The little trailers come into view, and Famka wonders what nosey Mrs. Billbray might see if she looks out her window. This, she is likely to do, given that it's early afternoon now.

"She'd see us, Momma," whispers Parran into her mind.

"Anything you can do about that?" asks Famka.

"With ya help," he says.

"All right, what?" asks Famka.

"Page twenty-three," says Parran. "You'll find the spell ya need."

A sheet flies up out of the mass of swirling papers and floats in front of Famka's face. She scans a spell called, *Seeming to be Disbelieving*. She smiles and says to herself, "Of course."

She releases Ophelia's hand, which freaks out her best friend. Ophelia waves wildly before she grabs ahold of Famka's arm for support. Beside Ophelia, Milly is still clinging tightly with her eyes shut.

"Sorry," mouths Famka then looks downward toward the approaching island. It's quickly growing from a green dot in the ocean to a large land mass encircled by a sandy beach. Famka points both of her hands toward the little trailer park and closes her eyes, trusting that Parran's spell is authentic.

She imagines what Mrs. Billbray would see looking up as Parran descends in a whirling mass of papers encircling three suspended witches.

Famka bends sunlight like scooping handfuls of water out of a warm bath and wraps it around them. She bathes them in yellow light and is surprised that she cannot see her own hands when she opens her eyes. She looks down at her bare feet, but they're gone too. A flash of nausea runs through her, threatening to shoot that morning's eggs up the backside of her throat. She swallows hard as they slow their descent into the swamp. The trees come up to meet them, and they glide alongside thin, patchy white trunks until they are finally and safely back on the ground. Famka slides her hands down her body and releases the sunlight keeping her invisible. It flies up and away like a bird. She's thankful that she can see her hands again. Then she pulls her hair into a bun at the back of her head and releases the light from her companions.

"Oh, thank goodness," says Milly. he lets go of Ophelia's hand and drops to her knees. Her puffy blonde hair is a windblown mess. She kisses the ground, sits back up, and breathes in heavily. "I've never been so happy to be in a swamp in all my life."

"We should get to Momma Nay's cabin fast," says Famka. She looks down a dirt trail that cuts between a long line of skinny white trees covered in yellow, browning leaves. Ankle-high grass borders the dirt path as it bends out of sight and the leaves rustle above them from a light breeze.

"Here, take my hand," says Ophelia helping Milly to her feet.

"Thank you," says Milly breathing in big gulps.

"Ho ho," says Parran. He's transformed back into his manlike form and is looking up curiously. "I feel ya Nay's spells. She's quite lovely and dangerous as a tornado." He reaches overhead and runs his paper hand through the air as if skimming his fingers through a pool of water. The air shimmers as waves roll away from him.

Watching the air shift, Famka realizes that Milly cannot see the effect that Parran has on his surroundings. She wonders how much of a witch Milly really is.

"Are we safe from Milly's ghost?" asks Ophelia watching the waves disappear.

"Depends on ya Nay's Tuning," says Parran.

"Can I even go home?" asks Milly.

"Best not to," says Parran.

"What about my parents?" Milly asks showing a rare concern for them. She tucks her frilly white blouse into her shorts then pulls the bottom back out, so it's not too tight against her stomach.

"He won't hurt them without alerting the Ghostal Holly," says Famka. "He won't want to bring attention to himself."

"Who's the Ghostal Holly again?" asks Milly.

"Ghost government," says Ophelia.

"They watch over the dead, but they also monitor all Tuning done by witches, Wigglers, Drolling Dragons, and Bombadoes. Well, no one really watches Bombadoes," adds Famka.

"Or the Woodlot," says Ophelia. "But I guess there aren't any of them left."

"You guys know so much," Milly says in amazement.

"Ghostal Holly are a bunch of thievin' liars. To be true," growls Parran.

Famka wonders what his experience has been with the

ghost government, and then she has an idea. "We should tell Miss Turtlebalm about Berny," Famka says, primarily to Parran. "She's the Resident Witch for this area. Maybe she can help us."

"What can she do?" asks Milly.

"I don't know for sure, but I think she's like a town sheriff. She keeps the peace between ghosts and witches and any other creatures with a Knack," says Famka.

"Let's go," says Ophelia. "Maybe Uncle Guncle can give us a lift into town. He should be back in the Horseshoe from tending his traps by now."

"Good idea," says Famka starting down the trail. "Come on."

"We not be leaving ya swamp with any ease," says Parran after her. "If'n we do, ol' Berny be finding us. To be sure."

Famka stops, turns back to the paper man, and asks, "What do you mean, Parran?"

"Berny'man will do whatever he has ta, to get what he wants," says Parran.

"And what exactly does he want?" asks Famka.

"A powerful witch such as ya self and a Growgan such as I," says Parran, "to help with his dirty deeds."

"For what?" asks Ophelia. "What could be so important that he'd risk the Ghostal Holly coming down on him?"

"The bawd man Bernard Trankler ain't just a ghost haunting a rich man's mansion. No, no. He's got something on his mind." Parran looks at Famka real serious and continues, "You seen it, Momma. These ghosties floating around ya swamp ain't got nothin' to do. Most of them can't be bothered doing much more than telling they what-if stories. They looking back at they lost lives saying what if I'd done this?

What if I'd done that? But not Berny. No, no. He got a hope in mind. It drives him like a mawd man."

"Bernard Trankler," says Ophelia. "Where do I know that name?"

"Wait a minute! That's Bernard Trankler, as in a Trankler's Hold It?" says Famka her green eyes going wide in her face. "That's his spell, isn't it? He authored it?"

"The very one," says Parran.

"Wow. Fallen Arts," says Famka. "He wasn't bragging when he said he authored more than half of all the dark Tuning was he?"

"He be exaggerating a bit," mutters Parran.

"Are you saying that my Berny is really some kind of powerful witch?" asks Milly.

"Not just any witch," says Famka. She looks to Ophelia. "But the father of the Fallen Arts."

"That means…" Milly pauses. "I can't go home?"

"Bess not ta," Parran repeats.

"So, I'm stuck here in this swamp?" Milly asks, looking like she just ate something rotten.

"It would seem so," says Parran.

Chapter 16

First Lesson

"This mattress is so lumpy. What time is it?" asks Milly. She's lying in a twin bed in Momma Nay's cabin. Famka, who's lying in another bed several feet away, turns to her side and looks at Milly. Milly's face is still covered in yesterday's makeup, and her poofy blonde hair looks like she stuck her finger in an electrical socket. Ophelia snores lightly beside Famka as the sun barely peeks through the window above the kitchen sink.

"Early." Famka glances past her brown feet, which are sticking out of the blanket that she's sharing with Ophelia. She scans the room for Parran until she finds him. He's returned to his book form and is sitting on the kitchen table closed. "Go back to sleep, Milly."

Milly rolls onto her side, stuffing a pillow between her legs, and pulls the blankets up to her neck. Famka stares at the arched ceiling for only a moment before getting out of bed. She's anxious to talk with the book man. She slips her feet into a pair of flip-flops, grabs the Growgan, and steps outside into the morning sun. Slivers of light cut between the tall trees as she places the book on the same makeshift table the Drolling Dragon was born on just a couple weeks prior.

She closes the front door and whispers, "Hey. Are you awake?"

"Aye, Momma," says Parran. The cover opens on its own, the pages flutter into the air, and he transforms into the shape of a man. She realizes that he must have had shoulder-length hair, a beard, and mustache when he was alive. Not very tall, perhaps slightly taller than the average girl, Parran looks as if he may have been a pirate or a smuggler trading in illegal goods down the Mississippi perhaps during the 1800s.

"What happens if Bernard finds us. I mean you and me?" she asks.

"He gets what he wants," says Parran.

"Which is what?" she asks impatiently.

"A downright awful book," he says.

"But you're a book," she says. "So, what's the big deal?"

"Not just any book, Momma," says Parran shaking his paper head. He looks around as if he's about to share a secret he'd rather no one else hear. His paper face crinkles, and he lowers his voice to just above a whisper. "The *Kitab'i'Mordanee*; the book that began all Tuning for ya living types."

Famka looks at him, confused. She's never heard of the *Kitab'i'Mordanee*. Even saying the words in her head sounds foreign.

"What's the Kitab'ee–" she tries saying, but Parran leaps toward, covering her mouth with his paper hand.

"Naw, Momma," he says sternly. "I say the name to ya once so you know it, but never repeat it. Ya gives it power when ya does."

He removes his hand from her mouth.

"Apologies for having to do that. I not lay me hands on ya in vain, but I see from ya look that ya no idea the significance. Dat horrid book be known as the Bastard Book. Never repeat its true name," says Parran. "Let's have a little sit down then." He gestures to the large pond out in front of the cabin. "Might we have a chat near the water."

"Why?" she asks suspiciously.

"I not ya threat, Momma," says Parran. "Ya done me a kindness taking me out of Berny's dirty mitts. N' you and I done imprinted on one another up there in them clouds. Ya know the truth of it."

"Is that what I'm feeling; this connection with you—imprinting?" she asks.

"It is," says Parran. "It happens with we Growgans. Ya broke me tie to Berny somehow, which I'm sure has him good and angry. I am thankful to ya. Ya no idea what it be like in that bawd bawd man's head." He takes a small bow. "Now me be yours."

"So, you have to do what I want?" asks Famka.

"We Growgans aren't slaves, but we aren't free, either," he says. "Without a witch we grow weak. Some die. Others go to sleep and neva wake. After Berny was murdered, I went to sleep until Milly began seeing ghosts. At dat time, her Tuning began to improve, and I began to stir. It was because of you that I woke after three centuries. Berny tried to use ya friend Milly to wake me, but she be weak. At most, she might hope to be what folks call a Kitchen Witch. A spell here and there, but nothing of real use."

"What about Ophelia?" asks Famka curiously.

"Aye, Momma," says Parran. "She's a fine witch, but she ain't ya. No, ma'am. You a Momma in da old ways. Ya just donna know how to use ya Knack yet."

"Oh…I see," says Famka feeling excited, but trying not to show it.

"Come now, Momma," says Parran. "Bess I 'splain a few tings over da water."

"Over?" Famka looks at him like he's a crazy person.

"Aye," says Parran stepping off the porch. He turns back to Famka and adds, "Ya need to be seeing what ya Nay hid in dis here pond."

Famka follows him down the short trail that bends slightly until it meets another dirt path, which goes all the way around the pond.

They step to the edge of the trail, and Famka looks down. Near the water's edge, turtles sit perched on a fallen branch, basking in the sun. Spikes of sedge grass poke out of the water all along the perimeter of the pond. The sunlight bounces off the glowing ripples formed by the many fish swimming about in the eerie green water. Despite the early morning, the heat is already rearing its ugly head, and Famka wipes her forehead. She pulls her long thick hair into a bun at the back of her head and ties it off with an old shoestring.

Parran steps out onto the water. She expects his paper feet to sink, but the surface is as stiff as a board. He continues across the pond until he reaches the very center. Once there, he turns to her and says, "Come now, Momma. It be the same for ya."

"Are you sure about that?" she shouts not wanting to get wet.

"Ask yerself and see if I tell ya true," he responds.

Famka doesn't have to pose the question to her soul to know that he's telling the truth. Whatever else it might mean to be Imprinted, Famka realizes that Parran cannot lie to her. She takes a step, and the water instantly hardens beneath her foot. Another step, and it happens again, but only where she steps, leaving the rest of the water unaffected by her. Turtles now swim lazily around the fallen branch, and the yellow fish dash away.

Once in the center of the pond, Famka says, "Now what?"

"Ya know da first rule of Tuning, I suppose?" he asks.

"Of course," she says.

"Say it to me," he requests.

"Are you serious?" she asks, feeling stupid.

He nods his paper head.

"To see the dead is to do as the dead do."

"That's a rough way to see things," he says. "That's not truly it. I know that sounds nice, 'cause ya dream of flying, swimming deep in ya ocean without the death catching ya, or what not, but ders more to it. Did ya Nay 'splain the very nature of Tuning to ya?"

"I thought so, but I guess not."

"Da old timers, those in da Knack that is, they started calling it Tuning 'cause of how dey saw da world. They knew dat if they could tune themselves properly, then anything was possible. Tuning isn't how ya change the world, Famka, but how ya change yourself. Like a piano string stretched just right so that when it's plucked, it creates da most beautiful notes. A person is the same, and they become somethin' truly magical when they tune the way dey see tings. Ya little friend Milly, she too busy with petty tings to get ta seeing what matters. If'n ya can get passed them petty tings, then you can truly Tune."

"Let me get this right." She runs her forearm across her brow. "You're saying that if I can see the world… more truly… then I can do anything?" asks Famka feeling like she just heard a whole pile of mule matter.

"Aye, Momma," says Parran. "Dis world is a shadow, and ya living in a cave, convinced that this is all there is. This"—he gestures to their surroundings—"is only da beginnin'. I not realize as much when I was still breathing, either, but I dreamed for over two hundred years while I slept. I studied the very spells written on me pages, and I put a few tings together. So, I tell ya true as I know. Ya have to break up with life."

"You mean die?" she asks.

"No, no." He shakes his paper head "Ya do that in ya own good time without me lessons. What I mean is that ya need to forget what ya tink is real. Folks make up all sorts of nonsense to fill dey lives. I seen so many new tings while I slept. Milly, da butler and the servants watchin' da Dumb Dumb box for hours. Den go spend what little money dey have on da tings they seen on dat very box, only to sit and do it again."

"Dumb Dumb box?" asks Famka. "You mean a television?"

"Aye, Momma. Dumb Dumb box," says Parran. "N' Milly's fadda. He breaks men and takes what dey have. You know what that gets ya when ya dead?"

"Um, no. I guess not," says Famka.

"Nothing," says Parran. "Except for some very angry ghosts chasin' ya for centuries. Ho ho. I seen it more than once, I have."

"So, I can't enjoy watching TV or buying things if I want to Tune?" she asks.

"Naw," he says, "Enjoy what ya will, but spend ya time building tings dat last. Nice homes be nice, but they not last.

Riches be built on lies, but heaven be built on kindness. Don't cost nothing to be decent."

"I see. I think," she says. "Momma Nay never spoke of Tuning like this."

"No, me guessing not," says Parran. "Me seeing ya Nay is a voodoo queen. She got her own ways of seeing and doing Tunings. She not lead ya wrong, just not very far."

"So where do we start? I mean, I assume you're going to teach me."

"Aye, Momma," he says happily, "now ya talking. Look there." He points into the distance where the sun is climbing through the trees. It's about half way up, not quite cresting the tops of the bushy leaves. Shimmering beams cut through the branches like knives.

"Take me hand," says Parran. "We a pair now. It be faster if I show ya what I see. N' close your eyes and do what ya did yesterday. Climb into me mind. Careful not to poke around too much. I got me sensitive spots like any soul do. Them places are mine, understood?"

Famka nods her head then holds his hand carefully, so as not to crush his paper fingers. His inked hand curls around hers, and the same trees pop into her mind, only now, she is seeing them through his eyes. The sun is still poking between the branches, but she can also see cracks in the air. The small openings lead to another place. It's like looking at a familiar picture, but she's unsure where she's seen it before. Compared to the gaps, the normal world—the one she's lived in her entire life—appears in black and white and is superimposed on a brightly colored masterpiece, in an almost haphazard way. Through the small openings, she sees a city made from light and water. Waves roll away from her, forming shapes that resemble buildings, houses, and streets. Bright reds, yellows, and greens glisten with such intensity that she nearly yanks her hand away from Parran, but he clamps down harder than she thought him capable. The unreal scene swims through the air, vibrating like notes.

Aye, Momma, says Parran in her mind. *Ya see why the old-timers started calling the Knack* "Tuning."

"Yes," Famka says, amazed. "It's so beautiful. What is this place?"

He ignores her question and says, "Now look down with me but keep steady."

With her eyes remaining closed, she points her head downward and nearly falls right over.

Water fills the pond from one massive hole. Parran carefully leads her to the opening. Inside are red-clay passages with beams of yellow sunlight breaking up shadows into random splotches of darkness. Thousands of ghosts, strange creatures, and witches fly through the tunnel at breakneck speed. Many of them have to duck out of each other's way or risk crashing into one another. A giant man resembling an Easter Island statue slows his pace. He is suspended in the air and looks up at Famka as he passes by. His head is flat, rectangular, and his face is so long that his chin ends below his neck and over his gun-barrel chest.

"That's a Bombadoe," she says surprised. "Giants."

"Aye, Momma," says Parran.

A second later, the giant is gone.

"Ever wonder how ya Nay comes and goes from dis place?" asks Parran.

"Yeah," says Famka completely amazed. "Ophi and I never see her leave. One day she's gone, and the next she's back."

"Now ya know, Momma," says Parran. "Dis below ya is da entrance into the Hallowed Halls. Dey take ya anywhere ya want to go in da whole of da world."

Her eyes pop open, and the tunnels disappear. She looks at Parran, who's now looking back at her.

"Can you teach me to get into the Halls?" asks Famka excited.

"Aye, Momma," says Parran. "But it not that easy to get into the Halls if you're alive. Ya must learn to use ya Knack first. Dis entrance be locked to ya for now."

"Holly Moly," yells Ophelia from the water's edge. Famka turns and looks at her best friend, who's standing alone and is dressed in her shorts and running shoes ready for her morning run. "What are you two doing out there? You're standing on water."

"Hi, Ophi," says Famka excitedly. "Parran is teaching me how to use my Knack. It's so amazing, and you'll never believe what I just found out…" However, as she takes a step toward her best friend, she falls right into the pond and is drenched from head to toe.

Ophelia starts laughing. So much for walking on water.

Chapter 17

A Second Lesson

THE FOLLOWING DAY, the three witches sit at the kitchen table eating breakfast. Bits of scrambled egg litter the three plates, and the smell of slightly burned toast still hangs in the air.

"Did ya Nay teach ya nothing of da Fire Thief?" asks Parran out of nowhere. He's floating in the air beside the kitchen sink with his legs crossed. Behind him several dirty pans rest on the stovetop along with a couple of pieces of uneaten bacon.

"A little," says Famka staring up at his ink-covered arms. The hundreds, no, thousands of the spells cover his body like tattoos. She wonders just how many he knows. "Only that most folks are afraid of the Fire Thief and that he hated the Ghostal Holly."

"That be part of it. Seems ya Nay talks in half-truths," says Parran.

"Hey, that's my great granny you're talking about." Ophelia gives Parran a stern eye. "Watch your old tongue."

"No offending to ya, Ophelia," says Parran. "I suspect she's only trying to protect ya from da part of life that's too big to be knowing. It be a good ting she do."

"That's all right. I'm just joshing," says Ophelia smiling. "Momma Nay teases us about our Tuning sometimes. She says that if we don't do it right, the Fire Thief will sneak into our rooms in the middle of the night and eat our feet."

"I used to hate that when I was little," says Famka. "I believed her for years."

"Berny talked about the Fire Thief all the time," says Milly through a mouthful of toast. "Sorta like he loved him, in a way."

"Those dat knew him well, did love him," says Parran.

"Then why is he so feared now?" asks Famka. "That doesn't make any sense unless someone is trying to make him look bad on purpose."

"Never met him meself. Got dangerously close once," says Parran. "The Fire Thief was at his height during the Great War. They called it the Battle of Bloodberry Bloom. Centuries before yee was born."

"What year?" asks Famka.

"More like years. 1600s," says Parran.

"The whole hundred years?" asks Ophelia.

"Mostly," says Parran. "Give or take a little and depending on who ya ask. Anyway, I was trading in goods, smuggling in others up 'n down da Mississip, but I neva picked up a bad spell in use against another witch. Unless they came looking for what I was taking, o'course. I neva wanted nothing to do with the war."

"So, you were a thief?" asks Milly disgusted.

"I was, but a murderer I was not," says Parran. "The Fire

Thief... Ya can't even count a number that high. He killed so many of those in the Knack that it nearly wiped us all out."

"But why would he do that?" asks Ophelia. "There must have been a reason."

"Lots o' stories. Some say he was betrayed by the Ghostal Holly somehow. I dunno if anyone actually knows how or why, but an old pirate once told me that the Fire Thief lost his family. Mum, dad, brother, sisters. Saw them all butchered. Others say he's a Woodlot of the old; an immortal, who hates his own self."

"So why does Berny follow him then?" asks Ophelia.

"Ah dat be me point in telling ya about da Fire Thief," says Parran. "Ya see one ting about da Fire Thief is certain. Somehow, he broke into heaven and stole the Motherbook of all tings. The Bastard Book. Ya knows not to repeat its true name. It say that the Nyre King himself wrote down everyting he did when creating da world. So, anyone dat have it can do anyting dey can imagine. That's how Tuning came to be."

"You mean the Fire Thief... invented Tuning?" asks Famka.

"Aye, in a way, yes, but more like he gave Tuning to the living," says Parran. "Ya see there were those that knew a bit o' Tuning before the Fire Thief ever came along. Lots a folks had a little of the Knack in them. Mostly though, it weren't too useful. Some called it magic or sorcery, others called it witchcraft. However, calling Tuning any one of those would be like calling a drowning baby a good swimmer. Ya follow?"

"So, the Fire Thief *is* the father of Tuning," says Famka.

"Most Tuning, but not all came from him. Some of what ya know was also invented by two great witches known as Wyndom and Wyndomier. Since that time, there are those that have come up with a fair bit on dey own, but the truest beginning can be traced back to the Fire Thief, Wyndom and Wyndomier. It was during the Great War that most of what we know about Tuning came about."

"Where are Wyndom and Wyndomier now?" asks Milly.

"Far as I know, the Fire Thief killed them," says Parran. "Then Wyndomier's Sky Builders' brought the war to a close ya know."

"The Sky Builders were created by Wyndomier?" ask Famka excitedly.

"Aye, Momma. He did so to train witches to join in the war," says Parran. "The Ghostal Holly was desperate to fight the Fire Thief after he done stole the Bastard Book out of heaven."

"Is that what Berny believes is in the gazebo behind my house?" asks Milly perking up.

"He believes it to be true. 'N he needs be having me spells too," says Parran. He glances down at his ink-covered arms before looking to Famka and adding, "And a great witch as well."

"Great witch!" yelps Milly. "Why not me instead of Famka? I am a witch too."

Famka flashes a look to Ophelia but remains quiet, because she doesn't want Milly to feel bad. Ironic, since she isn't sure that she actually likes Milly all that much, but something in Milly's tone gave Famka pause. They sit quietly, and Famka runs Parran's words back through her head like replaying a tape. Why would the Fire Thief want to destroy the Ghostal Holly? Could it really be as simple as revenge or was that a lie and he is after something else altogether? And is the Bastard Book hidden in the gazebo?

"What does Berny need of me?" asks Famka.

Parran opens his paper mouth, but then stops and speaks into Famka's mind instead. They remain silent, but Famka moves her lips as if she is talking to herself.

"What's going on with you two?" asks Milly after a long silence.

"Say it out loud, Parran," says Famka.

"He needs ya blood, and ya soul to break the spell around the gazebo," says Parran.

"What happens if he gets the book?" asks Ophelia.

"Lots o' folks die," says Parran. "Berny is twisted as they come. He wants nothing more than to free the Fire Thief from the Sea of Chall and return that beast to power."

"What if we go to the Ghostal Holly and tell them about the Bastard Book?" asks Famka.

"No, no!" says Parran. "No one must ever know of dat book. If anyone in the Knack becomes aware of it, dey will come here to ya little island and tear it apart until they get it. There are those that would have it at all costs. Berny not being the only one who wants it. Bess we can do is get away from Berny."

Chapter 18

The Fire Thief: A Wyndom Window
(Long before you were born)

HIS FINGERNAILS WERE missing, and the pink flesh behind them, which had turned milky white, looked to be lumpy and filled with pus. The Fire Thief tapped the rim of his hat, then stretched out both of his arms and looked at the back of both of his hands as if admiring expensive jewelry.

I've killed so many with these hands.

The Fire Thief smiled. The details of his face where hidden, but his teeth were perfectly straight and unusually white. Then he dissolved and reappeared on the lawn near them. There was something peculiar about his appearance. It was as if he was there and not there all at once.

"Mum, we have to go!" yells the boy. "We have to get to the barn."

They both ran toward the old barn. Several horses moved about uneasily inside. As they rounded the back wall, a shimmering black cloth hung perfectly still in the air. Even as it rained heavily and wind blew all around them the cloth did not move. The boy yelled, "Uncle Albert's!"

The boy and his mother disappeared into the black cloth.

The Fire Thief was always slow and careful in his pursuits. He planned with plenty of preparation and was methodical to a fault. He was only slightly bothered when the boy he so desired turned and ran. The mother was inconsequential. He knew that he would get his prey one way or the other. Sooner or later, he always did. What was it that he had heard once and liked very much? *Patience is a virgin. No that's not it. Patience is a virtue. Yes, that's it exactly.*

The dead move very fast, but the boy's mother was too young in her death to know all the secrets her preternatural body would reveal. So, who had taught the boy then? How did he know how to use a Wyndom Window? This was something the Fire Thief had not prepared for. *A minor oversight, but it will not happen again.*

Within moments, the boy and his beloved mother were many hundreds of miles away.

The Fire Thief, not really being dead, but not really being alive, either, could move very fast. He dissolved instantly from the man that he was, back into the shadow he preferred to be, in order to pursue his two victims. From a distance, he looked like the smoke coming from an oil fire and a swarm of moths fighting violently for the same crowded space.

Mother and son now stood in a cornfield near an old barn in the English countryside close to the home of some distant relatives. The boy thought naively that perhaps they would help.

"Mum, what are we going to do?"

"I don't know, honey. Let's go into the barn and see if we can warm you up a bit. In the morning, we will talk with your uncle."

The barn was warm, and several animals became alert as they entered. His mother could see perfectly in the dark with her preternatural eyes. The boy reached out to take her hand and felt a moment of relief even though she was so cold now. Moonlight poked through an open window as they sat on a bale of hay.

"How did you know what to do?" the mother asked her son.

"Poppa taught me. He was a witch. Sometimes, we would go places. He said that if we were ever in trouble to use it. The thing we traveled into is called a Wyndom Window."

For a moment, the boy's mother thought that they were safe and wondered to herself, *What am I going to do now? How do I take care of my son now that I'm—I'm dead?*

"It'll be all right, Mum," said the boy, as if he somehow knew what she was thinking.

Sadness and despair ran through her heart as she looked upon her sweet child. His bright green eyes gazed back at her, and she felt a world of emotions engulf her.

Chapter 19

A Memoroff

Famka was growing increasingly worried that Berny would somehow find a way past Momma Nay's protection charms that surrounded the swamp and steal her away. Famka tried her best to pay attention to all Parran was teaching her, but she was distracted by what she'd seen when she snuck out to the Horseshoe the other night, which was not the smartest thing for her to do. Already, strange things had begun happening there. Just two days ago, all the normal ghosts had disappeared from the Horseshoe entirely. On a typical day, old Mr. Tildon could be counted on to fish in the moonlight, despite never actually catching a single thing. He'd curse through the night, often keeping Famka and Ophelia awake. And then, there was the ghost of Wink Tree Lane, who was always mindlessly wandering the little dirt path leading between the Horseshoe and Wink. The poor spirit was simply a shadow. There was no more crying through the night, not even a single whisper. Even this morning, the water in the pond shot straight into the air, spouting like a geyser for several minutes before it returned to normal.

Ophelia and Milly had joined in the lessons, but as Parran had said, Milly was barely a witch, so she naturally struggled with Tuning. Milly had never worked very hard for anything in her young life, so something as simple as focus was difficult. Combined with Parran's teaching methods of placing a reward on any technique mastered, the days were trying at times and funny at others.

On the first day, Milly tried lifting one of Mrs. Billbray's homemade pies into the air, using nothing more than a simple levitation spell. Parran felt it best to leave Ophelia beneath the pie as an incentive for Milly to focus. Milly did manage to hold the lemon meringue in the air for a moment, but when it fell, it made quite the sticky mess in Ophelia's round bushy hair.

Ophelia had no problems following all of the paper man's lessons. Not quite as adept as Famka, Ophelia nevertheless found a fluidity to Tuning. She thought of it like running and didn't overthink it the way Famka did. To Ophelia, it was a matter of finding the correct pacing. There was a rhythm to the world, similar to placing her feet perfectly with each step, heel to toe, as she jogged across her favorite beach. And Tuning was no different. Always one step came before the other, heel to toe.

The very first thing that Parran had taught them was a spell of forgetfulness called a Memoroff, which as Milly found out, was difficult to remember. It wasn't a major spell, but not a minor one, either, and an important one. Every few days, Famka had to help Milly reinforce the spell, or it would collapse and her parents would wonder where she had gone off to for the past few weeks. Given the distance between the swamp and Milly's home, the spell needed considerable attention to keep it in place. Parran explained that it was best to use a Memoroff in close proximity to the subject or victim as distance made it less effective.

On this particular midweek morning, Famka stares up at Parran, who's standing on the porch of Momma Nay's cabin looking down at the three witches like an orator. "Da Memoroff is generally used by a cheatin' husband or wife. It's been the cornerstone of long-lasting marriages for centuries and a delight for young witches wishing to avoid dey parents when rules are broken. It be said dat many a king enlisted the use of witches for no other reason than to keep dey screaming queens at bay. Wars on the battlefield were fought by soldiers with swords, but in da bedroom, it always be a Memoroff."

Famka agrees with the reasoning but marvels that Tuning hadn't been put to better use over the centuries. There were so many larger problems than an unfaithful husband or a mischievous teenager. Famka longed to solve what she felt were real world problems, including saving her skinny behind from Berny. Anything else she simply didn't care about.

What she did care about that morning was why the Memoroff placed on Milly's father by way of his college class ring, which he'd given to Milly to wear as a necklace, seemed not to be working as well as it had before. The three witches stare down at a thick gold ring in Milly's open hand. The sun overhead barely cuts through the trees, shining light on the jewelry as it slowly begins glowing bright red.

"Why does it keep doing that every few days?" asks Milly frustrated.

"Because the spell isn't working right," Famka responds even more frustrated.

"Maybe we should try the spell again," offers Ophelia.

"I've authored it three times already," says Famka. "It should have worked by now."

"But my parents will come looking for me if the Memoroff stops working," complains Milly.

"I know that, Milly," says Famka shortly.

"Can't Parran help?" asks Milly.

"Quit interrupting. Let me think a minute," says Famka.

"I not have much need for such a spell in me day, so I not know all the properties," says Parran. "I know da spell because it was written in me pages long after I was a Growgan. But as a witch, I neva had reason to try it."

Famka glares down at the ring like it's offended her. She reads the name Rien, which is engraved around the inside of the band, before stepping away. She begins pacing in front of the cabin trying to understand why the spell continues to fail. Her long brown hair flows out behind her like a cape, as her bare feet pad quickly across the dirt.

"We need to hurry," says Ophelia. "Uncle Guncle came by this morning before either of you woke. He said the police were asking questions about Milly. I think your folks are looking for you."

"Hm, I doubt it. What if we try the spell together?" Milly suggests.

Famka ignores her as she continues walking in a big circle in front of the cabin. After a moment, she stops and calls out, "Parran."

"Aye, Momma," he says from the porch. He shuffles to the edge and looks down at her.

"Could Berny have anything to do with the Memoroff failing?"

"It be possible. I not know for sure."

"Do you think Bernard could tamper with the spell without having to come here to the swamp?"

"It does ring possible," says Parran. "But I'm not certain."

"Ohhhh," says Ophelia suddenly.

"What is it, Ophi?" Famka turns to face her friend.

"I think you're right. It has to be Bernard," says Ophelia.

"How do you know?" asks Milly.

"He can't get in here, right?" Ophelia asks Parran.

"Dat's right. Ya Nay's spells protect dis swamp from the likes of Berny."

"But the police can walk right in here?" Famka interrupts.

"You got it," says Ophelia smiling brightly. "And if they show up, they'll take Milly home and maybe us to jail for kidnapping or something."

"Kidnapping, really?" asks Milly.

"Sure. Think about it," says Ophelia, a certain excitement in her voice for having solved the mystery. "You haven't been home in weeks. Once the spell fails and they remember you, your parents will come looking for you. I'm sure they'd involve the police, and if they find you out here with us, me and Famka will be taken in for questioning, for sure. Even if we're not arrested, they'll take us in to the police station. Then we won't be in the swamp where we're safe from Berny."

Frustrated, Famka starts pacing again then abruptly stops and says, "We need to go to town and put the spell directly on your father, Milly. That way, it's stronger."

"What about my mom and the servants… the butler?" asks Milly playing with the ring.

"I can author a Sneezer and combine it with the Memoroff, so that when your dad gets home, he spreads the spell like a cold." Famka then turns to Parran and asks, "That will work…won't it?"

"Not bad tinking, Momma," says Parran. "But be certain. If we leave da swamp, we is open to Berny. I not believe dat we have time to put da Memoroff on Milly's papa."

"You think maybe that's what he's expecting us to do?" asks Ophelia. "Just leave?"

"Wouldn't put it past him to try and get us out of here any way he can," says Parran. "He's a clever one."

"Could he burn the swamp down?" asks Famka unexpectedly.

"Naw," says Parran. "Spells here are too strong for natural tings to affect da swamp. Only Tuning can get him in here."

"I don't want to go home," says Milly looking at Famka fearfully. "I know I complain about this shack, and I'm sorry. I'm used to…nicer, well you know, but I'd rather stay here."

"You don't have to go home," says Ophelia placing a hand on Milly's shoulder. "You can stay here as long as you like."

"Or as long as her parents don't bring the police here." Famka gives her best friend a stern look.

"Are there any other options, Parran?" asks Ophelia.

"Naw, Momma," he says.

"So, let me this straight," says Ophelia. "We stay here where we're safe from Berny, but not the police. Or we go into Wink where we're exposed to Berny, but safe from the police and Milly's parents."

"Seems like a mess," says Milly. "Sorry that I got you guys into this."

"What if we can get to Miss Turtlebalm in Wink? You know, before Berny notices that we've left the swamp," asks Famka. "She is the Resident Witch of Wink. So, she can help."

"She could help to be certain," says Parran. "There is only

one problem with ya plan."

"What's that?" asks Milly.

"Berny be watchin' the swamp day and night. He not need to sleep, being a ghost," says Parran.

"He can't watch the whole place, can he?" asks Ophelia. "The swamp is pretty big. And then there's the Horseshoe too."

"Naw, he cannot be in more than one place at a time," says Parran. "But how far is Wink from here? How ya planning on getting there quickly?"

"Parran," says Famka," weren't you a smuggler?"

"Aye, Momma. I was," he says. "But of tings not folks."

"So, what's the big difference?"

"Tings can lie still for hours, weeks without needs," says Parran. "Folks are patient for minutes at most."

"All right then," says Famka firmly. "I know what we can do." She turns to Ophelia. "We hide in the back of Uncle Guncle's truck before he drives into Wink with his morning fish delivery."

"With all the fish?" asks Milly scrunching up her nose.

"With all the fish," Famka confirms, looking less than satisfied.

"Berny will sense ya witchiness the moment ya step out o' these spells surrounding us," says Parran.

"So, we'll need you to create a diversion," says Famka. "Uncle Guncle leaves the Horseshoe each morning after checking his traps. He sells his fish to the Bacas, which is a few doors down from Turtleburgers."

"What does ya have in mind?" asks Parran.

"Can you fly us out of here again?" asks Famka.

"I not be thinking that work two times on the likes of

Berny," says Parran.

"What if you fly on your own? You know… as a way to distract him?" asks Milly.

Parran looks at Famka, clearly not thrilled with that suggestion.

"I have an idea," says Famka.

"I really don't like it when you say that," says Ophelia. "The last time nearly got you killed."

"You won't like this one, either," says Famka.

"Some way to distract Berny that puts you in harm's way?" says Ophelia.

"You got it," says Famka.

Chapter 20

Tricks Be Lies

"IT STINKS IN here," says Milly squished in between Famka and Ophelia. The three witches lie side by side beneath a black tarp in the back of Uncle Guncle's pickup truck. Famka's heart is beating louder than anyone's, having just offered herself teasingly up to Berny as a distraction before stealing away into the back of the truck. She couldn't have achieved it without Parran's help, and only hopes he can delay Berny long enough for them to make their escape.

Ophelia hugs a backpack across her chest. Coolers filled with fish slosh beside them as they bounce down Wink Tree Lane. The dirt road tosses them against the hot metal bed like popcorn kernels, and a basket of crabs nearly tips onto Ophelia. She pushes it back in place as one of the trapped critters tries to pinch her.

Within minutes, Famka is dripping in sweat. Her T-shirt sticks to her back, and she's right up against Milly. She tries to scoot away, but she's pinned tightly against a cooler. The smell is nearly suffocating as the tarp holds in the stench, baking the girls in a pickup-truck fish pie.

"I'm not sure I can stand this stink much longer," says Milly pinching her nose.

"Shhh," shushes Famka. "Keep your voice down. We don't want Uncle Guncle to hear us. The back window of his truck is always open. He doesn't have air conditioning."

"Do you think Parran is all right?" asks Ophelia quietly.

"What he did back there…!" says Famka.

"There's no doubt he's on our side. I like him," says Ophelia.

"Yeah, me too," says Famka.

"Do you think he'll be able to buy us a bit of time?" asks Ophelia.

"We'll find out soon enough," says Famka. "So far so good."

They continue down the bumpy, dusty, dirt road slowly and in silence. The heat beneath the tarp is near unbearable, and sweat runs freely. Uncle Guncle is generous with his braking, and more than once, Famka bumps her head against the cab of the truck. She looks up at the black tarp as it ripples from the wind running across the top. She closes her eyes and reaches out to Parran with her mind.

What if this doesn't work? she asks concerned.

Do what we planned, Momma, says Parran cautiously. *But if—*

"Could this truck move any slower?" Milly complains, breaking Famka's concentration. "It's so hot in here."

"Uncle Guncle doesn't want to upset the fish," says Ophelia. "Treats them with respect."

"That's weird," says Milly.

"If you tried his fried catfish, you'd change your mind,"

says Ophelia.

"I'm not sure that I can ever eat fish again after this trip into town." Milly pinches her nose again.

"I have to agree," says Famka scrunching up her face at the relentless odor.

They travel on for a while in silence, baking beneath the tarp. The side of the truck digs into Famka's back leaving her feeling terribly uncomfortable. She wonders why Berny is intent on dragging her back to Milly's home. Is the Bastard Book really there? Is it really worth the Ghostal Holly coming down on him? If Miss Turtlebalm spotted Berny it would all be over for him.

"Except for the stink, this is easier than I expected," says Milly. "I was worried that Berny would catch us right away."

Famka ignores her and tries to reestablish a connection with Parran, but a siren blasts to life right behind them. Milly jumps nervously beside Famka as the pickup truck pulls over and slowly comes to a stop. Uncle Guncle steps out of the truck, slams the door, and grumbles as walks toward the police car, his boots crunching on the dirt road. Famka looks out of a small slit where the rear gate meets the bed wall and sees a policeman stepping out of a black and white cruiser. Her eyes go wide in her brown face as she turns to Milly and Ophelia. She places a finger to her lips telling them to keep quiet before trying to peek out again.

"Why are you bothering me, Sam?" Uncle Guncle challenges the policeman.

"Calm down, Moses," says Sam the policeman.

"Turn them lights off before you disturb my fish," barks Uncle Guncle.

"Whatever you say, Moses." Sam reaches through the open

window of his cruiser, and the spinning red and blue lights go still. "Where you headed?"

"You pulled me over for that?" growls Uncle Guncle. "You'd better come up with something better, or I'm going on my way. You know exactly where I'm headed."

"I am the law, Moses," says Sam sternly.

"That maybe, but I've known your daddy and your momma since before they got tangled up in their sheets and brought your thick head into the world. I suspect they'll be upset if I pay them a visit and tell them their son was pestering me while I was trying to deliver my fish. Everyone loves my fish, son. Everyone! Especially your momma. What do you think she's going to say if she can't fry up her Sunday special after church this weekend? Oh, maybe she'll take a frozen pot pie out of the freezer. Or maybe one of them pizza bread things she forgot about that's covered in freezer burn. Oh, I'm sure either of those scenarios will go over real well with her and that clucking church group of hers."

"There's a young lady missing," says Sam ignoring him entirely. "The Rien girl."

"Haven't heard anything about it," snarls Guncle. "If'n that was true, being that her uppity daddy is one of the most well-known lawyers in Texas don't you think I'd o' heard about it? Pulling me over on account of some rumor seems a little suspicious to me."

"Are you sure all you have back there is fish?" Sam takes a step closer to the pickup.

"Goodbye, Sam." Uncle Guncle turns away from the policeman.

"I-don't-think-that's-a-very-good-idea." With each word, his voice grows unnaturally lower. "Moses Guncle, I am th-the law. The law. You will obey me."

Famka sees the policeman leaps out of sight and hears shuffling noises, then a thud against the truck, and Uncle Guncle groaning in pain. She can hear what she thinks is Sam growling like a dog, and something large drops to the ground. Milly clutches Famka's forearm while Famka squints through the tiny opening, trying to see where the policeman went. A red eye suddenly appears in the slit, the back gate is ripped from the hinges, and the tarp goes flying through the air.

Something sorta like Berny is standing at the back of the truck, grinning. Only it's not entirely him. It's as if Berny's ghost is wearing the policeman's body like a poorly fitted suit. Famka pushes against a crate as Milly screams. Berny's red eyes poke out of Sam's face like two small beads. He smiles, revealing two sets of teeth. His filthy yellowed ones sit in a curved line in front of the policeman's more polished, younger teeth.

"Three thieving little witches," says Berny nastily. "Tisk tisk."

Uncle Guncle steps clumsily alongside the pickup, holding a shotgun. Famka, Milly, and Ophelia quickly sit up and cram against the cab of the faded green truck huddled together.

"What are you supposed to be?" Uncle Guncle asks the creature standing at the back of his truck. He clicks the gun into ready to blow a hole right through Berny. The dead man leaps into the bed of the truck like some kind of gangly monkey. The fish slosh in their coolers, and two of the traps fall over.

"If you shoot me, you shoot your little friend, Sam." Berny smiles wickedly. "I'm sure his momma won't buy another one of your filthy fish if she finds out you killed her poor little Sam the policeman."

Berny kicks one of the coolers with his policeman's black boot. It falls onto its side, and fish spill out. Water runs out of the back of the truck. A dozen of Uncle Guncle's morning inventory bounce wildly as they desperately search for breath. Two fall off the end and flop onto the dirt road. Uncle Guncle looks down at the poor little fishes, somewhere between irritated and sad.

"I'll take my chances," says Uncle Guncle as he points the gun at Berny.

"No!" says Famka reaching out. "Don't. You really will kill Sam."

"Smart little witchy," says Berny smiling his disgusting double row of teeth at her. For a moment, Famka imagines the ghost as a used-car salesman straight out of the devil's backyard.

"What do you want, Berny?" demands Famka.

The ghost looks at Famka, turning his head sideways a few inches further than seems natural.

"I assume you must know," says Berny. "I can't imagine Parran has been sitting around your dirty little swamp silently. He is a chatterbox, that one. Even if he didn't teach you anything, he must have told you about me."

"Actually, he hasn't said a word about you," Famka lies. This elicits the expected irritation from Berny. "He's strangely loyal to you. I have no idea why."

The ghost turns his head another inch, making him look as if Sam's neck is now broken.

"Not a good liar, I see," says Berny.

"Believe what you want," says Ophelia. "If we knew how to Tune well, we wouldn't have taken your book."

"Another bad liar," says Berny.

"So… What is it that you want?" Famka laces the question with irritation.

"Well, you, of course," says Berny. "And my Growgan. Where is Parran by the way?"

"We don't know," lies Famka.

"Somehow, I doubt that," says Berny. "But I have a good way to find out." He spins his right hand in small circles, and Ophelia rises about five feet above the truck bed. Her gray-green eyes go wide, and her arms fly out as she kicks trying to gain balance.

"Put me down!" demands Ophelia.

"With a simple flick of my wrist, your friend flies into the air. I promise not to be here when she lands."

"No! Don't. I'll go with you, but you leave my friends be," says Famka. "And you never come back to the Horseshoe or the swamp."

"Famka," says Uncle Guncle concerned. "What are ya doing, girl?"

"It's the only way," says Famka. "Do we have a deal, Berny?"

"Deal," says Berny.

"Your word," says Famka. "State it loudly, so that we all hear it."

"I, Bernard Trankler, promise to never return to the Horseshoe or that disgusting swamp if you come with me now," he says, extending a hand. "And you bring my Growgan."

"No, baby," says Ophelia. She tries to reach out to Famka but is too high. "You can't go with him. There's no telling what he'll do to you."

"It's the only way he'll let us be. What else can we do? He has us beat," says Famka taking a step toward Berny.

All of sudden, the ghost screams in pain. He spins around and looks at Uncle Guncle, who just smashed his knees with the butt of his double-barrel shot gun. The ghost falls off the edge of the truck and onto his side, lying crumpled on the dirt road.

"You didn't say that I couldn't hit him, Famka," says Uncle Guncle glaring down at Berny. "Just that I couldn't shoot him."

The ghost raises the policeman's hand clumsily, as if it's being controlled by strings like a marionette doll, and points at Uncle Guncle. His fingers shake, and Famka jets across the bed. She leaps off the edge of the truck and shoves Uncle Guncle out of the way, both of them tumbling to the ground. A spell fires from the ghost's hand barely missing them both. A second later, Ophelia falls back into the truck then jumps off the edge and sits on Berny's chest, pinning him to the ground. She places her hands over his heart and mumbles a spell. Milly comes up beside them and pulls Berny's arms back over his head.

"Please, Berny," says Milly, "calm down. I'll come home with you."

"Get off me, witch!" demands Berny as he squirms under Ophelia.

"You're stuck in there aren't you?" says Ophelia. "You have a bad habit of creating spells that backfire on you."

"Now, Parran!" Yells Famka jumping to her feet.

The book man bursts through the open window of the truck cab. He begins as a book, but instantly transforms into his paper man shape in midair before landing silently beside

Famka. She grabs his paper hand, his inked fingers wrapping through hers, and they dash forward to descend on Berny, who continues to struggle beneath Ophelia's weight. With their free hands Famka and Parran both reach in and pull Berny's pathetic slimy soul from the policeman's body. Berny sticks to the policeman like gum on the bottom of a tennis shoe before finally snapping free. The force throws both Ophelia and Milly.

"That was foolish," says Berny. He yanks free of them and floats into the air, growing in size the higher he gets. His body flattens out like a giant kite as his white sleeping gown spreads wider. His head resembles a tiny flat rock covered in black hair resting on top of his large square shoulders. His feet dangle downward and are now the size of Uncle Guncle's pickup.

Famka releases Parran's hand and rushes to Ophelia's, whose hands are covered in mud. "He sure likes doing that," says Ophelia.

"That's what I'm counting on," says Famka looking up.

Milly crawls beside them, and they huddle together.

"Can I shoot him now?" asks Uncle Guncle cocking his shotgun.

"It won't help," says Famka.

"Famka Meadows," bellows Berny loudly. The sound of his voice reverberates through Famka's bones like a crack from a lightning storm. "Trick be lies, and a deal is a deal. Come with me now, and I won't crush your little witchy friends."

She stands up and says, "I'm sorry, but I can't hear you. What was that?"

He rotates to face downward. His body is now lying flat in the air like a giant sheet, and his gigantic face slowly moves to within several feet of hers. His flat head is well over six feet in length and nearly two-dimensional.

"Do not think that I don't know what you are trying to do," says Berny. "I applaud you for knowing that the local Resident Witch would feel my presence and come to your rescue. But I have been at this much longer than you have. No one is going to hear me, no matter how loudly I call out. I assure you that your Resident Witch, Turtlebalm, is far from Wink on an errand of my own making."

Famka's heart sinks, and Ophelia clutches her hand tightly. The witches were counting on Miss Turtlebalm to save them from Berny. Any good Resident Witch would have spells set in their territory that would alert them to any unsanctioned Tuning of this particular size. Mocha Turtlebalm was one of the best Resident Witches around.

"Come now." Berny glares at Famka with his red beady eyes. He turns to the book man, who's standing nearby. "You, too, Parran. Now that you're finally awake, we have much work to do."

Berny swoops down behind them, forcing them down the road.

Intermission

"I WOULD LIKE to stress a point you brought up earlier. You see, anyone can read the Bastard Book." Famka sits across from me in the studio, dabbing her mouth with a napkin.

"Anyone?" I say confused. "But it's written in the language of heaven."

"That's exactly the point, Blue," she says excitedly. She leans forward as if she's about to reveal a secret. "The Nyre King wrote everything in the language of heaven. Plants, animals, the trees, the oceans, the fish, and the planets were all written in that ancient language. Physics is an attempt at understanding what the Nyre King wrote on a physical level. Religion is the opposite side of the physical coin: simply an attempt to understand what Nyre King wrote on a spiritual level. From that perspective, there is no difference between any of us. Even your belief that as a Skeleton you are less than other species is incorrect because you, too, are written in the language of heaven."

I'm not sure that I believe her as I look across the table at Famka Meadows. I consider her words as I turn and look at a pair of puffy white gloves floating in the air beside me that type every word we say as if clicking on an invisible typewriter. They are called Composers, and I use them as a backup to my recording equipment located in the control room of my studio. The four-fingered gloves move quickly and silently, making only the occasional mistake. I sometimes find that reading what has been said rather than listening allows me to put facts together or search for clues that I may have otherwise missed.

"Did you know where Lady'Witch Turtlebalm was when Berny was after you?"

"Lady'Witch Turtlebalm," Famka repeats and then looks away as if considering her next words carefully. "No, I did not, but I later learned that she was in chambers in the Plaza of Giants with the Sky Builders' Guild while we were trying to trick Berny as we sneaked out of the Horseshoe. Apparently, she'd been sent on an unnecessary request to mediate over a minor dispute for what should have been a few hours."

"Seems strange doesn't it," I say. "Her being gone right when you would need her."

"I agree," she says. "Berny had a hand in that."

"Do you know what she was doing in the Plaza?"

"I only know that on her way home, Jorge the Alien requested her attendance at a council meeting of the Sky Builders. There had been rumors that summer of a western tribe of Wigglers locating the *Kitab'i'Mordanee*. Naturally, Jorge was concerned that if the lost tomb was found, war would be upon us again."

I feel immediately tense at her relaxed use of the Bastard Book's true name. Shifting in my chair, I try to hide my discomfort.

"I see that you believe in the superstitions around the book too," says Famka.

"I guess I do," I say. "It's the reason for our cursed skin." I glance at my blue complexion in the glass window into the studio control room. "Did you think Jorge's concerns were legitimate?"

"It is the Sky Builders' edict to protect the world from the Fallen Arts, and as a Sky Builder, I'm sworn, as Lady'Witch Turtlebalm was even then, to investigate any such rumors. Wyndomier himself made our mandate clear during the war," says Famka. "And certainly, the Kitab... the book played a big part in nearly destroying everything."

"But honestly, if someone found it, what good would it do them?" I ask. "Is it really readable to the average witch? I find it difficult to believe that it is. The book was written in heaven's language as you suggest."

"The Bastard Book is nothing like a *Gravedigger's Handbook*," she says. "Unlike a *Gravedigger's Handbook*, which will only teach a witch what their capacity is capable of handling, the Bastard Book will reveal whatever you ask it. Imagine for a moment that kind of unlimited knowledge. Anyone with the smallest imagination could wreak such havoc. But someone skilled in Tuning and equally merciless, like LumLum the Wiggler for example, well, he could threaten the world at large. It is no simple thing what the Ghostal Holly does to maintain a semblance of peace among all the sentient races. Wigglers hate Bombadoes. Ghosts tolerate witches Tuning, and Drolling

Dragons have grown more uncaring the smaller their numbers have become over the centuries. Then there is we humans, the weakest of all sentient beings. With all of the resources at the Ghostal Holly's disposal, they struggle to keep humanity from destroying itself with each passing decade. Introducing a weapon of unlimited knowledge could very easily send this dear planet of ours into extinction."

"So serious, you two," says Zinnia walking into the room with a tray of burritos. Her long black hair falls across her face as she sets the platter on the table between Famka and me. "The salsa is from Grim's garden. He grew tired of cutting up so many tomatoes, so he finally grew a proper salsa bush. Delicious too. I'm quite surprised. I must admit that I still enjoy cutting up my tomatoes, but that's just me."

I stand up and introduce my wife, "Famka this is..."

"Oh!" says Famka standing. "Your song "The One" is so touching. Your voice, it leaves me feeling... oh, I'm sorry I can't explain. Please don't think me a foolish admirer."

I stare at the most famous witch I have ever met, and I'm left feeling completely dumbfounded. She is here telling me about her unbelievable life, and I presume that she wants me to write about it as I have Charli Wonkers. Even without her story, that she is in my home is overwhelming, but now she is talking to my wife with admiration. I've studied Famka Meadows at length. She invented new spells, which are taught to young Sky Builders during their second- and third-year terms. She alone managed to rethink a Trankler's Hold It and use the shield in a way no one else was ever able to do. Not even Bernard Trankler himself had considered her approach. Watching Famka and my wife, Zinnia, makes me see that this is one heck of a weird day.

"Please, Famka. Sit," says Zinnia still clasping Famka's hands. "I'm so happy to meet you. Blue talks about you with such conviction. I think he's read nearly everything written on you. I have no doubt that he will be dancing out of here after you leave."

Good Lord, now I'm embarrassed.

"Oh, Zinni, please." I try my best to keep my blue face from turning red.

"You're not a witch?" asks Famka curiously.

"No," says Zinnia. "If I have any magic in me, it's in my songs."

"And yet you live here on this side of the Graveyard?" asks Famka.

"Mostly," Zinnia answers. "We travel back when we can."

"So interesting," says Famka. "I'm surprised the Ghostal Holly allows you to remain."

"I think they do so mostly because they don't know," says Zinnia.

"I see. Not to worry," says Famka. "Your secret is safe with me."

"Thank you," says Zinnia. "So nice meeting you, Famka. I'll let you both get back to your work."

"And you," says Famka. "Any new music out soon?"

Zinnia stops at the door. Her eyes flash to me before she says. "Actually, Blue finished up some final touches late last night. Soon I hope. Bye for now."

Famka sits down again then picks up a burrito and takes a bite. "Hm... the salsa is good."

Famous witches like salsa. Funny how celebrity works. I've got it in my head that she's some other-worldly being, that she can do no wrong, but she is flesh and blood just like me. Of course she'd like the salsa. Grim made it, and he's a great cook.

A terrible thought occurs to me, and I'm almost afraid to ask my question, because I'm reasonably sure that I already know the answer. Drumming my fingers on the table top I look at my burrito, which I haven't touched. If I don't eat it, Zinnia is sure to be upset with me. She hates wasting food, and rightfully so. As I take a bite and swallow a mouthful, I decide to ask Famka my burning and potentially stupid question. I say stupid because, sometimes, ignorance is fan-freaking-tastic. Despite my endlessly hungry curiosity, I often wish that I could remove certain things from my memory forever. There are details about people that I would love to un-know. Just pluck the thoughts right out of my head and toss them into a garbage bin.

"If everything is written in the language of heaven, can the *Kitab'i'Mordanee* unwrite the world?"

She nods, and now I'm certain that I didn't want to know that.

"Not only the world, but everything in existence."

Fan-freaking-tastic!

Chapter 21

Wink, Texas

"WHAT WILL IT be?" snarls Berny, still hanging in the air. His body is flat and gigantic spreading out over the road.

Famka looks over at Parran, who's staring down the road back toward the Horseshoe. The long dusty path bends alongside the ocean spraying the occasional mist from the Gulf. Wild, marshy grass runs away from them on the opposite side of the road across a large uneven field. Normally, the waist high grass rolls in faded yellow waves back and forth all day long, but somehow, the wind has come to a complete stop and the blades are still. Even the waves of the ocean have settled, and the blue water lies completely flat.

Someone be coming, says Parran in Famka's mind.

Who? asks Famka through their silent link.

Dunno, Momma, says Parran. *Be ready to move.*

"What is that?" Milly asks, suddenly pointing back toward the Horseshoe.

In the distance, the dust along the road slowly gathers into whirling columns of brown funnels. At first, there are only a few, but within seconds, there are dozens marching toward Famka like soldiers in a ghostly army. They form perfectly rigid lines, and as they move closer, more funnels join them.

Angrily Berny shoots into the air, arches his back, and puffs out his chest. He now resembles the sails of a pirate ship. With a large exhale, he blows like he's suddenly the big bad wolf, but it does nothing to slow the approaching columns. "Turn away," bellows Berny after his failed attempt. "This is no concern of yours."

But the funnels continue unperturbed by his ranting. One by one, they trudge forward with a single-minded determination. The sky is now so full of dust that the sun resembles an angry red dot in the far distance, and a plume of dust rolls out over the ocean, obscuring the blue-green water entirely. Berny reaches out, his arm extending unnaturally long like some kind of freaky puppet, and cuts across the tops of the funnels chopping them in two. They fall to the sides but continue, only making the procession wider.

Berny soars into the air, roaring like a beast, and descends on the dirt army.

"Let's go!" yells Famka. She grabs Ophelia by the hand and pulls her to her feet. Milly scuffles behind them as they run around to the passenger side of the pickup truck.

"Parran, book!" yells Famka, and he returns to his normal form, landing in her hands just before she dives into the pickup behind Milly and Ophelia. Uncle Guncle jams his key into the ignition and turns the engine over. The old truck grumbles to life, the rear tires spin, and they fly forward toward the little town of Wink. The rear of the truck swerves until the tires catch and they jerk into high speed. All the remaining fish and crabs fly out of the back of the pickup.

Famka spins around to look back at the battle scene.

"Hurry!" barks Famka as she watches Berny, who is now high in the air and larger than a barn. He is crisscrossed in funnels of dust. The brown snake-like ropes spin around him, pulling tightly like belts around his ghostly frame. They quickly turn his body into a freakish hour-glass shape. His mouth falls open as he continues to struggle wildly. He thrashes in the air with all his might, but he can't break free. Beneath him, a gigantic funnel of dust flows up from the road, opening widely. A moment later, it swallows him. The last thing that Famka sees before they are too far away is the outline of Berny's giant face pressing against the inside of the dust funnel.

"What on earth happened back there?" asks Ophelia seated beside Famka.

Famka turns to face forward, no longer able to see Berny. The little town of Wink is slowing growing on the horizon, and the ocean on their right is visible, thank goodness.

"God forsaken fuzzy floaty ruined my fish," grumbles Uncle Guncle. "Lost my shotgun too."

"Uncle Guncle, you can see ghosts?" asks Famka.

"Not so much. I got a bit of the Knack, but nothing like Momma Nay and, I suppose, you girls too," he says. "I couldn't see that ghost clearly, but I know he was one heck of a booger. Angry as all can be too. Hadn't felt one that bad in ages."

"What do we do now?" asks Milly.

"I think we should find Miss Turtlebalm," says Ophelia. "Let's check her shop in Wink. Maybe she's there."

"Maybe that was her back there, saving us," offers Famka.

"That weren't the work of no witch," says Parran from Famka's lap. The top edge of his dark brown cover moves in the shape of a mouth as he talks. Uncle Guncle flashes a quick glance at the book before hunching sternly over the steering wheel again like what he just saw is normal.

"Who was it?" asks Famka.

"Or what?" adds Ophelia.

"Bombadoe maybe. Perhaps a Wiggler. No telling, but it was old Tuning dey used, whoever it were," says Parran. "We stepped into a bit o' luck, Momma. Someone protect us for now."

"We still have to reinforce the Memoroff on my parents," says Milly reminding them why they left the safety of the Horseshoe to begin with.

"Do you think we're safe from Berny now?" Famka asks Parran.

"Naw, Momma," says Parran. "I won't count on it. We need be finding ya Resident Witch Turtlebalm."

They continue down the dirt road until they reach Wink's town limits. They quickly pass a sign that reads...

Welcome to Wink.

Winter population: 875.

Summer population: Good God, y'all!

They slow to a crawl when they reach a long row of wooden shops filled with junk for selling to tourists. Famka rolls down her window as they pass the buildings, each painted in a bright color. Some are blue, others are yellow, and occasionally one is red. Although the red ones are sorta frowned on by the locals. A covered boardwalk that runs in front of the shops is already crowded with moms buying ice cream and dads lugging bags filled with flip flops, towels, and suntan lotion. Excited children run chaotically around their parents and into the street. Two hotels are sandwiched between the shops, and to the right of Wink Tree Lane lies a large beach filled with pale sunbathers just waiting to burn in the hot Texas summer sun. A beach ball flies in front of the truck, and a boy dashes after it, forcing Uncle Guncle to brake hard. Parran flies onto the floor by Famka's feet, grumbling.

"Sorry, Parran." Famka reaches down to pick him up.

"There on the left," says Ophelia pointing to Miss Turtlebalm's Turtleburgers shop.

"'Course there ain't no parking," growls Uncle Guncle. "I'll drop you girls and come back when I find a spot."

He pulls over to the left, blocking in a couple of cars. Famka jumps out holding Parran, followed by Ophelia and Milly. Coming around the driver's side, Famka leans through the open window, kisses Guncle on the cheek, and says, "I'm sorry about your fish, Uncle."

"Ain't your fault, girly. Fish I can replace." His dark face remains flat, but his bright eyes smile as he pulls away. She knew what he meant. He'd spent his entire morning tending traps and gathering his fish in the blistering hot sun. It was back-breaking work, and often when he came back to the Horseshoe at the end of his work day, he was so tired that he could barely stand up straight. He wasn't the young man he'd once been, and his body often ached. More than once, Famka cooked him dinner, stewed up a potion for his aches, or tucked him into bed as he had done for her when she was a child. But after all of his effort hauling in his catch, it didn't matter to him as long as Famka and Ophelia were safe. That was the thing about the Horseshoe. Everyone loved each other. Despite Famka's burning desire to escape, she knew it was a place she could always call home.

The three little witches step onto the boardwalk and up to the blue door of Turtleburgers. There are so many tourists milling in the way, they don't see the closed sign right away. Milly pulls on the golden handle, but the door is locked.

"Where is Miss Turtlebalm?" Famka cups her hands around her eyes as she peers inside the empty shop.

"Berny said she was gone," says Ophelia. "He must have done something to get her to leave."

"Do you think she's all right?" asks Famka.

"I hope so," says Ophelia.

"What do we do now?" complains Milly.

"Parran?" whispers Famka to the book. "Can you get us inside?"

"Aye, Momma," says Parran. "It be not a worry. Problem be all da folks. Dey can't see us Tune. Else we bring the Ghostal Holly down on us."

"Let's go around back," says Ophelia. "Come on."

"What about Uncle Guncle?" asks Famka.

Milly looks out into the crowd of tourists along the boardwalk.

"We have a bigger problem," she says.

A stern-looking man, with enough mustache for two men, strolls toward them with an angry scowl. He cuts between the many bumbling tourists purposefully. A black suit covers his medium height, and his thick hair is combed back against his head.

As he approaches, he glares down at Milly disapprovingly. He stops and doesn't say so much as a how do, but stares at her as if he could burn a hole right into Milly without so much as a magnifying glass.

"Hi, Daddy," she says, fidgeting with her hands.

Chapter 22

Trapped in Turtleburgers

MILLY IS SHOVED inside the soda shop as the door flies open despite having been locked a moment ago.

"Hey!" yells Ophelia chasing in behind Milly's father. "You can't treat Milly like that. I don't care if she is your daughter."

Milly flashes a pathetic look at Ophelia then looks down at her own feet sheepishly.

As Famka steps inside, the door closes on its own behind her. Red-cushioned booths line the wall all the way to the back of the shop. Across the room, the old jukebox sits patiently waiting for requests, and to Famka's left, a row of stools, each anchored to the checkerboard-tiled floor, sit in front of a long white counter. She clutches the Growgan to her chest and realizes that the sounds from outside have gone silent. Famka can see the busy tourists through the glass, but she is certain they cannot see her.

"Who are you really?" asks Famka turning to Milly's father.

The mustached man breaks into a large smile before transforming into a small, ugly, stone-like elf. The black suit fades away into puffs of wispy tendrils, and he shrinks down to just over a foot tall. His leather shoes walk across the shop and leap into a trash bin in a corner. Finally, his mustache disappears with a funny sound like bubble gum popping. Appearing in place of Milly's father is a Drolling Dragon, whose long floppy ears are pinned behind a bald head, and large, bulging orange eyes stick out of a gray elephant-like skin.

"Heiki?" says Famka happily surprised. She walks toward the little Drolling Dragon closing the gap between them.

"Famka." Heiki leaps into the air and lands on the countertop. "Where is Momma Nay? How have you gotten into so much trouble in such short amount of time?"

"What is that thing?" Milly asks as she backs away from Heiki.

"Thing?" says Heiki insulted. "That's a fine way to talk to me after saving your butt from that Fuzzy Floaty out there." She points a tiny finger toward the Horseshoe without taking her eyes off Milly." I am a Drolling Dragon, young lady."

"We don't know where Momma Nay is," says Famka. "We've been trapped in the swamp for weeks hiding from that ghost out there. Was that you that saved us?"

"It most certainly was," says Heiki. "Ghost, huh? Well that's not going to do. We need to get rid of him right away. Who is he?"

"Bernard Trankler," Ophelia says, taking a seat on one of the red-topped stools and leaning against the counter.

"Gorilla biscuits and gravy!" Heiki crosses her arms across her little chest. "That can't be. Are you certain about that?"

"That's what he calls himself," says Famka.

"He was killed during the war," Heiki says. "And thank

goodness!"

"Why, what did he do that was so bad?" asks Ophelia.

"Father of the Fallen Arts and First Chair to the Fire Thief during the Battle of Bloodberry Bloom. Are you certain your ghost is Bernard Trankler?"

"Well, no," says Famka placing the Growgan on the counter. She looks down at the book, wondering why Parran hasn't spoken up yet. Normally, he's quite chatty.

"I don't understand what's so bad about him." Milly grabs a lock of her puffy blonde hair, nervously twisting it in between her fingers. "He was my mentor. He was tough, because he wanted me to Tune really good, but I never saw him hurt anyone," says Milly.

"Stupid witch," says Heiki. "As First Chair, he was the closest confidant to the Fire Thief and helped to bring about the near ending of my people. For one! How's that for something bad? There are countless horrific spells attributed to him. The most popular one is a Trankler's Hold It."

"I heard a story that Bernard had first invented the spell so that he could lock some poor young girl inside. I guess she didn't return his affections," says Ophelia.

"How did he invent such strong spells?" asks Milly.

"He not be dat strong," says Parran leaping from the counter and into his manlike form. He stands beside Famka next to the counter and looks at Heiki. "That maggot!"

"Gorilla biscuits and gravy," says Heiki surprised. "A Growgan. Is there anything else you girls would like to tell me about?"

"This is Parran," says Famka gesturing toward the book man. "He's been helping us."

"Happy to make ya acquaintance." Parran takes a step

back, then bows low before leaning against the counter. "Never thought to see another of ya kind again. A Drolling Dragon by the name of Hellman was a mate of mine, a great many years ago. Perhaps you know him."

"You know my Hellman?" asks Heiki, her voice rising slightly.

"I... I do," says Parran. "We ran supplies together during the war. He and his Nightcoach brought tings was needed down to the Mississip, where I took them up river under da Fire Thief's nose."

"Wait a second. You're Parran Papillon?" she asks in an accusatory tone. "The butterfly."

"I am," Parran responds. "Because no one suspects a butterfly."

She walks across the counter, leaps into the air, and whacks him across the face.

"What be dat for?" he asks, shocked and rubbing his cheek.

"Spring of 1698. May fifteenth. You Creole weenie. You owe me for that."

"Ahhh," says Parran. "That I do."

"Either of you want to tell us what that was about?" asks Famka. She looks at Ophelia and shrugs her shoulders.

"Your Growgan," snaps Heiki, "took my Hellman with him on a raid of the Wilds after I explicitly told Hellman not to go. But do you think he listened? He thought the world of you, Parran. Loved you like a brother. My idiot husband would have followed you anywhere. I hope it was worth it."

"It was," says Parran looking distant.

"What in the name of the Nyre King happened to you, Parran?" asks Heiki. "No one ever saw you again. Hellman looked for you for years. He flew his Nightcoach from the

Middling Side of the Graveyard to the Other. It was maybe fifty years ago that he finally gave up, but if you ask me, he never really let go of you, ya creole weenie."

"Ya not put the pieces together, Heiki?" asks Parran.

"Hellman said you went back after he and the rest of the crew were safe aboard your dinghy boat. No one ever saw you after that."

"Ho ho," says Parran. "There was one that saw me."

"Berny," Famka interrupts.

"Aye, Momma. Ya clever one. Put da pieces together. I slipped back into the Wilds after I knew that Hellman be safely away."

"What are the Wilds?" asks Milly.

"Fire Thief's stronghold," says Heiki. "It got its name because of its endless confusing corridors and tunnels. Many leading no place at all. There weren't high walls surrounding it or strong doors that might keep intruders out. No guards or even a mote."

"You mean that you could walk right in the front door of the Fire Thief's fortress?" asks Famka amazed.

"Yes. And many did," says Heiki. "In many ways it goes to show the arrogance of the Fire Thief. It was where the Fire Thief trained his army of witches."

"It be true," says Parran. "So much death lined those halls. Bodies upon bodies left to rot. The stink of the Wilds never released me."

"Why did you go back?" asks Famka.

"Me own foolishness," says Parran looking at Heiki.

"You went back because you're greedy," says Heiki. "Hellman told me enough about you to know that."

"That be part of it. I don't deny it," says Parran. "But I not all bad. Hellman was me friend. I knew he loved ya with all his heart, Heiki. I did. He wanted so bad to relieve ya pain after ya momma an' daddy was murdered. But I knew he shouldn't go with me. On that last raid, I lied to him. Told him I was going elsewhere, not back into da Wilds. So, I sent him down the Mississip and then made the biggest mistake of me life."

"So, what were you after?" asks Famka.

"Wyndomier Wicks," says Parran. "Hundreds of them. That's why we started, but there was one ting I wanted even more."

"What's a Wyndomier Wick?" says Milly.

"A witch's strongest tool," says Ophelia. "It resembles a policeman's baton. They are usually black with different markings carved along the sides. They help a witch channel their Tuning. They're almost all gone now."

"Kind of like a wand?" asks Milly.

"Similar, I guess," says Ophelia shrugging her muscled shoulders, "but rounder, so maybe more like a thick candle stick."

"I've never seen one. Can we buy one?" asks Milly looking excited.

"Probably not. The Ghostal Holly destroyed most of them after the war," says Ophelia.

"Now the only ones left are handed down by family members or purchased at a very high cost," adds Famka.

"That be right," says Parran. "The Wicks be something to fear to be sure. Da Fire Thief did everything he could to steal as many as possible from Wyndomier. Nearly had them all for himself until Hellman and I dealt him a blow. Took hundreds we did. Would have done more damage until Berny tracked me down that very night."

"Did he kill you?" asks Famka.

"Aye, Momma," says Parran. "Struck me dead and combined me with a rare book of spells, then changed me into a Growgan before me soul could take flight."

"Your soul wouldn't take flight, Parran," says Heiki nastily. "You're too heavy with life."

"Ya judge me too harshly, Heiki," says Parran. "Where you think all them Wicks came from? Da ones that helped win the war. Ya thinking they just appeared there by accident?"

"That wasn't you," states Heiki flatly. "You couldn't have hidden so many on your own."

"It was," says Parran. "Hellman not be knowing all that I hid. I not be doing all of them honorably I admit. Wyndomier Wicks went for a pretty penny, they did. I helped in the war but was going to be rich by the end of it too."

"That part, I believe, but the rest, I call mule matter," she says, crossing her little arms over her small chest.

"I can prove it," he says.

"How?" asks Famka with concern. She realizes that Parran has grown on her. Being Imprinted with him has given her a sense of kinship that she imagines she might feel with a sibling.

"There be stash that I buried in a place that I only know," says Parran. "One of the Wicks is no ordinary Wick." Parran drums his paper fingers on the counter and smiles. "I be stealing Wyndomier's Wick. The very first one."

"That God Wand?" says Heiki sounding shocked "You're lying!"

"I not," says Parran. "After da Fire Thief's witches took the Plaza of Giants and killed Wyndom, many of us, including Hellman, couldn't abide the war anymore. I tink maybe we lost our minds that night. Why else would we risk going into the Wilds so many times, Heiki? Ya think you the only one who lost during the war? Ya be thinking 'ol Parran be all alone for no reason? Naw, I lost too. Hellman, me, and me crew—we was gonna bring a hurting on da Fire Thief, and we did. I took Wyndomier's Wick right from beneath da Fire Thief's nose, and it cost me what I had left, but I wasn't going to risk the only real friend I had in the process. So, I lied to Hellman, knowing that if'n I told him the truth, he be following me back."

"He's telling the truth," says Famka coming to his rescue.

Heiki looks at Famka strangely and says, "You've Imprinted with Parran?"

She nods.

"All right," says Heiki. "I believe Famka over you. So, let's say that you're telling the truth. Where is it?"

"It not be that easy," says Parran.

"Of course it isn't," says Heiki sarcastically.

"Heiki, ya angry and not tinking straight," says Parran. "We can't just go grabbing the most famous Wick in history without caution. If'n it not be Berny chasing after us, then it be any of the other races in the Knack. Be terrible if a Wiggler got it. Can you imagine? What if a Pilgrim had it? What if the Ghostal Holly knew about its existence? Then we'd be brought in by the Guardians of the Ghoul and courted before the Tribunal of Burning Banshees. Maybe even locked up until one of us confessed of its whereabouts."

They all sit silently for a moment. Famka thinks about all that she has learned in the past few weeks. The Bastard Book stolen out of heaven in order to teach the living to Tune only to start a war. But why go through all the trouble? How could anyone hate with so much conviction? Then there was Wyndomier's Wick, the God Wand, Heiki had called it. Could it be that it was still hidden after all these years? Berny behaving very unghostly like. And what about a new baby Drolling Dragon after so many centuries without one?

A curious thought occurs to Famka, and she asks, "Heiki, is it possible that whatever caused you to have a baby is also making Berny stronger?"

"Oh!" says Ophelia. "Momma Nay is always saying that Tuning is dying. Could she be wrong?"

"Yeah, maybe she's wrong," says Famka.

"I would've agreed with Momma Nay until recently," says Heiki. "But now that Heaven is here, I'm not so sure."

"Who be Heaven?" asks Parran.

"Our daughter," says Heiki. "Mine and Hellman's."

"Ya be having a baby?" asks Parran looking delighted. "That's wonderful, Heiki."

"That fool of a husband wanted to name her Butterfly." Heiki shakes her head then turns to Famka with a stern look to her strange orange eyes. "If Tuning is returning to the world, then your ghost will get more powerful. I must say, though, that I still have my doubts about him actually being Bernard Trankler."

Chapter 23

If You Can't Beat 'em...

Heiki left to locate Miss Turtlebalm two very boring days ago. The three little witches spend their days trapped in Turtleburgers, trying to figure out a way to escape Berny. Ophelia thinks it's best to wait it out until Miss Turtlebalm returns, but Famka, thick headed as ever, thinks otherwise. Milly questions Parran endlessly about the war, completely unconcerned about their situation.

Knock! Knock! Knock!

"Momma?" says Milly.

Famka spins around on her stool and faces the window, which looks out onto Wink Tree Lane. A very angry and larger version of Milly is glaring back inside. Like Milly, her hair is a ball of blonde cotton candy, but her skin is showing the years of time in the hot Texas sun.

"Millicent!" she yells. "I know you're in there."

"Oh no," says Milly. She stands up from a booth, walks toward the window, and stands beside Ophelia. "What do we do?"

"How does she know we're here?" Ophelia waves her hand in front of the window. "She can't see us. Thank goodness."

"Berny," Famka declares, walking toward the glass. "Look."

The disfigured ghost floats behind Milly's mother. He's somehow shrunk to the size of a baseball. His arms are stretched, his fingers are splayed wide, and he's moving Milly's mother like a marionette doll. As he bangs his tiny fist in the air, so does her hand pound against the shop window.

"What is he doing to her?" asks Ophelia.

"I wish I could do that," mutters Milly.

"Hoodwinking," says Parran. "It be a way for a ghostie to steal control of a human body. But he can't be doing it for long."

Bang! Bang! Bang!

"Millicent!" yells her mother. "I'm going to the police if you don't get out here this very instant."

"Can she do that?" Famka asks Parran. "Can Berny make her go to the cops?"

"Aye, Momma," says Parran nodding his paper head. "He can. We be needing to hurry."

"They can't just break in here," says Ophelia. "That's illegal."

"My mother can do whatever she wants in this town," says Milly.

"Ophi, you know the cops will listen to whatever Milly's momma says," confirms Famka. "Her parents practically own Wink."

"That's it, young lady," says Milly's mother. "I'm going to the police. And your allowance is suspended."

As Milly's mother turns away, Berny shoots the witches a snide smirk. The scar on his face twists into a grotesque grimace as he attempts to smile.

"My allowance," says Milly. "That's not very fair. What is her…"

Famka cuts Milly off mid-question. "Parran. Tuning is all about doing what the dead naturally do, right?"

"Aye, Momma." He's sitting in a booth where Milly had just left him.

"If Tuning belongs to the dead, can the dead use a Wyndomier Wick?"

"Ho ho," says Parran nodding. "Aye. They can use them."

Ophelia turns from the window and asks, "Does Berny know about the God Wand?"

"Naw," says Parran. "He no way of knowing for sure."

"But he followed you after you stole it from the Wilds?" asks Famka.

"He not knowing that's what I took. That not be all that I stole, neither," says Parran.

"What else did you take?" Milly chimes in.

"Ya name it," says Parran. "Several pieces of Ghost Armor, Wyndomier Wicks by the dozens, a tub full of Earthquake Glue, two Wyndom Windows." He pauses, thinking. "I believe. Could o' been more. Several other tings that I no longer recall."

"What's Ghost Armor again?" asks Milly.

"It resembles a piece of cloth," Famka explains. "If a witch wears it, they can become invisible."

"Or change yer appearance, so ya be looking like someone ya not," adds Parran.

"You're kidding!" says Milly practically jumping.

"Can we use Ghost Armor to hide ourselves from Berny?" asks Famka. "At least until we figure out how to get the

Bastard Book from the columns of blood in Milly's backyard?"

"Aye, Momma. It work on ghosts," says the book man. "Ya be whoever ya want while wearing Ghost Armor."

"Are you joking, Famka?" says Ophelia flabbergasted. "You want to try and get that book?"

"You see what Berny is willing to do. I don't see how we have a choice?" says Famka turning to her best friend.

"Of course we have a choice," says Ophelia. "We wait right here until Miss Turtlebalm arrives and then tell her about Berny and that book."

"What do you think will happen then?" asks Famka. "That book started a war. We have no idea who else might want it. If it's really in Milly's backyard, we need to get it first. Otherwise, we'll have our own little war right here on our island. Can you imagine what kinds of creatures will come looking for it?"

"Then we find Momma Nay," suggests Ophelia. "She'll know if we should try to get it, and what to do with it."

"I agree with Famka," says Milly. "We should get it for ourselves."

"No," says Famka, "Not for ourselves. If the Fire Thief couldn't handle it, then neither can we."

"What makes you say he couldn't handle it?" asks Milly.

"Because of his eyes," says Famka. "When he took the book out of heaven, it destroyed his eyes."

"His eyes?" repeats Milly. "Is something wrong with them?"

"Yes," answers Famka. "They resemble matchsticks."

"Is that really true, Parran?" asks Ophelia.

"It is," say the book man. "I never got too close to that beasty. Once I seen him across a field. His eyes be burning in they sockets where peepers should'a be."

"Momma Nay told us that the Fire Thief looked upon heaven, and it was too beautiful. It's what burned his eyes out," says Famka.

"Some be saying dat burned his soul away too," says Parran. "It was a punishment put on him by the Nyre King hisself for stealing dat book."

"If we're going to do this, we need a plan," says Ophelia shaking her head unconvinced. "And if I know you, Famka, you already have one."

Famka smiles mischievously and says, "You're not going to like this, Ophi, but yeah, I got an idea."

"What is it?" asks Milly impatiently.

"First, we need to make sure your parents don't come looking for you. I don't want to ever see them or the police near the Horseshoe. I have no doubt that your momma could cause us all kinds of problems," says Famka staring at Milly, then turns to Parran. "Can you get us into the Hallowed Halls?"

"Naw, Momma. I'm physical like you. Only the dead can get in on their own. We need to be finding us a cemetery with a proper Porter. Dey can be opening up the Hallowed Halls from there," says Parran. "Be mindful, though. The moment we leave this shop, Berny will sense it and come down hard, so we must be quick about it."

"Why didn't he catch Heiki when she left, then?" ask Milly.

"Drolling Dragons be too fast," says Parran. "And for the moment, Berny be too weak."

"All right," says Famka looking at Ophelia again. "Babyhead Cemetery is five blocks from here. If we sneak out of here fast enough, maybe we can make it."

"I think I can make it," says Ophelia, "but what do we do

when we're there?"

Parran says, "There be a Porter in every cemetery that can get ya into the Hallowed Halls. We get there fast, locate it, and get to the Plaza of Giants right away. Once we there, we be safe from Berny. Even if he dares to show his ugly face, they be too many Guardians around. They will protect us."

"You mean run five blocks?" whines Milly all of a sudden. Her voice rising through the statement. "There's no way we're going to make it that far with Berny out there."

Famka knows that Milly is right. She doesn't want to admit it, but it's true. Famka stares at Milly. Pieces fall into place inside Famka's mind as she runs around blind alleyways in her imagination. After several dead ends, she concludes that there is only one choice. She repeats several possible scenarios but still reaches the same conclusion.

Ophelia steps up beside Famka with concern in her gray-green eyes. "I know that look. It's the same one you had when you tried Devil Digging into the ocean."

"Famka!" says Milly surprised, her mouth slightly open now. "You just spontaneously appeared in the middle of the Gulf?"

"It wasn't a big deal, and I wasn't Devil Digging. If I was, I'd be dead. I was trying something else," says Famka before adding, "We have to leave here."

"Maybe if I run fast enough, I can make the cemetery and get help, but that's risky. I really think we should stay here until Miss Turtlebalm shows up." Ophelia points to the boardwalk in front of the shop. "Not go out there."

"No, leaving here is the only way. Miss Turtlebalm should've been here by now. I think something happened to Heiki," says Famka flatly. "We can't defeat Berny, but maybe we can fool him."

"That didn't work when we left the Horseshoe," says Ophelia. "You remember what he tried to do to us in the painting. He doesn't care if we live or die. He'll kill us to get what he wants," says Ophelia placing her hands on her hips. "If we stay here long enough, eventually Miss Turtlebalm will show up, and she can deal with him. We don't have the training to fight him. We're not Sky Builders."

"What about the Bastard Book?" asks Famka with concern.

"Not our problem," says Ophelia suddenly angry. "You can't go trying to save everyone or everything, Famka. I'm sorry, but you just can't. We can't beat him, and you can't join him."

A long silent pause stands between the three witches as Famka considers Ophelia's words. She knows that her best friend loves her and is only trying to protect her, but still, Famka knows that she is right. They can sit in the shop and wait passively for help while sipping on milkshakes and eating burgers, or they can try to do something great, even if it's a little nuts.

Famka scans the room until she spots Ophelia's backpack. She is cautious not to look at it for too long, lest she give away her intentions. The purple and black bag is hanging on a tall silver coat hanger near the front door. She walks to the window, her bare feet tapping on the checkerboard floor, and looks outside. As she looks across Wink Tree Lane at the beach beyond, it looks more crowded than it had been earlier that morning. Families wind between each other chaotically. Children dash across the street excited for the sandy beach, bringing any cars, that brave Wink Tree Lane, to a grinding crawl. A silver pickup plods along, and Famka realizes that she's seen it nearly a dozen times that day.

Inside, she is burning with frustration. A rage is welling up in her belly and not for the first time. It's been with her as long as she can remember, but now, as she's gotten a little older, it has grown in both size and strength. She knows that she can be more than she is. She has more to offer the world, and she is ready, even if the world is not. She puts a hand to the glass and leans her forehead against the window. At that moment, she feels like that stupid truck outside: moving slowly and for no reason what so ever.

"You're wrong, Ophi," says Famka suddenly.

"About what?"

"Berny doesn't care if you or Milly die, but he cares if I do. So, I'll go."

Chapter 24

That Dang Third Witch

P ARRAN IS STANDING by the jukebox at the far end of the shop, fascinated by the truly magical device, as he calls it. Having never heard rock music, he decides that the Kinks are his favorite, and he plays "Lola" about a million annoying times. He asks more than once where he can meet this *Lola*. He also concludes that the Beatles are highly overrated.

The three witches are seated in one of the booths lining the wall. Ophelia is to the right of Famka, who's against the wall. Their arms touch lightly. Milly is on the opposite side of the black-topped table.

Famka places a zipper-like device on the table top. Milly watches Famka's hands work the spell. Her long slender fingers move with natural grace and dexterity, something Milly has never had. She hates looking at her own thick hands and often shoves them into her pockets or clasps them together, interlacing her fingers into their own self-made hiding places. Watching the spell come to life, Milly is certain that she hates Famka. As her jealousy rises to unexplored heights, she imagines putting Famka in a cage and tormenting her like she had her mother's stupid Scottish fold cat.

Finally, Famka pulls the zipper across the surface of the table as if opening a jacket. In the surface is an image of a clay-colored tunnel bending downward and out of sight like a worm's burrowed hole.

"That's it. You've done it, Famka!" says Ophelia looking down at the tunnel, her eyes going wide in her dark face. Milly nearly bursts into laughter, because with Ophelia's bushy round hairdo, when she gets excited, her head resembles a large black beach ball. But Milly reminds herself that Ophelia has been nice to her even if sometimes it felt fake. It was still nice, however, that she was… well nice.

Milly often heard her own mother's voice in her head. It persisted like a stalking butler always snooping just out of sight, always checking in even when unnecessary, and always silently commenting on everything Milly does. Milly knew what her mother would say if she saw her here with Famka and Ophelia. She tried not to care, but even still, her mother's negative voice soldiered onward. Always, it was there. Her stupid whiny negative voice.

What are you doing with them? They're beneath us. What will people say?

Shut up, Mother, she thinks. *They're my friends.*

But were they really? Milly had only known them a few weeks, and Famka had barely been nice to her at all. Still, she didn't want to be alone again, and certainly in hindsight, Berny had made a terrible friend. She decided to put her mother's imposing thoughts out of her mind. She has much Tuning to learn and her mother had never done anything but make her feel inferior anyway. She would prove her mother wrong.

"You've almost got it," says Milly. Her puffy blonde hair bounces with excitement.

"Shhh," shushes Famka as she concentrates on the spell.

Milly frowns and tries not to be insulted.

The tunnel moves like a snake bending through the darkness until it opens on an ornate office. Brown paneling lines the walls, many of which are covered in framed diplomas and pictures of important men standing side by side in suits. A man with slicked-back, dark hair sits in a plush leather chair behind a thick mahogany desk that is probably worth more than all of the Horseshoe and then a tiny bit more. The man jerks upward, surprised probably from hearing the music playing from Parran's insistent jukebox. His mouth falls open, and his eyes scrunch up as he tries to understand what he is seeing. Surely, his daughter and two other young girls suddenly appearing above him in his office while the Kinks "Lola" drifts in from the background is not something he has ever seen before.

"Milly?" questions the man, as if not believing his own eyes.

"Hi, Daddy," she says, leaning forward and peering down into the tunnel. Sometimes, Milly is surprised by the tone of her own voice. To her, it sounds like some other person, because there is no way she is such an insufferable suck-up. She takes pride in making other people believe she's kindhearted, and sometimes, she actually is. Although now that she's considering it, that's probably not very often.

"What is going on, young lady?" demands her father.

"Don't worry, Daddy," she says. "In just a minute, you'll forget about me. It's not like you're actually concerned. All you care about are your expensive friends." She pauses then adds, as if remembering to say something that she forgot, "Oh! And you and Mom are both the worst parents a daughter could have." Milly suddenly feels fantastic. For years, she's wanted to tell her father how horrible he's been. She has fantasized about it in hundreds of different scenarios, but this little bit of reality isn't so bad, even if she isn't strutting away as her parents' house burns down behind her. A missed birthday here, a late meeting there, it all adds up.

Milly can't remember a time when she sat in the same room with her parents without having to put on a show for a guest. There were many parties of course when they were all together, but never just the three of them. Milly does have a few precious memories from her childhood. Once, the three of them went to the beach for an afternoon. Milly figures that should've happened more often, considering they live on an island. Of course, her mother complained of the sun giving her a headache. Another time, they visited Milly's grandparents in Austin. Dinner at the restaurant was nice, but as soon as they returned to her grandparents, the conversation quickly spiraled out of control. In sixty seconds flat, her father stormed away from his father in a huff. Thirty seconds later, the three of them were speeding back toward the Gulf.

When Milly looks up however, she is surprised to see both Famka and Ophelia staring back at her with shock. Surely, they can understand how Milly feels. Famka's parents, whoever they may have been, are dead. As for Ophelia's, well, they seem to be gone an awful lot. Near as Milly can tell, the only real parent either of them has is Momma Nay, and she is gone half the year on some adventure, or walkabout, or whatever she does. No one really knows, so the two girls might as well be alone.

"What?" says Milly shrugging her shoulders. "It's true. My parents couldn't care less if I ever came home. So, can you hurry up, Famka? The sooner they forget about me, the better."

"You know it's not permanent," whispers Famka. "But go ahead. Here." She hands Milly a tall metal cup and waves her hand dismissively. "Pour some in."

Milly snatches it out of Famka's hand. "Daddy," says Milly looking down again. "I want you to know that I hate you... and Mom. How you tolerate her complaining, I'll never understand. Her stupid cat Miss Hopkins is never coming home, either. I let her go in a swamp, and I'm pretty sure that she was eaten."

Milly turns the cup over, shaking it liberally to make sure that every drop falls into the tunnel.

"Not all of it!" Famka snatches it back from her, but it's too late.

A great glob of milkshake falls through the surface of the table, floats for a few moments in the tunnel, and then drops again, covering Milly's father in chocolate ice cream. His perfectly slicked-back hair, black suit, and gray-striped tie are smudged brown by the sticky mess. He leaps from his leather chair, sending it spinning in circles behind him. His hand jerks out and knocks a yellow note pad from his desk, then his body grows stiff, slowing his excited movements. The ice cream begins to dissolve into his skin and through his clothing. His blue eyes glaze over, and confusion rolls across his mustached face as he goes completely still. For a moment, he doesn't move at all as if he were sculpted from stone.

"Daddy?" says Milly sounding regretful for a second, but

he doesn't respond. "Daddy?"

"We didn't kill him, did we?" asks Ophelia turning to look at Famka, looking panicked.

"No, Ophi," she responds calmly. "The Memoroff is taking control of him. His mind is just fighting it. People don't want to forget important things… or people." Famka's eyes flash to Milly as if silently making a point that Milly's father, despite his workaholic nature, cares for his daughter. His face suddenly twists in agony, his back arches, and he drops to the ground. Milly leans almost completely over the table, peering closely into the portal and placing her hands on the edge.

"Careful," says Famka to Milly. "You heard Parran's warning. This isn't the Hallowed Halls. This portal can't support living beings. It could pull you in and crush you."

Milly jerks her hands back and looks up at Famka, feeling mildly surprised. *Maybe Famka is my friend, after all,* Milly thinks. *Maybe she isn't so bad.* But even still, there is something about the pretty witch that rubs Milly wrong. First off, Famka's strange green eyes stare out of a light brown face with strikingly beautiful perfection. It leaves Milly jealous. Despite Milly's mixed feelings about Famka, she is taken back by her beauty. Milly longs to be beautiful. To Milly, Famka is too perfect, almost like an artist has toiled for years creating the ultimate specimen of what a woman should resemble. Her long hair is thick and never a single strand runs away from the other hairs. Her small nose sits above beautiful thick pink lips. Her shoulders and arms are thin, yet well-defined with a small rise in the bicep. Milly feels self-conscious of her own arms. To her, they are fat and flabby, especially when she stretches during a morning yawn. Unlike Famka, Milly would never wear a sleeveless garment. Even when the summer temperature reaches the Oh-My-God stage of heat, she insists, at the very least, on short sleeves.

Famka wiggles her fingers, and the portal slowly closes. Milly's father disappears, as does his office and any signs that the three little witches had dumped the entire contents of a milkshake spell on his head. The wormhole-like portal slowly slithers toward them, ending right at the surface of the table. Famka reaches across the table and pulls the zipper from between the salt and pepper shakers and back across the surface. Milly stares at Famka's delicate fingers again, feeling a slight wave of jealousy. Famka reaches down and places the device in the front pocket of her shorts. Milly decides right then and there that she deserves to have the magical device. If Milly can't work the Tuning, then surely, she should have the little device to help her with her magic. *What was it called?* she thinks. *Oh right, a Winzi.*

Even if Heiki had given the Winzi to Famka as a gift for saving her daughter Heaven, Milly feels that she deserves it instead. Milly did have a book of spells, which is now somehow connected to Famka. Yet another instance that makes Milly dislike Famka. So, she'll steal if from Ophelia's backpack the moment she can.

Chapter 25

Shooting a Ghost

With Milly's father spreading the Memoroff to the remainder of his household and the sun finally down, Famka leaps up from the table and storms toward the coat rack. Her rage has been building since yesterday, and another day stewing in it is not something she is capable of. Despite her best friend's warnings, Famka needs to act. She hopes that with night finally arriving, and the street clear, she can confront Berny without incident.

"What are you doing?" asks Ophelia turning on the bench.

"Stay here!" barks Famka. She yanks Ophelia's backpack from the coat rack, opens the front door, and dashes outside. The sun has set over the distant horizon, leaving only faint pinks and oranges streaking the sky. The ocean falls upon the sand, sounding faintly across the beach. The street is now almost completely empty for the evening, but still several late-night youngsters linger along the sand.

"They're going to be in for quite a surprise," Famka says under her breath as she steps into the middle of the road. She doesn't care if anyone sees her Tune in public. She isn't part of the Ghostal Holly or the Sky Builders' Guild. She's never been officially trained and isn't subject to any of the so-called Tuning institutions. As far as she's concerned, she's free to do what she wants, and being as angry as she is, that's exactly what's she's going to do.

"Famka, are you crazy? Come back!" yells Ophelia from the door of Turtleburgers.

Famka ignores her and instead looks down the road toward the Horseshoe. Closed shops line the righthand side of the road, and the beach is on her left. A line of streetlights flicker along the boardwalk. Insects flock to the round yellowish globes hanging from dark green posts. Running between her feet is a solid yellow line painted on the asphalt, which is still warm from the hot day.

"Bernard Trankler!" she yells. "Come out. I want to strike a deal."

A couple scurries by, eyeing Famka like she's a crazy person and quickly disappearing down an alleyway. Several people laugh from the beach near the water's edge, and a dropped bottle clanks to the ground nearby. A breeze suddenly flows down the road, blowing Famka's hair back and her shirt flat against her body. The wind picks up speed, applying more pressure and spitting sand into her eyes. With the backpack slung over her shoulder, Famka throws her hands into the air and calls upon her Knack.

"Trankler's Hold It!" she yells. A whirl of power flies from her outstretched fingers, and an invisible shield springs up around her, blocking the powerful wind. Berny's face suddenly appears like a giant balloon above her. It's the size of a pickup truck. She can clearly see his red eyes and rotten teeth as he smiles widely. The pores of his nose are even more pronounced than before and resemble large black dots. His head floats around her, but she follows him, tracking his every move. She remains crouched careful to keep her hands up and the shield in place.

"Little witch," says Berny, "you are improving, but you cannot beat me."

"Are you sure?" she asks through gritted teeth.

"Most certainly. I'm touched that you have learned my most famous spell so quickly, but do not think you can use it against me. I invented it, after all. You would-be Sky Builders have struggled with it for years, yet it's so simple," he says arrogantly as he moves to within inches of the forcefield and lowers his voice. His gigantic red eyes glare like two bleeding suns in his pale scarred face. "The strongest shield is only ionized air and a mouthful of spit. Ingenious, isn't it? The spit is what gives you the connection to the spirit. Odd, I know, but it works, even if a young witch like you finds it disgusting. I must admit, though, that I miss using it. Now that I'm dead, I have little reason for such spells and, of course, no saliva."

Then he floats a few feet away just above the beach. A swarm of sand rises up, enveloping Famka completely. She falls to her knees and covers her eyes. Hunching over, she closes her body to the onslaught, trying her best to call up more shields, but even the one she had conjured is gone. She tries spitting into her hand, but the moisture flies away as it becomes difficult to breathe. The skin on her knuckles becomes raw as each grain cuts across her skin. She falls onto her side, careful to keep her eyes tightly shut. Slowly she runs her hand along the warm pavement until she feels a slight rise from the painted yellow stripe. She calls upon her Knack and pulls the divider away from the road. Then she forces herself to stand, pulls on the yellow stripe, and whips a long piece of it at Berny like a rope, slapping him in the face. The wind stops, and a red welt across his cheek is revealed, along with a very shocked expression. Not giving him a moment to retaliate, Famka whips him again and again, forcing his big head back out across the beach toward the ocean.

"Clever," growls Bernard. "But your little friends aren't as strong as you are, are they?" His eyes flicker to Famka's right, and he flies toward Ophelia and Milly, who are now standing in the street nearby. He descends on them, his mouth outstretched and grotesquely large.

Use a Hold It, Momma, shouts Parran into her mind.

Famka has no idea what he's planning, but she doesn't hesitate. She spits in both of her hands then flicks them both open. Two Trankler's Hold Its spring up in front of her friends. Berny smashes into one, howling loudly. He flies back into the air and turns on Famka with rage in his red eyes. Ophelia runs to Famka and picks up the dropped piece of the yellow stripe. It looks like a long yellow rope in her dark hand. Parran joins them, followed closely by Milly.

The four of them stand in the middle of Wink Tree Lane, staring up at the ugly poltergeist as several people look out from a bar down the street. The beach is now deserted, and all is silent except for the rolling waves.

"We're not going with you, Bernard Trankler," says Famka loudly.

"Wrong again," says Bernard.

The ground beneath them shakes. It crumbles beneath their feet and each of them drops a foot. The asphalt clamps down around their ankles imprisoning them. Famka tries to jerk away and nearly falls, but Ophelia snatches Famka by the hand steadying her. The shield Famka has created fades, and Berny floats toward them again.

"You are nothing but trouble," he says. "I'll tell you what. Here's my final offer. If you come with me without any more problems, then I promise not to destroy your home. I'll even leave your friend Guncle alone and stop antagonizing poor Mrs. Billbray. How does that sound?"

"You are just horrid," says Ophelia.

"I have a better offer," says Famka.

"Oh yes?" says Berny sounding almost delighted. "What would that be?"

"First…" Famka whips a gun out of the backpack still hanging on her shoulder. She aims the old gun and pulls the trigger. With a loud explosion, a hole appears in Berny's forehead. It looks like it's melting, like those chalk pavement pictures in *Mary Poppins* when the rain comes. His big head disappears, replaced by his normal body. Famka is once again surprised at how small of a man he really is, perhaps just over five feet tall. She pulls the trigger again, and he slams into the pavement. The asphalt gripping Famka's feet relaxes, and she pulls free, slowly walking toward him. She stares down at Berny and pulls the trigger again and again, blowing holes in his face, chest, arms, and legs. With each shot, more of his body melts away. Strangely though, she notices sprinkles of dirt from the bullets on the ground beside him.

"I was only going to shoot you once," says Famka, mentally filing away the observation, "but you threatened my friends, and I don't like that. So, here's my deal. We're going to the Plaza of Giants to tell the Ghostal Holly who you are. I'm sure after what you did during the war, they will love chatting with you. How many Trankler's Hold Its did you use to crush witches to death? How many Drolling Dragons did you murder with Salamander Matter. How many Malamanders did you kill? I won't feel bad for you when the Ghostal Holly finally destroys your sick twisted soul."

"You foolish child. It is now our secret for life. Tell them of me, and I tell them of the book. I'm sure you don't want every ghoul from the Other Side of the Graveyard here on your little island. We are bonded by our secrets despite your illusion of freedom," he slurs like a drunken sailor, laughing in between the odd gurgling sounds in his throat. "If anyone should learn that the Bastard Book is hidden here, do you know what would happen to this little island of yours? Every race in the Knack would swarm this place. The fighting would escalate into a bloody mess. No, Famka Meadows, we are bonded now in secrecy. So, you see, you can't beat me. Be a good little witch and come along now." He tries to sit up but falls back again. "I will find you. You cannot destroy me. Already, I am healing." He laughs again as he pokes a finger into one of the holes in his chest, which is closing on its own as if he was never wounded.

Famka bends down and lies right through her teeth. "You think I like this place? This island? Let them come and tear it to pieces. I don't care."

"Don't, Famka. Think of our friends. The Billbrays, Mom and Dad. They care about this place. Just leave it… Let's go," says Ophelia pulling on her arm.

"Aye, Momma. She be right," Parran adds.

"I don't know," says Milly, looking around. "Do you really think it would matter? I mean, they may as well… I certainly don't care what they do to my home!"

"I care!" shouts Ophelia. "Famka, come on!"

"Where to?" Famka asks as they step away from Bernard. "He's right. There's nothing we can do."

"We have to try," says Ophelia urgently.

Famka shoves the gun into the backpack, and the four of them take off running leaving Berny half splattered, but quickly healing on the pavement. He lay sprawled within a ring of light cast down from a lamppost. With one last stop to look at Berny, Famka follows the others as they dash up Wink Tree Lane before ducking down Deep Elm Street. The many touristy shops give way to homes as they run away from the ocean. Ophelia is already far in front as Famka passes Milly, who's huffing loudly. Humidity hangs so thick in the air that Famka feels like she's running in a gym sock. Her bare feet slap against the asphalt, the sound echoing occasionally off the little wooden houses. A porch light flickers on as they turn down another street.

"Hey, what are you kids... What is that?" yells someone from behind them. Famka is certain they are referring to Parran, who easily keeps up with Ophelia. The book man doesn't so much run as he hops, covering several normal steps with one of his.

"There's the cemetery!" yells Ophelia from up ahead. After another block, Famka watches Ophelia dash underneath the wrought-iron archway that sits on top of stone posts on either side of the path leading in. Rising to an arched half circle, the wrought iron is a design of ornate vines woven in metal. Famka notices words in blue light above the arch. They float in the air, burning dimly. She's been to this cemetery several times but has never seen them before. She wonders if her companions can see. As she gets closer, she stops to read them.

Let the hollow in your heart rest, for in Ban'Hallow you are blessed.

"Come on, Famka!" yells Ophelia stopping to look back. "What are you doing?"

"You don't see those words?" asks Famka pointing above her.

"See what?" asks Milly between heavy breaths as she comes to a stop beside Famka.

"No, I don't," yells Ophelia. Then she points behind Famka back toward Wink. "But I see that."

Famka spins, her dress swirling then settling, as Berny limps toward them. He's still a block away, but his distorted outline is visible. He flickers in and out of sight like a broken television set trying to find a signal. Every time he reappears, however, he's a little closer. Milly screams and dashes into the cemetery after Ophelia and Parran. Famka considers shooting Berny again as he approaches but decides against it and runs into the cemetery after her friends. She knows that they have to find a way to the Plaza of Giants, and right now, the only way there is through a cemetery stone.

Chapter 26

Porter of Babyhead Cemetery

F AMKA RUNS BEHIND Milly, who's so scared that she's nearly caught up with Ophelia. Parran leaps into the lead with his peculiar style of hop running. He barely seems to be touching the ground as his paper feet skim across the dirt path. Famka speeds up, hearing Berny growling behind them like some kind of feral animal. Years of being barefoot around the Horseshoe has conditioned her feet, so the gravel path does little to bother her, despite it being filled with numerous sharp pebbles.

Overgrown wildflowers border the path on either side. An unkempt rock edge barely keeps the flowers from spilling over onto the pathway. Smoky gravestones stick up through a green blanket like unwelcome intruders in an otherwise beautiful meadow. Small structures dot the cemetery, some with large arching doorways leading to rooms where whole families sleep for eternity. The grounds are largely ignored except for a fenced area in the very center of the graveyard.

As the last remnants of the sun disappear, turning the sky

into a dotted black canvas, ghosts begin floating up through the ground. Dozens of them. Glowing figures rise faintly, turning this dark, depressed evening in the cemetery into a carnival of blue bouncing light.

"Come on, Milt," says a ghost. "Two rounds of Cheater's Wild."

"I beat the pants off ya last night," says Milt. "You ain't got much more to give up. I done taken your *Gravedigger's Handbook*, over half your crypt, and every jug of Minor's Malt you had. Pretty soon, you'll be sleeping at the church with Father what's-his-face."

"He's a preacher not a priest," says the first ghost. "And his name is Mike. Preacher Mike. So, have some respect. Now, are we playing tonight or not?" The two ghosts float away across the cemetery, and the remainder of the conversation fades away.

Not far away, Parran stands at a crossroads in the path, talking with a ghost. Ophelia and Milly catch up and wait beside him, listening eagerly as Famka finally comes up beside them.

"A spook you say?" says the small ghost. He's wearing an old-fashioned brown suit. A golden pocket watch chain dangles from his right pocket, and resting on his head is a ten-gallon hat, which is way too large for his little frame.

"That be correct. Chasing us for days now," says Parran. "N' we need to be finding ya Porter."

The ghost chuckles before saying, "My dear Growgan, we are far too small of a barrow for a full-time Porter. Why it's been Lady'Witch Turtlebalm who's been kind enough to perform Porter duties here at Babyhead Cemetery. For small matters of governance, or when the newly dead wake and require assistance transitioning, I often fill in, but only when the citations are elementary. Perhaps you simply require someone with proper communication skills. How big of a problem can your ghost really be?"

Why do ghosts always behave as if nothing matters? Are they all crazy? Famka thinks to herself. Having heard her thoughts, Parran smirks, his eyes flashing toward her. She looks back the way they'd come, but Berny is nowhere to be seen. Thank goodness! However, she doesn't trust his disappearance. So far, he seems to just show up, always knowing where they are. A young couple floats toward them hand in hand. They look to have died in their prime. Neither of them looks much older than mid-twenties perhaps. The man smiles at Famka, which annoys the dead girl at his side. She jabs him in his ribs, and he turns to her innocently. Slowly they rise into the air and away from Famka before disappearing between several tall trees in the distance. Their blue hues fade through the leaves.

"Might ya point us to an entry point?" asks Parran. "If ya not be having a proper Porter, then we need to be getting into the Hallowed Halls and onto the Plaza of Giants before that spook be showin' up again."

"You just came from town," says the ghost. "Where's Lady'Witch Turtlebalm?"

"We don't know, sir," says Famka butting in. "We're in a hurry, and we're in danger. Can you help us or not?"

The ghost tips his cowboy hat back and wrinkles his eyebrows together. "Then you'll need to be asking Herbert if he'll let you into the Hallowed Halls. But I warn you, he's as cranky as can be," says the ghost turning and pointing across the cemetery. "He's over yawnder. Look for the crypt with the dragon's head above the door. It's the biggest one here."

Famka stares off into the darkness, wondering how on earth they are going to find it in the dark. Three ghosts suddenly go zipping by in a flash of blurred blue lines, and she realizes they've run out of time.

"Without permission from a Resident Witch," adds the ghost, "you won't... Wait, where are you going?"

Famka is already running in the direction he pointed as his last words trail off. Ophelia, not missing a beat, is right beside her. It takes a moment, but Milly and Parran catch on. The four of them turn down a path that cuts through yellow sunflowers as several more ghosts zip by, resembling faint blue lights. The moon offers little help, and Famka stumbles, but Ophelia catches her before she falls.

"Thanks," she says.

"I can feel him, Famka," says Ophelia.

"Me too. Keep going."

Against the dark sky, Famka sees the outline of a single mausoleum. She hopes that it's the right one and turns toward it. They round another corner, and the dirt path comes to an abrupt end at the foot of a bloated stone crypt. It stands taller, wider, and deeper than any other they've seen so far. Several stone steps lead from the path, along a long brick walkway, and right up to a large rounded door. Engraved above the stone archway is the name Rien.

Milly runs her hands along the stone, which frames the thick wooden door. "This is my family's tomb," she says proudly.

"It sure is," says Berny suddenly poking his head through the door.

Milly stumbles and falls on her behind as Famka yanks out

the gun from the backpack and fires it at Berny. He disappears back into the tomb as red, blue, and yellow paint splotches decorate the door, certain to make the groundskeeper angry. Famka spins around, but Berny remains invisible. Strangely, there are no other ghosts in sight.

"There!" says Milly pointing upward. Berny sits crooked and gargoyle-like on top of the tomb, smiling wickedly, but then he disappears again. Ophelia is crouched and looks like she's ready to run when Berny reappears, jerks the gun from Famka's hand, and tosses it away. He shoves Famka to the ground and leaps onto her chest, pinning her painfully in place.

"Get off her!" yells Ophelia trying to shove him. She falls through Berny and stumbles over Famka's outstretched legs instead.

"You know what I want," says Berny.

"I don't really care what you want," says Famka struggling beneath him. She pushes her arms up against his firm hands, but that only increases the pain around her wrists from his grip.

"I would very much like to stop chasing you," says Berny almost sympathetically. "Despite being dead, it's exhausting. So, I'll ask one more time. I'm a gentleman, after all. Come with me and no more trouble will come to you."

Famka looks closely into his scarred face again, and a wave of nausea hits her. A lock of his oily black hair falls across his forehead. *How is he pushing his magic onto me so forcefully?* she wonders. He's a ghost, but he has both mass and weight. Despite being dead, he is also warm and stinks like he hasn't had a shower in at least a month. Famka turns her face as he breaths out, feeling like she might vomit from the putrid smell.

He smells like an old pickle jar. That's weird.

With limited options open to her, she decides on the only obvious choice and kicks him in the gonads. Unfortunately, her shin moves through him like he is made of smoke.

He smiles that creepy smile of his again, exposing his rotten teeth. "I can't fault you for that. I suppose I would have tried the same thing, but do not forget that I'm still a ghost. What you feel is simply your mind filling in the gaps of what you believe to be real. Perhaps I smell bad to you, or you feel my body weight resting upon your stomach. You see my teeth, and you imagine that my breath is warm, but how can that be when I'm spirit and not flesh? You must break up with life to truly Tune, Famka. Your weakness gives me strength. You must stop believing that what you were taught was real, and then, perhaps, you will have a chance to beat me. In the meantime, I must assume that you are not going to come along easily and I will have to take you by force."

"Miss Turtlebalm will find you," says Ophelia beside them. "We'll find you."

"You're right," says Berny. "It won't matter though. By the time she does, our work will be done."

He yanks Famka to her feet, then quickly slips behind her, grabs her under the arms, and lifts her into the air. The bottom of her dress waves loosely around her ankles as she kicks her feet. She tries to pull free of Berny, but his grasp is too strong. Again, she wonders how he has mass and strength. *Break up with life*, she replays his words in her mind. He's not alive, but somehow, he feels physical. Beneath them, the cemetery spreads out in a perfect grid. Oddly, there are still no ghosts floating about. Famka presumes Berny must have scared them off.

Parran leaps up into the air, breaking apart from his man-like form and into a ruffle of pages. Papers fly up around Berny and Famka like a tornado spinning with white sheets. A second later, however, Parran looks like he is being sucked into a vacuum as all of his pages are pulled to a single place. He immediately reshapes into a book in Berny's hand.

"Nice try, old friend," says Berny. "That worked last time, but not twice. You know what they say, fool me once shame on you. Fool me twice... Well, you know."

Sorry, Momma, whispers Parran in Famka's mind.

How is he so real? asks Famka.

Naw. He's not. What Berny said down there be true. Your mind is filling in the gaps, because ya need to be seeing the world the way ya know it.

Break up with life. How can I break up with life? she wonders. *Wouldn't I die?*

The three of them travel lazily above the cemetery, but within moments, they will be over Wink. Famka looks down and sees Ophelia and Milly running beneath them, but they quickly fall behind as they come to a fence enclosing a portion of the grounds.

"Famka!" yells Ophelia from the ground. "Famka!" She leaps over the fence easily, but Milly is unable to follow and gets stuck. Famka glides just above the pointed rooftop of Babyhead Cemetery church, and her friends fall out of sight. Famka closes her eyes, trying her best to concentrate, but also knowing the ground is growing more distant with each second. If she doesn't figure out how to get away soon, Berny will take her and Parran back to Milly's, and they'll be trapped.

If Berny can apply weight to me, then maybe I can apply weight to him. But how?

Famka figures that she has nothing to lose and tries something that makes her feel silly. An image of a cartoon character leaps into her mind, one that she's seen from Saturday mornings. She imagines herself growing in size. Her feet turn into puffy balloons with ten stubby, rounded toes. Her legs and thighs swell like pillows, her hips widen, her stomach spills over her waist. Her chin becomes two. Her cheeks are like two round balls of cotton candy.

"What are you doing?" Berny grumbles. "Stop it!"

When Famka opens her eyes, she isn't just heavier, but she is actually fat. She's shocked that her thin frame is gone, replaced by a much larger and rounder version of herself. Her hands are twice as big as normal, resembling meaty bear claws. Slowly they begin to descend back down toward the cemetery.

"I'm doing the same thing you did to me," says Famka. "For all of your big talk, you haven't broken up with life, either. You're stuck and you need me."

"If you don't stop this," threatens Berny, "I'll hurt your friends."

"I'm only doing as you told me, Bernard," says Famka staring into his ugly face. "I'm breaking up with life."

Berny growls as he strains to pull her upward, but Famka closes her eyes again.

That's it, Momma, whispers Parran in her mind.

She fills in the image of her overweight self with more detail, which forces them even further downward. Finally, they land softly in the sunflowered cemetery between long rows of tombs.

Frustrated, Berny drops Parran to the ground and slams his hand into Famka's chest. Her mouth falls open as pain shoots through every part of her body. His ghostly fingers clutch her heart and squeeze as she tries to pull free. She screams out. Parran immediately transforms into his man form. He grabs Berny's arm and tries to yank it off Famka, but Berny cuts through Parran with his free hand. The book man flies apart. Pages float all around them and scatter to the ground.

"I've waited for centuries," he growls. "I can wait a little longer for the right witch to come along. Don't think I won't kill you. You are not the only witch."

Ophelia dashes around the corner of a tomb breathing heavily.

"Berny!" she yells.

He jerks up, releasing Famka, who falls to the ground. Berny spins around, but Ophelia fires the gun, getting in a lucky shot before he can dash out of the way. Half of his head flies off in a splatter of paint, spraying a tomb behind him in bright colors. Ophelia fires again and again with anger burning in her gray-green eyes until he is little more than body parts barely held together by the threads of his white sleeping grown.

She keeps firing the gun, which will never run out of bullets.

"Ophi," says Famka finally. She stands up with great effort. "Ophi. Ophi. Stop!"

Ophelia breathes in large deep breaths. She is fixated on Berny with brutal focus.

Famka waddles up beside her best friend and pushes Ophelia's outstretched arm downward. After a moment, sweetness returns to Ophelia's eyes. She turns to Famka, and a wave of tears slide down her cheeks.

"His hand was in your chest," says Ophelia suddenly

throwing her arms around Famka and pulling her tightly. "He was killing you."

"I'm all right, honey," says Famka. "He didn't do any damage. I think he was only trying to scare me. He can't get what he wants without me."

"Did we beat him?" asks Ophelia looking at Berny over Famka's shoulder.

"I don't know," says Famka. She turns as Ophelia releases her and looks at what remains of Berny. "Maybe."

He resembles a painter's discarded easel. The door to one of the tombs is covered in splotches of bright colors. They blend together without beginning or end, invading one another haphazardly. Near the top is a single closed eye amongst the stains. It's the only part of Berny that is recognizable. The only part that might give away that he was once a person.

"He's gone," says Ophelia sounding relieved.

Famka isn't so sure, however. She is skeptical. Berny has been persistent. She doesn't completely understand the nature of ghosts. Most of them seem aloof, while others are compelled to complete some task with absolute resolve. It's as if they are afflicted by some mental disorder. Famka is convinced, though, that all of the dead behave oddly.

"Oh, Parran!" Famka looks down at all the pages scattered around her on the ground. "Ophi, help me put him back together."

They gather all the pages and, one by one, place them neatly into a stack on a soft bit of grass that borders the long path. Finally finishing with the brown cover, Famka hopes that Parran will return to normal. She didn't have to wait long. The book suddenly shoots into the air, and Parran transforms back into his manlike form before landing softly.

"Ho ho! I thank ya, Momma," says Parran excitedly. "Ya figured it out. The spell is in me cover. That's how I have life. You are a clever one."

"Is Berny dead?" she asks, ignoring his praise. "Do ghosts die?" She realizes that she's never thought about it until now. There are a number of ghosts that she's seen wandering aimlessly around the Horseshoe for years, many of them the same boring old farts.

"Not easy to tell if Berny be dead or not." Parran is careful to keep his distance from the Berny smudge decorating the door. "But ya did some real damage to be sure." Parran looks at Ophelia. "That there gun ya pulled out of the painting be handy in your hand. Ghosts can be destroyed, but they don't die in the way ya be thinking. Me guessing Berny be down for now, but he be back. I only knowing a Wyndomier Wick can be killing a ghost good and dead."

"Oh no! What happened? Where's Berny?" Milly asks as she comes around a corner a moment later. Her gaze falls to the door, and she is out of breath. "Oh… Is that him?" Her voice rises slightly.

"What be left of him," says Parran.

Milly walks up to the door, but like Parran, she's careful to stay back. It's difficult to tell from the shadow falling across Milly's profile, but for a moment, Famka thinks that Milly looks sad. Her usual chipper face turns slightly downward. It is subtle, so Famka decides to ignore it.

"Is that paint?" asks Milly scrunching up her nose. She reaches out but jerks back, seeming to remember that even in this state, Berny might be dangerous. "That's kind of gross. It looks like blood."

When Milly turns back, her eyes goes wide with surprise as she looks at Famka. "Holy moly. You're fat."

"Milly! That's not a very nice thing to say," says Ophelia, who is doing her best not to laugh at Famka.

"My spell worked, so the two of you can keep your mouths shut," says Famka looking down at her fat hands. "I really hope I can undo this."

"Not me," says Ophelia cheekily. "Now, you can come running with me in the mornings."

"Very funny, Ophi," says Famka looking distressed. "You know how much I hate running. Come on, let's get out of here before he pulls himself back together!"

Chapter 27

Herbert the Drolling Dragon

IT TOOK SEVERAL tries, but Famka finally managed to shrink herself back to normal. Well, mostly normal. Her chin still hung low with two full folds drooping like brown-leather luggage bags. Ophelia, of course, enjoyed teasing her, while at the same time seeming to feel bad for Famka.

"Come on, fatty," Ophelia jokes as they step up to the large mausoleum that belongs to Milly's family. A dragonhead above the round doorway looks down at them with frozen eyes. Beside them, Milly snickers, but doesn't comment.

"That's not funny," says Famka massaging the flesh beneath her chin. "Why isn't this going away?"

"Sometimes, Tuning be slow," says Parran gliding up beside them, "when ya trying new spells."

Famka is happy that her thighs no longer rub together but is still annoyed with her inability to Tune properly. She should know more spells by now, and heaven knows her Knack could be better. She believes she could be a great witch and is beyond frustrated that she still struggles with rudimentary skills. But the Sky Builders wouldn't have arbitrarily sent her an invitation, right? There must be a reason she and Ophelia received them, even if they aren't attending. *Thanks, Momma Nay,* thinks Famka. At the very least, someone at the Sky Builders' Guild had faith in her even if she didn't always have it in herself.

"What do we do now?" Famka looks at the door and does her best to put her double chin out of her mind.

"It be a door," says Parran pointing out the obvious. "We knock."

"That's it?" says Milly, her voice rising. "Just knock. If I'd known that, I would have come here ages ago."

You wouldn't know what to do, Famka says to herself as she knocks three times.

They wait, but nothing happens. After a long pause, the three girls look at each other. Ophelia shrugs her shoulders and asks, "Should we knock again?"

"Sure, I guess," says Famka.

Ophelia reaches out but is interrupted by a very grumpy voice.

"What?"

Famka looks around but doesn't see where the voice came from. Milly lifts up onto her tiptoes and speaks into the dragonhead, "Hello, sir. We need to go to the Plaza of Giants. Can you help us?"

"What an idiot," says the grumpy voice. "Down here."

"Oh God," says Milly jumping back. "Another one."

Famka looks down, and a Drolling Dragon is seated on a tiny green chair with plush armrests. She is certain that the chair wasn't there a moment ago. He is uglier, if that is possible, than Heiki. However, he is well dressed as if he is the owner of an art gallery. His long, floppy ears are pulled tightly back against his bald head and fall down his back like a ponytail. A pencil-thin mustache is perfectly trimmed above his top lip, and his dark green suit is fitted to his small body, ending perfectly above tiny black polished shoes.

He leaps into the air rising just above them so that they are all forced to look up and then crosses his tiny arms over his tiny chest.

"Nyre King be true," grumbles the Drolling Dragon. "What do you dummies want?"

"That's not very nice," says Milly. "We're witches not dummies. Maybe you're a dummy."

"Don't get lippy with me, young lady," scolds the Drolling Dragon. "You are here because you need something from me. *Not* the other way around. I am perfectly content to let the lot of you stand here all night." His bulbous orange eyes look behind them. "Crickets and Toadstools. Where is everyone? What did you four do? There isn't a single ghost in sight. Milt and Jose ought to be playing Cheater's Wild by now. And Mrs. Hernandez is usually complaining that Milt is ignoring her. And where is that young couple? They were just buried in here last week. They hadn't the skills to leave the graveyard yet. At the very least, they should be here somewhere."

"We need to go to the Plaza of Giants and find Miss Turtlebalm," says Famka looking up at the Drolling Dragon floating slightly above her.

"She'll be back soon. I'm sure whatever problems you have can wait until her return."

"This little creature is so rude," mumbles Milly.

"Please, sir," says Famka. "It's really important that we get to the Plaza."

"I've been watching this here entry point for over two hundred years. Everyone that comes to me says it's important. What's your excuse?"

"There's a very dangerous ghost chasing us," says Ophelia. "He kept us from leaving our home for weeks and terrorized us on the way here."

"I'd say that poses a problem for you then," says the Drolling Dragon, "because without permission from Lady'Witch Turtlebalm, you'll not be getting into the Hallowed Halls from *this* entry point, unless of course you have a Skeleton Key from the Ghostal Holly? Or perhaps invitations from the Sky Builders? Do you have either of those?" He pauses and Famka is really annoyed now, because she has invitations, but there's no chance of retrieving them quickly, certainly not before Berny shows up again. "I see from your dour expressions that you do not. Well then, I'll be going back to sleep. Come back should you find yourself in possession of any of the items."

"Master Dragon. It be important that we get to the Plaza," says Parran. "Lady'Witch Turtlebalm be misplaced, otherwise we not come directly to ya."

"I see someone of the old ways," says the Drolling Dragon. "I be no master. Name's Herbert. And you Growgan?"

"Parran Papillon," says the book man with a bow. "At your service."

"Papillon," says Herbert with recognition in his grumpy voice. "The butterfly. I remember ya. You owe me a case of Minor's Malt."

"We don't have any Minor's Malt," says Famka nervously. She can feel Berny growing strong again. "We really need to find Miss Turtlebalm. She's in the Plaza. It's very important, sir."

"You'd better find me at least one case," says Herbert flatly. "Your friend here robbed me blind on more than one occasion in the middle 1600s."

"Those were tough times," says Parran. "We was in the middle of a war. Lots of things happened. Many I'm not proud of."

"No Drolling Dragon alive cares spit about that war," snaps Herbert. "Not me, not then and certainly not now. We are a dying species, book man. We must enjoy what little time we have left, and I would like some Minor's Malt. If you hadn't robbed me, I'd be more likely to let you into the Hallowed Halls."

"That's not true, sir," says Famka to the little man, who's now floating at head height.

"It most certainly is," gripes Herbert. "Ya friend robbed me blind. Probably got himself turned into a Growgan for robbing someone else too."

"Well, that part is actually true," adds Ophelia nodding her head. "You know, we could just stay right here until Berny shows up again. Then maybe you'll believe us."

"That's not helping, Ophi," says Famka irritated.

Ophelia shrugs her shoulders as Famka continues, "You're not a dying species anymore. Heiki had a baby."

"Pass the cornbread!" says Herbert. "Hold your tongue, little missy."

"I promise it," says Famka. "Momma Nay delivered a little girl just a few weeks ago. Heiki named her Heaven."

"That hasn't happened since the Fire Thief killed off all the Dragons," says Herbert astonished. "That means that a Dragon is to come. Can't be." He looks off into the distance then snaps his fingers and disappears, followed by a funny sound. SWISH!"

"That didn't work out very well," says Ophelia looking annoyed. She squints her hazel eyes, creating a crease between her eyebrows.

"What do we do now?" asks Milly sounding depressed.

"We have two invitations back in the swamp," offers Ophelia. "Maybe I can make it. I'm pretty fast now."

"Ophi, the Horseshoe is at least five miles from here. Then, you'd still have to get through the swamp and to the cabin in the dark. There's no chance," says Famka looking off into the dark graveyard. She pauses then and adds, "Berny will be here soon."

SWISH!

The ugly little man suddenly reappears.

"Why didn't you say you were Momma Nay's girls?" barks Herbert. He hits his head on the dragonhead above the doorway. "Crickets and toadstools! I'd love to tear that thing off."

"Hey, you can't do that," says Milly. "This is my family's crypt."

"Never thought I'd see a wee one again," says Herbert ignoring Milly.

The little man retrieves a handkerchief from a pocket in his little trousers and wipes his big ugly eyes.

"Are you actually crying?" asks Milly rudely.

Famka jabs her in the side, and Milly glares back.

"I heard what you did for little Heaven," says Herbert looking at Famka. "You should have said as much. We Drolling Dragons owe you a debt forever, Famka Meadows. I be your servant in all things. Call upon me where ya are. I'll hear ya."

"Thank you, I think," says Famka.

"Are you sure that you don't want to wait until Lady'Witch Turtlebalm comes back from the Plaza?"

"There's no telling when she'll come back, sir. Heiki left several days ago to find her, but she still hasn't shown up," says Famka. "We're going to find her."

"It would seem that Heiki hasn't returned," says Herbert worried.

"Do you think she's all right?" asks Famka.

"I couldn't say," says Herbert. "But Heiki is quite resourceful."

Famka isn't sure how to read the emotions of a Drolling Dragon. Herbert's bulbous orange eyes betray little, but she suspects that he's keeping something to himself.

After a moment, the Drolling Dragon points to Famka's face and says, "And that won't do." He runs his tiny index finger in a circle in the air, and with each rotation, her chin shrinks. Within just a few seconds, her jawline is back to normal.

"So much better," says Milly before turning back to Herbert. "Could you do that for me? I have a few places that could use some trimming."

"No, I cannot," says Herbert annoyed. "Tuning isn't for vanity."

"But you made Famka look better," argues Milly.

"I simply undid what she could not," says Herbert. "Now then. You wish to go to the Plaza of Giants?"

"Yes, please." Famka is feeling the burn again inside. "That would be very helpful."

The little man snaps his tiny fingers again. This time, an

entranceway appears behind him. The tomb's heavy wooden door evaporates like mist burning off a cold lake. In its place is a red-clay cavern larger than several football fields. Tunnels break off from the cavern, leading in different directions. And the room is filled with all sorts of odd creatures, including witches and ghosts flying by at incredible speeds. Famka leans over and looks down the side of the gray crypt, because the tomb is so much smaller than the cavern inside. She is excited to see real Tuning.

"Is this how we get to the Plaza of Giants?" asks Milly with a shaky voice.

"Don't worry, Milly," says Ophelia. "We'll go in together."

Someone powerful must have created the Hallowed Halls, Famka thinks.

Parran whispers in her mind, *No one be sure how that Halls came about. Some say the Nyre King made them when the world be created. May have used them himself to travel about easily.*

They're so wonderful, whispers Famka in her mind, smiling to herself.

"Would you two quit that," says Milly looking from Famka to Parran. "It's so creepy."

Chapter 28

Little ol' Berny

B<small>ERNY IS FURIOUS</small> and in a lot of pain. He must reach Famka before she disappears into the Hallowed Halls. He tries to sit up and peel his body off the stone crypt, but he's stuck. Like paint splattered against a wall, his body resembles a child's messy afternoon. He hadn't felt discomfort like this since he was alive. How is it that a country witch like Famka Meadows can inflict so much agony? She is just a simple girl from Nowheresville, Texas. He isn't accustomed to feeling his ghostly body hurt. He thought for sure that he was beyond it when he'd died several hundred years ago. He is thankful for that, too, for his body failed him when he was alive. He is small, never a big man. Even as a child, other children considered him weak. Even when his body showed muscles, they were never very large. His feet are big, however. Size eleven. A strange oddity for a man at five-foot-three, whose delicate hands are like a small girl's. Which, as fate would have it, works in his favor because he can work spells that other witches struggle with. He can move his fingers in such a way that he can pull Tuning out of the air as if it were long pieces of pasta from a never-ending bowl of spaghetti.

He'd once mentioned to another witch how he invented spells and considered the intricacies of certain dishes as a model for his enchantments. He was laughed at, of course, but by then, Berny had grown accustomed to being overlooked. It had happened throughout his entire childhood, even when he was accepted into the newly founded Sky Builders' Guild, he was still just little ol' Berny.

Even Wyndomier himself, the father of modern Tuning, the creator of the Sky Builders' Guild, didn't see Berny's potential.

After betraying the Sky Builders, Berny had worked hard to ensure the Fire Thief's success. He poured his life and soul into the Struggle, as he'd come to call it: the movement the Fire Thief had begun at the hands of an oppressive government—the Ghostal Holly. How he hated the Ghostal Holly too! He had come to think, as the Fire Thief had, that Chairman Boo, the head of the Ghostal Holly, had for too long meddled in the affairs of the weak race, as Chairman Boo called human beings. So, it was ironic that human beings nearly brought down the Ghostal Holly. The weak ones! The Fire Thief hadn't been weak, nor had Berny. No, they had been strong, but still they had failed.

For now...

But Berny was not a man to give up. The Fire Thief had taught him the virtue of determination. Sometimes, the simple act of continuing on when everyone else had stopped was enough. And certainly, Berny was the bulwark of dogged determination. He had tried every day for over three hundred years to retrieve the *Kitab'i'Mordanee* from where the Fire

Thief had left it hidden. He would not call it the Bastard Book as so many had come to know it. And only Berny knew of its whereabouts.

Looking down as his arm repairs itself, Berny thinks it odd that the Nyre King hasn't come for the book himself or herself. This simple act made Berny wonder if the Nyre King was, in fact, a myth—a fable told to children because life would be hard. He figured that if the Nyre King existed, then the Nyre King simply didn't care. Or perhaps if the Nyre King is all-powerful, then he isn't all-powerful all the time. Berny sometimes wondered that, when he made people suffer. If God was all merciful, then why didn't God show up when Berny's victims cried out. Perhaps the Nyre King isn't all-merciful all the time?

Berny figured that was all nonsense and that reality was largely up for grabs. He often thought that right and wrong wasn't up to a final judge sitting on a mighty throne, but subjective, and it gave his sense of morality a certain fluidity. This is what brought him to the Fire Thief's attention. That and his tiny delicate hands, of course.

In no time, Berny had risen above the others in the Struggle to be the Fire Thief's First Chair. With his help, Berny mastered spells and created new ones that are still unmatched.

So that is why Berny can't understand why a simple country bumpkin like Famka Meadows has so successfully blown his ghostly body to pieces, with a gun yanked from a painting no less. Not that it matters, because in a few more moments, he will be his normal small self again.

He can hear Famka talking with a Drolling Dragon as he watches his nose reform between his eyes. He knew Herbert, of course, that little rude raccoon. Ugly as all heck, too, and there were so few Drolling Dragons left, which Berny thought was probably a good thing. They were so terrible on the eyes. Strangely, Drolling Dragons had been one of the first races in the Knack just after Bombadoes. They knew of Tuning long before human beings even began to walk upright, still eating ticks off one another's backs. Sometimes, he would come here to Babyhead Cemetery to talk with Herbert when he grew frustrated. Berny never let Herbert know that he was in fact Bernard Trankler, the Fire Thief's First Chair and why that would have ended with Berny in prison.

"I will be your servant forever, Famka Meadows," says Herbert. This is not exactly what Herbert says. Berny has a bad habit of hearing what he wants to hear. It helps him shape the world as he prefers, and it has gotten him into trouble on more than one occasion. It even lost him the few friends he'd ever had, which weren't many. Hearing Herbert's vow of service to Famka, Berny immediately grows angry. A Drolling Dragon servant is no small thing. The secrets they keep about Tuning are legendary. The irony is that they don't seem to care about their vast knowledge. Drolling Dragons feel that what they know about the world should die with them, and in the last few hundred, they relegated themselves to service of some kind or another. This might be the third most ridiculous thing Berny had ever heard, next to religion and morality. To have so much knowledge of Tuning and then sweep floors with it truly blew Berny's mind.

"Oh," says Famka excitedly. "I'm so pretty now."

Berny imagines Famka jumping up and down like a giddy schoolgirl. This, of course, didn't really happen, but in Berny's mind it did. *Already, that Drolling Dragon is helping her*, he thinks angrily. How many decades had Berny come here and complained to Herbert without him so much as lifting a finger on one of his little hands to help?

Berny is growing furious. He is madder than a wet hen. If he wasn't expending so much energy trying to put his body back together, he might explode and resemble a messy painting again.

"Can you make me pretty too?" asks Milly.

Of course Milly would ask that ugly Drolling Dragon to make her beautiful. That spoiled idiot of a child! Berny had spent years trying to improve Milly's pathetic skills, but to no avail. She couldn't Tune her way out of a wet paper bag. Famka, however, is the prize. With her, he could undo the spell locking away the *Kitab'i'Mordanee* and finally free the Fire Thief. Then as two brothers, they'd continue their most glorious work and overthrow the Ghostal Holly once and for all. The world would be remade in a proper fashion. Chairman Boo and his insufferable Ghostal Holly would be wiped away, make no mistake about that! Human beings, the supposed weak ones, would take control. They were the true witches.

Bombadoes, Drolling Dragon, and Wigglers were all limited in their willingness to go the distance. None of the other races had it in them to change life as it had been given to them. They all accepted fate as something concrete and unchangeable; as if life were simply a pair of hand-me-downs forced upon them at birth.

Well, Berny couldn't accept that. Life hadn't fit him comfortably, and certainly death hadn't been much better. His hand-me-downs fit loosely and had holes in the knees. He wanted a form-fitting version of life, tailored specifically to him, even if it meant that everyone else on earth suffered.

And Berny was great, after all.

All he needed now was Famka Meadows. She was a *real witch*.

He needed her to locate the God Wand.

To free the *Kitab'i'Mordanee* from its prison.

To liberate the Fire Thief.

To level the Ghostal Holly, that retched controlling government.

So many steps, but the Fire Thief had taught him determination.

He didn't care if Famka died in the process. What did it matter? It wasn't like anyone in the heavens was watching. And even if the Nyre King was, it appeared that he didn't care.

Chapter 29

Into the Hallowed Halls

"Simply tell the Halls where you wish to go," says Herbert still floating near the Dragonhead above the doorway. "And the Halls will take you there."

Famka thinks back to Momma Nay's wording when she had taken her and Ophelia through the Hallowed Halls to Baton Rouge last summer. The phrase was very specific, and Momma Nay was also stern when she taught the girls, so Famka was careful to say it correctly, "With all intents and purposes, we intend to go to the Plaza of Giants."

"Perfectly said," says Herbert with a strange smile on his strange face.

A blue string appears from the center of Famka's stomach and stretches out through the doorway, across the massive cavern, and disappears into a tunnel, which resembles a tiny black dot. The cavern is crammed full of folks zooming through the air, and even when someone flies through the string, it remains unmolested. Famka leans into the entrance and looks up at the reddish-clay walls that rise dozens of stories high. Her stomach jumps as she looks at the floor, which is too far below to see. The first step is always the scariest. After that, she'll be flying, and flying is crazy fun!

"Follow the blue string," says Herbert. "If you get lost, find the nearest exit and get out of the Halls as quickly as possible."

"Why quickly?" asks Milly concerned.

"Because there is no oxygen in the Hallowed Halls," says Herbert. "They were built by the Nyre King for the dead, not breathers like you three."

Famka nods, and Herbert adds, "I stand by what I said, young Meadows. You have done we Drolling Dragons a great service in saving Heaven. If you should need my assistance simply call out. I will hear you."

"Thank you, Herbert," says Famka.

"I will do what I can to delay your ghost. After such losses as we suffered during the war, we Drolling Dragons do not like getting involved in the problems of humans. I make you an exception. Make haste and go to the Ghostal Holly and tell them of what you know. A final warning. Do not Tune in the Hallowed Halls. It is illegal. The Halls are a safe place for all species to travel freely. There are no exceptions. Good day, little misses," Herbert says, then disappears, followed by a funny sound.

SWISH!

Famka looks over at Parran, who's standing beside Milly. "Sorry, Parran. Inside," says Famka holding the backpack open to him.

He shrugs his paper shoulders and says, "I've hidden in worse." He leaps into the air, transforming back into a book, and then lands perfectly inside the bag. Famka zips it up then places her arms through the straps, securing it to her back.

BLUE SKELETON

"Are you ever going to return my backpack?" asks Ophelia.

"I'll buy you another one," says Famka feeling a little irritated.

"With what money?" asks Ophelia.

"After we get paid from the Whirly Bird harvest, I'll get you a new one," says Famka.

"I don't really care, baby," says Ophelia with a smile lighting up her gray green eyes. "I'm just teasing you."

"I've got one at home you can have," offers Milly.

"No!" says Famka. "I'll take care of it." She shakes off her frustration and turns to face the doorway.

"Take a deep breath," says Famka excited to be finally leaving the island.

She grabs Ophelia's hand, and they leap through the stone doorway and into the massive Hallowed Halls. Unfortunately, Ophelia didn't take Milly by the hand, so Milly flies chaotically through the Halls beside them and nearly crashes right into a family of three witches, who duck out of the way just in time. Milly flails in the air, hands and feet waving wildly. Panic runs across her face as her eyes widen and mouth stretches open. Frustrated at Milly's constant lack of control, Famka debates letting Milly fly away. No matter what Milly tries, she doesn't seem to understand the basic intricacies of Tuning. Flying through the Hallowed Halls is no different. With resignation, Famka pulls on Ophelia and they glide up to Milly until Ophelia can take her hand. All three girls finally zoom hand-in-hand through the Halls, following along the blue string.

All around them, witches zip by in a flurry. Having little time to cross the Hallowed Halls, witches are always moving the fastest. Momma Nay had once told Famka that the other races, such as Bombadoes and Wigglers, were more adept at holding their breath for extended periods of times. As for ghosts, well, they were the biggest time-wasting lollygaggers ever, so more often than not, they were in the way. There had been times in the early days of Tuning when ghosts had kept witches from exiting quickly. Several witches died, prompting the Ghostal Holly to mandate laws regarding the Hallowed Halls. Now, if a ghost interferes, causing the death of a witch, the ghost is placed into a teacup-sized box that is placed on a shelf, and the ghost is left to their own thoughts for quite a long time. As some ghosts are already a bit off once released, lunacy is known to take over. This has happened only three times since the modern age of Tuning began approximately four hundred years ago, so any ghost in their right mind, pardon the pun, makes certain to avoid witches in the Hallowed Halls.

Having been raised by Momma Nay in the witchy arts of Tuning, both Famka and Ophelia have been in the Hallowed Halls before. Most recently to visit Baton Rouge.

Famka was always taken aback by the sheer size of the Halls. The cavern could be described as having sipped half the water out of the Gulf of Mexico and still be thirsty. To call it huge would be an understatement. Famka looks up at the curved ceiling high above them, careful not to crash into any oncoming travelers. Its rounded ridges remind her of ripples of sand left standing after a windstorm. Around them, tunnels run away in various directions. Some of them open onto city streets, others into living rooms, and one on the deck of a ship before closing again. Down below, pink sand flows along a pathway broken up by large random white rocks. Sporadic beams of yellow light break through openings in the ceiling, dotting the floor in circles of sunlight.

Far below, a Bombadoe floats beneath her. Unlike the three witches, who fly facedown like Superman, the Bombadoe is completely upright, standing tall as he moves slowly across the vast space. Even at such a far distance, he's big. Famka figures he might be well over fifteen feet tall and is mesmerized by the giant. His head is flat and rectangular with a chin so long it extends beyond his neckline, ending just over his gun-barrel chest. He is thick with a round belly, but not overly fat, and reminds her again of an Eastern Island statue brought to life. She'd seen a picture of one in an old magazine once when reading about islands in the South Pacific. *Bombadoes were the last to see Dragons*, she thinks. She is so distracted that she doesn't see four rat-like creatures, not much larger than a five-year-old child, flying right at them. Fortunately, Ophelia sees them. She reacts quickly to jerk Famka and Milly out of the way. *Wigglers*, she thinks, looking back over her shoulder.

Ophelia shoots Famka an angry look and takes control of their flight. Her firm grip on Famka's hand tightens, and they rise higher into the cavern but careful not to stray from the blue string, which leads them to the Plaza of Giants. A long single line of witches dressed in orange with hooded black pullovers flies beneath them. Stitched onto each of their chests is a Gris Gris, which is the image of the Fire Thief within a circle. Toward the top of the circle, where his eyes should be, are the famous burning matchstick eyes. She recognizes the uniform as that of a first-year Sky Builder.

It reminds Famka that she and Ophelia had missed the Try Outs again, which really burns her up. She is suddenly so angry that she nearly lets go of Ophelia's hand. If it wasn't for Ophelia gripping down hard, Famka might have flown away. She turns to her best friend, and Ophelia mouths, "I'm sorry," followed by a sympathetic expression. Ophelia's big hair frames her warm face, but Famka is still furious.

However, Famka doesn't have time to be angry. On the other side of Ophelia, Milly begins choking. The blonde girl yanks free from Ophelia and clutches her throat. Milly opens her mouth in a natural reaction to take in air, but there isn't any available. She looks over at Famka and Ophelia with a look of terror. Pudgy fingers scratch frantically at her neck, and she tumbles away, spinning in circles. Famka is certain that Milly didn't take a full breath before the three girls entered the Hallowed Halls.

She could die in here, thinks Famka, as both she and Ophelia dive toward Milly. Even though the cavern in massive and the distance between walls is several miles, Milly is in danger of crashing into the far edge. Faster, she spins toward the rock and flies right through a ghost, who looks back angrily before continuing on his way. Blonde hair, white shirt, and blue-jean shorts blur into one another as her speed increases.

Witches, ghosts, and all manner of odd creatures swerve out of the way as the two girls dive after Milly. The stone wall grows closer, and Famka isn't sure they can reach Milly in time. The wall is so close now that it looks like an ancient God hovering high above, watching over misbehaving children. Hundreds of tunnels dot the cliff wall, similar to alcoves in a theater setting. Some of the tunnels are crammed full of folks coming and going, while others open to the outside world. That's when Famka has an idea.

She tugs on Ophelia's hand to get her attention then points to an exit that looks out over a small body of water. Famka figures that they can't stop Milly completely, but they can slow her down enough that the crash landing in the water won't kill her—or them—hopefully. At the speed they're traveling, it seems terribly close, but Ophelia nods, and they dive even harder. Barely missing another young witch, the two girls reach Milly, and with a tug to slow her down, followed by a light shove, they send her toward the opening. Unfortunately, the same group of young Sky Builders has circled back around the massive cavern and suddenly stop between Milly and the exit she's heading toward. The students fly uneasily, looking as though today might be the first time any of them have been in the Hallowed Halls. Young, fresh faces straining to hold their breath stop in mid-flight, as an instructor with a scar across his left eye keeps his hand up in a closed grip. Famka waves her free hand to get their attention, but none of them notice her. She screams out, but there is no sound, of course, because there is no air.

This isn't good. Eyes darting back and forth, she scans for an option, but there isn't one. Milly flies closer toward the students, her arms still trying to grasp ahold of something solid, a flash of fear in her blue eyes. Famka's heart is pummeling the backside of her rib cage like an angry boxer, as she watches the inevitable crash approaching. She isn't sure what will happen when they collide, but someone is going to get hurt or worse, killed.

Tuning is illegal in the Hallowed Halls. If she knew a Displacement spell, she could shove several students out of the way and create an opening for Milly to fly through, but she doesn't. All she can think is *move*.

Move! Famka screams in her mind.

She reaches out, fingers splayed wide, blue veins pushing against her brown skin, and a burst of Tuning flies from her fingertips, but it's not exactly what she expected. She's wasn't expecting to break the law, but when she Tuned, she always imagined that something great might happen. Instead, chocolate-chip cookies suddenly appear in the air, pummeling the students in chocolaty goodness. They immediately fall away, which creates an opening just as Milly flies through them and out the exit. The last thing Famka sees as she and Ophelia fly behind Milly is one very angry mentor.

Chapter 30

The Barrow of Shady Grove

THE THREE WITCHES fly out of the Halls through a portal high in the air above a tree line. Greenery resembling broccoli spears surrounds a large pond in the center of a massive graveyard. Air returns, and with it sound, with a funny swishing noise as they exit. Humidity envelops Famka as she crashes through leaves, breaking a branch with a loud snap. Milly is still ahead of them, and Famka is fearful as the impending water approaches. Famka breathes in large gulps of air as she frantically tries to think of a spell that might slow their descent. Would a Trankler's Hold It work? No, too hard of a surface. If only she knew how Ophelia had used a Mending spell to strengthen her muscles. She should have asked. So stupid! Milly screams out seconds before she crashes into the water. A second later, Ophelia hits it with a hard dunk that shoots water high above her. On the far side, Famka splashes into the large pond. Warm water rises all around Famka and then collapses over her, forcing her downward as she sinks beneath the surface. In seconds, she's deep enough to blot out any light from above. Fortunately, her skirt doesn't weigh her down, so she kicks easily to the top. Breaking the surface, Famka takes in a huge breath followed by a coughing fit as water shoots out of her mouth and nose. Thankful to finally have oxygen, she whips around in search of the other two witches, but only gas-fired lampposts look back from the top of a nearby landing.

Milly pops up across the pond, looking flushed. Famka jerks in her direction and sees Milly's tanned skin, now pale in the moonlight, her blonde hair wet and plastered to her head. Makeup running down her round cheeks, she looks like a sad clown.

"Where's Ophelia?" Famka yells out frantically.

"I—I don't know," says Milly looking around.

A great beach ball-sized welt of panic hurls through Famka's stomach. She spins around again, looking for her best friend.

Where is Ophelia?

Dear God.

Did she crash into a tree?

Famka imagines her best friend lying half dead and tangled in limbs, her body twisted. She whirls back around in the direction from which she thought they'd exited the Halls, but there is no doorway floating in the air. No escape and no obvious possibility of returning to the Halls. All she can see is a thick blanket of broccoli against the night sky.

A moment later, Ophelia pops up near Milly.

Thank goodness!

Ophelia's head barely crests the water as she struggles to take in air. Hair in her face and splashing wildly, she's unable to remain at the surface and slips underneath, before emerging again.

"Help!" she screams out, trying to grab ahold of anything solid before she slips back down again. "Something has my..." Ophelia disappears.

Famka immediately swims toward her, but she's on the farthest side of the pond and too far to reach Ophelia quickly. Desperately she swings her arms outward and kicks hard, pushing against the water. Between strokes, Famka sees her best friend's hand break the surface again, but then disappear, as if something is yanking her downward. Famka kicks again and again, but she's still too far away.

Dang it!

Fortunately, Milly is closer and reaches the spot where Ophelia was a moment ago. Milly dives down, and for a moment, Famka is alone in the pond with only ripples remaining where the two witches had just been.

"Ophi. Ophi!" Famka yells out then takes in a giant breath, prepared to dive down. Ophelia and Milly burst through the surface, gasping for air. Ophelia chokes out water and looks frightened. Famka pushes Milly's hands away, spins Ophelia around, and grabs her beneath the arms from behind. She holds Ophelia tightly, dragging her toward the water's edge. She can smell the pond on Ophelia's hair, which strangely reminds her of cotton candy.

"Calm down," says Famka firmly as Ophelia continues to take in air in short breaths. "I know you're scared, but if you don't stop struggling then you'll drag us both down."

Famka pulls Ophelia behind her, but despite kicking with all her strength, it's like swimming against a riptide.

"The pond is enchanted," says Ophelia as the two girls go under.

Milly splashes toward them.

Famka grabs ahold of Milly's hand, and the moment she does, the pull on her releases and she and Ophelia easily remain at the surface. The two girls drag Ophelia to the edge.

Crawling onto a well-manicured lawn, Famka helps Ophelia out of the water. Despite the warm weather, Famka feels an immediate chill. Blades of moist grass cut between her splayed fingers as she plops down beside Ophelia. Famka shares a rare smile with Milly, who smiles back. Despite Famka's previous feelings about Milly, she's thankful for her help. Without Milly, Famka could have lost her best friend; the only family she really has.

"Thank you," says Ophelia, now on her hands and knees. "Something had me by the ankle. Hurt like the dickens too."

Famka looks at Ophelia's bare skin, and sure enough, there are red welts around her ankle.

"What was it?" asks Famka.

"Did you see it?" Milly interjects.

"Dunno. I didn't see it." Ophelia drops onto her stomach and turns over.

"Might have been that mentor with the Sky Builders. The one with the greasy black hair," says Famka suspiciously. "He was pretty angry as we flew by him."

"Yeah, probably," says Milly looking relieved and lying down beside Ophelia.

Famka hesitates but suddenly feeling exhausted, throws off her backpack and flops down as well. She grabs Ophelia's hand as the three lie side by side, breathing heavily and staring up at the night sky.

"Isn't it illegal to Tune in the Hallowed Halls?" says Ophelia in a hushed voice.

"Yeah. I was thinking the same thing," Famka answers. "Kinda weird that a mentor would fire a spell at us."

"Do you think he followed us?" asks Milly.

The night is still, but the moon now sits in an unusual spot in the sky. It appears somehow closer, as if it's within reaching distance and one could simply reach up and yank it out of the sky. The white surface is brighter than normal. Its round edges are clearly rimmed by a thick black line like it's been outlined by a child's marker. Famka wonders how far they are from the Horseshoe as she pushes a lock of her wet hair away from her cheek. The stars are unusually bright, too, so she figures they are nowhere near a large city, but even still, the stars are too bright even for country stars. That's when Famka realizes where they are.

"Where are we?" asks Milly, as if reading Famka's mind.

"The Other Side of the Graveyard," says Famka.

"Really?" says Milly with surprise in her voice. "I've never been here."

"Really!" says Famka. "Ophi and I have been here a couple o' times with Momma Nay. You can usually tell you're here, because everything looks clearer. Like it's all somehow cleaner or well taken care of. Dunno exactly how to describe it. Just somehow nicer, I guess."

"That's neat." Milly yawns and stretches her arms out. "I'm so tired."

"Me too," says Famka realizing that her body aches and she can barely keep her eyes open. She's happy to be alive, but worried that she cannot stay awake. It's too early to be falling asleep. They've been running from Berny for quite some time. Perhaps she's just tired. They did leave Miss Turtlebalm's shop sometime around nine p.m. Then ran to Babyhead Cemetery, fought with Berny, and convinced Herbert the Drolling Dragon to let them into the Hallowed Halls. That does seem like a lot, but should she really be this tired?

"A Sleeping spell!" Ophelia slurs then turns her head toward Famka and closes her eyes.

She feels Ophelia's hand go limp in hers as she, too, slips off into sleep. It seems like only a few minutes before she's dreaming. Blue turtles in the thousands crawl out of the ocean and onto the beach near the Horseshoe. The water parts behind the turtles like a zipper opening a giant blue jacket. One by one, the small turtles crawl forward across the sand. Famka runs with them toward the Horseshoe. First, the turtles smother the trailers, then the swamp, and finally the little tourist town of Wink. When the southern end of the island is covered, even Milly's palatial mansion is gone. The gazebo—the one hiding the *Kitab'i'Mordanee*—is completely engulfed. Finally, the entire island is engulfed in blue turtles. Famka is left feeling that the dream is a blessing and not a dark omen. The turtles are like toddlers, innocent and cute.

When Famka wakes, she is disoriented. She has no idea how long she's been asleep, and her muscles ache with the sting of running. She wipes moisture from her face. When her vision clears, the sun is bright and she is alone.

Chapter 31

Death of a Friend

Realizing that she's alone, Famka leaps up in a panic. She's still beside the pond where she crashed last night. At least, she *thinks* it was last night. The hot sun beats down from high overhead, leaving her feeling like she's missed half the day. Her clothes are dry and smeared in grime with brown stains running along her skirt. Flecks of dirt dot her arms, and she smells of cotton candy, much like Ophelia had yesterday. Well-manicured grass blankets the landscape around the water, stretching away from her toward a flat landing. Trees with bushy tops line the entire perimeter and crowd around wood-slated benches that are spaced out evenly every thirty feet or so. Famka turns in a circle, eyeing all the benches, hoping that Ophelia might be sitting in one, but they're all empty.

Someone or something moves behind the nearest bench. The thick green bushes ruffle loudly.

"Hello," Famka calls out on guard, leaning slightly for a better look.

Fortunately, Milly steps out from behind the bench and not Berny. Letting out a long breath, she asks, "Where's Ophelia?"

Milly walks down the hill toward Famka. "She wasn't here when I woke. I went to pee. I thought maybe she had done the same." Milly shrugs her shoulders. "What happened last night in the Hallowed Halls?"

"I think that mentor with the Sky Builders fired a spell at us," says Famka. "But it's supposed to be illegal to Tune in the Hallowed Halls. I'm not sure. We need to find Ophelia."

"Maybe there are exceptions to that Tuning rule when witches get into trouble?"

A knot tightens in Famka's stomach, and a flash of worry runs across her face as she realizes that she can't feel Parran nearby. Since Imprinting with him, he's been a constant in her head. Quiet most times, but always there, like a humming bird darting between trees. Now, however, he's gone, and Famka feels exposed without him. "Something's not right."

"What it is?" asks Milly concerned.

"Parran," she says ruffling through her backpack. "Where is he?"

"Maybe Ophelia has him?" Milly offers.

"I doubt it. Why would she do that?" asks Famka suspiciously. "Ophelia's gun is gone too." Famka glares up at Milly. "What were you really doing up there?"

"You think I took Parran?" Milly puts a hand to her heart as though offended.

"It makes sense," says Famka. "You've been jealous of me since we met. You think that Parran belongs to you, but he doesn't."

"Oh, get off it, Famka," snaps Milly. "Get a grip. I saved

Ophelia last night. You were too far away. If not for me, she would have drowned, and if you don't believe me, then go up there, behind those bushes, and take a look for yourself. I didn't take Parran from you. Go on. Go see for yourself. Just be careful not to step in anything wet. You're barefoot."

The two girls stand quietly for a moment as tension floats between them. Famka doesn't trust Milly, but she did save Ophelia, so she has doubts.

"Come on." Famka finally breaks the silence. She closes her bag and swings it over her back then starts walking up the hill. "Let's find Ophelia and figure out where we are. Then we can get to the Plaza of Giants and tell the Ghostal Holly what Berny has been doing and be done with all this nonsense."

"Wait!" says Milly. "What's this?"

When Famka turns around, Milly is picking up a piece of paper from the ground.

"Where did you find that?"

"It just fell off your back," says Milly.

"For real?" asks Famka skeptically.

"No, I just pulled it out of my butt. Yes, for real," says Milly angrily.

"It's from Bernard," says Milly. "I told you it wasn't me. He has Ophelia and Parran."

"Well, what does it say?" Famka steps beside Milly and reads the note...

My Dearest Witches,

This has been a real treat chasing you young ladies, but time for playing is over. I have your little friend, and I've taken back my Growgan. Meet me after midnight at Tattoo Statue. It is located on the far west side of

Shady Grove near the amphitheater. Make sure you come alone.

Regrettably,
B. Trankler

Guilt pinches Famka's stomach for accusing Milly of betrayal. Maybe Ophelia was right and Milly isn't so bad after all. Milly saved her best friend last night, or so she keeps telling herself. Milly had tried repeatedly to fit in with the two witches, most noticeably trying to impress Famka. Milly was clumsy, naive about Tuning, and often foolish about what was possible, but mostly, Milly had been excited to have the two other witches to share her time with.

Famka tells herself that she will be nicer to Milly from now on.

More words suddenly appear on the paper scrolling by themselves as if by magic.

P.S. Remember that I asked nicely and more than once. Now that I've made my point, please be on time. There is nothing worse than waiting around for no good reason. As a token of my sincerity, turn around and look at the pond. Now, I know he meant a lot to you. Shame you'll never see him again.

Famka and Milly face the water as bubbles begin gurgling at the surface. A series of pops splutter through the water and into the air, but for a moment, nothing else happens. They look at each other confused before turning back as a low rumble draws their attention. An old green pickup truck suddenly emerges from the murky water. The windshield is shattered, the front bumper has been torn away, and a there's a large dent buckling the driver's door into a bowl. The familiar rust stains cresting the edges of the wheel wells tell Famka exactly who it belongs to. Uncle Guncle.

One dark hand clutches the steering wheel.

"That son of bitch!" snaps Famka. "Trankler killed Uncle Guncle."

"I'm sorry, Famka," says Milly as they watch the truck sink back down again. "Were you close to him?"

"Yeah," says Famka. "He was kinda like… Yeah, I knew him."

Famka lets out a long breath, her shoulders slumping. She didn't know her father, but she'd often sought Moses Guncle out for fatherly advice. He could be counted on even if he was exhausted, which was most of the time. Even after a long day baking in the hot Texas summer sun fishing for his livelihood. Which often meant feeding those folks in the Horseshoe who couldn't afford to take care of themselves. Famka suddenly feels horrible. She had inadvertently dragged him into this mess when they hid in his pickup while trying to escape Berny. She didn't think that Berny would kill, could kill. All the ghosts she'd known before were harmless and filled with boring stories. Perhaps at times, some of them were horrible to look at with noses missing or ears detached, but they were still harmless.

Fish I can replace.

Those were the last words Uncle Guncle had said to her. She knew what he'd meant. That she was more important than his daily catch.

Famka wipes her eyes. *This isn't fair,* she says to herself as she looks down at the note again.

The words disappear, leaving just a piece of plain white

paper. Famka takes it from Milly, crumples it up, and shoves it into her pocket. Despite being able to see the dead, that didn't ensure that Uncle Guncle would be a ghost. Some people remained on earth after death, while others moved on. No one really knows why.

In any case, Uncle Guncle was dead and likely gone.

More tears slip from Famka's unusually green eyes, and Milly places a kind arm around her. Famka looks out across the water, filled with regret. *Be strong,* she tells herself, but she'd rather rage, which is exactly the feeling building in her now. A tightening in her stomach spreads out along her limbs until her hands begin shaking. She imagines hurting Berny violently in a way she'd never allowed herself to think before.

"What do we do?" asks Milly in barely a whisper. For a moment, Famka glares into her thoughts before turning to Milly. Her hair has dried out and is now a big poofy mess of blonde wisps circling her head. Her typically makeup-covered face is clear of color, leaving her looking just a little pale.

"We get that son of a bitch," growls Famka. "And we break him."

It takes a few minutes, but the two girls turn away from the pond and begin walking up the hill in silence. It's hot as heck, but a light breeze takes the edge off. Blades of grass poke between Famka's bare feet, but all she can think about is hurting Berny and hurting him bad.

They find a dirt path in between the trees and follow it until it breaks off and cuts between two tall bushes. Stepping onto a brick walkway and having no idea which way to go, they turn left and continue alongside a line of short gray tombstones. Famka tries to remember how she manipulated a Trankler's Hold It before, because if she can, then she will use it on Berny. She'll trap him inside one and crush him just like he had done to his victims when he was still alive. She almost laughs to herself, like a half-crazy person, at the thought of using his own spell against him.

The worn brick walkway is warm against Famka's bare feet as they continue onward. The bricks curve beneath her heels, and not so much as a single pebble stabs against her skin. Above her are dark green gas-fired lamps, which are sleeping for the day. Surrounding the two witches, the graveyard spreads out in a mixture of low gray tombstones, large crypts, thick bushes, and trees for miles. Had this been any other day, Famka would have loved to explore the Barrow of Shady Grove. It seemed delightful, but she was not able to see it that way, not really. Finally reaching a crossroad, a wooden sign nailed to a post in the center of the path reads…

Behind you: Sadness
To your left: The Haint.
To your right: Amphitheater
Up ahead: Plaza of Giants.

Famka furrows her brow at the sign, wondering if it's a coincidence that it states so clearly how she's feeling. At that moment, she doesn't like Tuning because the sign makes her feelings for Uncle Guncle seem trivial. What she feels isn't anyone's business; nor is it something to be advertised on a sign of all things. Famka glares up at it angrily, and the word *Sadness* changes to read: *Angry as a badger.*

"Yeah, you're dang right," yells Famka to the sign.

"Come on, Famka," says Milly taking the lead. Famka follows for a while in brooding silence with a mixture of anger and sadness. How could she have let that Berny kill Uncle Guncle? It was her fault. She was certain that Momma Nay would give her a big *I told you so*. Tuning is dangerous, and some of those who Tune are too. Famka let herself down, let Uncle Guncle down, but mostly, she thought about how she would tell Ophelia. *Oh dear God.* She has to get to Ophelia before Berny murders again.

"There they are. That's them!"

A familiar man with scar across his left eye yells from farther up the pathway. He's pointing a stern finger at Famka and Milly. Beside him are two ghosts dressed in Old West policeman's attire complete with cowboy hats, black knee-length dusters, button-down brown shirts, bright badges, and of course, cowboy boots.

Milly dives into a nearby bush and disappears without a sound. Famka looks at the bushes as they ruffle from Milly's hasty departure; several leaves fall to the ground behind her.

"Get that one," barks the scarred man, and the two deputies fly after Milly.

Not in the mood, Famka stares up at the tall thin fellow as he approaches. When he comes to a stop just a few feet away, she asks, "What do you want?"

"Do not pay lip service to me, young lady. What is your name?"

"What difference does it make?" she snaps.

"I suppose it doesn't matter," says the tall man. "I am Thalban Rankor. You may refer to me as Mar'Witch Rankor. First Chair to Chairman Boo of the Ghostal Holly, Chief Architect and Wizard of the Sea of Chall, mentor at the Sky Builders' Guild, and most recently, winner of the Wyndom and Wyndomier awards for Finest Craft."

"Don't care," says Famka noticing that he keeps his left hand behind him, as if he's hiding something.

In any other circumstances, Famka would have be excited to meet him. A Sky Builder, an actual Sky Builder, but at this very moment, she couldn't care less who he is. *What a pompous donkey butt*, she thinks, glaring up at his pronounced nose, which sits squarely between his dark brown, almost black eyes, set in a chiseled, stone-like face. A scar runs across his left eye. His cheekbones protrude like shelves buttressing out from a fortress. His skin is sallow with an almost greenish tint. She wonders if he isn't, in fact, sick despite a seemingly strong physical body. His short black hair is combed perfectly to the side and trimmed neatly around his ears.

"Yesterday, you were seen Tuning in the Hallowed Halls," he says, "which is a highly punishable offense. Minimum term is five years in the Sea of Chall. Not to mention that you nearly killed two young Sky Builders during their first foray into the Halls. One boy fell to the ground and broke his back. Right now, he is undergoing extensive bone regrowth at the Saint Jude's Blessing. What say you?"

Standing alone, under the brooding gaze of Thalban, his heavy brow sits like a rock ledge above his eyes, Famka is overwhelmed with guilt along with a heavy dose of sadness. She is responsible for the death of Uncle Guncle, and now some poor boy's back is broken. This hard-looking fellow is right. She should probably be locked up, but she has to push onward, nonetheless. She has to persevere despite the weight of her circumstances beating down on her right now. She has to save Ophelia. The rest, she can deal with later.

"What say I?" she says as confidently as she can manage. "I say that Bernard Trankler has been terrorizing me for weeks.

He's kept me a prisoner in my home, attacked me more than once, and murdered a friend. So, what do I say?" Famka pauses then finishes, "I say that I don't really care what you want or your laws. I'm going to find him and save my best friend. Goodbye."

"Bernard Trankler," repeats Thalban, followed by a laugh.

Annoyed, Famka turns to leave, but Thalban steps in front of her, blocking her path. "Likely story. He's been dead for centuries, and no one has ever seen his ghost. Not even once."

"What happened to your hand?" asks Famka noticing again that he keeps it hidden behind him.

"That is none of your business," says Thalban nastily.

"I recognize you," says Famka. "You came to Momma Nay for help after you tried using a Cauldron thing."

Oh boy. If Thalban didn't look mean before, he does now. His pale face almost appears to go dark if you can imagine such a thing. Famka takes a step back, certain he's about to do something bad, but luckily for her one of the deputies returns.

Thalban turns to the ghost and barks, "Where is the other girl?"

"She got away, Mar'Witch Rankor," says the deputy. "We'll locate her."

"How does a young girl out maneuver you? Aren't you a Guardian of the Ghoul?" growls Thalban. "Never mind. Arrest this one."

Chapter 32

Ghost Armor

"Y͟O͟U͟ ͟H͟A͟V͟E͟ ͟T͟O͟ listen!" yells Famka as the deputy drags her through a crowded police station. His cold, ghostly hand is tight like a vice. It is clamped down on her arm painfully.

"Please. Bernard Trankler took my best friend. He's keeping her prisoner. He'll kill her. You have to listen to me," she pleads, but no one listens. Several faces turn at Trankler's name, but not a single person steps in to help.

Passing through a set of swinging saloon doors, they continue down a hallway until they reach an empty room. The walls are thick, made of stone, and cold. The silent ghost leaves her alone without another word. A single bolted bench sits against the middle of a wall. All sound from outside suddenly goes silent, leaving her with nothing more than her thoughts.

She can't help but wonder how Milly disappeared in the Barrow. Somehow, Milly outran two ghosts. So often, Milly seems like a dunce, a clumsy fool who can barely Tune, but she managed to escape.

And why did she abandon me? I've got to get out of here.

Famka looks up at the Trankler's Hold It in the doorway. She can see through the shimmering barrier out into the hallway, but she cannot leave the room...or can she? She's removed a Trankler's Hold It once before, when she foolishly interfered with the Sky Builder at Momma Nay's shop, but she has no idea how she actually did it.

Thinking back to that night in Lotty Laveau's, Famka hears Momma Nay's words in her head. *This will come back on us.* Momma Nay was referring to helping Thalban, and she was right, but Famka couldn't let Thalban die just because he wasn't the nicest person, even if he was clearly breaking laws laid out by the Ghostal Holly. It wasn't her job to enforce their prerogative, but it spoke volumes about the nature of the man Thalban was; that he would easily break the law he was supposed to help enforce. He was, after all, some kind of insider to Chairman Boo at the Ghostal Holly. Something about that struck Famka as wrong. Why make laws if you're going to break them? Why not simply write better laws?

She walks up to the Trankler's Hold It and places her hands carefully on the field. Closing her eyes, she calls upon the Song of the World, but hears nothing. She squeezes her eyes tightly shut, concentrating, but still only silence greets her.

"Ugh!" she yells out, throwing her hands down in frustration. She storms back to the bench where she plops down, resting her elbows on her knees. She rests her chin in her hands and scowls at the Trankler's Hold It with a vendetta. She tries several more times without success. Time passes slowly, like it does when Famka is in school. There is no clock, however, to torment her. Finally, she lies on her back, realizing how exhausted she is. Her back aches, and her legs are sore. She stares up at the ceiling fighting sleep, but finally slips off.

Hours later, she pops up, awake and fearing that too much time has passed, leaving Ophelia in danger. Determined to get out of this jail, she walks up to the Trankler's Hold It again and places her hands on the field. She closes her eyes, but her thoughts are a jumble, running like undisciplined children. She tries to concentrate, but she's so worried about Ophelia that she can't bring any Tuning into focus.

"For the love of God," she mutters in frustration.

She tries again, and this time, opens her eyes, knowing that somehow, the field is gone. A large ghost of a man floats in front of her instead of an empty exit. Her heart jumps, but she shows no emotion. His square head sits on his shoulders, framing a thick gun-barrel chest. The most obvious part of him is his ridiculous mustache, which is so bushy and wide that it extends at least six inches on either side of his big head, which is covered with a black cowboy hat.

"I am Constable Cockney," says the ghost in a low, rumbling voice. "Might I come in?"

"Do I have a choice?" asks Famka. She turns away from him and sits on the bench again.

"Do you understand why you are here?" He floats into the cell.

"Not really," admits Famka. "The only thing I understand is that no one will listen to me. Is this how you treat people on *your* side of the Graveyard?"

"Some serious charges have been brought against you," says the constable.

"I didn't do anything wrong." Famka crosses her arms over her chest defiantly.

"That is not entirely true," says the constable. He floats to the bench and sits beside her like he's still alive. "You've been seen Tuning in the Hallowed Halls. Mar'Witch Rankor has confirmed it along with several young Sky Builders. One of them you hurt terribly."

Famka looks down at the floor, feeling terrible. She never wanted to inflict any kind of pain on anyone. She thought of Milly and felt another sting of regret.

"I didn't mean to," says Famka quietly. "And I didn't know, either. Well, I did, but I was trying to save my friend. If I hadn't done something, Milly and those Sky Builder kids would've been really hurt."

"I believe you," he says calmly.

"You do?" asks Famka surprised.

"Chocolate-chip cookies," says the constable with a smile, which pushes his big mustache into his nose. "If you had meant to be malicious, you would have used something else."

"So, can I go then?" ask Famka.

"Tell me of Bernard Trankler," says the ghostly policeman. "You see, I must investigate all accusations regarding the Fallen Arts, and certainly Mr. Trankler qualifies. It is an edict passed down from the Ghostal Holly. I personally do not believe that the man is still in existence. Since the war, I have looked into no less than three thousand alleged Bernard Trankler sightings. Not one of them has turned out to be true. Personally, I think ghosts invoke his name to cause fear in witches."

"Well, it's really him," says Famka, but even as she says the words, she realizes that maybe it's not. Maybe it's a witch wearing Ghost Armor. His face has changed more than once. Admittedly, Famka doesn't know much about the nature of ghosts. They rarely speak to her, and when they do, they're usually boring and self-absorbed.

"How can you be so sure?" asks Constable Cockney.

Famka pauses and wonders if perhaps the constable is right. Not only is he potentially correct about Bernard, but she also questions if the Bastard Book is, in fact, dangerous. Famka considers telling the constable about the *Kitab'i'Mordanee*, but what if Bernard's warnings are true? Her home would be overridden with witches and ghosts fighting to get it. Famka longs to leave the Horseshoe but doesn't want to see it destroyed.

"Once," says the constable, "a ghost broke into the Cabish building. You may have seen it on your way here. It's the large stone structure at the top of the Plaza."

"What is it?" asks Famka.

"The seat of the Ghostal Holly," he adds. "The ghost, his name was… Wiltern. Yes, I think that was it. He broke in and stole one of the few remaining pieces of Ghost Armor. Then he pretended to be Bernard Trankler for the better part of a decade. He terrorized a small town in south Texas. Probably not far from where you're from."

"How do you know where I'm from?" asks Famka suspiciously.

"You are Famka Meadows from Wink, Texas, in the Horseshoe trailer number six," says the constable. "I am an old friend of your Nay. Now then, may I finish my story?"

Famka nods.

"Wiltern had convinced many witches and ghosts that he was actually Bernard. For a short time, he ran the small town like a king. Witches did his bidding and ghosts ran his errands. Fortunately, Wiltern was lazy. He never had any intention to hurt anyone the way Bernard Trankler had during the war, but by simply invoking Bernard's name, folks can get scared. With the right circumstances, it can be a very simple thing to gain control over others."

He removes his hat and places it on the bench between them. "And so, I'll ask again. Do you have any proof that this ghost of yours is Bernard Trankler?"

Looking at the stern policeman, Famka considers Bernard's words again. But what is she to do? Despite a convincing argument, Famka still believes that Bernard is who he says he is and is a real threat.

"What if it is him?" asks Famka feeling trapped.

"Then I—along with several of my deputies—will have to investigate your claim, the location he's been haunting, and any other disturbances related to his actions."

Famka's heart sinks. She can't let the constable know that Bernard has been haunting Milly's home. That could mean the Bastard Book would be discovered.

"Maybe you're right," says Famka. "I don't really know what the real Bernard looks like. I guess this fellow could be anyone."

The constable reaches into his black vest. His arms seem to go in farther than seems possible, but then he withdraws a picture of a small man.

"Is this him?" asks the ghostly policeman.

Famka takes the picture, and it sort of resembles Berny. The edges of the photo are worn and the image is faded. The only clear distinction is Bernard's smirk and scarred face. Otherwise, the photo is too blurry to make out any more details. Famka is left wondering if the Berny she knows might be a fraud. Is it possible that someone who doesn't know exactly what the real Berny looks like is trying to imitate him? Like Wiltern had done in the constable's example? But she feels conflicted because she doesn't trust the constable enough to tell him her suspicions and get to the truth. So she lies.

"No, that isn't the ghost who's been chasing us." Then she asks, "Is this Bernard Trankler?"

"The one and only. Although not much of a photo." Constable Cockney takes the picture back. "Well, that's settled. It would seem that your ghost also doesn't know what Bernard looked like. And that means he doesn't have Ghost Armor. That's good. No laws broken. No harm, no foul."

"Can I go then?" asks Famka.

The constable places his hat back on his square head, covering his thick brown hair.

"About that," he says floating up. "I'm afraid that I can't let you leave without you first going before the Tribunal of Burning Banshees. It may not seem like much to you, but Tuning in the Hallowed Halls is a serious offense."

"Why?" asks Famka feeling confused.

"Because the Hallowed Halls belong to the dead," says the constable. "As I'm sure you know, the dead don't want the living Tuning. As more witches began to Tune, the Hallowed Halls became overrun. The Ghostal Holly set laws in place to keep the dead happy. Or at least calm. It wouldn't take much to provoke them, and the Hallowed Halls would be off limits to everyone but ghosts. Can you imagine what this would do to the magical community?"

She did kind of see his point, but it still seemed ridiculous that she'd have to go before a judge just for shooting chocolate-chip cookies at a couple of first-year Sky Builders. She was trying to save them, after all. Plus, she didn't have time to deal with some law that she didn't understand or care about anyway. What she cared about was her friends, and they were currently being held hostage.

The constable floats toward the exit. Before he leaves, he turns back to her and says, "Did I tell you that Momma Nay once saved my life?"

Famka shakes her head.

"It was a very long time ago. Remind me to tell you about it sometime. Much like Wiltern, it involved Ghost Armor. You see that's the thing about Ghost Armor. It allows you to look like whomever you want to look like." He smiles through his ridiculously large mustache. "And it can make you invisible too."

Frustrated, Famka watches him go. The Trankler's Hold It springs to life behind him, and she is locked in the silent room once again. When she looks down, there is a strange black cloth on the bench where he was previously seated. She picks it up, and it shimmers in her hand as if it's made of water. Embroidered in the surface is the face of the Fire Thief with his burning matchstick eyes. They stare up at her, and she realizes that this must be Ghost Armor and the constable left it for her. She looks again at the exit where the constable just floated through, thinking this is why Momma Nay always helps folks. It makes the world a better place when people look out for one another.

How terrible Famka feels for lying to the constable.

Chapter 33

The Fire Thief
(Long before you were born)

"Mum, what happened at home?"

Her answer was in the tears that leapt from her eyes, like escaped prisoners, and slid down her face. She knew he would need, as all children need, to be loved and raised safely in a proper home. But that was gone now, shattered in one cruel moment.

"It isn't fair. It simply is not fair."

"Life never really is, is it?" said the Fire Thief.

Startled, the boy turned as he reappeared. His polluted mass came through the barn wall and landed silently on the hay-covered floor. The animals in the barn all moaned miserably. The Fire Thief raised his hand, and they all fell to the ground instantly, either dead or merely sleeping.

"You cannot have my son."

"Circles. It's always about circles. Repetition. Patterns. I found the pattern."

"What do you want?" But she knew the answer.

"Circles. It's always the circles. They always come back, but not this time."

"You cannot have my son!"

"They always come back, but I got here in time. Yes, I did. I understand the pattern now. The Nyre King is a fool."

"I don't understand." She put her arms around her son and rocked back and forth against the bale of dry hay.

The Fire Thief did not speak again but tilted his head in quiet contemplation. The same curious expression as before drifted across his face.

They looked at each other, the monster and the mother. She wondered what he could be thinking, and for a moment, she saw the man that he once had been instead of the grotesque and distorted thing that now stood in front of her.

"You were human once, weren't you? You were like me?"

He looked at her quietly, as an indiscernible emotion darted across his indiscernible face. The brightness of his matchstick eyes flickered in their sockets, but he did not respond to her question.

"Circles. Only circles," he repeated instead.

"I will not give him to you."

The Fire Thief ignored her and slowly reached into his coat pocket, into the pocket that was not really a pocket, and removed the long black stick he had used to destroy her husband.

"Wyndomier Wick!" says the boy. "Mum, let's go."

It turned into a beam of red light as the Fire Thief raised the device into the air and then pointed it at his victims.

But they were no longer there.

Sometimes, the dead, like certain animal species, are born into their new lives knowing instinctively certain actions. Not all such dead are like this, but on this cold night, the boy's mother knew instinctively what to do.

Holding her son's hand, she did not wait to see what the Fire Thief's evil device would do. She ran at an incredible speed, gripping her son's hand as he ran beside her. Through forests, farms, villages, and towns, they ran. She did not know where she was running, and she didn't look back. Within moments, they had reached the end of land and stared out into the open sea. There was a port below, and ships with tall sails were docked with sleeping crews in their bellies. The moon was sitting like a giant orb at the edge of the horizon above the deep dark water. It hung lazily in the cold evening sky, smiling upon those that looked carefully. Cautiously, she looked down and over the cliff's edge.

"It's all right, Mum. We can jump. I'll be fine as long as I'm holding your hand."

"I don't know. Are you sure?"

The boy closed his eyes tightly as they both fell several hundred feet to the water below. He expected to feel the rush of cold water, but there was no splash when they landed; it was as solid as earth. But they were not harmed. Without sinking, they now stood on the surface of the water, holding hands tightly, amazed that such a thing was possible.

Chapter 34

Tribunal of Burning Banshees

THE NEXT MORNING, a deputy appears in the entrance of Famka's cell. He floats for a second before the near invisible Trankler's Hold It disappears. Noises flood the room from down the hallway like water rushing in through a broken dam. Someone is yelling, not unlike Famka was when she was dragged into the police station against her will.

"Famka Meadows. Come with me," demands the deputy over the commotion. She reluctantly stands, unlocking the soreness in her legs, and looks closely at the ghostly policeman, hoping for an opportunity to escape. He's alone and the brick wall behind him is visible through his pale face. The only thing on him that appears solid is the five-point star badge clipped onto his chest. She wonders if there is a way to outrun the dead man.

"Where are you taking me?" asks Famka fingering the Ghost Armor stuffed deep into her front pocket.

"You will go on trial before the Tribunal of Burning Banshees for your misconduct in the Hallowed Halls," says the ghost calmly. His southern accent drawing out each word.

"Trial," she snaps, thinking this is all some kind of a bad joke. She made cookies appear in the Hallowed Halls as a distraction and only so that Milly wouldn't crash into the line of young students. Famka had noticed many of the young Sky Builders struggling while attempting their first flight in the Halls. Even though she hadn't expected cookies, of all things to appear, it had worked. A gap had opened between the students that allowed Milly to safely pass through them without anyone getting hurt.

"That doesn't make any sense. What am I on trial for?" asks Famka.

"For the murder of Sky Builder Watanabe," says the deputy.

"What!" snaps Famka confused. "What are you talking about?"

"The young Sky Builder that fell in the Hallowed Halls. He died at Saint Jude's, while the nurses where trying to regrow his bones," says the deputy.

"From chocolate-chip cookies?" says Famka flabbergasted.

"The boy was struck by a Breaking spell," says the deputy flatly. "Not cookies."

"But I didn't do that," insists Famka. "I don't even know any Breaking spells."

"The spell came from your proximity," says the deputy sternly.

"But it can't be me," Famka argues, feeling terrible and also questioning if she had inadvertently hurt the boy. She had authored difficult Tuning before, but only by accident. And she had managed to pull a Trankler's Hold It down once, but a Breaking spell? It was part of Wyndomier's Nine original spells and incredibly difficult to master. She has no idea how to author one. Her heart sinks, and she wonders if this week could get any worse. First Uncle Guncle is murdered, and now a poor boy dies. Famka wonders if she actually deserves to be locked up. Maybe she's dangerous and hasn't realized how lethal she is. Tuning has always come relatively easily to her, even when she was a small child. She might not be a Dragon, for who Tuning runs like lightning through their veins, but she has talents, nonetheless. But how could she author a Breaking spell? For a moment, she considers Parran, who was folded into her backpack at the time they were flying through the Hallowed Halls.

Could he have done it?

It doesn't seem likely, but she hasn't known him that long, and there's no way Ophelia could've done it, because Famka was holding hands with her at the time. Milly wasn't an option, either. She was spinning wildly out of control.

So, who was it?

"It is not up to me to determine your innocence or guilt," says the deputy clutching her by the arm. His cold, firm grip sends a chill down her spine. "Come with me."

Famka doesn't struggle as he leads her from the cell and down the hallway. They don't return to the main lobby but continue in the opposite direction down a series of brick corridors lined with other cells. Over and over, she thinks of the young boy falling hundreds of feet to his death. She runs the scene on repeat, torturing herself as she pictures his broken body on the rocks below in the Hallowed Halls. What will his parents feel when they find out? Does he have siblings that will cry for him? A girlfriend who loves him? Grandparents who will never again spoil him on a birthday?

Am I responsible for that?

As Famka continues onward, she's in a daze. She barely realizes that the deputy is taking her from the jailhouse, across a large, open wood-paneled lobby, and into a massive courtroom. They enter through a set of thick, dark wooden doors and walk slowly between rows of benches filled with folks waiting to be judged. They reach a single circular riser where Famka is guided to stand. The room is eerily quiet as she steps onto the riser before three towering pillars that rise high above her. At the top of each pillar is a single light that splashes a faint purple hue against the high, curved ceiling. The dark chamber weighs heavily on her as if the walls themselves sit in judgment of her.

Four distinct shields spring up, encasing her in a box. The near invisible Trankler's Hold It rises to chin height, which will allow her to hear, but keeps her from leaving.

Panicked, she looks back down the aisle toward the exit doors, but they're closed now. The benches are crammed with ghosts, witches, and what she's pretty sure are two Wigglers. One of them glares at her like she's done something terribly wrong to him. Deep-set, black beady eyes sit above a long nose with spindly whiskers poking out of either side. Neither Wiggler is much larger than a five-year-old child, and both remind Famka of rats. Despite their peculiar facial features, they're dressed in the gaudiest clothing she's ever seen. Bright purple cocked hats lined in white crystals sit on their little heads. Diamond-encrusted purple knee-length jackets cover their small bodies. And despite the crowded courtroom, there are several available seats on either side of the Wigglers.

Like a first performance, Famka feels like she's on display, sitting high above all these magical folks. So many eyes looking up at her leaves her feeling vulnerable. Out of all those in attendance that morning the Wigglers glare at her. She quickly turns away, feeling as if she's eaten some undercooked fish.

"Don't stare at them," says the deputy cautiously. "You'll get the Collywobbles."

"What's that?" she asks, rubbing her face through a wave of nausea. A bead of sweat trickles down her brow even though the room is cool. The back of her Led Zeppelin T-shirt feels wet along her spine.

"Wigglers can make you nauseated if you make eye contact with them for too long," he says. "They take offense when you stare at them for even a moment, so try not to." He floats away and then hovers beside the exit doors with his arms crossed. Famka wipes her face again as a Drolling Dragon suddenly appears beside her followed by a funny sound.

SWISH!

"Famka Meadows," says the ugly little talking statue. His bulbous orange eyes look out of his gray head like those of a porcelain doll. He's dressed in a very tight dark-blue suit. A tiny, dark black tie hangs from his neckline. Unlike the other two Drolling Dragons Famka has seen, this one is fat. If it wasn't for his tucked-in shirt, his belly would spill right out into the open.

"My name is Hewitt. I am a Drolling Dragon."

"I know what a Drolling Dragon is," mutters Famka trying to push the nausea from the Wigglers away.

"Fine then," says Hewitt floating at head height. He places a notepad under one arm, pressing it against his fat little body. A pencil sits above one of his large floppy ears, which are both tied back like a ponytail of sorts. "I assume that you presume innocence? You might as well. Everyone does."

"Of course I do," says Famka turning away from Hewitt. She's frustrated, and words that she doesn't mean leap out of her mouth. "What's the big deal, anyway? I Tuned in the Hallowed Halls."

"Young lady, you presume incorrectly," says Hewitt insulted. "Tuning in the Hallowed Halls is strictly forbidden and for good reason. Without that particular law, the Halls would be off limits to those of us still in need of our lungs. You do know that the Hallowed Halls belongs to the dead? We get to use them only by their grace."

Famka scrunches up her face as she considers what the Drolling Dragon said.

"Can you imagine trying to get here in a car?" adds Hewitt.

Famka looks surprised that the little creature even knows what a car is.

"Yes, I know what a car is. Trains, airplanes, and many other inventions that *your species* dreams up." Hewitt has a particular tone of annoyance and emphasized *your species* as if they were curse words. "Murder is as illegal on the Middling Side of the Graveyard as it is on the Other."

Famka isn't certain if she was the one who hurt the young Sky Builder or not. She runs the events through her head again, and it doesn't make sense to her. How on earth did she manage a Breaking spell? Despite knowing numerous other spells, she only knows one of the nine Wyndomier spells, and that one is a Mending spell. Sure, she can talk with animals, avoid Bernard's protective enchantments surrounding Milly's home, and somehow tear down a supposedly unbreakable barrier, a Trankler's Hold It, but Wyndomier's Nine are far beyond her Tuning abilities.

Momma Nay has always been careful about teaching her

and Ophelia any of them. Even when Famka tried to learn them on her own, she wasn't able to complete a single one. Certainly not a Breaking spell and certainly not by studying the *Gravedigger's Handbook*, which up until meeting Parran, was the only spell book she had. It taught the user only what they were capable of knowing, and apparently, Famka wasn't capable of knowing even one of the three Breaking spells. Maybe she's responsible somehow, but she's certain that only cookies appeared and purely as a distraction. However, if she doesn't act soon, there will be another death. This time, it might be Ophelia, and when it comes to her best friend, the world could catch fire for all Famka cared. She'd let it burn to the ground and dance on the ashes.

"Are you my lawyer?" asks Famka glaring at the stone Drolling Dragon.

"Lawyer?" says Hewitt pausing, at what Famka guesses might be confusion. "Ah right. Representation. We have no need for such things here. The Tribunal can see into your soul. They will know if you are lying or not. Argumentative narratives aren't necessary for presuming innocence or guilt."

"So, they can read my thoughts?" Famka panics at the thought.

"No," Hewitt says, his frustration evident in his tone. "I see that you don't listen, either. The Tribunal can see into your soul. They cannot read one's mind. Even if they could, it would be a violation of laws set down by the Ghostal Holly."

"So, you just throw people in jail without letting them defend themselves?"

"No, we do not just *throw* people in jail," says Hewitt sarcastically. "The Tribunal will know if you are guilty or not. To them, your soul is like an open book. They are infallible." The

Drolling Dragon points to the three tall pillars. "Proving innocence or guilt based on observation is archaic. It is a wonder your species hasn't killed itself off."

"So why are you here then?" Famka can no longer hide her own frustration.

"Mar'Witch Rankor has suggested that you somehow took down a Trankler's Hold It. Chairman Boo was curious to know if this was true, so he sent me. I told him that it was a waste of time as no one has ever been able to do such a thing. The chairman insisted. I personally don't find much of what Mar'Witch Ranker has to say useful. Despite his achievements, he is still human, after all." Hewitt shakes his little stone head. "He also suggested that you are a practitioner of the Fallen Arts. Perhaps you are a witch of the old guard still dreaming of the return of the Fire Thief. That I find easy to believe. Given the Breaking spell you authored in the Hallowed Halls, I'd be certain of it."

"You found me out," Famka declares. Growing angry, she scowls at the little Drolling Dragon, who tilts his ugly stone head. "I'm a witch of the… What was it you called me? The old guard."

"Sarcasm," says Hewitt. "You're not taking this seriously. That is the problem with witches from *your* side of the Graveyard. You foreigners don't understand our ways. No matter." The Drolling Dragon turns his attention to the three tall columns. "The Tribunal of Burning Banshees has arrived. They will know if you're telling the truth or not."

When Famka looks toward the top of the three pillars, three of the strangest creatures are standing where the purple light had been. Red hooded robes cover each of the three judges, who aren't ghosts despite being called banshees. In fact, they look more like very tall stick insects; the kind you sometimes seeing crawling on trees if you look very carefully. Two round green eyes are set in long narrow faces. Their skin, if that's what you could call their exterior, resembles the bark of an old tree. Dark cracks run down their faces between rough gray surfaces. In some ways, Famka sees them as so unreal that she imagines them as cartoon characters that have somehow come to life.

How can something that looks like that actually be alive?

On the other hand, there is something kinda scary about the banshees too.

"You! One Famka Joy Meadows," says the banshee in the middle. His voice is low and gruff as if speaking is perhaps something he doesn't do very often.

And how does he know my middle name?

He points an unusually long finger, which also resembles tree bark. His hand, however, has only three fingers, and his wrist is strangely thin, as if it might snap with the slightest resistance.

"I am Root," says the banshee in the middle. "To my left is Stem, and to my right is Branch."

"Um, hello," says Famka cautiously, looking up at the three banshees.

"You are accused of performing a Breaking spell in the Hallowed Halls, causing the death of Sky Builder Watanabe, as well as a reported practitioner of the Fallen Arts and somehow capable of disabling a Trankler's Hold It."

"I didn't hurt that boy," barks Famka with more confidence than she feels.

"Perhaps," says the banshee picking up a document on the bench before him. "And the Trankler's Hold It?"

"I'm... I'm not sure about that," says Famka. "I only did it once."

"Highly unlikely," mutters Hewitt, floating beside her.

"Only a witch practicing the Fallen Arts could have succeeded in tearing down a Trankler's Hold It," yells a voice from the back of the courtroom. When Famka turns, Thalban Rankor is storming down the aisle toward her, his face hard and his dark eyes unblinking. The doors slam shut behind him, echoing throughout the cavernous room.

"Mar'Witch Rankor," says Root. "You were not summoned to our presence. Leave now."

"Forgive me," says Thalban bowing. Famka notices that his hair sticks to his head even when he's bent over. "I feel that it is my duty to report directly to your highest council what I have witnessed."

"You did that already when you spoke with Constable Cockney. He gave me his report," says the banshee. "If you have something more to add, do so with the constable unless we summon you, which I've already mentioned that we did not."

"This young girl was seen with another witch, who easily outpaced a Guardian of the Ghoul," interjects Thalban. "Most certainly the Fallen Arts."

"Why are you doing this?" asks Famka turning to Thalban, who's now standing between her and Hewitt. She looks down at his clawed hand. "We saved you. When you came to us with your injuries from that... that Cauldron of whatever it was called. Momma Nay was right about you."

"We are aware of Mar'Witch Thalban's use of a Cauldron of Names," Root interjects. "He reported himself immediately to the Ghostal Holly. He has been absolved of any crime."

"But…"

The banshee holds up his strange wooden hand, his three fingers long like thin twigs splaying out at odd angles.

"There are no known instances of a witch Tuning or using the Fallen Arts to remove a Trankler's Hold It once it has been put in place, despite what has been suggested. Perhaps what you saw was an illusion, Mar'Witch Rankor. However, I have no doubt that this young witch is caught up in questionable circumstances. I find you, Famka Joy Meadows, innocent of the Fallen Arts."

Oh, thank goodness. Relieved, Famka says, "Can I go then?"

"No, you may not," bellows the banshee. Famka jumps, as it's louder than she expected. The banshee leans forward and glares down at Famka. "There is still the matter of Tuning in the Hallowed Halls, which resulted in the death of a young Sky Builder."

"I told you, I didn't do that," Famka shoots back angrily. If she doesn't get out of here soon and find Ophelia and Milly, there could be more deaths. Berny showed his willingness to murder when he killed Uncle Guncle. Somehow, no one seems to believe that Berny is who Famka says he is. It's as if everyone is traumatized and refuses to believe in the possibility that Bernard Trankler is still in existence. But maybe she has been too cautious, trying not to tip off anyone about the *Kitab'i'Mordanee*. Perhaps she hasn't provided enough information. Despite not having lived through the Hundred-Year War and not fully understanding its ramifications, it's difficult for her to understand or empathize with those who did. But she doesn't want a war near her home. Up until recently, she was just a young witch, desperately hungry to learn more about Tuning, but now she is caught up in a struggle that she doesn't fully understand. There appear to be so many rules, laws, and personal desires floating around her that she doesn't really comprehend. And in many ways, she simply doesn't care.

"We believe you," says the banshee in his strange low voice.

"The infallible wisdom of the Burning Banshees has once again… Wait, what?" says Hewitt.

"However," says the banshee, "you have not told us the entire truth. Your soul is humming dissonant. To our souls, it is deafening."

"I'm sorry, but I cannot tell you more," says Famka standing up straight.

"If you wish to go free, then you must," says Root.

Famka folds her arms across her chest in an effort to stand her ground.

"We appreciate your strength of character. You will have time to reconsider," says Root. "Deputy, take young Meadows back to her cell."

"No!" she yells. "I have to go free. You don't understand. If I stay here, my friends will die."

"Tribunal," says Thalban. "You must reconsider. This girl is a danger to our society. On my honor as a Sky Builder, she tore down a Trankler's Hold It before my very eyes. I swear it. She is a witch of the old guard. Certainly, you can see that she performed a Fallen Art in the Hallowed Halls."

"One must wonder why you are so interested in her, Mar'Witch Rankor," says Root.

Famka looks at Thalban, and he almost seems to shrink beneath the heavy gaze of the banshee. He shoots her a nasty look again, and she's left wondering why he's trying so hard to discredit her. Does it have something to with Momma Nay? No, it can't be so trivial. No one is that petty. She wonders if it's because he's aware of the *Kitab'i'Mordanee*'s location. What did he say when they saved him? Famka thinks back to that night when he showed up in Momma Nay's shop. He must know about the Bastard Book. That makes sense. He would understand the importance of keeping its whereabouts safe, because he wants it. Of course. And if someone else found it, then he would have trouble keeping it for himself.

The deputy floats up beside her from the back of the courtroom, but the Trankler's Hold It remains in place, so he lingers close by as a reminder that she has no place to escape. Famka glances around the crowded room, feeling trapped.

Weighing her odds, she rolls the dice and takes a chance, figuring she'll dance on the ashes later. "Thalban is looking for the *Kitab'i'Mordanee*," Famka yells out, to a visibly shocked Thalban. He stares back at her with contempt in his dark eyes.

But Famka doesn't stop there. "He knows where it is and wants it for himself. That's why he used the Cauldron of Names. He was trying to figure out who authored the spell that's hiding it, so he could figure out its location."

The folks waiting quietly in the benches grow agitated. What begins as a murmur slowly grows from whispers to arguing. Famka looks at one of the Wigglers again, and he's smiling a wicked smile at her. His nostrils rise up and expose his large front teeth.

Oh Lord. What have I done?

"Bastard Book. Do not say it's true name!" yells a witch dressed in a green poncho. Her hair is covered in a black shawl.

"If she knows where the stolen book is then you can't let

her leave here," yells a ghost from the back row. He rises into the air, shaking violently. For a moment, he flickers like a light bulb trying to hang on to life. "I w-was t-there during the war. I saw what the Fire Thief did. That book!" Then he blinks out of sight like a soapy bubble popping out of existence.

"Do you know of this book's location?" asks Root. He seems to grow even taller as he glares down at her.

"No," Famka lies.

The three banshees leap from their pillars, turning into smoke that swirls down in front of her. Their bodies instantly materialize, but now their red robes are open wide, and Famka realizes they are actually wings. They open out around them like large kites. Red and green translucent netting spreads thinly across them in a membrane, which allows the light from the crylight bugs behind them to come through faintly. Their ashen wood bodies are extremely thin, reminding Famka of twigs. Despite fearing for her safety, she sees something beautiful in their strange appearance. More so than ghosts and other assortment of bizarre creatures, she feels that she's witnessing some kind of other worldly beings.

"That was the first lie you told, Famka Joy Meadows," says Root, who is standing in the center. This whole time, the other two had remained quiet, but now, the one called Branch says in a rough voice, "*Kitab'i'Mordanee*. Where is it?"

"The book must be returned to the Nyre King. It cannot remain here," says Root.

"I don't have it," says Famka. She stumbles back and bumps into the Trankler's Hold It. Losing her balance, she grabs the edge and pulls it free, which sends her tumbling onto the floor. Famka looks stunned at the silky field between her fingers. It hangs loose like a satin blanket.

"Fallen Arts!" yells a witch, who's pointing a finger at Famka. The room breaks into chaos as witches bolt for the exit and ghosts pop out of sight. The banshees slowly step toward Famka, who's still on the floor.

"Take her captive!" barks Hewitt to Thalban.

The master Sky Builder yanks a Wyndomier Wick seemingly from out of nowhere and fires it. Famka instinctively raises her hand, and the Trankler's Hold It protects her from the spell. Looking stunned for a gnat-sized second, Thalban fires another spell, but not before Famka rolls away. She spits into her hand and then wraps the invisible shield around her like a cloak. This time, it doesn't pop but covers her completely. She leaps to her feet surrounded by the blurred flailing arms of the deputy. He tries to grab her again, but his hands pass through her like she's a ghost. She shrugs her shoulders and spins around. Halfway down the aisle, Thalban now stands between her and the exit door, which has been thrust open by the escaping witches. He's crouched and grinning back at her confidently. With the banshees behind her and Thalban blocking the exit, Famka scans the room for more options.

"Tell us the location of the *Kitab'i'Mordanee*," says Root. "And no harm will come to you."

Famka looks over her shoulder at the odd creature and says, "Now *you're* lying."

Time to dance on the ashes.

She bolts right for Thalban, who's shocked when he's thrown back. He flies across the room and lands with a thud between benches. Famka stops for only a moment to see what happened to the Sky Builder. In that second, the exit doors slam shut.

"Try getting through that," says Hewitt grinning.

Behind the floating Drolling Dragon, the banshees transform into three columns of smoke. This time, Famka doesn't hesitate and dashes for the exit, hoping she's right. She bursts through the doors, smashing the thick wood to splinters. Debris explodes and sprays out from her, covering the marble floor in dust. She removes the Ghost Armor from her pocket, pulls it over her head, and whispers, "Invisible."

All color vanishes as everything around her turns black and white. She looks down at her hands, and they're gone, but there is no time to investigate. She slams herself against a wall as a mob of witches dashes by.

"Where did she go?" demands Hewitt floating out into the hallway.

"Fallen witch," yells a witch pointing toward Famka. "She just disappeared right over there."

"Are you sure, Florence?" asks Hewitt. "The only Tuning possible in these chambers is from the Tribunal."

Three columns of dark purple smoke zoom out of the courtroom, past the Drolling Dragon, and toward Famka. She bolts down a hallway, clumsily knocking into a witch as she turns the corner.

"Hey!" yells the witch falling to the ground.

"Sorry," says Famka ducking in between a group of Sky Builders dressed in their typical orange and black ponchos.

"What was that?" says one of them.

Famka ducks into an empty office, holds her breath, and squeezes her eyes tight. It takes only seconds before the banshees find her. Even without looking, she immediately feels them. She peeks out as the three columns of smoke materialize before her. The face of Root is the only one that takes form. His bark-like face remains impassive, as he prods her soul like an unwelcome visitor.

"We are impressed by your skills," says Root. Famka remains quiet. "We have not seen Tuning such as yours in quite a great many years."

"I can't stay here. I have to help my friends," says Famka. "If you believe me to be a danger then you'll have to force me to stay."

"Our Tribunal does not believe you to be of malicious intent, but you have broken a law. You must be accountable. However, we are not without compassion and understanding. Find your friends, do as you must. When your task in complete, return here for your judgment."

And with that, the banshees disappear.

Chapter 35

A Revelation

Famka bolts out of the courthouse and onto the Plaza of Giants. Witches and ghosts crowd the massive park-like grounds. Shops are filled with folks purchasing goods, and clusters of ghosts sit idly, many playing cards in the center of the plaza. After being cooped up in her cell, the warm sunshine feels great against Famka's skin, but the sun appears to be a white dot in a gray sky. Being that she's invisible, she finds it difficult to navigate. First, she can't see her own feet. To her surprise, this slows her down. Secondly, she keeps having to dodge folks as they go about their day. Twice, she fell to the ground, and one time, she nearly flopped right over a park bench. She caught herself on the armrest just before she went butt over barbecue and hit a body part that would really, really hurt.

Frustrated, she decides to try something new. She sidles up beside a lamppost as a barrier. As she stands at the edge of the brick street that encircles the large plaza, Famka whispers the only name that comes to mind, "Make me look like Miss

Turtlebalm."

All of sudden, hands appear where there weren't any before, but they aren't hers. Old palms belonging to Miss Turtlebalm look up at Famka. Lines along lengthy fingers stretch out, and thin wrists rise up into a long-sleeve poncho. Famka dashes up to a shop window to inspect her reflection, and sure enough, it's Miss Turtlebalm looking back at her. Famka smiles, and so does the reflection. She touches the top of her head where her gray hair is pulled into a bun and runs her hand along a wrinkle on her thin face. Silver-rimmed glasses sit at the tip of her pointy nose, and stern blue eyes look back, demanding respect.

Famka is about to leave when a small witch, not much taller than a big dog, tugs on her sleeve. When she looks down, she is surprised to see a strange little man with a mustache shaped in a half circle and wearing large round glasses.

"Lady'Witch Turtlebalm," says the little man squinting his brown eyes up at her. "I found the book you were looking for."

Oh no, Famka thinks. *What do I say? Ophelia is so much better at this.*

"Um, yes," says Famka uncomfortably. "I'm sorry, but I'm really in quite a hurry. You'll have to excuse me."

She begins to walk away when the little man says, "But you insisted that I alert you the moment I found the book. And it was no simple thing."

"I did?"

"Yes!" says the little man loudly. "You did."

"Um, well. Do you have it then?" Her voice rises higher than normal. *I sound like an idiot,* she thinks.

"As a matter of fact, I do," says the little man. He reaches deep into a pocket, his arm going much farther than seems possible, before withdrawing a rather large tome from a very small opening in his poncho.

"Here you are," he says, handing her the book.

"Oh!" She takes the weighty book in her hands. The rough cover smells like a used bookstore; a smell she is not fond of.

"You might be right, by the way," says the little man just as he's about to turn and leave.

Famka looks at him with no idea what he's about to say. She's just trying her best to hold it together because her insides are bouncing like excited children on a trampoline. *It's so weird that he doesn't realize I'm not actually Miss Turtlebalm. Oh, I hope he doesn't figure it out.*

"Trankler may have been just as responsible for the atrocities during the war as the Fire Thief was. I found several records in the deepest part of the Ghostal Holly's archives that suggest as much. Let me tell you, they weren't keen on me poking around in their restricted section, but an old friend owed me a favor. He manages one of the more obscure sections and he was able to get me inside for a few hours. You can thank me with a case of Minor's Malt."

"Um, that's sorta crazy," says Famka.

"Yes, crazy," says the little man with an odd look.

Why's he's looking at me that way? Oh, good grief, Miss Turtlebalm wouldn't talk that way.

"That's, um," Famka fumbles, "a bit over the top. Wouldn't you say?"

"No more so than suggesting that Bernard Trankler has been hiding out for the last several hundred years on that remote island you chose to live on," says the little man. "But it turns out that you were right about part of it, anyway."

"Which is?" says Famka.

"That island was, in fact, his home before the war. At least for a time. He may have come over from Europe on one of the first ships to America and wrecked on the shores. There is some evidence to suggest it." The little man steps closer and then looks around cautiously before adding in a quiet voice. "As far as Trankler having the Bastard Book after the fall of the Fire Thief, well, that's a bit over the top, even for you, Mocha."

Mocha? Oh, that must be Miss Turtlebalm's first name.

"I wouldn't suggest it aloud again. If word gets out that it's even a slight possibility, your little home will be ravaged. Don't forget the last time rumors like that crept up."

"Rumors?" says Famka. "What do you mean?"

"Mocha, where is your head?" says the little man. "I'm talking about the girl, Famka. Poor, poor dear." He shakes his head. "Losing her parents like that. It's a travesty, and all over a rumor. Had you not found her, Nyre King knows what would have happened."

Famka reaches out and steadies herself against the shop window.

"Mocha, Mocha," says the little man. "Are you all right? I say. You look like you've seen a ghost."

"Um, yes," says Famka doing her best to focus on the little fellow. She looks at his bushy mustache as a distraction, an anchor. "A um... long day at the Ghostal Holly."

"I can't imagine. How you tolerate that government nonsense is beyond me," he says. "Well, good day then. I look forward to your next batch of odd inquiries. As usual, you are nothing if not interesting. And don't forget my case of Minor's Malt."

The little man turns and walks away. Within seconds, he disappears into the crowd.

Famka lets out a long breath and nearly falls backward. She grabs hold of the windowsill, trying her best to keep track of everything she's just learned.

If only Ophelia was here. She would know how to put these puzzle pieces in order. If nothing else, she would comfort me. Miss Turtlebalm knew my real parents. I need my best friend.

"Why, Lady'Witch Turtlebalm," says a ghost suddenly floating before Famka.

Good grief how popular can this old lady be?

Frustrated, Famka rushes away from the ghost, hoping to lose him in a crowd, but he floats right up beside her and says, "I was wondering could you hel…"

"I'm not Miss Turtlebalm," barks Famka loudly.

"Well you certainly look like her."

"Well, I'm not. Invisible!" With that, Famka disappears, leaving the ghost stunned as she runs toward the Barrow of Shady Grove to save her friends.

Chapter 36

A Final Conflict

MILLY SITS, HER back against a stone wall, sulking. Beside her, Ophelia sits quietly, with only the sound of her steady breathing to indicate that she is even there. The crypt is dark, and despite having been there for what feels like forever, it's still difficult to see. Stale air lingers in the room, reminding Milly of death. More than once, spiders have crawled on her, leaving her less than happy.

She is irritated that Berny continues to treat her so poorly. Her little brain can't work out exactly why he has turned his back on her. To Milly this little escapade has all been a game. She is happy to have left Wink, but now she stinks and wants a bath, so she wants to go home. She doesn't believe that Berny is really going to hurt Famka, or Ophelia, and certainly not her. Milly had studied hard with Berny, after all. She had always done everything he had asked, even when it was boring, which was often.

"Come on, Berny," says Milly in her complaining tone. She leans forward, so that she might catch glimpse of him in the adjoining room. "Berny…"

He remains silent, which irritates her to no end, so she leaps up, bonking her head on the low ceiling. Dang it! Carefully she makes her way to the next room, running her hands along the stone wall so that she doesn't trip, and leaves Ophelia alone. Once in the other room, Milly stands before Berny as he pores over Parran, who's now back in his book form and resting in Berny's lap. He's floating cross-legged as he continues to read page after page of new spells. He has obsessed over Parran since regaining the spell book.

"Millicent, you are the worst possible witch I have ever known," he says without looking up from the book.

"Don't call me that. You know I don't like it," says Milly. "Anyway, I helped you. See, your book works again. It's good that you came back."

"No. Parran returned to life because of Famka," says Berny. "All you did was manage to fumble nearly every spell I taught you. That you were able to call forth bugs and toads from the swamp to ruin your parents party is… well, I don't understand it."

"So why are you keeping us here?" asks Milly. "I want to go home."

"You may go when I have Famka," says Berny. "In fact, we will all go home. I must get to work on retrieving the *Kitab'i'Mordanee*. Now shut your mouth. Already the spells in this Growgan are fading. If Famka doesn't return soon, Parran will be of little use. I would like learn a bit more before they are all gone."

"Fiiiine, but you're not very nice, Berny," says Milly. "I thought we were friends."

"You know what? You're right. We are friends," says Berny

with a nasty grin. His yellow teeth spread out between his thin lips, making Milly uncomfortable. "And friends share."

"Oh great," says Milly. "Are you going to teach me a new spell now? Finally."

"Teach?" says Berny with his wicked grin. "No, no. We're done with that. But I will share with you something new that I have recently learned. It's a spell called a Handmaid's Mind. Would you like to venture a guess at what it does?" He drums his fingers across the book and squints at Milly, narrowing his eyes to snake-like slits.

"Um, maybe not," says Milly feeling apprehensive.

"It renders the victim speechless, compliant and best of all speechless. Oh, did I mention that already? It has an unusual way of keeping you quiet. You see, seconds after I've authored the spell, your mouth will close up and your lips will disappear, leaving no trace that they were ever there."

"I don't think I would like that very much," says Milly. She yanks the book out of his hands, but Berny doesn't seem bothered. Instead, he says with a wicked grin, "It's your lucky day. It would seem that Famka has finally arrived."

"Fine. Can we go now?" asks Milly as she walks back into the first room where Ophelia is stills seated quietly on the floor. "Come, Ophelia, we're going to leave now," says Milly.

Ophelia leaps to her feet, snatches the book from Milly, and throws it at the crypt wall, which explodes into a pile of rubble. Fresh air spills into the room as Ophelia jumps through the hole and out into the dark graveyard. Out of the debris, Parran transforms back into his man form and runs behind Ophelia as Famka comes up beside them. For a moment, Milly is stunned. She didn't expect Ophelia to do anything, because Ophelia had been silent for hours. Milly runs toward the exit, but stumbles and crashes to the crypt floor, scraping her bare legs against the stone.

"Stay there!" yells Berny, who disappears after Famka, Ophelia, and Parran.

Chapter 37

It Was the Butler's Fault

Famka, Ophelia, and Parran race down the hill along a brick pathway at supernatural speed. With Parran's aid, they move unusually fast. To anyone watching, the three refugees resemble a blur followed by a trail of dust and leaves. Glowing lampposts, tall trees, and gravestones fall behind them in an instant. It takes only a moment before they come to a stop beside a row of bushes, beyond which is a flat area of overgrown grass about the size of a small park. Tall bushes surround the area like prison guards, and the moon peeks between tall trees in the distance. They step through an opening in the hedgerow and walk between barely visible gravestones. Many look to have been forgotten and have faded over time. More than once, Famka nearly trips over one. Finally, Parran stops at a nearly invisible stone.

"Is this it?" asks Famka, her toe throbbing.

"Aye, Momma," says Parran looking down.

Weeds and vines surround the tiny gravestone. Parran bends down and brushes away grime and overgrowth until a name appears…

Francis Papillon
I missed you even before you were gone.
1658-1682

"Parran, you were married?" asks Ophelia.

"Naw," says Parran. His paper eyes frown at the edges as he looks at the name. "Me baby girl."

"Oh… I'm so sorry, Parran," says Famka.

"Me too, Momma," says the paper man. "Come on now. No time for dis sadness." Parran moves his hand in concentric circles over the gravestone whispering, "Francis, my Francis, I bless you with kisses. I bless you with kisses, my beautiful princess."

The grass surrounding the stone peels away like carpet curling itself into a roll. The stone unseats itself and walks to Parran's feet like a puppy. Chunks of earth begin leaping into a pile until the wide hole exposes a full-sized coffin.

"Parran, is there a body in there?" asks Ophelia pointing down. Her dark brown face scrunches up.

"Naw," he says then leaps onto the moist ground beside the coffin. "I never found me baby's body." He looks up at the two witches. "Dis grave was a place for me tears."

"We need to hurry," says Famka turning back into the darkness between the bushes. "Berny will find us soon."

"What about Milly?" asks Ophelia. "We can't leave her with him."

"Don't worry, Ophi. He won't hurt her." Famka climbs down into the hole.

Once the three of them are in the hole, Ophelia says,

"What's that?" She points to the outline of a silver shimmering hand that is clamped down around the lock of the coffin.

"Ho ho," says Parran. "Someone be trying to take me stash."

Famka immediately recognizes the hand. It belongs to Thalban Rankor.

"Dey be using a Cauldron of Names to find me goods."

"How do we get rid of it?" asks Ophelia.

"Like this," says Famka. She kicks it several times, and each time with satisfaction.

A painful howl cries out as the hand disappears.

"How'd you do that?" asks Ophelia.

"Remember back home when I was trying to Devil Dig in the ocean?"

"Yeah," says Ophelia stretching the word out with worry.

"Well, I wasn't Devil Digging. Despite what you might think. I was trying to wrap a Trankler's Hold It around me, and I finally figured it out," says Famka with a smile.

"Are you saying that there's one around you now?" she asks.

"You got it."

Parran opens the coffin and retrieves a moldy leather bag. He unties a leather strap, and dozens of Tuning Tensils spill out, including Wyndomier Wicks, two shimmering cloths, each with a Gris Gris sewn into it, a clay pot filled with something labeled Earthquake Glue, and two round black clothes.

"The God Wand," says Parran now holding a stick the size of a policeman's baton. It's black and weathered with scars along the sides. It's nothing special.

"What is all this stuff?" asks Ophelia.

"A gold mine," says Berny above them.

Famka spins around, and Berny floats, arms crossed, with a satisfied grin. "You've out done yourself, Parran. You stole the God Wand. Time to go, my little witches," says Berny. "Bring the bag would you, and don't forget the God Wand!"

"Go where?" asks Ophelia.

"Why home, of course," says Berny.

"Why did you have to kill Uncle Guncle?" demands Famka.

"Uncle Guncle is dead," mutters Ophelia sadly.

"You wouldn't listen. I asked you more than once, and politely, I might add," says Berny. "You only have yourself to blame."

"You're a monster," says Ophelia.

"Perhaps," says Berny. "Come now. We must be going."

The three of them drag the bag out of the hole and climb out. The gravesite restores itself, leaving no trace that it was unearthed only moments ago.

"I think that's enough." Famka drops the bag and lets the contents spill out. "We aren't going anywhere with you."

"Don't make me hurt another of your loved ones," says Berny, his eyes darting to Ophelia. Ophelia pulls Famka back as Berny floats toward them. "I could break her. Just like I broke that old man from the dump you live in."

"I've wondered about something," says Famka standing firm.

"Famka, what are you doing?" whispers Ophelia tapping Famka's side.

"It's all right, Ophi," says Famka clutching her best friend by the wrist. "He can't hurt us. He never could."

Berny's body explodes in size. He resembles a giant kite

again, stretched thin across a bony frame. His giant pockmarked nose comes within inches of Famka's, and he growls at her.

"I could tear you to pieces. Shred your body into tiny bits and sprinkle your remains over your precious Sky Builders' Guild."

"Then do it," says Famka. "I dare you."

Berny howls into the night. His voice reverberates through Famka like an earthquake, but she doesn't move. Ophelia winces, but Famka clamps down on her wrist to keep her from falling. Berny's body grows even larger, and his ribs push against his shirt. The pores in his face resemble black saucers. "This is your last…"

SMACK!

Famka punches Berny square in the nose.

He immediately deflates to his normal size and cradles his face. When Famka looks at her hand it's covered in mud.

"What's wrong, Berny?" asks Famka. "Did that hurt a little?"

"How did you do that?" he asks, his voice muffled behind his hands.

"I'm using your own spell against you. With a few modifications of course. You see, I figured out how to wrap a Trankler's Hold It around me. It was an accident the first time, and I wasn't sure I could do the same for Ophelia and Parran, but it's there," Famka lies. She is not able to wrap the field around her friends, but hopes that Berny doesn't realize it. "Go ahead and try to attack them. See where it gets you."

"Stop! Stop!" yells Milly. She runs toward them from out of the darkness.

"You can't hurt them, Berny." Milly stops several feet

away, rubbing her nose. She looks at Berny, pleading. "Please. They're my friends."

Berny glares at Milly with disgust but blinks out of sight for a moment. When he returns, his yellow teeth shine out from between his thin lips like little worms. His eyes have turned completely black, but he now appears faded like a giant pencil eraser just ran over him.

"Then I'll attack Milly," he threatens. He turns toward her, and she steps back. Her blue eyes widening in her tan face.

"I don't think so," says Famka. "You see, I wasn't certain at first, but now I am. You have no power. You can't Tune. Maybe you never could. Although I admit the talent you displayed in the painting at Milly's seemed dangerous." Famka takes a step toward him. "You might even be able to wield a Wyndomier Wick with some effect, but I doubt it. You see, I can feel the Trankler's Hold It around me. I can feel the personality that went into authoring it, and it feels nothing like yours. Whoever wrote the original spell was powerful, intelligent, and detached. You on the other hand are a liar and a manipulator. And you care too much. You are weak and needy. You can only intimidate through threats."

"How dare you!" he barks at Famka.

"I dare," she says, taking another step toward him. "I won't run, so I dare. I won't be intimidated by you anymore, so I dare. I'm not afraid of you, so I dare."

"Oh, Famka," says Milly. "I dare, because you weren't smart enough to figure out everything."

"Milly!" says Ophelia. "What are you doing?"

When Famka turns, Milly is holding the God Wand, it's glowing orange in her thick hand, and Berny is gone. The only thing remaining is a pile of grass and mud where Berny had been floating just a moment ago. Blades of grass fly through the air, with several landing in Famka's mouth.

"She's doing what she's been doing all along," says Famka. "She's been lying to us from the first day we met her."

"How did you figure me out?" asks Milly.

"Almost from the beginning," says Famka. "The first was the swamp when you made a stick figure out of grass stand up on its own. Then your butler gave you away. You used a Memoroff on him. For a witch who claims to be so ignorant, that is a very powerful spell. And you knew exactly what you were doing when you dumped the entire contents of the Memoroff on your father. The second time was when we fled the Horseshoe. Ophi's hands were covered in mud after pinning Berny to the ground. And then again in Wink outside of Turtleburgers. Both times, Berny smelled like earth. No ghost stinks."

"Famka, are you certain?" says Ophelia skeptically.

"I'm absolutely sure," she answers. "Remember when we were first running from Berny? We ran right into the butler on our way out of Milly's house. He was angry with Milly, but then out of nowhere, he didn't seem to care that we tore up one of her father's prized painting. And that wasn't the only thing, either. Did you ever wonder why we rarely saw Milly and Berny together? It's a lot of work keeping a golem moving isn't, Milly?"

"It's not as difficult as you think, but yes, it's hard," says Milly.

"And not once did Berny actually hurt us," says Famka.

"I'm not sure I understand…" says Ophelia.

"Milly and Berny are one and the same," Famka explains to Ophelia, then turns to face Milly. "Or at least since we've known you. I assume the real Berny must have taught you the Fallen Arts. But all this time, your Berny was nothing more than a golem made of twigs, dirt, and of course, Tuning." Famka glares at Milly. "You must have known Berny quite well at one point. Some of the things your golem said made me question my own instincts, but you made a few too many mistakes."

"Very good, Famka. You figured it all out, after all," says Milly pausing. "You're right. I knew Berny very well. He spent years teaching me the Fallen Arts. That is until your friend Miss Turtlebalm came around. Berny didn't want the Ghostal Holly finding him. He is a war criminal after all. But then he left me, just like my parents. Believe it or not, I really liked spending time with you and Ophelia. You are both great witches. Especially you, Famka. But we must be going. I still need your help to get the *Kitab'i'Mordanee* out of its prison in the gazebo. And I'll be taking these."

Milly quickly rifles through the bag, withdraws one of the two black cloths, and throws it. It sticks in the air as if it is against a solid wall.

"A Wyndom Window," says Milly. "Very handy."

She closes the bag, drags it toward the window, and says, "Home."

The cloth slowly expands until it is large enough for a person to walk into. A moment later, the Hallowed Halls appear in the surface. A clay tunnel opens to a huge cavern, which is filled with witches and ghosts zipping by.

"You can't take everything…" says Famka.

"You're right," says Milly. "I'll be sure to send the empty bag to the Horseshoe. Come on, Famka. Time to go home."

"The boy died," Famka blurts out.

"What are you talking about?"

"The one you hit with a spell in the Hallowed Halls when we were traveling here."

Milly shrugs her shoulders.

"So, it was you?"

"Yes," says Milly. "I Tuned in the Hallowed Halls, killed some idiot Sky Builder, and now I'm going to get away with it."

Famka is instantly furious. How can Milly be so callous? A boy died. A boy whose entire life was in front of him. Anger explodes in her and bursts like a popping tire. Her gut cramps as she points her splayed fingers at Milly. Grass, vines, and dirt move beneath Milly's feet, creating a hole that she sinks into. Two vines climb up her ankles and wrap themselves around her legs tightly until Milly screams out.

"Back off, Famka!" threatens Milly. She points the God Wand, and it begins to glow more brightly in her hand. It resembled a policeman's baton before, but now, it looks more like an angry torch.

"You can't hurt me," says Famka. "I'm protected by a Trankler's Hold It."

"I believe you, but I don't believe that you are able to put one around your friends," says Milly, and she fires a blast.

Chapter 38

A Drolling Dragon to the Rescue

OPHELIA DIVES OUT of the way before Milly can fire another spell. And an ugly stone statue appears between Parran and the next blast from Milly.

The spell smashes the little Drolling Dragon in the chest, and he falls to the ground unconscious, his little orange eyes rolled up in his head.

"Hellman!" yells Parran as he leaps to the little creature and picks him up. His tiny cowboy hat falls from his head revealing his long floppy ears.

"That was the wrong thing to do," says Heiki, who just popped out of nowhere followed by a funny sound.

SWISH!

Heiki snaps her tiny fingers, and the God Wand flies from Milly's hand. It lands in the grass far out of sight. Across the clearing, Miss Turtlebalm walks briskly out of the dark, a glowing Wyndomier Wick in her long thin hand. She fires a spell at Milly's legs, the vines slip away, and she falls on her butt.

"Bernard Trankler," barks Miss Turtlebalm still pointing her Wick at Milly. "Is he here?"

"N– no," says Milly suddenly looking very scared.

Miss Turtlebalm offers her a hand and helps her stand up.

"What are you doing?" asks Famka.

Miss Turtlebalm does the most unexpected thing… She bonks Milly right over the head with the end of her Wick. Milly's eyes roll up, and for a moment, it looks as if she might faint, but Miss Turtlebalm catches her around the shoulders before she falls then releases her, but instead of falling, Milly stands perfectly rigid.

"Milly, when did you last see Bernard Trankler?" asks Miss Turtlebalm.

"Three months ago," she answers.

"Do you know where he is now?"

"No," says Milly.

"You can't trust her," says Famka. "She's a liar."

"She is under a temporary Speaker spell," says Miss Turtlebalm. "It becomes painful to lie. The more she lies, the worse it hurts."

"Why did you come to the Horseshoe, Milly?" asks Ophelia.

"I was alone. I wanted friends that were like me," she says. "Berny was my only friend, then he left. Just like my mom and dad. Everybody leaves me."

"You could have just said that," says Ophelia.

Famka looks at the blonde girl with a mixture of pity and anger. Mostly, she is disturbed. Milly murdered Uncle Guncle and a young Sky Builder, or at the very least, she is responsible for his falling in the Hallowed Halls because of her spell.

"Milly, I'm going to send you to Saint Jude's Blessing."

Noticing the confusion on her face, Miss Turtlebalm adds, "Saint Jude's is a hospital for witches. I believe that you need tending to. You are a victim of the Fallen Arts."

Lady'Witch Turtlebalm bonks Milly over the head again, and Milly unfreezes.

"Um, all right," says Milly rubbing her eyes.

"Girls, come here please," says Miss Turtlebalm to Famka and Ophelia. "Help Millicent toward the Wyndom Window."

The last thing Famka wants to do is help Milly, but reluctantly she and Ophelia steady Milly as Miss Turtlebalm walks to the Wyndom Window still hanging in the air and says loudly, "Saint Jude's Blessing." Suddenly a long hallway appears in the surface. Marble floors run the length of the hall ending at a dark wooden counter where two nurses sit.

Looking up, one of the two nurses asks, "Lady'Witch Turtlebalm. What can we do for you?"

"This young witch is Millicent Rien. She was misguided by Bernard Trankler and has been actively authoring spells in the Fallen Arts," says Miss Turtlebalm.

"Oh dear," says the nurse. "Send her right away."

"Go on now," says Miss Turtlebalm, gently ushering Milly into the Wyndom Window.

Once inside, the nurses assist Milly around a corner and out of sight. A second later, the window goes blank, returning to its normal shimmering black surface.

"I don't understand something, Miss Turtlebalm," says Famka "Milly was behind everything. The only thing that Berny did was try to scare us."

"And it worked," adds Ophelia.

"Was Berny ever real?"

"Bernard Trankler is very real," says Miss Turtlebalm.

"From what I can determine, he spent quite a bit of time with Milly throughout her childhood. He taught her a considerable amount about the Fallen Arts. I believe the Berny you knew was Milly authoring a spell that created the golem."

"So where is he?" asks Ophelia.

"I do not know," says Miss Turtlebalm. "For centuries, he has evaded capture. I suspect he has gone far away for now. I do wonder what made him leave."

"Milly said that Berny thought she was bad at Tuning," says Famka. "That she was no longer useful to him."

"It is too early in her Knack to know if that is true. Some witches come into their abilities much later. I did catch wind of Tuning coming from her home a few years ago. I went out there on several occasions but had no idea Bernard Trankler was teaching her. If he was there, then it is possible that my presence eventually scared him off."

"What about the boy, Miss Turtlebalm?" asks Famka. "The one who died?"

"That is very unfortunate," she says. "As an under-age witch, Milly cannot be held accountable."

"But Milly authored the spell that killed him," argues Famka.

"Yes, that is true, but Milly never attended the Sky Builders' Guild, so she has no official training. The law does not permit an untrained and underage witch from being held accountable for spells that could have been authored by accident. It is perhaps a flaw in the legal system upheld by the Ghostal Holly, but it has also saved many young witches from being imprisoned in the Sea of Chall."

"Doesn't seem fair," says Famka sadly.

"Lady'Witch Turtlebalm," Heiki calls out. "Would you

knock some sense into this fool husband of mine."

Miss Turtlebalm tenderly places a hand on Famka's shoulder before walking toward Heiki. She bends down beside the little Drolling Dragon, who is holding one of Hellman's tiny hands. Beside them, Parran sits cross-legged.

"Why do a foolhardy thing like that, Hellman?" asks Heiki.

"Parran is my best friend," says Hellman as he rubs his chest. "I wouldn't be here if it wasn't for him. He saved me more than once. I owed him."

"I thought I was your best friend," says Heiki, her voice going a little higher than usual.

"You're both my best friends," says Hellman taking both of her tiny hands in his.

"Hm," she grumbles, dissatisfied.

"How are you feeling, Hellman?" asks Miss Turtlebalm.

"Not bad considering I was hit with a Bility Burglar. That's one heck of a spell," says the little Drolling Dragon. He sits up and waddles over to his cowboy hat and places it back on his tiny head. "If I wasn't as old as I am, I might be lying here paralyzed for some time."

"Well, I'm glad that you're so old then," says Miss Turtlebalm in a rare joke.

"Let's go home, Hellman," says Heiki. She takes him by the hand, and they float up into the air.

"What about Parran?" asks Hellman.

"I guess he can visit some time," says Heiki, "but none of your shenanigans, you creole weeny. We have a child now."

"Me thanks to ya, Heiki," says Parran with a little bow.

"Hm," she grumbles again.

"How is Heaven?" asks Ophelia.

"Oh, she is my greatest blessing," says Heiki.

"I thought I was your greatest blessing," says Hellman.

"You both are, old dragon," says Heiki. "Famka, Ophelia, you are both welcome in our home anytime. Lady'Witch Turtlebalm, might you bring us one of your pecan pies on your next visit?"

"I'd be happy to," she says standing.

"For now," says Heiki, then she and Hellman disappear, followed by a funny sound.

SWISH!

"For now," whispers Miss Turtlebalm.

A second later, Hellman reappears. He flies to Parran and hugs the paper man around the neck.

"Missed ya too, old friend," says Parran.

SWISH! Hellman is gone.

"What ya be doing with me stash?" asks Parran looking to Miss Turtlebalm.

"Considering you and Hellman stole these items from the Fire Thief and he stole them from the Ghostal Holly, then I must return them to the Ghostal Holly," says Miss Turtlebalm stepping up to the Wyndom Window. "Ghostal Holly, Cabish building."

The Hallowed Halls reappear in the surface of the Wyndom Window. A clay tunnel runs away from her toward an opening into a massive cavern.

"Would ya be leaving me with a piece or two?" asks Parran.

"I do not think that would be wise," says Miss Turtlebalm. With a flick of her Wyndomier Wick, the bag lifts into the air, whisks into the Window, and is gone.

Before stepping into the Wyndom Window, Miss Turtlebalm says to Famka and Ophelia, "Why don't you two stay and explore the Barrow. I've always enjoyed Shady Grove this time of year. I think you'll find it to be a special place." At the last second, she adds, "You might even find something special here."

Chapter 39

The Fire Thief: Skeletons
(Long before you were born)

But the Fire Thief was coming. The boy knew it. He could feel it like worms crawling through him, piercing his veins.

The boy with his inquisitive green eyes and thick brown hair said, "We can't stop, Mum. He's coming. Run!" The boy looked over his mother's shoulder and could feel the Fire Thief's brutal intent.

The last Dragon and his dead mother flew across oceans, and they flew across seas. They reached other countries, other lands, and kept running through forests and trees. They were a bright, fast, moving light. Those who might have seen them were left with a good story and nothing else, because no one would ever know that a dead mother was trying to keep her living child alive and safe. They only knew that a bright blue light came flying by them at an unusual speed, flying in a way that was not possible, as they sat safely in their own lives, protected in the knowledge that reality was something you could touch and see.

It is true, however, that the Fire Thief knew when they had left England and reappeared in the Americas. The Fire Thief knew, because like any good killer, the Fire Thief would always know what needed to be known. He knew that he would pursue them even to the ends of the earth or beyond, if needed. For the Fire Thief must have what the Fire Thief must have.

And today, he must have the boy with inquisitive green eyes.

The Hundred-Year War was nearly over. The Ghostal Holly and their champion Wyndomier would fall once the last Dragon was slain. Already, the Skeletons had fallen, blamed for something they weren't responsible for.

Their skin turning blue, spirits broken.

"Sometimes, destroying a race is so much more fun than killing them."

The Fire Thief would relish in watching the Skeletons brought to the lowest and most base rung in society. They would suffer for betraying the Struggle. They will remember every day what they did to bring the Fire Thief's wrath upon them.

When he was done with this final task of killing the last Dragon—a very delicious task, indeed—he would have to deal with Berny. The little man thought too much of himself. He had been handy, yes. The Fire Thief could not deny it. Berny had a fluid morality, which allowed the little man to create spells that were quite effective. The Trankler's Hold It alone had imprisoned thousands of Drolling Dragons, witches, members of the Ghostal Holly, and of course, those meddling Sky Builders. The Fire Thief had enjoyed watching them each die as the field slowly crushed each one.

Then there was the matter of Parran Papillon's betrayal. The creole pirate had been helpful in the Struggle's efforts, but something had recently changed with his loyalties. His deliveries had become sporadic before ceasing altogether and finally stealing the very Wyndomier Wicks that he had delivered. If that very action alone didn't spell out Parran's true nature nothing else would.

No matter. What's another dead witch?

Perhaps he would take the blade to each of the betrayers, because nothing was like the blade.

For now, however, he was so close to the very last Dragon. Oh, so very close, indeed. So many centuries of waiting and killing at long last will come to an end. The last Dragon, an English boy with the vivid green eyes, a once happy boy belonging to a disgustingly happy family will die. The boy with the ironic name. The Fire Thief wasn't devoid of humor, so the irony wasn't lost on him. He found it ironic that such a happy family would have, well a macabre name.

Marshall Macabre.

One stab, two stabs, three stabs, four.

The rhythm always drumming in his wicked head. His very wicked head.

Chapter 40

Back Home

THE TWO WITCHES sit in rusty metal chairs on Famka's porch in the Horseshoe. Floating above the Gulf, the sun sets behind a mildly cloudy day. Thickness still hangs in the air even as chitter bugs come out for the night. They buzz loudly as they zip through the air. Parran rests quietly in his book form on a worn wooden crab crate beside Famka.

"Maybe we'll get into the Sky Builders' Guild next year," says Ophelia plucking her bushy hair with a pick.

"Yeah, maybe," says Famka shrugging her shoulders. Her long brown hair hangs over the back of her chair, which squeaks rhythmically when she rocks back and forth. "I guess it doesn't matter now."

"I hope that we do, anyway," says Ophelia.

"Did you understand half of what Lady'Witch Turtlebalm taught us today?" asks Famka.

"Nope. Maybe the first quarter of the first half," says Ophelia. "We can ask Momma Nay to help us when she gets home."

"Shouldn't she be back by now?"

"Yeah, it's getting late in the season," says Ophelia. "But you remember two years ago? She was on the Other Side of the Graveyard all the way into November. She even missed Day of the Dead."

"She's not far from missing it again," says Famka "Maybe Parran will help us then."

"I likes me pages the way they is," says Parran, his book cover moving like a mouth.

"Sounds like Parran is afraid of Lady'Witch Turtlebalm," teases Ophelia. "Big scaredy cat."

"Leave him be, Ophi," says Famka.

"Oh, come on, Parran," says Ophelia. "Just explain how to use Kinderhook."

"Naw," he says. "And ya bess keep that there God Wand out of sight until you learn something more complicated than a Kinderhook spell."

"Why would I want to know how to do that spell?" asks Famka. "The only thing it's good for is making grownups act like kids."

"Perfect for you," teases Ophelia.

Famka looks at the Wyndomier Wick sitting on the crate beside Parran. It's old, worn out, and in such poor shape that it's difficult to believe it's the original Wick created by Wyndomier himself.

"Lady'Witch Turtlebalm did ya blessing by lettin' ya keep it," says Parran.

"Yeah." Famka reaches over and picks it up. It's rough in her hands and feels to be of a personality so intense that it borders on foreign. She thinks back to that night in the Barrow of Shady Grove when she first saw it. Some of the events still don't make sense to her. Even though Milly is at Saint Jude's for treatment, poisoned from working the Fallen Arts, Famka can't help but not trust how that night transpired.

"You think Milly will be home soon?" Famka asks Ophelia, who's now standing.

"Don't know." Ophelia leans against a porch post. "It's going to be bad for her when she gets here."

"I can't believe the news about her dad," says Famka. "His mind is completely gone."

"You think she'll have to move?" asks Ophelia. "If he can't be a lawyer anymore, then they'll go broke. I'm not sure her momma has money enough to keep that giant house going."

"Probably."

"That's sad."

"You really think Milly was Berny all along?"

"It's hard to believe isn't it?" Ophelia shakes her head.

"Well, there's something I keep wondering."

Ophelia raises her eyebrows annoyed.

"This will be the last time. I won't bring it up again," says Famka. "Now, listen. When Heiki left us at Turtleburgers to go find Miss Turtlebalm, she said that someone stalled her. How on earth could Milly have done that if she was with us in the soda shop?"

"Girls. Girls," yells Mrs. Billbray from her trailer next door. She's hanging out of her kitchen window like a gawking bird, as usual.

"Oh, thank goodness," mutters Ophelia. "Hi, Mrs. Billbray."

"My mister's feet are aching again. You think you can run a pair of socks out to Momma Nay for me?" asks the old woman.

Famka rolls her eyes at Ophelia then says, "She's not back

yet, but I think Ophi and I can figure something out for you."

"That would be rightly kind of you," says Mrs. Billbray. "I've got some leftover pot pie. Make sure you girls stop by before it gets cold."

"Thank you," says Ophelia just as the old woman disappears back inside. "That old bird is always in a hurry."

"You know what else I don't understand?" Famka watches Uncle Guncle limp toward them from across the Horseshoe. The truck in the Barrow had been a trick. Despite losing his pickup, Uncle Guncle is safe. But something still bothers her about that night in the Barrow.

"Oh, come on, Famka," says Ophelia annoyed. "Enough already."

"No, seriously," argues Famka. "Listen."

"Fine," says Ophelia.

"If Milly isn't very good at Tuning like Berny... I mean if she was such a bad witch, then how did she manage to get Uncle Guncle's truck all the way through the Hallowed Halls and into the Barrow of Shady Grove?"

"I don't know," she says kicking a rock off the porch. "And you know what? I don't care. We're home and we're safe. We may not be in the Sky Builders' Guild, but we have a great mentor in Lady'Witch Turtlebalm. Oh, and let me also point out that the Tribunal of Burning Banshees let you off with a slap on the hand."

"Still... an entire truck. We can barely lift a stone," says Famka. "Even after weeks of lessons."

"Famka, I have no idea. Can we just enjoy what's left of today without over-thinking everything? Come on, let's get Uncle Guncle and go enjoy some of Mrs. Billbray's pot pie. I'm sure it's delicious, even if it's leftovers."

"Fine, but something still ain't right," says Famka standing up. She quickly stashes Parran and the God Wand in her trailer before running after Ophelia. "I can't wait to see Heaven tomorrow."

"Me too," says Ophelia. "That'll be fun."

Famka smiles at her best friend, and for a moment, she feels good being home. Things aren't what she expected, but for the most part, they're not so bad, either. However, there's still a nagging feeling that something isn't quite right, but for now, she'll fill her belly full of pot pie and do as her best friend suggests. Enjoy the rest of the day.

In a small town in Texas, live three little witches: one is a magical, shining diamond, the second is an innocent babe full of life, and the last is now a seasoned murderer.

Epilogue
Goodbye Famka

I LOOK DOWN at my notes, which are hastily scribbled in pencil on a notebook. Despite the Composers clicking away on the invisible keyboard over my shoulder, I always write my own version. I've filled another notebook entirely, and fortunately, Zinnia brings me several more when she returns from visiting her parents on the Middling Side of the Graveyard.

"She killed Ophelia," says Famka from out of nowhere. Her revelation is startling, and I sit up straighter. After her story, I did not expect it, but there has been a hint all along.

"Who did?" I ask, suspecting what she will say but wanting her to say the name anyway.

"Milly," says Famka. "Milly Rien. Not then of course. Not while we were still in our teens. It was years later, after we had all joined the Sky Builders' Guild and had children of our own."

"How did Ophelia die?"

"Milly placed a Speaker spell on Ophi," says Famka. "But Ophi couldn't abide by the terms of the spell and spoke aloud what she shouldn't have. It killed her."

"What was she supposed to keep quiet about?"

"It wasn't what she said, but to whom she said it." Famka wipes her eyes. "The spell prevented her from speaking to her daughter, Dorthea. When I found them, Dorthea was crying in her arms and Ophi was gone."

"Why are you telling me this?" I ask, staring at her intently.

"Because I, too, am trapped within a Speaker spell," she answers frowning slightly, the edges of her full lips falling slightly. "As I mentioned earlier tonight."

"Then by telling me this, you endanger your own life," I say.

"True, but I wasn't sure until just now," she answers.

"You mean you could have died?" I ask astonished. "Right now, by telling me?"

"I had a suspicion that I might not. You see by telling you, a Skeleton, the spell wouldn't kill me."

"Why a Skeleton?" I ask, feeling uneasy.

"Because your kind aren't considered people. When Milly authored the Speaker spell, she stated that if I ever told anyone the truth, there would be consequences. My death being one of them."

"I see." I feel crummy because what she says is the truth. We Skeletons aren't even considered a threat, so we are always overlooked. "I suppose that I should be insulted, in a way, but I guess your outlook on us is normal."

"No, Master Skeleton." She addresses me like I'm someone important. "You misunderstand me. I have high regard for Skeletons and all that you have been through. Regardless of what happened during the war, enslaving your race for the mistake of an ancestor is deplorable. And that phrase the Ghostal Holly has made law. The one you have to repeat when anyone asks. I do not understand why it has stood all these centuries."

"I am nothing, and I am no one." I mumble the words and let them hang in the air for a moment. I stare at my blue reflection again in the glass window between the two rooms and think about those wretched words. Children have stopped me on more than one occasion in the Plaza. It is a joke to them. Like a rite of passage; they dare each other and force Skeletons to say it. Sometimes, they make us repeat it loudly, yelling for all standing nearby to hear. It's humiliating to say the least. By the time those children are adults, the belief is engrained and the constant reinforcement has imbued them with a superior sense of themselves, leaving us Skeletons looked upon as a race of servants.

When I look at Famka again, her green eyes stare back at me with concern. They are not the cold eyes I often see in the Plaza; the angry stares I am accustomed to. They are filled instead with compassion.

"So that's why you came here to me?" I ask finally understanding my place in her story. "You figured that you could tell me what happened without dying, and that I will tell everyone by writing your story."

"Yes," she says. "I would have sought you out sooner, but I didn't figure it out at first. In fact, it's taken me years to find a way around this spell; a loophole, if you will. I should have seen it sooner, because it wasn't a secret that Milly is an elitist. In her mind, some people are better than others, because of their lineage, which for her, goes directly back to wealth. Since Skeletons are considered lowly, I took a chance coming here and telling you this small part of my story. If Milly had thought to include Skeletons in her spell, then I would be dead right now."

"But why?" I wonder if I'm missing something critical. "What's so important that she would risk imprisonment by authoring an illegal spell just to keep you quiet? A Speaker spell is a Fallen Art. Surely, she knew that the Ghostal Holly would arrest her if she'd been found authoring that spell."

"I wrestled with your exact questions for years. I could not figure out why she did what she did, but sometimes, the simplest answer is the right answer. The problem was that I was thinking like me and not Milly. You see, she is petty and wanted to hurt me, in addition to gaining power over those she felt threatened by. Look at what she did to her own parents."

Looking away, she goes quiet. Sounds from outside glide into the studio from the hallway. I'm sure that Zinnia, Grim, and Jimmy Bum Skeleton are getting ready for this evening's show. Uncle Keeno and Humphrey are probably glued to the Busyboo in the other room as usual. They won't be any help, and I'm sure that the dance hall will be full tonight because Shouting Through Demons is playing. Their record, *Writing, Drinking, Sulking, Smoking* was well-received on this side of the Graveyard.

Famka sucks in a sudden deep breath. I look over as tears well up in her eyes, and I'm a little taken aback. Famka Meadows is a legend, after all, and I'm not accustomed to seeing legends behave like the rest of us. Not that legendary people come walking through my front door every day, but even still, this leaves me feeling uncomfortable. I don't know her well enough to offer comforting words. Whatever she is going through is her own private nightmare. I don't prod, either, so we sit for a long moment in silence. Famka turns away, chewing the right side of her bottom lip. I feel awkward, so I look up at the Composers as they float patiently in the air. The white fingers are curved and ready to type the moment we begin talking. When I glance at Famka again, her face is a mask, leaving no sign of her emotions only a moment ago.

"The worst part… is that I have a daughter," she tells me. "I believe that you know her. Charli Wonkers."

"You're kidding!" I say, nearly leaping out of my seat. "Charli was just here recently. Maybe two months ago. She told me her story. She's looking for you."

Famka wipes her fresh tears away.

"Here let me get you a tissue." I start to stand, but she stops me.

"No, I'll be fine. Thank you." She wipes her eyes with the back of her hand before continuing. "Milly murdered my best friend, but she didn't stop there. I can't prove it yet, but she killed my husband and at least two residents of the Horseshoe."

"Your husband?"

"Charli's father. Oh, my husband. He was a sweet man. All he wanted was to love me and provide for our Charli. And Milly took that from him."

"You read *Charli's Story*, didn't you?" I say, realizing that she sought me out specifically over all other Skeletons.

"I did," says Famka. "Charli is wrong about me. I know

that she is angry, but I would have never left her or her father. I was forced, because of my choices. The witches of the Horseshoe. That's how we thought of ourselves, Ophelia, Milly, and I. More like three little idiots."

"What do you want me to do with your story?"

"Print it… please," she says. "I know that I ask a great favor of you, but you printed Charli's story, so I hope that you'll do the same for me. It is the only way I know to reach her."

"I cannot promise that," I say. "But after I've gone back through all my notes, I promise to consider it."

"Thank you." She rises to leave.

"I feel that there is still quite a bit more to your story, though," I say before she leaves.

"Yes, there is more, but I have other things to attend to now," she says cryptically and then pulls a black cloth from her front pocket. "Perhaps if the circumstances allow, we will meet again. I have enjoyed meeting you and your lovely wife and being in your gracious home. Thank you for your time."

I follow her out of the studio and walk her down the hall to the front door. The tapping of our feet on the worn wood floor echoes off the walls. Just before she is about to exit, she stops and pulls the cloth over her head. It's shimmering black with a Gris Gris on the face. That is the image of the Fire Thief with his burning matchstick eyes blazing with hatred. They look back at me, and I know it's not him, but even still, those eyes worry me. I feel dread every time I see them, and I have to remind myself that it's only cloth.

"You really do have Ghost Armor?" I say surprised. "So rare."

"A gift from a friend," she says, then pulls the cloth tightly and tucks the excess material into the neckline of her shirt.

"A Skeleton," she says loudly and instantly transforms into one of my kind. She shrinks approximately a foot, her long dark hair changes from brown to jet black, and her skin, of course, turns blue, like mine, followed by bone markings like tattoos along her forehead, cheeks, and jawline. She now looks like a Skeleton. She smiles up at me before turning to go. I watch her disappear into the audience of Skeletons already filing into the dance hall through the large sliding barn doors across the room. A second later, she is gone, swallowed by the crowd.

A couple of hours later, I sit on the patio outside the dance hall. The sun has slipped over the side of the earth, and the night has come out to play. The music inside is too loud for me, mostly because my thoughts are arguing loudly in my head. Ever since I published *Charli's Story*, lunatics have come out of the woodwork. Some seeking fame, others fishing for information on Charli's supposed Dragonhood. I'm still not certain, but I suspect two inquiries were informants for the Ghostal Holly. I'm guessing the same will happen once enough folks have read Famka's story. Despite everything that I have learned about her, I have so many more questions. What went wrong with the three witches as adults? What happened when they joined the Sky Builders' Guild? And the most intriguing question...

Where is Milly now?

I decide right then that I will research it for myself even if Famka never returns. Like me, some of you, my dear readers, will also want to know the final fate of the three witches.

I try to let me thoughts relax as I breathe in the summer air, which is still thick from the hot day. I find it comforting, like putting on a familiar pair of pants. Strings of white lights run between the trees above me, and the smell of smoked meat wafts from a large open-topped smoker made of yellow limestone. All around me, Skeletons sit at picnic tables eating Grim's barbecue. So many blue faces. So many tired and worn-out blue faces.

We, too, had been Dragons once.

I have no doubt that all of my fellow Skeletons spent the day toiling at work they'd rather not do. Postures are sloped forward, expressions are dower, but laughter rings out from a few of the tables nearby. That is one of the notable things about Skeletons. We are resilient, and we have music. This is the one thing the Ghostal Holly hasn't taken from us.

In the corner of the courtyard, my wife, Zinnia, steps onto a stage. Her thick black hair flows out behind her as she crosses to the middle. There is an old piano that barely hangs on to its tuning waiting for her to sing a song. My brother, Jimmy Bum Skeleton, sits down at the piano as Zinnia pulls a microphone free from a stand. Without a word, she begins to sing Famka's favorite song, "The One," that she and Jimmy Bum have been practicing.

Like a spell, her lips make everything right. She is a reminder that the world is still filled with beauty. Her happy brown eyes twinkle along the edges with laughter. They are both innocent and playful as if she has a wonderful joke to share with me later tonight.

I hope that she does.

As the day comes to an end and the evening finally goes to sleep, Zinnia and I slip back into our home for the night. Outside, everyone has gone, and Grim has already begun smoking his meats for the next day. He'll feed the flames with logs and then drift off himself. I swear he never leaves his barbecue throne. Zinnia and I crawl into bed together, and she clasps my hand under the blankets. Humphrey floats into our room and blows out a candle, surprising me since he is quite lazy, before heading back to his little room upstairs in the attic.

"Stop thinking so much," Zinnia says. "You've been up since five a.m. You should get some sleep."

"Aren't you curious about what she told me?" I ask. "You know that was Famka Meadows here all day? In our home."

"Of course I'm curious, but you'll tell me tomorrow and the day after that and then probably again the following day."

"Very funny," I say, tucking the blankets around my feet.

"But it can wait." She kisses me goodnight then turns onto her side.

Several silent minutes pass before Zinnia unexpectedly asks, "Do you think she'll come back?"

"I don't know," I say.

"I hope so," she says in barely a whisper. "She was really nice."

Be good, be well…
Blue Skeleton

Afterword

I hope you enjoyed the first installment in the Witches of the Horeshoe series and that you are eager to dive in to book two! Books two and three are now available exclusively on AMAZON.COM.

Dragon and Mr. Sneeze: *Witches of the Horseshoe*, Book Two
Dragon and Mr. Sneeze: *Witches of the Horseshoe*, Book Three

If you want to be kept up-to-date on new releases, you can sign up for my newsletter by going to my website. (And sometimes, I send my readers free stuff!)

I enjoy hearing what readers think about my stories, so if you are inclined to share your thoughts, you can email me at blue@blueskeleton.com.

What are people are saying?

Blue Skeleton has created a unique world in which blue skeletons and Drolling Dragons and other fantastical creatures live side by side with witches and ghosts and even humans. It is a world in which handkerchiefs can become windows through which characters can step into other worlds and eras, and coat pockets can be universes deep. It is a world in which good battles evil in the form of the Fire Thief, a terrifying creature who has burning candles to fill its empty eye sockets. It is all marvelously told, and I can't wait for future episodes.

~*Mary Balogh – New York Times Bestselling Author*

Fun, vivid, and endearing. The utterly absorbing story and the deeply rich characters draw you right in and make you want to be a sidekick in their world. Highly recommend.
~*Gladys Rodriguez - TV Writer, "Sons of Anarchy"*

Blue Skeleton didn't write a book. He wrote a papery escape. A glorious, compelling, vibrant papery escape. As much as he needed to write it, I needed to read it. And with all going on in the world, I want—and demand—more escapes. There will be more, right, Mr. Skeleton? RIGHT?!
~*Bob Oschack - TV Writer, "Late Late Show"*

I'd like to hear what you have to say, too!

If you enjoyed this first book in the Witches of the Horseshoe series, you can make a big difference by sharing your thoughts. Reviews are the most powerful tools in my arsenal when it comes to getting attention for my books. Much as I'd like to, I don't have the financial muscle of a New York publisher. I can't take out full-page ads in the newspaper or put posters on the subway. (Not yet, anyway.) But I do have something much more powerful—an effective, committed and loyal bunch of readers.

Honest reviews of my books help bring them to the attention of other readers, and I would be very grateful if you could spend just five minutes leaving a review (it can be as short as you like) on on the book's Amazon page, or on my Author's Page.

Thank you very much.

About the Author

Blue Skeleton is the author of the Dragon and Mr. Sneeze Series. He makes his online home at www.blueskeleton.com, where you can sign up for his newsletter so you can be among the first to hear when the next books in the series become available.

You can also connect with Blue on Instagram or on Facebook, and if the mood strikes you, please send him an email at blue@blueskeleton.com.